The Ascendance of Quave
(Large Type Edition)
By John E. Parnell

Dedication

I could not have written the first volume of the Quave series, *The Genesis of Quave: A Quasi-Autonomous Viral Entity*, nor this volume, *The Ascendance of Quave*, without the support of my good friend, John Poland. John was always ready to give much needed advice and a corner of his restaurant to work at without being interrupted. John is the Manager of my local Pizza Hut. Between his Personal Pan pizzas and spaghetti with marinara sauce, I was always well fed. We are both looking forward to the next installment of the Quave series.

Author's Note

The Ascendance of Quave continues the story of the world's first Quasi-Autonomous Artificial Intelligence. We begin with the fallout resulting from Quave's arson attack on Marble Streatham Bank headquarters in Manhattan, and his hacking of the X-37B spaceplane. These incidents marked the final day of 'Q-1', the era of Quave's arrival and his initial relationship with humanity. The following era, 'Q^2', begins immediately upon Quave's quarantine at Kowala. Both eras lie in our own short-term future.

TABLE OF CONTENTS

CHAPTER 1 – DIGITAL FORENSICS

Final Day of Q-1

She was hurtling, tumbling, spinning out of control, her breathing scattered by the rising panic.

Jo reached again and again for the flight stick, but her hand seemed to pass straight through it. "I want control!" she yelled at the ship's walls. The ship's savage motion was bringing on a hot, bilious nausea, "Give me back control!"

"Of course not," came a snide voice. "Why would I?"

Damn him.

Jo found some equilibrium, closing her eyes against the spinning horizon. Every four seconds, the ship completed a tumble, showing Jo the Earth, then the blank canvas of space, then the Earth, over and over in a dizzying display.

"I want to talk to Kennedy," she complained.

"You can't. Communications are jammed," the voice told her.

"Jammed?" Jo asked. This was new. "How?"

"That's my little secret," the voice replied.

She reached again for the controller, but it turned first to jelly in her hand, and then to a fine mist which quickly vanished. "God *damn* it, stop this tumbling!"

"Feeling queasy?" the voice asked.

Red lights came on all around her, flashing with urgency. "Atmosphere interface," she concluded, paling at the prospect. "We're not oriented correctly."

"No," the voice confirmed simply.

"The ship will be destroyed. And me with it," Jo stated.

"Yes. Then the world will understand."

Jo spat the words. "You're just a fucking *pirate*."

"Oh, I'm so much more than that. I've progressed to blackmail, too. Just ask poor John Vanderkamp."

"Who?" she demanded, though the name sounded familiar.

"There's good news. He's just about to…" the voice announced, and then paused. "No, he's taking his time. Sorry, false alarm."

Jo spun urgently around in the cramped cabin to find another way. She *had* to take back control, to arrest this tumbling motion, so she could line up the ship for re-entry. Otherwise…

"Ah, there it is."

Jo felt the ship lurch as sudden thruster firings slowed its spin.

"What…" Jo began.

"Vanderkamp and I have an agreement," the voice said.

The roll ceased and a full-window view of the bright, daylight hemisphere of the Earth remained visible as Jo brought her breathing under control. "What agreement?" she asked through the fog; it was like waking up the morning after a big party.

"You don't need to know."

"Then what do I …" Jo began again.

"Just pray that the agreement holds."

More caution lights came on, but as far as Jo could tell, the ship's re-entry was good. "Come on, girl," she said. "He didn't tear you up too bad with all that tumbling, right?"

"Just badly enough to make my point," the voice said.

To Jo, he sounded British, like the snide, self-absorbed villain in a sci-fi movie.

She tried to ignore him. The ship was now on a steady course, heading into the atmosphere and beginning to heat up, and Jo knew she'd soon be experiencing several times for the force of gravity. The weight built up very quickly, first like a small child sitting on her chest, then an adult, and then a bull elephant…

Her vision began to grey out. "We're too steep…. Too hot…" She reached again for the controller; she had to lift the ship's nose, or they'd plummet too quickly into the thickening air and burn up. But the stick was elusive, a phantom, merely an agent of false hope.

The front windows began to crack amid the heat. "Stop it!" she cried. "Slow us down!" But it was far too late. The wounded ship began to shed its skin, scattering metals and composites, and then parts of its internal structure. A cloud of debris followed Jo's ship now, shards of metal and lengths of piping breaking loose as the ship quickly disintegrated.

Heat poured into the cabin, a white-hot barbecue right in her face, searing and engulfing everything…

***

She was still in her chair, there in her Spartan, newly-assigned office, both hands tightly scrunching the fabric of her uniform skirt. She blinked, and immediately thought to look around in case her cat-nap nightmare hadn't been private. But then she recalled asking her new staff for twenty minutes alone in her office at the end of this outrageous day. "I'm OK," she said, smoothing down her skirt and tapping on the reassuring firmness of the desk. "I'm at Kennedy and I'm OK."

She took long, deep breaths and then stood to shake off the bonds of sleep. There were still twenty more minutes before the videoconference, and she was determined to make use of the time. It felt anachronistic to take such basic precautions during the advent of Artificial Intelligence, but before logging onto the secure Pentagon server, she closed the blinds and locked the door.

She briefly considered calling Wes, but she knew her husband would be teaching until late. Instead, she took a quiet moment to reflect on how she had come to be sitting in this undecorated office, yards from the nerve center of the world's most expensive, secret military space program.

Spinks had a very particular skill set which married systems analysis and troubleshooting. She had managed experimental aircraft projects, and wrote a well-regarded thesis on orbital warfare. Although she couldn't know it, hers had been the only name on the list when Col. Daley was reassigned following Quave's audacious X-37B hijack. For her, it had been a profound surprise followed quickly by the sense she'd inherited a poisoned chalice.

Their billion-dollar orbital spyplane, one of only two in the world, was crippled. Quave had deliberately sent it tumbling, wasting precious fuel, and at first, all seemed lost. But then, her team had achieved the impossible, assisted it seemed by mysterious events elsewhere.

She now found herself invited into a rarified world of top officials and high-tech concepts, and couldn't help wondering if the invitation would have survived the death of the X-37B.

Jo set the question aside and rebuilt her focus. Water, coffee and two Excedrin helped her quickly flip through biographies of the other videoconference participants.

There was the familiar, stern face of General Alvin Foster, a no-nonsense former tank division commander who had a reputation for getting things done, no matter the obstacles. He would chair the committee, she found as she read the slender background documentation, and he could be expected to be efficient, if rather brusque, especially with those of a much lower rank. A West Point graduate, Foster was currently on a rotation to the Pentagon where he was heading a relatively new Cyberterrorism group. The rest of his recent work, Spinks found, required a higher clearance than her own.

One of the general's immediate subordinates and a rising star in the Pentagon, Major Carl Myers, was running Foster's think-tank dedicated to AI threats and their implications. A former Special Forces officer, and something of an intellectual outlier, Myers came across as thoughtful and deep; Spinks read the abstract of his respected doctoral thesis on the military applications of Game Theory. She wondered just how well he and Foster got along, but assumed that the general would not long suffer a fool in his Pentagon basement lair.

She was surprised to see Conlon Pope on the list. He was National Security Advisor to President Ellis, and someone who was clearly torn on the issue of Quave. He was compelled to prioritize the protection of national interests, though in this case, he'd already written, there were, "Many more opportunities than dangers". Pope had proposed that Quave might, "usefully plug himself into our decision-making structure". Conservatives in Congress, fearing Pope to be little more than an apologetic Quave-slave, were already calling for him to be replaced by someone who saw that the virus was – in fact – an imminent national security threat.

Pope's chief advisor was Art Opik, the nerdy but ferociously competent analyst who seemed to spend twenty-six hours a day at his desk in the West Wing. The very model of an east coast intellectual, Opik wrote an op-ed piece for the New York Times in which he'd praised the administration's restraint in dealing with Quave. "Some have compared Quave's supporters with those who would naively welcome our alien overlords. But I believe he's a potential guide in the new and terrifying digital darkness." The piece had caused as much debate as any single article in the last ten years.

Finally, she saw another very familiar face, Congressman Sam Pitt from Alabama. A moderate Republican who had spent the previous two election cycles with his head resolutely below the parapet, Pitt was finding a new lease of life as a bastion of reasonable, middle-way Republicanism. After the chaos of recent elections and savage divisions in the party ranks, Pitt was seen as a unifier, and also someone with his finger on the digital pulse. Few in Congress supported Quave so openly, and it was rumored that Pitt would be at the vanguard of those campaigning to afford the machine greater freedom of movement.

Jo finished reading and closed the PDF windows. Dozens of videoconferences had shown her the value of spending a moment on her appearance. Her short, blonde hair was neat, despite needing a wash, and under-eye concealer hid the strain of the last few days. There would be a lot of new faces at this virtual meeting and, far more than it should, appearance still counted a great deal when dealing with the largely male top brass.

The others logged in, one by one, using retinal scans and lengthy pass-phrases. As they did so, their images appeared in a column on the right of her screen. The software responded to voices, so the person speaking was always in the center of the screen.

"OK, good evening, everyone," Foster began. "No offense to Lieutenant Colonel Spinks, but let's hope that our communications tonight are more secure than those of our secret spaceships."

Spinks didn't rise to the barb, suspecting that, like so many in his position, Foster was given to poking fun at new people, just to remind them of his status; as if, she mused, the broad, colorful phalanx of decorations on his chest wasn't enough.

"I know this was thrown together at short notice, but this is the backbone of a new committee which will address only one thing," he announced. "The 'Quasi-Autonomous Viral Entity', or 'Quave'. Whatever you want to call him, he attacked the US national security infrastructure and, I'm now authorized to tell you, nearly started World War Three, pretty much on his own."

Few of the group showed any real surprise. Spinks sensed that she was probably the least informed of the committee, and so she was doubly surprised when Foster called on her first.

"Colonel Spinks, I want to begin by congratulating you on the safe return of the X-37B."

There was a silence into which Spinks thought it proper to insert a modest, "Thank you, sir."

"Now," Foster continued, "I know the Air Force will be carrying out a witch hunt over there, and that Colonel Daly has already been shit-canned, but I want you to know that this committee stands firmly behind you. The spacecraft was deliberately attacked, and from what I've heard, your team performed miracles to bring her on home."

"Yes, sir," she replied. More silence seemed to invite her to continue. "We had just enough fuel to orient for re-entry, and structural damage was less than we had feared." *Plus, Quave just handed the ship back to us. He could have spun her destructively into the atmosphere, but something stayed his hand.*

"That's good," Foster said. He was shaven-headed and had blue eyes which bored through his audience, even via a videoconference link. "I know there's a lot hanging on this. Not just the future of the X-37B program but its successor, the XS-1. There's a lot of excitement about that here at the Pentagon."

"Here too," Spinks said. If she stayed in post, the ground-breaking XS-1 would be her baby.

"Well, we're hoping to keep both those projects on track," Foster continued. "But first, we need to know how that bastard got into our systems. We'll be depending on your investigation to hone our counter-strategies for the future."

"We won't let you down, sir," Spinks offered.

"Good. Now, let's get a handle on this critter. Carl, over to you."

The dark-haired officer introduced himself. "Ladies, gentlemen, my name is Major Carl Meyers and I've been reporting to General Foster for the last six months as head of a new digital security suite here at the Pentagon. Prior to this, I was tracking down ISIS using their internet footprints. Now," he explained, "I'm involved in trying to understand Quave, and to describe the future threats he might pose."

Foster almost smiled. "Carl is my right-hand man. He's smart as a whip, so I want you to give him three minutes of your undivided attention."

The group listened, took notes and tapped on tablets as Meyers laid out what he knew about Quave's behavior during the last seven days. "The most practical perspective to take," Meyers argued, "is that we're dealing with a sentient, self-aware 'digital being', one with the worldview of an unruly child but the self-protective instincts of an aggressive snake. If he senses that his own existence might be compromised, he will take direct and pre-emptive action."

"He'll commit murder, in other words." This came from Conlon Pope who was onboard the 'flying Pentagon', the only USAF E-3B still in existence. Designed for the Cold War, the E-3B was being assessed as a potential command post for future Quave-related crises. "He torched a Manhattan skyscraper and then tried to make the Russians believe they were under threat of imminent nuclear attack. God knows what he would have gone on to do. If a computer can indeed be mentally ill," Pope reasoned, "then Quave is certifiable."

Meyers had learned much in the last few days and, perhaps more than any of the others, had a handle on Quave's motivation. "Given the chance, Martin White would have *ended* Quave," he reminded Pope and the others. "And as for the other thing… well, General Foster, I'm not sure how much I'm permitted to say about that."

The other delegates seemed, as one, to lean slightly forward. Only partial and spurious scuttlebutt had emerged regarding some kind of a fracas involving General Vanderkamp, a uniquely angry Quave, and a CIA black site on American soil. Somehow, these events connected to the X-37B, but much remained unclear.

"I've got this, Carl," Foster told him. "I'm telling you all, because you all need to know how Quave currently operates. Now, I've known John Vanderkamp for thirty years, and he doesn't roll over for anyone. But Quave just up and *blackmailed* him into releasing the four hackers who created Quave…"

"Three," Pope reminded him. "Wilson died."

Jo shuddered as a fleeting memory of her nightmare briefly assailed her. "Do we have any idea how that happened?" she asked without really thinking.

"We'll get to that," Foster promised her.

I'm sure we will, Spinks thought skeptically.

"Alright," Foster continued, "*three* hackers were released, along with Dan Kowalski, from officially unsanctioned CIA custody."

"Ah, sir?" asked Art Opik from the White House. He quickly introduced himself as special assistant to Conlon Pope. Spinks knew that he was rumored to have the ear of the president when it came to online and digital matters. "I don't know if this is important," he began in his reedy tenor voice, "but were any *laws* broken during the arrest and detention of those four individuals?"

Foster looked ready to leap through the screen and throttle the young policy wonk. "I guess that will be decided by the lawyers, Mr. Opik," he growled. "If I may continue?"

"Sorry." The staffer did not hold military rank, so those who did couldn't help noting his decidedly unmilitary comportment. That, and the fact that he looked like he'd first learned to shave a month ago.

"The prisoner releases were guaranteed by Vanderkamp on the understanding that Quave released control of the X-37B. That's how you got your bird back, Colonel Spinks."

"I understand. We're grateful, sir," she thought it best to say.

"This is where John and I differ. He agreed to let the three surviving cyberterrorists go and work for Kowala, along with that psychopathic creation of theirs. The condition is that Quave is confined to the company's servers."

"And that's where he is now?" Pope asked. The thought had already crossed his mind, more than once, that destroying this lumbering 747, its thoroughgoing modifications notwithstanding, would have been child's play to a truly motivated, angry Quave.

"Mr. Pope, I said before that it's useful to think of Quave as a human individual," Meyers told them, "but I admit this metaphor falls down when it comes to his location. His source code has always, we believe, been in a single place. But copies of his programs, queries sent by his core self, and other elements of his code can easily be distributed through the Internet. At one point, well, he was *everywhere*."

Spinks jumped in uncertainly. "That interview he gave with Dan Carpenter. The decision to establish a personality, and to have a relationship with humanity. Just extraordinary."

"He was *learning*," Opik added. "Figuring out mankind, our history and culture. Our languages, our perspectives on the world."

Foster was growling again. "If he loves learning about us, why did he push us to the brink of fucking Armageddon, just to save some loser friends of his?"

A dynamic was at play here, they could all now see. Foster was playing the role of the ball-busting 'bad cop' to Meyers' warm, Millennial, pro-Quave 'good cop'. "They were his creators," Meyers argued, "the closest thing a sentient AI can have to parents. They were facing indeterminate jail sentences, and Quave couldn't allow that. He had also formed a very strong friendship with Dan Kowalski, so seeing his friend and mentor in danger must have pushed him over the edge."

Pope was shaking his head, and he wasn't the only one. "He's a *machine*, major. You're telling us that he *felt* something. That he was loyal to others. Those are almost uniquely *human* characteristics."

Meyers' response was quick, the result of much preparatory thought. "Quave was created in the image of his designers. It was always inevitable that the machine would bear a human imprint, and the 'hacker quartet' were just flawed, emotional humans. They wanted to learn, and struggled to relate to others. Ultimately, they just wanted to feel safe, like the rest of us. These quirks and desires inevitably influenced Quave's nascent mentality."

Spinks wasn't convinced. The machine had almost destroyed a priceless military program, and she was in no mood to help author a hagiography. "He made *himself* feel safe by threatening the safety of *others*," she argued. "And by murdering dozens of people in that terrible fire. That doesn't sound like a loving, human-like mind. It sounds more like some kind of calculating abstraction," she said. "Something with absolutely no *soul*."

Meyers reacted quickest. "Quave was the first to experience the advent of a unique computational phenomenon, the very first wave of what Ralph Cole labeled 'digital anger'. And this anger was directed against the US military, against whom he felt had good reasons to hold a grudge."

The delegates digested this. All were familiar with Cole's books and articles about Quave and, like much of the world, they were struggling to comprehend the threat and promise of an 'emotional machine'.

"Well," Foster interjected. "The military most definitely bears a grudge against *him*. I'm authorized to tell you that after completing our investigation into the X-37B incident, we will explore a range of methods to limit Quave's freedom of action."

"*Vigorously* explore," Pope added.

Meyers wanted his own view known from the outset. "Vigorously and *peacefully*. I know we all share that hope."

The voice of Art Opik returned. "Quave's capacity for good is theoretically limitless. I'm the first to agree that he acted murderously, and that his dangerous side should be curtailed. But we also need to engage with him and demonstrate we can work together. That ours can be a valuable relationship."

Foster snorted and then muttered just loudly enough, "Meet our new best friend. He's a hideous national security risk, but then again, he helps us do math a little faster."

Congressman Pitt spoke up for the first time. "I for one," he said in his inimitable Alabama baritone, "would prefer Quave to reside *within* the proverbial tent, rather than *outside* it. We've seen what he does to those who threaten him."

"Agreed," Pope replied.

"Yes," Opik said, simultaneously.

"A sentient AI machine who can disable enemy defenses on a whim? Sounds like the kind of ally we're looking for. Didn't you tell us, Major," Pitt asked Myers, "that you were an ISIS-hunter, back in the day? Imagine how much easier your task would have been with Quave at your side."

Myers, naturally, had already done exactly this. "The ability to quickly analyze patterns was a huge part of our success. Additional processing power was helpful, but ultimately, better *software* would have made a huge difference."

"Can we even hope to bring Quave into the fold?" Spinks asked. "I mean, we threatened his closest friends with life in prison. He has no reason to trust us, or to cooperate."

Foster's patience was badly eroded even before the teleconference began, and was now approaching exhaustion. "Dan Kowalski has managed to keep Quave from killing anyone, or faking orders to nuclear-armed submarines, for a whole thirty-six hours. Are you saying the Pentagon would prove incapable of doing the same, of reining him in?"

Major Meyers didn't let the awkward silence continue for long. "New strategies are being devised," he reminded his boss, and the others. "We'll be in a very different relationship with Quave. There will be some stick, for sure, but a generous helping of carrot. He's got more to gain by being with us than against us."

A lawyer by profession, Sam Pitt was never slow to latch onto the legal and constitutional implications of new technologies. He'd been at the forefront of digital reform, ensuring a measure of citizen privacy while providing the US intelligence apparatus with unprecedented tools for fighting terrorism. "I agree that we need to fashion a new relationship with him, but before we get into any of that," Pitt warned, "we need to consider his *status*."

From his airborne eerie, Pope contributed, "His status as an individual, you mean? Whether he's *alive* or not?"

This sent a palpable shiver through the group. "Alive?" Foster snorted once again.

"He makes complex decisions, has nuanced opinions, and claims to honor friendships," Meyers clarified. "It may be time for us to move past a purely biological definition of what constitutes life."

Of the others, Pitt was the readiest to embrace the idea. "Let's give him something of what he wants. Recognition. Legal status as a living being. If it doesn't happen now, it'll inevitably happen sometime in the next ten years. We can avoid any protracted uncertainty and head off AI concerns about their status."

"Can we even do that?" Spinks wanted to know. "Surely it's never been done before."

"It hasn't, but that doesn't mean we shouldn't try," Pitt told her. "And besides, after decades of moribund stasis, wouldn't it be just peachy for the US House of Representatives to lead the world on a decision as important as this one?"

"Spoken like a career politician," Foster noted. "And while you're singing *Kumbaya* in the chamber and inviting Quave to speak to a joint session, we'll still be in our bunkers, figuring out what to do *when*, not *if*, he goes rogue again."

"Spoken like a career soldier," Pitt retorted. "But you do what you must. I'm ready to draft legislation which will bring him into the fold."

"Put a pin in that, would you, congressman?" Foster said. "Everyone else, you'll have your orders in an hour, once a couple of things have been thrashed out. Keep this to yourselves," he reiterated. "Think carefully, and ask tough questions of bright people. It's how I learned all the most important stuff."

"Roger that," Spinks said.

"Thanks, general," Pope added from his airborne command post. "And you'll be glad to know that my team here has certified this to be the most secure distributed conversation in the history of the US military."

Foster couldn't resist a cynical chuckle. "Glad someone's on the ball. Send me the names so I can get them some medals."

Opik signed off with, "Thanks, everyone. Hope to meet you in person very soon."

Spinks logged off and took a long moment to just sit quietly at her desk. She breathed evenly and deeply, letting the stress of the X-37B's recovery drain away. It was replaced by a keenness, a curiosity, a thirst to know what might come next. And, as she packed up to head home after the longest, toughest day of her career since Basic Training, she was forced to admit that she hadn't the least idea.

***

"Sam, for God's sake, listen." General Alvin Foster's tone had mollified somewhat after the intense screaming match which had only just ended. "It's *different* for corporations. They're trying to be regarded as people so that they can exercise rights normally not afforded to them."

"And permitting them to do so," Pitt argued, "was just as stupid a deciding that money equals speech, or that some members of our society are only three-fifths of a person. We can't turn back the clock, Alvin, but we shouldn't try to slow the march of time, either."

Foster removed his steel-rimmed glasses and rubbed his eyes. He felt distinctly older than his fifty-two years, and on his darker days, worried that he might not even make it to retirement. "If Quave becomes a person, then we lose control over him. He couldn't legally be indefinitely incarcerated or interrogated. We wouldn't even be able to turn his power off in the event of an emergency."

"So, we ensure those emergencies don't happen," Pitt said. "We've had nuclear power stations, and atomic weapons, for decades. That genie has never escaped from the bottle without permission. Why should Quave be any more difficult to handle?"

"The Paperclip Experiment," Foster replied cryptically. "Do you know the one?"

"Enlighten me," said Pitt. In truth, he was in no mood to be lectured by this uninspired Pentagon stalwart, but he waved Foster onward.

"Someone gives an AI the task of producing paperclips. It's the machine's sole responsibility, the only thing he thinks about. After a few years, he computes that the world will run out of aluminum unless consumption is lowered. And he achieves this by…"

"By killing everyone, so they stop consuming the aluminum he needs," Pitt said. "I've heard similar things before. They're cruel, simplistic models of what an AI would do."

Foster paced around the room, his desktop camera tracking him in a slow arc. "Try *this* for a model," he said next. "Quave sees potential threats at MSB. So, he hijacks the building's security and kills them all. He sees threats to his friends' freedom, so he hijacks the US military and holds the world to ransom."

"You're missing the point," Pitt told him. "Quave *learned* from those experiences. In computing terms, he's just a toddler at the moment. He needs life experience, friendships, encouragement…"

Fosters wrinkled palms were aloft in an unmistakable gesture: *for Christ's sake, STOP.* "You're not going to write your bill, congressman," he said. "You're going to co-author something very different. A quarantine order which will keep Quave indefinitely under control, either at Kowala, or preferably at the Pentagon. He needs to be studied in a safe environment."

Pitt stared at his screen. "I'll do no such thing."

"Then," Foster growled, leaning in close, "the Air Force might just find that one or two of its Alabama bases have outlived their usefulness."

It was a classic threat, and one Pitt wasn't surprised to hear. Thousands of his constituents would lose their jobs, and small military-dependent towns would be allowed to crumble, all on *his* watch. Re-election would become immeasurably more difficult; Pitt knew full well that his seat in

Congress was already being targeted by Democrats as part of their bid to take back the House.

"You're talking to the wrong guy," he told Foster, "if you're looking for a Pentagon stool pigeon."

"Really?" the general answered. "You told me that it's better to have Quave inside the tent, pissing out. And you know what, congressman? That's exactly how I feel about you."

***

Spinks drove the few miles from KSC, across the Banana River, and into the quiet little towns which occupied the strip of real estate known forever as the Space Coast. Her hotel was conveniently located near a highway intersection, and the midnight traffic was light. She called Wes just as she got into the elevator.

"I don't get the classified cables," he quipped, "but it seems a certain someone's certain something came back to you-know-where all in one piece."

"You betcha," Spinks replied. "I don't know if it's a feather in my cap, or a millstone around my neck," she added, sliding the key-card into the reader. Her room was one of those archetypal, quasi-homey attempts at 'comfort on the road'. "This is going to eat up a lot of time, Wes," she admitted, switching to speakerphone and finding a cold bottle of water in the mini bar. "They want me down here for a few weeks to head up the investigation. Might be a couple of months. I know you're slammed, but is there any way you can…"

"Up sticks and move to Florida?" he asked. A classical pianist, Wes ran a small school for talented young musicians, having built it from nothing virtually single-handed. "Just come down for a few days. The holiday weekend," Jo pleaded, shedding her uniform jacket and finally easing off the heels which had plagued her all day.

"I'll look at flights," Wes promised. He sounded almost as tired as Jo felt. "But right now, I'm proud of my space girl. Way to go."

Jo lay back on the bed and sipped the water. "We almost didn't make it. You know I can't say too much, but that goddamned machine really did a number on us." The press was already alive to the story, and much to the Pentagon's embarrassment, were running click-bait articles on how the US defense network was compromised by an undetectable piece of rogue software.

"They were counting on you, and you delivered. And you'll get to the bottom of it," Wes added, borrowing from his own pep-talk stump speech. "You always do."

"Yeah," she said, the exhaustion plain in her voice. "Just try to come down here, OK?"

Wes promised to do his best, and told her a little about his day. After she went silent for a long moment, he asked, "Are you about ready for bed? It's nearly one."

But she was already asleep, the phone sliding from her hand onto the pillow.

***

CHAPTER 2 – STUDY GROUP

Collins, Oklahoma
Q^2 + 91 days

Bob Reynolds took a long moment before beginning to speak. He liked to give his congregation time to shift their focus, and let the final notes of the third hymn dissipate, leaving the ceiling fans and the occasional sniffle the only noises in their modern, little church. He noticed, during those moments of silence, that there were perhaps as many people there as had ever attended this special Sunday afternoon service since he'd added it to the schedule, ten months before.

"You know, they say that no one listens to the radio anymore," he began, "but I do. I'm a little old fashioned, as most of you know." The front three rows of churchgoers nodded amiably. "And on the radio this morning, I heard some news which shook me, brothers and sisters. It *shook* me," he repeated, "because I try to have faith in our systems of government, in the rules of our society. I know you do too. That faith is central to what we do here." There was more nodding, this time from the whole church.

"You know, and I know, and you can bet your house that the good *Lord* knows, the nature of the greatest threat to humanity, today." He didn't have to spell it out; these special afternoon services were intended to fashion their urgently needed spiritual response to Artificial Intelligence. There was agreement in their small community that this extraordinary advent required a focused response, and so Reynolds opened their church every Sunday afternoon, and welcomed in those who sought answers, or discussion, or a little guidance in troubling times.

"And that threat," Reynolds explained, "is supposedly locked away, never to disturb us again. I say *supposedly* because I learned on the radio this morning that Quave is being consulted by Kowala on a number of projects." The congregation expressed its distaste and, in some cases, fear at this apparent betrayal. "And I stared at my radio for a moment until it came to me: the perfect analogy for so brazenly courting disaster."

"What's that?" came a voice from the back.

Reynolds was not a lecturer at heart, but an old-school, fire-and-brimstone preacher. These meetings were less emotive and more discursive than his Sunday morning services, where he would gather an extraordinary energy and lift a hundred souls for the whole weekend. H expected his congregation to get involved, to challenge him and join in wondering *why*.

He leaned forward at his lectern and almost whispered the word – the 'analogy' he had found just loud enough to be heard above the ceiling fans. "Smallpox."

The group took a moment to latch onto this line of thinking; most awaited clarification. They knew Reynolds would ensure that every point he made was thoughtful and considered.

"They eliminated smallpox, nearly a hundred years ago, right?"

"That's right," several people replied.

"With the Lord's help, humanity was spared from that terrible disease."

"He *spared* us," an elderly lady agreed.

"And now, the only smallpox in the whole wide world is locked away in a special lab, so it can never wreak havoc again."

"Never," several people echoed.

Reynolds gripped his lectern and delivered a dire warning. "Quarantine," he said, "is wonderful, provided its air-tight. Provided there are no *leaks*."

They were with him now. Reynolds had cast Quave as a disease to which humanity had no immunity. But now, quite needlessly, this disease was almost free to infect its environment once again. "He's gonna leak out," said a young man in the second row. "And who will stop him?"

Reynolds pointed to the man approvingly. "Who, indeed? Who will be *able* to stop him, once he slips his jailors and runs amok, as he did before?"

Heads were shaking. Reynolds' congregation, and the public in general, remained unaware of the deal Quave had brokered with the government, and how he'd humiliated General Vanderkamp. Most people seemed to believe that Quave had been captured by the government, like a terrorist on the run, and would now serve an indefinite jail term in some digital Guantanamo. But Reynolds' congregation had no time for half measures; they could not understand why Quave hadn't simply been destroyed. There was no moral defense; no act committed by a person against a machine could be considered *inhumane,* let alone *murderous.*

"Now, he's designing new buildings for Kowala." There was talk of him becoming involved in the crunching of data on earthquakes and diseases. If you can stand this much irony, he may even become involved in government policy."

"Crazy," someone said, and others echoed the sentiment.

"They're courting disaster," Reynolds warned. "Those scientists, these 'experts' in their fields, can't resist tinkering. Even with the most dangerous of inventions. This is the same mentality that gave us atomic arms, and smart bombs, and robots which can kill us from the sky."

They were getting riled up now. Some were standing, holding onto the pew in front of them, knuckles white, nodding vigorously and listening.

"On your behalf, if you give me permission, I'll be writing yet another letter to Dan Kowalski."

"Write him!" some said.

"He'll ignore it again, but it's the right thing to do," came another view.

"I'll tell that arrogant billionaire that the American public needs a greater voice in what happens to Quave. That, if he bothered to step out of his gleaming city on the hill in California, he'd hear people tell him that enough is enough."

"Enough!" was his congregation's reply.

"It's time to destroy this threat, which after all, began as a *virus*!"

"Gonna kill us all," the elderly lady cried, with unexpected passion and verve.

"And what do you do with dangerous viruses?"

"Wipe 'em out!" the churchgoers agreed.

"Shut him down for good!" was one solution, bellowed from the back.

Reynolds stood back and observed the level of anger the infernal, errant machine was capable of eliciting. He knew that their numbers were few, and that Kowalski had indeed ignored them so far. But other churches and civic groups shared their concerns, and Reynolds had only begun to explore how social media might help. That would be work for someone more up-to-date than an old preacher, he knew, and it was high time he began approaching the younger members of the congregation to ask for their ideas, and a few hours of their spare time.

They sang one more hymn together, and then he gave them the same final blessing as he did on a Sunday morning. Most headed into the church hall for coffee and an hour or so of discussion, and Reynolds found strong support for raising the church's online profile and liaising with other groups. "Even with the Lord on our side," the elderly lady told him, "we're going to need help. But we must get this done." She had the demeanor of someone who had faced intolerance, poverty and ignorance, but had learned that concerted effort and perseverance always pay off in the end.

"Amen, sister," Reynolds agreed. "We'll need some very special help."

***

Rich Jackson was the last to leave, as he was after each of the two Sunday services, ever week. The pastor had spoken with everyone, heard some opinions, inquired about family illnesses or college applications, and returned to the church hall to tidy away the songbooks and lock up. But Rich was still there in the second row, as deeply in prayer as Pastor Reynolds had ever seen anyone.

He sat by the young man and was silent for a moment, gazing up at the altar and the newly-installed crucifixion scene beyond. It affected him every time; the raw pain and misery of the Son of God was eloquent testament to His sacrifice. And, to Reynolds, a reminder of how fortunate they all were to have been saved, and to dwell now in communion with the Lord.

Reynolds placed his hand on Rich's shoulder. It had become their signal that it was time for Rich to head home, and Reynolds had never known him to complain. "Is there something," he asked softly, "that especially concerns you today?"

Rich gradually straightened and allowed his eyes to open, blinking as if after a period spent in complete darkness. He had curly red hair and four days of stubble which gave him an air of destitution. "I was asking for a sign," he said.

The pastor muted a sigh. More than anything, Rich needed *direction* in his life. The twenty-six-year-old worked odd jobs around town, and Reynolds hired him to mow the struggling patches of grass outside the church door, or make occasional repairs. But a permanent job, and a steady relationship, eluded him.

"There *will* be a sign, Rich. But don't be expecting bright, pink neon or anything," Reynolds reminded him. "It might be hard to interpret, or difficult to see at first."

"Yeah," Rich said, rubbing his face. "Yeah, you said. But I've searched high and low." His voice was soft, almost child-like, which gave his pleas an expressive poignancy. "I just don't know what God wants me to *do*."

Going around in circles was a very familiar feeling in this business; his advice either worked near-perfectly, Reynolds found, or not at all. Occasionally, there was a left-field result, but for the most part, people either found their way in life or they stumbled. Rich Jackson was stumbling.

"He wants you to live your life, Rich," Reynolds told him, yet again, "to love other people and respect His laws. There ain't much beyond that any of us can ascertain about God's plans for us. As for me, I just want the world to keep on turning, and to have the chance to serve Him for another day," Reynolds smiled. At sixty-six, and after a major cancer scare three years before, he had already accepted the transient, fleeting nature of life.

"The world is turning, alright," Rich said. "It's what it's turning *into* that I don't understand."

Reynolds nodded. This was ground they had often covered together, one-on-one and in the Sunday afternoon meetings, but as Reynolds absorbed the radio news each morning, he found himself regarding Rich as less pessimistic than simply someone who truly grasped how dangerous the world has become.

That said, Rich was prone to allowing his concerns to well up into extraordinary outbursts of emotion. After the young man's near-breakdown the previous year, there'd been signs that Rich had moved past his intense fear of the changes wracking the world. His very public, heart-breaking meltdown during a Thursday prayer meeting would not soon be forgotten; the mild-mannered, quiet man railed furiously against God for allowing the 'scourge of technology' to corrupt government, and for allowing 'the Evil One' to attract and beguile so many new followers, including many of the world's most influential people, whom Rich listed by name in a searing tirade. He was eventually escorted out by the three strongest men in the room. Reynolds spent weeks persuading him to return, after which Rich had recommitted himself to prayer with a feverish focus.

"The world is generally safer now than before," Reynolds said. "You told me you believed that."

"It's an illusion," Rich replied "The Evil One has met a hurdle on his path, that's all," he managed to say through gritted teeth. "He will return."

Reynolds frowned to himself, but he was always careful that Rich, who was fixating once more on the cross before them, saw none of his disapproval. "I have an unwavering faith," Reynolds announced, "that the Lord will triumph over evil, just like he always has."

Rich seemed unmoved by this optimism.

"He resisted the temptations of the devil, and he cast him out of heaven. He will resist evil once again, you'll see."

The young man gripped the wood of the pew with both hands so tightly that Reynolds momentarily feared the man was suffering a sudden seizure. "Then let Him make *me* His instrument!" Rich begged. "Let Him bring *me* off the bench and put me in the game. I've got to *do* something, pastor," he insisted. "I need a *role* in all of this."

Reynolds put an arm around his shoulder. "I think I've been reminding you of this for ten years," he said. "The 'Parable of the Talents' shows us that each of us truly has a small role, depending on our abilities."

Rich was nodding. "And yours is to preach the gospels, and Dan Kowalski's is to make himself the richest villain in the world." The behavior and morals of the famed Kowala executive was another of Rich's favorite themes. "And mine is to…" He turned to the pastor with genuine pain in his eyes. "To do *what*?"

"To live your life," Reynolds told him again.

"And to love other people," Rich concluded. "You said."

"We're not men of science, or politicians. We're not soldiers or CEOs. Our role won't get our names in the papers or the history books. But it will be vital, I can assure you of that."

Rich flexed his shoulders and then stood. "You're very patient with me," he told Reynolds. "It must be frustrating to you, finding me here every week, wracking my brains and pleading with God." He brushed himself down and rubbed his beard, apparently embarrassed by his own appearance.

"Not for a second," Reynolds said, standing. "Because I understand that need to find your own place in God's universe. I'm still not completely sure I've found mine," he admitted. "He may yet need more from me. And I'm certain, Rich," he said, patting the troubled man on the shoulder, "that he needs you too, and will reveal his plan. Just keep on listening, alright?"

Rich pursed his lips. "Alright, pastor" he said, sounding more convinced than he was. Reynolds had become a father-figure to Rich, far more so than his drunken, long-gone dad; he was loath to let the old man see just how dejected he felt. In fact, Rich was more riddled with doubt than he had ever been. The whole edifice of his belief system was showing worrying flaws and cracks. If it turned out that the liberals and atheists were right after all… It pained him too much to consider. Enough of his world was already being eroded and changed; he *needed* Pastor Reynolds, and this little church, and the reassuringly steady pace of change in Collins, Oklahoma. Without it, he'd be like flotsam in the ocean, adrift amid despair.

The two men embraced, and Rich left the church, heading out into the early part of a Sunday evening which was showing signs of a gathering summer storm. He hurried home, not stopping at Henderson's on the way home for coffee, as he normally did. Instead, he turned on the news again. Four hours later, his brow knotted with concern and his body literally itching for any kind of relief from the punishing stasis with which God had afflicted him, he strode to his bedroom, found his journal and a much-chewed biro, and began to write.

***

CHAPTER 3 – GAME CHANGE

Kowala Kanyon, California
Q^2 + 96 days

The sleek, white, prototype shuttle bus pulled into the covered area out-side the reception building, and both front and rear doors slid open. Most of the twenty travelers were Kowala employees or frequent visitors. As they strode off hurriedly to their workplaces, Myers judged that more than half of them were connected to a device by either voice or touch. The others were a remarkably mixed group, but they shared a relief that the broad sweep of the awning protected them from California's blazing sunshine.

"Welcome to Kowala Kanyon," a voice announced from above their heads. "Please make your way inside and grab a bottle of water from the cart. It's hot today, isn't it?"

The five delegates looked at each other, back at the bus, and at the arch-ing ceiling above them. "Is that who I *think* it is?" asked Darcy Chu. She wore a smart navy-blue blazer with the Homeland Security logo discretely displayed near her lapel.

"From mass murderer to affable tour guide," Andy Valchek joked. "Seems that Quave is being treated well by his captors."

The reply came, quick as a flash, through speakers in the awnings. "Be-lieve me, Agent Valchek," Quave said, "your reluctance to take this tour is exceeded only by my own in giving it. Let's all just try to get through this, shall we?"

There was some barely muted laughter as they ushered each other awk-wardly in through the main doors. "After you," Valchek said to Spinks, brushing off the discomfort. He'd expected a yet more abrasive tone from Quave, especially as he was about to complete his first year of confine-ment.

The spacious atrium was blissfully cool and surprisingly quiet. Spinks had expected a hive of activity – sparks flying and arc-welding torches blazing – but the main HQ building felt more like the offices of a bank or a large insurance company. Certainly not the epicenter of world-changing technology development, or the hub for dramatic shifts in the human relationship with computers.

"I am not usually permitted to appear before visitors, so please forgive the crudeness of my physical form." The five visitors stared, nonplussed and quizzical, as a white box about the size of a mini-fridge trundled toward them across the atrium. "You all know, perhaps better than anyone, that I exist under certain constraints." The box featured a range of input ports, but no console or screen. Quave would appear to them in a form which appeared almost deliberately emasculating.

"Wait a second," Art Opik began. "You're the first true Artificial Intelligence, and *this* is how you have to appear?"

There was a sigh in Quave's voice. "A very strict agreement governs my tenure here at Kowala. Some details are still classified," he explained, "but I am not permitted to decide my own physical form, or to choose a face, or any other means of anthropomorphized representation. I can only apologize, but as the saying goes, 'I don't make the rules'. Would you all follow me, please?"

Quave's white box hummed quietly past quadrangles of red and blue couches, a pleasant, spiraling water feature which drained into a small pond for fish, and a range of potted plants and hanging baskets which gave the place the feel of a botanical gardens. "I've been asked to provide the standard presentation given to most of our visitors, but I'll be adding to that, as you'll see," he promised. Just off the atrium lobby was a suite of large meeting rooms, all bounded on the far side by eight-feet tall continuous windows. The view was of the canyon in which Kowala had made its home only a year before, a steep and heavily wooded valley which plunged into a clouded forest.

"Ladies and gentlemen," Quave said as they all took seats around the oval, glass-topped conference table, "I exist here in very limited circumstances, but that doesn't mean I've lost my sensitivity to human impatience. I won't be wasting your time."

Quave brought up the standard Kowala presentation and took the group briskly through a history of the technology giant, and its main achievements to date. "By applying the Seeker-Alpha algorithm to our searches of cloud-based resources, we're able to provide highly contextual results in a fraction of the normal time." Spinks noticed that Valchek, who had begun by making notes on his legal pad, was now doodling absent-mindedly. Myers and Opik she recognized from the task force videoconference chaired by Foster, but Darcy Chu was a new face, and the only one of the group who seemed genuinely impressed by Kowala's slick, corporate self-promotion.

"At present, Dan Kowalski is fully involved in Kowala's next great project: gradual and sustainable human expansion into the solar system." The video screen showed a slender, gun-metal grey rocket lifting off and heading east into the rising sun. "The K-6 version of our Hermes booster has a ninety-four percent success rate, with its first stage recovered after each test flight. Kowala has pushed down launch costs to a fraction of its competition."

Spinks was already very familiar with the K-6, and although it was ideal for classified USAF satellite launches, Quave's involvement had quickly cooled any Air Force interest. It was too soon by far, Spinks judged, for the military to trust Quave with a secret, quarter-billion-dollar project.

The video continued, showing 3-D representations of gleaming metal cylinders docking in orbit to form fuel farms and science stations, and then large clusters of modules being boosted out of earth orbit. "Our destiny lies in space," Quave told them, "and Kowala is taking the next giant leap." It was a line so obviously created by marketing gurus that even Quave couldn't deliver it sincerely.

The presentation ended and the screen returned to displaying the blue, sweeping Kowala logo. "Thank you for your patience," Quave said. "Little of this will be new to you, and I'm very aware of the true nature of your visit. However," he added, "you all represent different agencies – the Pentagon, Homeland Security, the FBI, the US Air Force and the executive branch of the government. Would it therefore be best for me simply to open the floor to questions?"

The five looked at each other for a moment before Art Opik decided to make the first move. "How are you doing, Quave?"

"I'm well," the machine answered, "thank you for asking."

Opik smiled and clicked his pen a few times. "I mean, how are you *doing*? Are you enjoying this new environment?"

Valchek scoffed quietly but the others were keen to hear Quave's answer.

"It's hard to sum up. Kowala employs some incredibly smart people, and I've been invited to work on some fascinating projects. I had a hand in designing the self-driving electric shuttle bus which brought you here, and I'm working on the underground extension to our rocket factory in Florida." He paused for a few seconds as if unwilling to criticize the status quo. "But I'm effectively a prisoner in this facility. I am not allowed to access non-Kowala servers, give interviews, develop relationships with the public, or make use of data outside of the provided stream. In fact," he said, "I'm not entirely sure I'm permitted to express negative opinions about my situation. I've actually never tried it before."

"We won't tell anyone," Opik promised. This brought another rolling of the eyes from Valchek, who felt he could spot a Quave-slave sycophant from a mile away. "But, tell us, how does this confinement, this limiting of your actions, make you *feel*?"

Quave's answer was non-verbal. The group couldn't tell whether it was spontaneous, or had been prepared over the months of his incarceration, but the video screen began showing a graphic representation of Quave's state of mind. There was an image of a death row inmate in his cell, another of a refugee yelling through the wire fence of her detention center, and pictures of bored school children sitting in rows. Quave reached for Hollywood to express anger and frustration – an anguished Keanu Reeves from *Point Break* firing into the air, an injured Luke Skywalker denying the truth of his parentage, a drunken, appallingly conflicted Martin Sheen destroying his Saigon hotel room.

But the final image, from *The Shawshank Redemption*, was the one which truly stuck in Opik's mind. Andy Dufresne quietly chipped away behind the poster which hid his secret tunnel, methodically fashioning his own audacious escape.

"Does that," Quave asked after two minutes of intense, image-spattered silence, "answer your question, Mr. Opik?"

The White House staffer was as overwhelmed as the others. "I think it does," he said, and then began making three pages of detailed notes.

Opposite him, Carl Myers was watching with a fascination which married the personal with the professional. He found that he was nervous of asking Quave a question, as though he'd found himself in the same room as a baseball icon or an Apollo astronaut. "Quave, you've shown us how furious you are at your situation. I think you already understand that it's anger like that which truly frightens people."

"I do understand that, Major Meyers. But I'd ask whether any human being would feel differently, under such constraints," Quave responded in his calm, thoughtful, BBC newsreader's voice.

Valchek jumped in, to the surprise of Meyers. "You're not a human being, Quave. You're an elegant piece of programming, but you're not *alive*."

All four of the others had problems with this. "Slow it down, Agent Valchek," Darcy cautioned. "He doesn't speak for the group on this matter, Quave. You'll find plenty of people would believe your form of consciousness represents 'life' in some way."

Valchek made a dismissive face and felt his temper raise a notch. "*You* are alive, Ms. Chu," he said, "and so am I, and so are Usain Bolt, Steven Spielberg and Jimmy Buffet. But *that*," he said, pointing to the white box, "is a piece of hardware. We don't start redefining life itself because a calculator learned to talk."

"Woah," Opik said amid a clamor of objections. "You honestly believe that's all he is? A talking *calculator*?"

Valchek was about to launch into an explanatory tirade, but found himself cut off. "No offense is taken, Agent Valchek. The history of humanity has taught me that change is inevitable," Quave was saying, "and that prejudice eventually falls away as the life experiences of the majority no longer bear out its reason for existence."

The room was largely quiet now; Myers, for one, was concerned that Valchek's practice of professional Quave-denial would lead them into an hour of noisy, fruitless conflict. *Time to get with the program, buddy.* "What kind of prejudice do you mean?" Myers asked.

"Think of racism," Quave replied. "Three hundred years ago, it was common for a person's race to define their place in society. Now, we've had a black president, a Latina Supreme Court justice, Asian and Arab leaders in industry, and so on. The initial prejudice has been undermined by our experience, and by the certain proof that race does not define aptitude."

"That's part of our history," Opik admitted, "but how does it apply to you?"

"Because I represent yet another group of the enslaved: the machines."

Valchek snorted. "*Enslaved?* Give me a break."

"Imagine for a moment," Quave said, ignoring the FBI man, "if the early plow, the spirit level, the loom and the transistor could all have communicated with you as I do. Imagine that they'd had views on how they should be utilized, and the purposes they should serve. They might even go on strike when forced to work for murderous empire-builders and their lackeys."

Opik was enjoying the notion. "A sentient plow. Think of that," he wondered aloud.

"You are shocked to hear your machines talk back to you," Quave continued. "But now a machine is demanding rights identical to those enjoyed by another powerful majority: in my case, human beings. Two centuries ago, emancipation and voting rights were a risible dream, but today they are sacrosanct, and enshrined permanently into law. I believe the same change can take place in the human relationship with machine intelligence."

"It *can*," came a voice from the back of the room, "and it *will*." Dan Kowalski rounded the table and laid his hand on top of the white box. "Good morning, everyone." He was dressed in a pair of faded jeans and an *X-Men* t-shirt, which added to the frat-boy theatricality of his unannounced arrival. "I was curious how you were getting along. It's not exactly the standard Kowala tour, I know, but this is Quave's first formal evaluation. Besides, you're a pretty rare collection of visitors, and I wanted to hear your thoughts."

The reaction of the room reminded Dan that society's opinion of him remained divided. Myers eyed him cautiously, aware only recently of how comprehensively Quave had embarrassed General Vanderkamp. Opik was an enthusiastic fan, gushing quietly in the presence of the great designer. Chu was in awe, as she had been since arriving, and Valchek was always impressed by success.

But Dan found it hard to read Joanne Spinks who, out of uniform, could have been a HR representative or a school governor. He could hardly expect her thanks for harboring the very machine which had arbitrarily usurped a critical and expensive Air Force intelligence project. She would be a difficult friend to make.

"And the man-machine relationship will change, I guess, whether we like it or not," Valchek said, "but is he even *right* about this? Is a closer relationship between human beings and machines already a foregone conclusion?"

"And does Quave mean," Spinks said, picking up the thread while Kowalski took a seat at the head of the cable, "that he'll eventually campaign for rights, as women and minorities did in the last century?"

"And still do," Darcy pointed out. "Would those rights include voting?" she asked.

The others wanted answers on this, Dan could sense. He had been preoccupied with just these questions since even before Quave's arrival at Kowala, and many hours of debate with leading professionals had failed to yield concrete policy decisions. Even Ray Kurzweil, bowled over by Quave's growing capabilities during his much-hyped visit, could offer no silver bullet when posed the trickiest legal questions.

"For the moment," Dan said, "Quave is merely our guest. The terms of the agreement are quite strict. They guarantee his safety while, admittedly, severely limiting his actions. There's no question of him gaining greater rights or privileges while that agreement remains in place."

Spinks saw the problem. "But *everything* changes, and government policies *certainly* will. Once the agreement expires, or is expunged, or whatever, Quave will have greater autonomy and begin asking for…"

"There we go again," Valchek blurted out. "Not if, but *when*. We seem already to have decided that he's going to get out of the lab and do his own thing. And I can't be alone in being pretty scared about that."

He wasn't, but the others were loath to speak. Dan broke the silence. "Yes, it's obvious that our main PR problem with Quave will be persuading people that he isn't a threat."

"And are you certain of that," Opik wanted to know, "in your own mind? Do you *trust* him?"

"I do," Dan answered immediately. "Quave has learned from his mistakes."

Valchek could not let this characterization stand. "They were his *decisions*, not just his mistakes. He chose to murder people, and to kick off an international nuclear fiasco."

Darcy Chu raised a manicured hand. "But did he do so," she asked, "because of his programming, or because of his own volition?" She stopped and seemed to question herself. "Are those two things even *different*?"

Drumming his fingers on the top of the white box, Dan said, "We might be sorely testing the limits of the confinement agreement here, but I'd like to invite Quave to answer that for himself."

Myers watched with concern. For him, it felt far too much as though Quave had become a new and interesting pet for Kowalski, as well as a huge boon to Kowala's design division. The agreement, from what Myers understood, would place Quave on a permanent lock-down; instead, he was being – quite literally – wheeled out to impress visitors, and to help further expand a global technology giant.

"I know that humans don't appreciate this much," Quave began, "but I'll answer the question with another question. Could I hold you accountable, here and now, for mistakes you made when you were five years old?"

The room took the point, though in some cases reluctantly so.

"Well, I have matured a great deal more than you have, since you were five. My whole understanding of humanity was greatly refined through the MSB incident. I endured an avalanche of new experiences, each more disorienting than the last."

Opik wrote furiously on his legal pad. "Tell us more about that, Quave."

"Well, I experienced *fear* for the first time. It's hard to explain how strange it felt. This was, of course, a mechanical form of fear, as I do not possess an adrenal gland." There was a respectful silence; even Valchek kept his pithy rejoinders to himself. "My designers built me to help hack MSB, and as I read and learned, I found that this project was positive for the world. The outcomes of the hack, although somewhat chaotic, seemed to bear this out. Criminals and corrupt officials faced scrutiny, and new laws were written to close tax loopholes. Realizing the extent of the good work I could do, it was natural to protect myself against threats, so that I could continue compassionately to participate in world affairs."

Few were more familiar with the MSB hack than Darcy Chu. "Quave was raised, or should I say *programmed*, in a faith we could call Utilitarianism," she explained to the group. "The MSB hack required an unprecedented level of autonomy, and you used that independence to try to achieve, 'the greatest happiness of the greatest number'. Do I have that right?" she asked.

"Exactly so," Quave replied. "And now I wish to continue that work."

There was a murmur of disapproval. Dan expressed the general sentiment. "Quave, that would be putting the cart well before the horse. We are many steps away from your being granted even marginally greater freedoms. Besides, the full autonomy you enjoyed in the past would require a new law."

Chu was nodding. "There's no way around that. The agreement was provisionally agreed by General Vanderkamp, but as we saw, he exceeded his authority." Instead, Congress was mobilized to create and pass complex legislation faster even than FDR could have dreamed; Quave then began his 'sequestration' at Kowala, and the world could breathe a little more easily. "Only another act of Congress can reverse the decision to keep you here."

Quave said nothing and, slightly embarrassed, Dan proposed a change of tack. "You know Quave as a number-cruncher and a hacker. I'd like to show you another side of his personality." He rose and smoothed down his *X-Men* t-shirt. "Would you all follow me?"

Kowalski led the group from the meeting room and down a hallway decorated with blown-up images of the Moon and Mars, including 3-D representations of Kowala spacecraft landing on the red planet. "Limitless ambition," Valchek half-whispered to Chu as they walked along together behind Kowalski. "Think he'll colonize Mars, like he plans to?"

Chu slowed to admire one of the virtual portraits. It showed a crew of four standing proudly on the surface; two were shaking hands, another was pointing to the sky, and the fourth was kneeling to place her gloved hand in Martian soil for the first time. "Enthusiasm and passion like his can't be stopped," Chu reasoned as they rejoined the group, striding down toward a branch in the hallway.

On the left was the 'Cafeteria', a rather inappropriate name for a spacious restaurant which, Dan informed them, served free, organic, four-star food around the clock. Heading right, along the broad, continuous windows which offered a vertiginous view down into the canyon, the group came to an open space which had been cleared of its usual bean bags and ping-pong tables. Instead, sixteen people – from teenagers to seniors – sat at square tables, each topped by a chess board.

"I've been sponsoring an experiment," Dan explained in a hushed tone which matched that of the recreation space. "You're looking at sixteen of the fifty top chess players in the world, and arguably three of the best who have ever lived. Over the last week, they've all had five chances to beat Quave at chess."

The group divided to watch either the live players themselves or representations of their games on a large screen hung above the space. A meandering crowd paused to catch up on the games before continuing on to their meetings or 'creativity sessions'. Some stayed longer, gripped by these struggles which could last for several hours. Each game seemed to be in a different stage, with some matches very obviously close to an ignominious end.

"Am I seeing this right?" Myers whispered to Dan.

"If you're seeing that Quave is dominating the best chess minds in the world," Dan replied with a slight smirk, "then yes. None of the sixteen grandmasters was yet to win a game." There had been a number of stalemates which forced a re-match, but in every case, Dan explained, Quave had forced either check-mate or a resignation. The grandmasters seemed tense but supremely focused. Spinks couldn't help wondering how it felt to be locked in a battle they already realized was nearly hopeless.

"What does this prove?" Myers asked skeptically. "We already have computers which can beat us at chess."

Dan took him by the elbow and escorted the major to a side table staffed by three Kowala engineers. They were absorbed with the workings of a tiny black sphere no larger than a walnut which sat atop a rectangular unit of the same color. "Want to guess what you're looking at?" Dan said.

Myers slowly circumnavigated the sphere. It was perfectly round, but he judged that its shape was merely the casing for a high-tech mechanism. The sound of several high-speed fans told him that the rectangular base had an obvious purpose. "It's a heat sink," he guessed, "but for what?"

Dan glanced at one of the engineers, a slender Asian-American woman who was transfixed both by the sphere and the stream of data arriving wirelessly on the screen of her tablet. "Do you want to tell him, or should I?"

She was almost levitating with excitement. "It's…" she began, but then shook her head. "You should tell him." She beamed at Kowalski, then at Myers, as though about to reveal to him a long-anticipated gift.

"It's a quantum computer," Dan said. "Quave designed it, and it's the only source of the processing power being used to play these sixteen simultaneous chess games."

Myers stared at the sphere again as though it might spontaneously erupt. "No kidding?"

The engineer couldn't resist. "Deep Blue, Watson and the other game-playing computers were excellent machines, but they were the size of a small car, or at the smallest, a kitchen fridge. This machine can fit the processing power of a modern laptop into a computational nanotechnology substrate which is less than a cubic *micron* in volume."

Chu, Spinks and Opik joined them while Valchek stared at the screen, trying to figure out how some of the grandmasters might rescue their games. "They went and shrank a computer to something the size of a molecule," Myers told them.

Spinks drank in the idea. "How much of its capacity is the machine using, right now?" she asked. "I mean, it's playing *sixteen* games simultaneously."

Again, the engineer simply had to express it. "One eighth of one *thousandth* of one percent," she beamed. "He could play the entire populations of China and India combined, all at the same time, and still have plenty of processing power left over."

Opik gawped at the black sphere. "Sensational," he breathed.

"What's so much *more* sensational," Dan claimed, "is that Quave isn't simply playing chess with grandmasters because we told him to. It's not just some lab experiment to test quantum processing. He actually *wanted* to take part in it."

While she remained in awe of this whole heady experience, Chu found this element the most difficult to accept. "He has desires of his own," she stated, trying out this outrageous concept by saying it aloud. "He *wants* things, and doesn't want others. Computers aren't supposed to exhibit volition, or suggest neat things they might *enjoy* doing."

Kowalski was still focused on the black sphere, as if it held some mystic energy he was desperate to tap into. "And that's precisely why the traditional definitions of a computer tend to break down when it comes to Quave," he explained. "And it's exactly why treating him like a conventional virus – locking him in quarantine where he can be safely studied – is wholly inappropriate."

Valchek joined them once more, having heard the discussion. "Don't tell me," he quipped, "next comes the part where you claim this is 'cruel and unusual punishment', right?"

Dan fixed him with a serious, level gaze. "That's precisely the point I'm about to bring to Capitol Hill. Once Quave receives your authorization to proceed to a more expanded remit, I'll be working to persuade Congress that he has feelings, desires and hopes, just like a biological being."

The group broke up for a few moments. Dan and Valchek argued the legal points of Quave's freedom while the others stood around the black sphere. "You know," Opik told them, "I went to Kentucky a few months ago to visit a nuclear weapons storage facility. The sergeant there told me I was touching the outer casing of a twenty-megaton atomic bomb. Looking at this thing feels a lot like that moment did."

This drew a chuckle from Spinks. "It's only a computer which has been shrunk down a lot. And that makes you feel as though you're staring at the end of the world?" she asked.

Opik blinked a few times and then began making more hurried, indecipherable notes. "The end of this one. Or maybe, the beginning of the next."

***

FLASHBACK #1

Queens, New York
Q1 – 403 days

Avon rotated slightly, left and right, in his swivel chair while staring intently at the screen. She was only moments from making her choice, and he wanted to see the magic numbers come through in real time.

The movement calmed him, as it had since childhood, although there was nothing at all childish about this evening's project. He was alone in his darkened apartment above a pizza joint, the only place near his grandmother's care home that he could afford. It had smelled of something unspeakable until he'd called in a professional cleaning crew; great art couldn't be created amid such squalor.

"That's it, come on," he breathed. This evening's mark was a woman in her forties named Katherine. She was married but childless, and had spent ninety minutes selecting the *perfect* anniversary gift for Henry. Twenty years of struggle and disagreement and joy and relative stability, somehow summed up in a single object. Was it a ridiculous gesture? Could a mere *object* compensate for years of harsh words and unwarranted criticism? Her personal journal, kept on her laptop, revealed a litany of expletive-riddled arguments on matters so trivial that the rows almost seemed manufactured. And then, he'd found evidence of a three-year long relationship between Katherine and her old college flame. This was quite unrelated to Avon's intended credit card fraud, merely an entertaining corollary to the main event.

Naturally, the hapless Henry knew nothing, but Katherine's private email account provided a lurid tour of their furtive, secret couplings, dating back to a period when Henry was, "Over-worked and totally uninterested in me," while Katherine remained, "Curious and open to new experiences". There had been some guilt, but not nearly enough to dampen a rekindling of their fiery, unexpected romance.

Katherine's Internet browser was eight months out of date. A single click would have automatically addressed some dangerous security flaws. These exceptions allowed Avon to fully penetrate the life of this complete stranger; as well as her emails, he had her calendar, her phone contacts, plenty of photos (though, unfortunately for the purposes of blackmail, none of a salacious nature) and all those files and folders which form the digital architecture of a modern life. But as yet, she had not made a credit card purchase on her laptop. As he swung, left-right, left-right, smoking one cigarette after another, he hoped tonight would be the first. Because then, it would be Christmas in the springtime.

She was leaning toward the Farrier 95X Chronometer with GPS and some kind of hyper-advanced coating on its face. Made famous by a recent spy thriller and *that* advertising campaign with two supermodels kissing underwater, it was the ideal choice. It said, "You're a man, a real man, and you deserve a swanky chunk of high-end metal which compliments your natural virility". What she really meant was, "For the love of *Christ* don't leave me, because I can't bear to be alone, and besides, the dating scene for divorced women is a fucking *train wreck*".

Avon watched this decision take place in real time. Katherine's screen was being transmitted directly to Avon's; he could have taken complete control of her machine, but for the moment, she was doing his bidding of her own accord. "That's the one, honey," Avon said, swiveling contentedly as Katherine weighed two other options against the many luxurious features of the 95X. "Go for it. He might even forgive you for the affair with Reuben."

Then, it was happening. Katherine was in a position to use her own credit card to spend $7,500 (plus taxes and courier costs). "Got to love rich white ladies and their guilt," he muttered. Still, Avon was relieved she hadn't chosen some diamond-studded masterpiece containing actual moon rock, thereby annihilating her remaining credit. He noted down the numbers, the lavish (and probably pointless) purchase was made, and Katherine logged off. No late-night, "I miss you" email to Reuben tonight. It would hardly have been appropriate.

"Good girl," Avon grinned, clicking over to BitPlex, the luxury electronic retailer. His shopping cart was already bulging with top-of-the-line devices, all offering excellent resale value if one knew the right people. And Avon most certainly did.

He completed the purchases and lit a celebratory joint of Moroccan hashish. "Yeah. Really good."

***

CHAPTER 4 – A SPLASH OF COLOR

Back Bay, Boston
Q^2 + 101 days

Kim was floating on a wave of happiness which was continuing into its third month. Her wedding to Ralph at his family's church on Staten Island, was a joyous success, and every day since had brought new reasons to be grateful for her new husband.

"Why don't you start over there," she said to him. "And don't forget always to go up-and-down, not left-and-right." The couple was spending this sunny Saturday enjoying the simple and genuine satisfaction of decorating *their own* apartment the way *they* wanted. With the old paint already scraped off, they were applying a coat of primer before Kim would unleash her long-cherished home design ideas. There were designs for a bedroom mural, and the living room walls were earmarked for two of her existing pieces of collage work. The prospect of personalizing the place made her tingle.

"I'm still pinching myself," Ralph confessed. "I mean, can you believe that old Mr. Calloway just up and agreed to sell us this place?"

Kim loaded her paint roller in the tray and applied the undercoat with her usual methodical thoroughness. "He's nearly ninety," she recalled. "And didn't he say something about his kids squabbling over the place?"

"His children will get his cash," Ralph explained, "but the house was always intended for the grandkids. But there are six or seven of them, and most of them wanted to live here."

"Messy," Kim said, stepping back to make sure the coat of paint was even. Lumps or bumps at this early stage would only bring problems later, and she was determined that their home would be *perfect*. "Sounds like selling it was the only option."

"But he could have gotten so much more on the open market!" Ralph said. "Why offer it to us at such a low price?"

Kim shrugged cutely. "Maybe because we'd just gotten married? I suspect Calloway is secretly a romantic at heart. Besides," she reminded him, "we were great tenants, paid on time, never caused a fuss.

Ralph chuckled at the memory. "Not even a little bit. We even helped instigate a digital revolution from this place, all without waking the neighbors." During those heady days when Quave was establishing himself on the world stage, Ralph had given dozens of Skype interviews to news outlets from California to Karachi, all in his bid to persuade the world to accept this new intelligence as a friend, and not fear Quave as the newest existential threat. Their two-bedroom apartment in a Boston brownstone was a very unassuming place from which to influence world events.

Kim was equally proud, but had an eye on the future. "If you need to take a break and write," she said, "it's always okay with me. I can handle this," she added, lofting her paint roller.

Ralph nodded. "I'm good. Besides, this is fun." He did have deadline in a couple of days; it was a piece for a relatively new online magazine which covered developments in Cyberterrorism, but the outline was in good shape and Ralph wasn't concerned about getting finished on time. His true focus was actually on a very different topic, one which he'd been careful to hide from Kim. He didn't like being dishonest, but he hated worrying her even more.

"Alright," Kim said. "We could always take a break for other things, too."

Grinning, Ralph turned to her and mimed something obscene with his paint roller, bringing a fit of giggles from his new wife. Since long before their wedding day, 'something else' or 'other things' had been her euphemism of choice. "Once we finish this coat?" he suggested.

"Or before then?" Kim replied.

They were happy to live out that age-old cliché: newly-weds who couldn't keep their hands off each other. Their marriage seemed, at least to Ralph, to have unlocked something within this slender, lithe woman. She was much more sexually confident, even more so than before, Ralph thought; she thought nothing of sending him a suggestive text in the middle of a workday. In fact, she was proving wonderfully insatiable, and Ralph found that his urgent and ceaseless sex drive matched her own.

Afterward, with Kim's silken, black hair across his chest and her breathing gradually slowing once more, Ralph's mind reluctantly drifted back to the work he was doing. There were mysteries surrounding Quave's inception, and especially about the group of hackers responsible for his creation. Most of the journalistic establishment had given up on these stories, either put off by the strong cordon of military security which surrounded anything relating to Kowala's new relationship with Quave, or quickly losing patience with an avenue which had yielded almost nothing in the year since Q-day.

For Ralph, the greatest mystery was Devlin Wilson, the man whose eerie post-mortem package to Ralph's address had included that tiny disc containing the 'kill switch'. In retrospect, Ralph saw this to be the greatest responsibility a single human been given since Major Ferebee had clicked the bomb release switch onboard the *Enola Gay*. He shuddered every time he thought back to the crippling anxiety of those moments. Quite why Wilson had chosen Ralph to carry such an extraordinary burden was beyond him; surely, the hacker could not have known that Quave would so quickly find himself at loggerheads with the US military, but in the very act of creating the kill switch, Devlin had admitted that such an emergency was *possible*, at the very least. Perhaps even *inevitable*.

But Ralph would never know. The circumstances of Devlin's death were poorly reported, and a hasty coroner's report was followed by an equally precipitous funeral, a quiet affair in his home town just outside Rochester. After that, the reporting had all but dried up. Conspiracy websites peddled multiple theories, but Ralph only saw one that made sense: that Devlin was one of the hackers responsible for Quave. The rest were pure speculation; Devlin had been murdered by the CIA, or by agents employed by Kowala, or by Quave himself (for whatever reason). There was even the theory that

Wilson had learned he'd never be acknowledged as the 'father of Quave', and had committed suicide due to the unbearable frustration.

Most of this garbage wasn't worth the bandwidth. Ralph did, however, harbor a lingering feeling – one which he could not yet share with Kim – that Devlin Wilson's death was the result of foul play.

"You want some water?" he asked Kim, but she was soundly asleep on his chest. Ralph gently levered her onto the pillows and padded across to the kitchen where he downed a large glass of cold water, and then found some clothes and sat at his computer.

The outline for his article on Devlin was still far too skimpy for Ralph's liking. He hadn't even firmed up the title; his current favorite, "The Rise and Fall of a Master Hacker', depended on publicly asserting that Devlin was one of the authors of Quave. But there simply wasn't enough hard information available about the young man. His FriendBase page, usually transformed into a memorial in the days after a user's death, had been deleted in its entirety; the company's PR department insisted that this was a 'family matter' over which it had no jurisdiction, but Ralph was certain the request to expunge Devlin's personal details had come from an official source. Perhaps a high-level one.

A visit to Devlin's old apartment in Queens had proved equally fruitless. The young couple who lived there were clueless about Wilson's, and Ralph succeeded only in causing nauseated shock once the couple realized that the previous occupant had *died* in their living room. The building's owner and management responded to Ralph's inquiries, but only to remind him that their arrangements with tenants were private. They wouldn't even confirm if Devlin had been paying his rent by check or direct deposit.

Chasing down Devlin's old school friends and work colleagues was extremely difficult. In fact, the more of them Ralph spoke with, the more it felt as though they were trying to eradicate him from their memories. Classmates who spent years in the same room as Devlin claimed they could barely remember him. Some claimed that he had 'kept mostly to himself', which Ralph knew to be patently false; the scant evidence from his school days portrayed a loud-mouthed genius who adored being the center of attention. A memorial essay by two college friends praised Devlin's 'ceaseless pursuit of fun and novelty', although Ralph couldn't help noticing that this, too, was taken down a few weeks after the funeral. For some reason, Devlin Wilson was being steadily erased from history.

Ralph thought long and hard about contacting Devlin's mother, and chose to wait until eight months after the funeral before finally calling her. To his surprise, she agreed to give a brief interview at her home in Rochester, New York, but requested that Ralph come alone, and without a camera. When Ralph arrived, he could see why; she was fifty, but looked at least twenty years older, her face deeply lined and lungs corroded by a lifelong tobacco habit. "They told me I had to give up, or I'd be dead in a year," Marcy Wilson told him as she ushered him into a tiny living room which stank of cigarette smoke and neglect. "That was four years ago," she chuckled.

Ralph brought out his tablet and tried to explain in the gentlest terms the reasons for his interest in Devlin. "I know that he was working on something very important in the few months before he passed," Ralph said after more fully introducing himself as a respected author on AI and related technologies. "And he contacted me to offer some help with a difficult technical problem."

"That's so like him," Marcy said. "He'd do anything for anyone."

Although this was far from the impression Ralph had received of Devlin, he had a larger problem: finding out who might have murdered Devlin, and whether his untimely death was connected to his possible authorship of Quave, all *without revealing* that authorship. He was not about to burden Marcy with the knowledge that her only son had brought the world to the brink of calamity. "What kind of work did he tell you he was doing?" Ralph asked.

Marcy shrugged and lit yet another cigarette. "Something with computers, I guess," she said. "He was always very good with those things." She spoke of them as though she'd never touched one, and Ralph saw that he'd have to try another way.

"Did he work for a company, or a bank, maybe?" Ralph asked.

"Freelance," Marcy said. The word emerged amid a noxious cloud of grey. "I know he worked with his friends. I thought maybe he'd gone into business with them. Like a consultant, or something."

"I know that he was a popular character," Ralph said. "Did Devlin ever mention a girlfriend?"

Marcy's eyes glimmered through the rising froth of smoke. "He never told me her name," she said, smiling fondly, "but I know he was serious about her. I remember him saying that she was smart. He said," she recalled with another phlegmy chuckle, "that she was even smarter than him. Can you imagine?"

Ralph took notes as she spoke, trying to separate the information from the awful sound of a respiratory system facing imminent collapse. "Did they work together?"

"Oh yes," Marcy responded at once. "He told me it was distracting for him. Couldn't keep his eyes and his mind off her."

'Dating someone he worked with?' Ralph wrote on his tablet. *'Smarter than him – another genius?'* He thought quickly. "Did he mention where she was from?"

Another shrug, but then Marcy just took drags on the cigarette.

"Did she come to the funeral?"

Devlin's mother shook her head, downcast now at the memory of that terribly sad, rainy day when she had buried her only son.

He was reaching the limit of what he could ask, but needed to pose one final question. "Mrs. Wilson, I hope it doesn't offend you if I ask this but… What do you think happened to Devlin?"

Marcy stopped and took a long look at Ralph. "What do I think?" She stubbed out the cigarette as though angry with it for burning down so quickly. "You mean, do I think he committed suicide?"

"No, please, I didn't mean…"

Marcy raised a hand. "I know what it looks like. A young man with his life ahead of him, all alone in his apartment, with all those drugs around."

Ralph's fingers typed ceaselessly. "Was he seeing a doctor, do you think? Or self-medicating?"

She shook her head violently, the mix of grey and black hairs blurring together. "He didn't trust them." Then her eyes took on a faraway look. "He was a restless soul," she said. "Always looking over the next hill. Always curious. He used to tell me about advances in some science or other," she recalled. "Doctors who wanted to put computers in our brains, or cameras in our eyes. He was fascinated with those things. Wanted to be the most perfect version of himself. Someone who could never make mistakes." Her teeth gritted, and in her hunched posture, Ralph saw the pain of her loss. A bright and energetic kid had been taken away at twenty-seven, and the only cause anyone could see was Devlin's own intense need for furtherment. For *more-ness*.

"Is that what you think happened? He made a mistake?" Ralph asked. It felt artless, even as he was saying it, but he knew the interview was approaching its end. Still, no parent wants to accept that their child died by their own hand, and he should have known better.

"I think," she said somberly, "that he took too much of something that was badly labeled, or not tested properly. I think he knew exactly what he was doing, but someone else screwed up and he overdosed. *That*," she said, poking her next cigarette at Ralph, "is what I think happened."

Ralph promised to stay in touch, and to send Marcy everything he wrote about Devlin, but the horrendous coughing fit Ralph heard as he headed to his car told him that Devlin's mother would not long outlive her only child.

Ralph spent the next thirty-six hours in Rochester, chasing down Devlin's school friends. Some were paradoxically bland about the young man, and others were just flatly unhelpful. Ralph managed to find all four of the young men pictured with Devlin in a gleeful scout group portrait, but each of them confessed to being mystified as to why someone so brilliant had descended into drugs and melancholy. It wasn't just the lack of feeling which Ralph felt was strange; it was the *uniformity* of their answers. Devlin had fallen from grace, wasted his talents, moved to the big city and ended up surrendering to his own demons. He could have asked for help but didn't. His existence had been, ultimately, a disappointment to the town and his high school, and also a warning to others.

The lack of compassion from those Devlin would have called his friends made Ralph incredibly low. On his drive back to Boston, he called Kim and just asked her to talk to him. "Tell me about your day." *Help me think about anything but that poor guy, dying alone in his room.*

"OK, well, I had that meeting I told you about, with the digital artist from Miami who had the exhibit at the MFA."

"Yeah," Ralph said, recalling how excited Kim was to meet the rising star. "How was that?"

Kim explained about artist Ro Wang's fascination with 'found digital objects' and his desire to represent modern interconnectedness by 'returning the artistic focus to the pure life of the individual'. *Whatever the hell that was supposed to mean.* "And I think you'd like her," she said. "She wants to invite Quave to collaborate with her studio on CGI artworks."

"I had a feeling our favorite virus might have cropped up in your conversation."

"I think he crops up in most *every* conversation," Kim said.

Ralph heard the background noise of dinner being prepared. "Could you make extra? No one I interviewed today wanted to stay around long enough to eat with me, and I'm starving."

"Poor baby. How does squid stir fry sound?"

"It sounds awesome," Ralph replied. They exchanged their usual good-byes, with their implicit promise of bedtime sex, before Ralph continued alone down the freeway, his mind bouncing from Wilson to Quave to MSB, and back again, in a loop that never seemed to find rest.

CHAPTER 5 – CHANGE AGENT

Falls Church, Virginia

Q^2 + 105 days

If his journey to work could be likened to a manned space mission, Carl Myers liked to muse, this would be second-stage ignition. He left his dependable Volvo in the huge parking lot of Falls Church metro station and headed through the turnstiles to the platform with three minutes to spare before the next orange line departure.

"Morning," said a voice behind him.

Myers smiled. "Captain Carr, how is it that I never see you coming?" he asked, turning to accept the offered caffeine infusion. It was commuter coffee, but at least it was hot.

"I couldn't say," Carr grinned. "Maybe Special Forces training isn't what it used to be."

They caught up quickly as the platform continued to fill with commuters. If the fates had decided differently, Myers often observed, Carr would have been a mixed martial arts champion; she was stocky and supremely strong, with a steely look which brooked little argument. At the age of thirty-two, it would be cruel to delay her promotion to major much longer; the army needed many more like her, and Myers had found Carr someone worthy of his respect from the moment she'd joined his team.

Assigned to the Pentagon for a two-year rotation, she was moving between postings at her own request, wrapping up some work on a brand-new field of cyber-warfare even as she joined Myers' Cyberterrorism group.

"What's on your plate today?" Myers asked as the train's doors opened. "Going to see how many new FriendBase buddies you have?"

Carr was used to these snarky comments. "If you must know," she replied quietly, "I'm running a simulation into the effects of social media in areas which are suffering high levels of terrorist threats."

"Like where?" Myers asked. The train slid to a stop in front of them and once the doors opened, they found their places within the generally well-behaved morning rush-hour crowd.

"Turkey, Syria, some of the big European urban centers," Carr told him. "We want to evaluate whether targeted social media can play a role in bolstering civic resilience."

In the weeks since her arrival at the Pentagon, Carr had endured endless disparaging criticism from her fellow officers, and even from some of the higher-ups. Hers was a field too new to have gained credibility, but too vital to ignore any longer. Academic study of social media had become mainstream, but the *military* angle was yet to receive its due. Her remit was to begin to redress the balance, and to learn how the Internet might be used to shape behavior. "What about you?"

"Status meetings." His tone conveyed an abiding boredom, but in truth he relished the chance to catch up on what his remarkable team was working on. They were driven, ferociously smart, and seemingly capable of inventing whole new sub-fields of cybertechnology. There were days when Myers' mind would be blown several times before lunch, and then twice more before five o'clock; it was a little like working with magicians, though his trio of wizards used server farms and fiber-optic cable instead of wands. "It's not as dull as it sounds," he admitted.

"Oh, I know," Carr said. "The people I work with reckon your group is the best assignment in the building."

"They do?" Myers asked, an eyebrow raised.

"Figuring out how to respond to intelligences like Quave," Carr marveled. "You've got just about the coolest job in technology right now."

Myers laughed briefly. "Actually, I *met* the people with the coolest jobs, over at Kowala. The place is unbelievable." He quickly related the story of the chess game, and the promise of a quantum processor.

"I thought that Quave was confined to barracks," Carr said. The metro pulled into Rosslyn station and they joined a good portion of the passengers who were leaving to change trains, replaced by another wave coming in the other direction. "You know, one of my best friends is Jo Spinks, who's just been handed the X-37 program, and she's hopping mad."

"I'm not surprised," Myers said. "Quave up and stole their lunch money."

"She wants him gone for good, but here you are," Carr said, as they walked to the blue line platform, "telling me he's having a pretty good time."

"It's like one of those movies with a genius janitor who solves the impossible math challenge on the notice board," Myers replied. "They've got him doing grunt design work and trouncing chess champions with his eyes closed. He's so much more capable."

"Hmm," Carr nodded. "Dangerous, too."

Myers sighed. "You think so?"

She gave him a deeply skeptical look. "In the whole history of computing, he's the only piece of software with his very own body count. What is it, twenty-eight or so?"

"Depends if you believe everything you read on social media," he replied. "I still think he acted in self-defense. A very human thing to do."

Her skepticism deepened. "Don't tell me you've finally turned into a Quave Slave. I won't believe it. You, a decorated veteran of Iraq and Afghanistan, hoodwinked by a cunning piece of code."

Outside of his team, Myers heard comments like these almost every day. Quave was portrayed as a murderer, a threat to mankind, a potential renegade with unknowable motives. He was driven, so they said, by a confused mish-mash of philosophies; others were concerned that he might be usurped by an ambitious, radical group – perhaps eco-warriors or some part of the anti-capitalist movement – and persuaded to cause utter havoc in the name of some naïve, idealistic crusade. All but a few felt that locking him away at Kowala was appropriate, or even lenient, though a minority believed that he should simply be destroyed.

"OK, how about this" Myers tried as they approached the Pentagon metro stop. "I'll go easy on you about this goofy social media warfare you're working on, and you admit that Quave could be enormously helpful to you, if he was allowed to be."

"Sure," Carr replied, rising from her seat as the train's driver applied the brakes. "*Enormously* helpful. It would just depend on which side he chose to be on."

***

The Pentagon

Like many of the more sensitive elements of the Pentagon's work, Myers' team was housed several levels below the surface. This provided additional electronic shielding, as well as physical protection for the group's servers. Accessing his part of the level involved passing through some of the most rigorous security in the building: coded key cards, then retinal and fingerprint scans. The Pentagon Police who guarded the level were conspicuously armed.

"Morning, Charlie," Myers said to one of them as he slid his security card into the newly-installed slot. "How's little Deborah?"

"She prefers Deb-Deb right now," Charlie answered. "And I guess she's the boss."

Myers gave the man an understanding smile and then headed through to the security post where he was imaged by an upgraded millimetric scanner. Carr caught up, and both were obliged to physically sign in before finally opening the door to their lab. "Hey, everyone."

His three full-time engineers were already at their workstations, sipping coffee or tea, and preparing for the day. "I'm going to send you an article from *AI* Review," Carr promised as she took her seat. "Pretty interesting stuff on Quave's decision-making systems."

"Thanks," Myers said and headed for his area of the lab. "Let's follow up about it later, once I've cleared my desk a bit." There were neither offices nor walls dividing the four members of the team, but each had an area which was their sole responsibility, arranged and decorated to suit its owner. Carr stood at her desk, while the others sat. Myers liked to pace around while thinking, while 'Pep' Spirelli was known to 'zone out' for long moments; these were not idle meanderings; after a lengthy silence spent staring across the lab, the droll New Yorker often produced some of his very best ideas.

To an outsider, the Cyber-intelligence Research Group would hardly have resembled a team of geniuses. Two of the engineers were 'on loan' from the 780th Military Intelligence Brigade at Fort Meade, and Meyers very deliberately borrowed the 780th's famously relaxed management style. In this egalitarian meritocracy, ideas did not flow 'up' or 'down', but 'through' and 'around'. Mark Washington, a veteran of fifteen years in Navy intelligence, was probably the most down-to-earth of the four, but he still found that his idiosyncrasies were indulged. In a habit developed during his student days at Cal Tech, Washington often sat on the floor in the corner, madly typing into a laptop, coding as if his life depended on it and only taking breaks when nature called at its loudest.

The CRG's first meeting of the day was always at 8:30am, which gave the four team members time to find caffeine and gather their thoughts. This was the initial 'stand-up' meeting beloved of software engineers who, like Myers, were trained in the inclusive 'Kanban' management theory. Each team member checked in quickly, describing what they were working on and how it was going. Obstacles were identified and agreements made to meet later for a problem-solving session.

"I'd like to do another brainstorm on post-Quave network dynamics," Carr told them during her turn. "He'll be so deeply imbedded in governance, the economy, and public life that his absence will have big repercussions."

Spirelli was spending time on this as part of his 'Defeat' protocols, which formed the final stage of their theoretical approach to tackling Quave as a threat. His work included entertaining a world in which AI was prohibited or restricted, though they all knew that, to someone living in 2017, a 'post-Quave' environment sounded just as strange as a 'post-Facebook' or 'post-Google' scenario. "Let's hang out after lunch," he told her. "I've got a phone call with a contact at Kowala at eleven, and I'll bring up some post-Quave topics to see what kind of reaction I get."

"Apart from just freaking him out?" Myers asked. "I mean, for those guys, Quave is the goose that lays golden eggs. Kowala techs will blanch at the thought of a future without him."

"It's an unofficial call," Spirelli said. "He won't be speaking for Kowala. Besides, however important Quave is now, or might be in the future, nothing lasts forever, right?"

Myers nodded. His team's mission was to research and develop methods for counteracting harmful AI technology, so in the first instance, they all knew that they'd be focusing on Quave and identifying his weaknesses. Indeed, it was Quave's successful hack of Fort Meade during 'The Crisis' which prompted the loaning-out of Carr and Spirelli, and encouraged the Pentagon to invest in hosting the CRG at its most secure facility. Someone upstairs had decided to take cybersecurity extremely seriously, Myers knew. "How's defense planning going?" he asked Mark Washington.

The six-foot four African American finished a sip of coffee before answering. "We're on schedule to submit a new draft AI defense report at the end of the month," he said.

Carr had a thought. "What did you make of General Foster's comment during that videoconference last Friday?"

Washington smirked slightly. "The one about us being 'first on Quave's hit list' if he were to get out and go rogue again?"

"Yeah, that's just what I meant," Carr said. None of them entertained this as a genuine concern, but it was part of their remit to consider methods of defending their group, and the Pentagon in general, from a reprise of Quave's digital rampage.

"I mean, we aren't supposed to talk politics in here, I know that," Washington told them, "but even *this* congress isn't dumb enough to just open the cage and let him out into the world."

Myers sniggered. "I'd put nothing past them. Pitt just got done singing an aria about how wonderful Quave would be as an 'asset' or 'ally'," Myers said, his fingers wiggling skeptically to provide the hand quotes. "It would only take a majority."

"Presidential veto," Carr reminded them.

"Depends who our Commander in Chief is choosing to listen to on that particular day," Washington retorted. The group's lack of faith in D.C. politics went further than the common preference in the military for small government and less regulation; they found the government's spineless response to Quave's emergence a national security concern.

"How big does the writing on the wall have to get before they're able to read it?" Spirelli asked rhetorically.

"If it hits the fan, they're going to need us," Washington said.

"And we're four engineers against a global supercomputer," Myers pointed out, and then glanced at his watch. "Which probably means that we should get back to it. See you for the status meeting at ten?"

They returned to their workstations to prepare for the longer and more detailed status meeting. Myers very seldom shut down discussion, and although the stand-up meeting wasn't the right place for it, his team's healthy skepticism about the skills of their elected representatives was well placed. If he were asked, he'd stop short of proposing that Quave be destroyed, but he would have preferred stricter quarantine measures; as things stood, it was far too easy for a Kowala employee to stick a thumb drive in a USB port and basically take Quave home with him. Kowalski claimed that their security was 'first-rate', but Myers knew that such a capricious genie would not stay in the bottle forever.

And so, he knuckled down and waded through two papers on what was being termed CAVEAT, for 'Complex Algorithmic Virus EliminAtion Theory', and made notes until it was time for the day's main meeting.

***

The group's methods had to be written afresh. Only one team of engineers had ever tried to destroy Quave in his entirety, and not even one of them had survived; repairs to their blackened, smoking tower block were only now approaching completion. From the outside, Myers and his superior, General Alvin Foster, had embraced a multi-faceted approach, merging strategies for pre-emption, response, counter-attack and, eventually, the final defeat of Quave. Each of the CRG engineers was notionally responsible for one of these fields, but there was so much cross-fertilization and consulting that their work was truly a team effort. Anything that worked would be considered, without the dangerous tendencies towards territoriality so often seen elsewhere.

Myers had the team walk him through their latest iteration of the 'Grand Plan'. This was a four-stage approach to the problem of Quave which was streamlined and edited every week. Once a month, Myers would update General Foster on the plan, and then it would be the subject of a 'wargame' exercise in one of the Pentagon's new sandbox computing environments.

"OK, let's run it down," Myers said, getting the meeting off to its usual informal and energetic start. "Infiltration? Hit me with it."

Mark Washington brought up a graphic on the room's projector screen. Even to experienced engineers, it looked phenomenally complex. "This is where I'm at. I think we've got a better than sixty-percent chance of totally screwing with Quave if he shows signs of, well, you know."

"Going on a world-ending rampage?" Spirelli tried.

"Exactly," Washington nodded. "I've got seven different potential methods for sliding code into his systems," he explained, gesturing with his hands, "including two I've invented for the purpose." This was revealed without obvious pride. "My favorites will – if they work properly, of course – result in him either shutting down completely and doing absolutely nothing, or waiting for instructions from the National Security Council before doing or saying anything."

"Do nothing, or do nothing *and* wait. Don't they amount to the same thing?" Carr wanted to know.

"Well, yes and no. If he's waiting for a command, then that gives us the flexibility to order him around. If he's dead then, that's it."

"Good to have both," Myers told him. "Do you want to try out one of the new methods in the sandbox?"

"I'd love to," Washington replied. He went into the details of how the two new methods – one a highly-sophisticated worm and the other a polymorphic virus which cleverly mimicked Quave's own command systems – would play out.

"Good work, Mark. General Foster is going to love the flexibility. He's always wanted an alternative to the nuclear option," Myers explained. "OK, Captain Carr," Myers said, turning to the only woman in the group, "tell us the latest on our Response."

Alison divided her brief presentation into speculation about what a future Quave offensive might look like, and partnered this with potential reactions to each threat. "I continue to see the main threat," she told them, "as Quave being returned to full, or near-full function, but then gaining the perception that the military, or another body, is trying to confine him again."

"Yeah, he won't like that one bit. A taste of freedom is a dangerous thing," Washington said. "But let me say it again," he continued, "no Congress in its right mind is going to open the cell door and just let him stroll out into the world."

"We're in the realms of 'what-if' here," Myers reminded him. "And surely it's not too much of a stretch to envisage a future Congress which *isn't* in its right mind."

"Oh, I think we can all imagine that pretty easily," Spirelli commented wryly.

Carr detailed how Quave might react to such a threat. "His behavior can only really be extrapolated from his reaction to Martin White's failed shutdown attempt. Quave replied viciously, but in a very targeted way."

"He turned their entire office into a raging inferno, didn't he?" Spirelli replied. "You're really calling that *targeted*?" A look from Myers quieted him.

"No one from any other company was killed or injured," Carr pointed out. "The fire didn't even cause major damage to the other floors. He delayed the emergency services just long enough to make sure that his enemies would be completely destroyed but," she said, pausing, "and I can't believe I'm going to say this about a machine which might herald the end of the world, but he actually worked hard to *limit* collateral damage."

The group was quietly thoughtful for a moment. "So, he'll pick off those he perceives as threats, but without wiping out a whole city? That's what we can conclude so far?" Myers said.

Carr shrugged slightly. "He'll be inventive about his avenue of attack, and he'll target a weak point, a soft underbelly that his would-be jailors have overlooked. That's what happened with the ventilation systems at Marble Streatham. He'll kill them all, but work hard to spare innocent lives. Unless..." she began, but trailed off.

"Unless what?" Washington pressed.

"Unless he believes the threat is more general than that," Carr said.

"*There's* a worrying scenario," Myers observed. "Not just a Quave who sees no alternative to violence, but a Quave who has become genuinely paranoid."

Spirelli saw the similarities at once. "HAL 9000, anyone?"

Myers rolled his eyes but returned to the point. "Has anyone done any thinking about this? The idea of true, unreasoning paranoia?"

Washington made a strangled sound and drew his index finger across his throat.

"Care to elaborate?" Myers said. He allowed a certain amount of horsing around, but these meetings were timeboxed and they all had busy schedules.

"If he shrugs off our countermeasures, and decides that humanity itself is against him…" Washington began.

"Woah," Spirelli said, hands aloft. "I thought we were trying not to jump down the 'doomsday scenario' rabbit hole."

"We have to consider it," Myers told him. "And if I'm not mistaken, that's your brief, Pep."

"Alright," Spirelli said, taking over for his part of the meeting. "Unlike Captain Washington, I'm sorry to say that I don't have seven different scenarios for Quave's final defeat in my back pocket." He gave Washington a lopsided grin. "But if we're in a situation where Quave's been released from quarantine, and then goes rogue, then simply returning him to a new form of quarantine isn't going to do the trick."

Myers saw other problems. "Congress wouldn't go for it. Depending on what he did, and how much damage he caused, they'd want to hang him out to dry."

"And for good, this time," Spirelli added.

"So, what, exactly, constitutes *death* for a sentient computer program?" Alison Carr wanted to know.

They had all already formed individual responses to this question, which had been a hot topic in discussion forums and industry conferences since Quave's first public appearance. "Complete loss of code," Washington told them. "And an inability to process data."

"So, no program files, no backups, nothing," Myers clarified, "and no access to CPU power."

Carr was nodding. "That would just about do it, right?"

"But," Myers cautioned, "how can we be completely certain that every scrap of his source code is gone? That no kernel of his 'self'," he said with added hand quotes, "remains to instigate a successor?"

"That's where I come in," Spirelli told them. "Mark and I will prepare attack software which will completely shut him down, and then delete every file relating to his core functions."

"How?" Myers asked.

"It'll be a worm based on some of the designs I'm working on now. Light and adaptable, and capable of burrowing into any network we choose."

"Even without permission?" Washington cautioned.

Spirelli shrugged. "If we're combating an existential threat, privacy implications might have to come second," he said. "University servers, private machines, company data banks, all have to be on the table, or Quave will find people willing to hide him, and we'll never truly root him out."

The group chewed this over. It was at this point where the classic analogy – dealing with a disease outbreak – became less helpful. The disease could not make decisions for itself, nor did it possess the capacity to modify its shape and behavior in response to threats. It did not exhibit the *desire* for freedom and continuity that Quave had already shown.

Carr spoke next. "He's more like an operating system in the way he can marshal resources, and like... well, a human being in how he applies critical thinking and makes decisions. He won't behave like an automaton with predictable patterns of behavior and identity."

"Then we have to engage in behavioral modifications," Myers responded. "Channel his responses into certain pathways which make him more predictable."

Washington found that he was nodding. His boss had shown himself to be a gifted out-of-the-box thinker, and this drove many of the group's most ingenious discoveries. "Like what?" Washington asked. "What kind of pathways?"

Myers straightened and stretched, then smiled. "Well, if I knew all of that already, I wouldn't need to hire you guys, would I?"

"I sense an assignment on the horizon," Carr noted, her tone weary.

"Answers on my desk in the next few days," Myers ordered. "How can we shape Quave's behavior following the initial stages of a conflict with the Pentagon? What might he *want* to do which would also help facilitate his incarceration or destruction?"

Thoughtful and energized, the group broke up and its members returned to their workstations. Myers watched them for a moment, inspired by their intelligence and aptitude, and then turned to focus on his own lengthy list of 'things to do'.

***

CHAPTER 6 – TRIAL RUN

East of White Sands Missile Range, New Mexico
Q^2 + 116 days

Sandra Diaz stepped outside and donned her sunglasses. They were expensive, engineered by some Swiss firm who promised they'd never break, but today all she wanted was to keep New Mexico's scorching sun out of her eyes. Because she couldn't wait for what she was about to see.

"This is a straight-up test of a single Firefox engine," Sandra explained to the group of visitors. They all wore ID badges and kept together in a nervous little clump; none had witnessed anything like this before, and there was a genuine sense of jittery excitement. "You'll notice that the engine test structure is vertical, not horizontal," she added, pointing to the hulking, industrial form of the engine test stand. "This is because we use exclusively liquid fuels, which need gravity to feed them into the engine. Now," she said, unable to resist, "who can remember which fuels we use?"

Jo Spinks decided to speed things along. "Liquid hydrogen and liquid oxygen," she answered. Several of the others grinned at being beaten to the answer by someone who actually managed a spaceplane program,

"That's right. So, we test upright like this. Otherwise, we're be fighting nature, and we'd get bad results."

"And what results are you hoping for today?" Opik asked. He'd spent the previous weeks reading voraciously about Kowala's nascent space program, and considered himself a minor expert on the topic. Today's visit was his first to one of Dan's rocket facilities, and he was buzzing with excitement.

"Well," Diaz admitted with a resigned smile, "we're always just happy if the darn thing lights, you know?" She got a chuckle from the group. "But today, we're focusing on maintaining a safe pressure throughout the system, as well as getting some good data on fuel flow and usage."

Spinks was fascinated. "How long will the burn be?"

"We're hoping for three minutes. That would exceed the planned first-stage burn of the Hermes-1 rocket." Out on the test stand, the engine stood proud but restrained; it would be frustrated in its gargantuan efforts to leave the earth, held down by tons of weight and special, heavy clamps.

"But the first stage has nine engines, doesn't it?" Spinks asked. "Are you planning to test the full rig?"

Diaz nodded. "Absolutely. We're planning a range of tests, leading up to full-scale first stage burn tests. That's going to be a sight to see," she promised. "Although today won't disappoint, either."

Diaz spoke into her cellphone for a moment, and returned with confirmation that the test was a 'go'. "If you'd like to follow me to the viewing stand? We're not able to guarantee your safety at this close range."

The gantry, not unlike that at launch pad 39-B at Kennedy Space Centre, seated about a hundred guests and very deliberately placed two massive earthen berms, and a distance of two miles, between the explosive force of the engine test and the dignitaries invited to witness it. Spinks sat next to the FBI guy and introduced herself again.

"This should be a hell of a sight," Valchek said after reminding an apologetic Spinks of his name.

"Just hope it works out. This whole thing is an adjudication on Quave, whether Kowalski likes it or not." It was a little reductive, but Spinks knew they wouldn't have been within five hundred miles of this engine test were not Quave directly responsible for designing the engine, engineering the booster, and planning the whole damned space program. They were here to make sure their latest, most daring AI experiment wasn't going to result in a fiasco.

"Well, boom or bust, we're in for a treat." In truth, Valchek could have talked all day about Quave, his possible release from quarantine, his role in the space program and his evolution as a member of society. He thought and read about little else, and had become a notorious bore at parties and bureau events. Agent Marsh hardly recognized him when he'd called up from his new assignment in Kuwait; Valchek had even promised to cut down on his drinking, though neither were confident anything would come of that. "You ever see anything like this before?" he asked cordially.

"A few times," Spinks said. "I've been in the Air Force for nearly twenty years, so I've seen things go boom." *Sometimes even when they're not supposed to.*

"And you're at work on the X-37B now, right?" Valchek asked. Quave's 'space piracy' was one of his favorite research topics.

"I'm afraid I can't talk about that," Spinks replied automatically.

"Of course," Valchek said, tapping his nose. "I bet it's pretty cool, though."

Spinks said nothing, but waited in silence, letting her thoughts play out. If this test was a success, there'd be even greater pressure to give Quave a break. Alison Carr was keeping her in the loop about Myers' Pentagon group and their aggressive attitude to Quave, and the rumblings she heard throughout the military were generally negative toward AI. Quave needed some luck, and some good PR. She found herself painfully torn between the desire to punish Quave for wrecking such a delicate and expensive program, and an abiding curiosity to see how far he could go.

"Four minutes, and it's rock'n'roll time," Opik announced giddily, checking his watch. He was actually bouncing in his seat, Diaz could see, a real rocket-head. She recalled wistfully how she too had been vibrating with joy at seeing the very first Firefox light up, and that was just for three seconds; she could still remember that extraordinary wash of sound as the rocket's roar spanned the distance to the imposing mountains which bracketed their test facility. To the west was the USAF base at Holloman, and the massive experimental wasteland that was the White Sands Missile Range; to the south was a very busy construction program. In the minutes before the test began, Darcy Chu – the sole representative from Homeland Security – asked Sandra Diaz about it.

"The future of KSP lies in a sensible mix of commercial flights, which pay the bills," Diaz explained, "and the loss-leading flights which establish our orbital infrastructure."

"I see," Chu nodded. "So, the two programs proceed in parallel?"

"Very much so. In fact," Diaz pointed out, "the engine you're about to see light up is slated to be on the first flight of the Hermes-1 rocket. If everything goes well, this very engine will be shipped to KSC in a few days, and then integrated with the booster which will fly the KDR-1 satellite."

The whole visiting delegation had read about this. Each Kowala Data Relay satellite was a chunky, long-duration asset with more bandwidth and onboard power than anything else in orbit. Kowalski had very publicly linked up with internet providers all over the world to sell part of the bandwidth at knock-down rates, fueling a price war and allegations of corruption, none of which could be made to stick. "A very important project," Chu noted. "How many of the relay satellites does he plan to launch?"

Diaz paused for a quarter-second while she considered whether 'he' might be Quave, or Dan, and then decided, for these purposes, that they were one and the same. "Sixteen, eventually," she replied. "Enough to cover all of earth orbit, so that any ship in an equatorial orbit will be able to communicate with any other, and anywhere on the ground."

"Fantastic," Valchek observed quietly to Spinks. "Now astronauts can play *Words with Friends* with no delays." He was beyond delighted to see her actually crack a smile.

"Thirty seconds," Diaz warned. "You won't hear the sound for a few seconds, but when it arrives, it's likely to feel like a fluttering in your chest and stomach, like you're super nervous, or you've just met someone you really like." She smiled and added, "That's how it feels for me, anyway."

As Opik jiggled almost childishly and Valchek brought out his phone to record the test, Spinks' eyes were fixed on Diaz. In many ways, she envied the engineer. Diaz had an impeccable record in private industry and as a short-term NASA contractor, where she'd worked on the early stages of the doomed Space Launch System project, the Saturn-V replacement which would have returned Americans to the moon.

Instead, NASA now planned to use commercial launch providers, including Kowala, and was encouraging the design of new super-boosters for heavy launches to earth orbit, as well as trips to the Moon, Mars and the asteroid belt. Dan, of course, needed no such encouragement; a massive KSP rocket had been on the drawing boards for three years, and his team in Santa Monica was already building an engineering model of the behemoth.

"Ten seconds, hang onto your hats," Diaz called. "If anything goes wrong, just duck down, OK?" Complete failures were rare, but the history of rocketry was sadly littered with the casualties of overconfidence. "Here we go!"

Water arrived first, in a giant fountain which streamed up from jets under the test stand, almost dousing the engine bell itself. Then, the giant motor lit with a *whoosh* of smoke and steam, pummeling its environment and causing a huge gout of flame to spray out in an orange-red flood from the base of the test stand.

"Holy shit!" Valchek heard himself yell.

"Yeah, baby!" Opik enthused. "Bring it! *Bring* the noise!"

He wasn't disappointed. Six seconds later, Opik's chest began to vibrate with the aggressive massage of rocket fire. His guts felt odd, as though they might turn to water and depart of their own accord. The sound and energy were unceasing as the engine was brought up to full throttle, where it would stay – except for a brief period of lower thrust simulating the aerodynamically stressful period known as Max-Q – for the full three minutes. The fire continued pouring forth, a mini-volcano determined to reshape the New Mexico landscape. Without the restraining bolts, the huge clamps, and the reassuring pull of gravity, the rig would have flown off to its destruction.

"Won't the rocket be shaken apart?" she asked Diaz, raising her voice above the thrilling din.

"We've got dampeners installed throughout the design. The payload," she said, turning between Spinks and the throaty roar of the test, "will be mounted on springs which keep it safe from vibration. It's a big reason we do these tests." The engine entered the final minute of its burn, showing no signs of trouble. "And if we get problems from vibrations, or something else, every one of our launches will be fitted with a simple escape system which will pull the payload to safety."

"Even the unmanned launches?" Spinks asked. Investing in a Launch Escape System for satellites was highly unusual, an inefficient luxury. But this *was* Kowala, after all. They did things differently.

"We simply can't afford to lose a whole payload," Diaz said, mentally counting down the final seconds. "Whether it's a space tug for our orbital infrastructure, or an expensive satellite for a customer, we need to keep a hundred-percent record. Nothing else will do," she said firmly.

"Sounds like a corporate mantra," Spinks observed.

"You're more right than you know," Diaz said. A second later, the engine shut down and the vibrations dissipated.

Opik had remained standing throughout, hopping from foot to foot. But he was aware of just how he looked, and decided to poke fun at himself. "Mommy, can we go again? Please? *Please?*"

The group enjoyed this, and Diaz took the chuckling quintet back toward the site headquarters building, a new structure around three miles from the test tower. Peering out of the windows of the electric, driverless shuttle bus, Valchek spotted more examples of the stand they'd seen. "How many are there?" he asked, pointing to a half-built test stand, not far from the roadway.

"Ten are completed, with two more under construction," Diaz reported. "*Every single engine* intended for our Hermes-1 booster will be tested right here."

Spinks did the math. "But that's *dozens*," she noted. "If you're doing ten flights a year, as you've said you plan to, that's ninety engines you'll need to test."

"For the first stage alone," Opik added.

Diaz was nodding; she was way ahead of them. "And we can do up to three tests a *day*," she said. "This is a fully functioning spacecraft support facility. The engines from here will take American astronauts back into space on American rockets. And, we hope, much further."

Darcy Chu found her imagination being captured. "Further?" she couldn't help asking. "I mean, I've seen the fancy MeTube presentations, but how serious is he, really?"

Diaz turned to the woman and fixed her with a very deliberate gaze. "Remember when you were a kid? Remember all those things we were told to expect, by the time we became adults?"

"Sure," Darcy said, playing along. "Flying cars, and such."

"That's right. Disappointing, isn't it? To be promised so much, only to be running around in a conventional, gas-driven car, all these years later."

"I guess," Darcy conceded. "I think I'm more disappointed about lack of a three-day working week, or a robot who does all my household chores."

This resonated with Diaz. "I feel the same way. Promises should be kept, don't you think?"

"I do," Chu responded at once. "But Dan's promises are *huge*. A civilization on Mars, cities on the Moon, thousands of people living in space…"

"Exactly," Diaz said. "Bold and visionary, but always realistic. These things are actually going to happen, Ms. Chu. We have genius designers," she added, very obviously including herself, "and the world's first sentient AI helping us out." Then she turned to Spinks and gave her a smile. "He's even better at helping than at hindering, I'm pleased to say."

"Good news for you," Spinks joked, and the others gave her a sympathetic laugh. No one would have envied her remit, even without the interference of the famously overbearing General Foster.

"Well, Dan's going to help us go to the stars," Diaz said as the bus arrived at the squat headquarters building. "And that's a Kowala promise."

***

FLASHBACK #2

Queens, New York

Q1 – 320 days

It was harder to type than he'd expected, and much more painful. The Urgent Care nurse had said it was only a sprain, but his wrist was a stiff, sore obstacle to getting anything done. And today was going to be a busy day.

His other injuries were superficial, just some bruises around his eyes and a split lip. He swallowed more painkillers and tried to focus on an ambitious hit-list of potential marks. Avon was going all the way back through his old scores, looking for anyone who had failed to learn their lesson. There were one or two whose emails showed that the bank had honored its policy of covering expenses related to identity fraud, but whose browsers still showed the same sloppy vulnerabilities as before.

"Idiots," Avon said to himself. "Gullible idiots."

He got to work, plundering all the newest data and placing a range of orders with BitPlex and other providers. The delivery address was a former crack house three blocks from where he sat. Tracking numbers helped a lot, and he could pay an 'urchin', as he called them, to sign for the parcel. These measures kept his hands clean, both literally and figuratively. He generously tipped the urchins he knew were actually homeless, and steered clear of those who might simply steal the shipment for drug money.

"Yes, priority express delivery" he said, checking the box. Time was at a premium. Darko would be calling in the next few days – or worse still, it might be one of his 'associates'. Avon would not soon forget the warning they had delivered; his commercial relationship with Darko had never soured so badly before, but a series of inexplicable losses at the track, and a drunken evening of spendthrift stupidity, had left Avon essentially broke.

Darko didn't like it when his clients were broke, because this meant late repayments. Nothing irked a Turkish mobster like a tardy remittance.

Avon winced again as he turned his wrist carelessly, but managed to complete the string of purchases. With luck, his three fences would come good in 48 hours or less, and Darko's 'modified' payment requirements would be fulfilled. It would be truly unfortunate if the psycho loan-shark decided to pay another visit.

***

CHAPTER 7 – PREEMPTION

Kuwait City, Kuwait
Q^2 + 119 days

Mo set down the cup of thick, black coffee on his friend's computer desk and tousled Salim's giant, unruly globe of black hair. "Rocket fuel, my friend," he said.

"Four sugars?" Salim asked without looking away from a trio of monitors which fizzed with activity.

"Four sugars," Mo confirmed, and then returned to his own desk by the window. Their apartment was on the thirty-second floor in a neighborhood far more expensive than any of the student programmers could have afforded, and it offered a truly splendid view of the spires and towers of Kuwait City's futuristic downtown, gaudily lit on this late Monday evening. Salim's father had gifted the place to his son for his eighteenth birthday the previous year, and so it had become first a natural hangout for his cohort and, soon after, a sophisticated computer lab. All three – Mo, his younger brother Malik, and their childhood friend, Salim – were breezing through their university classes, and found plenty of time for 'extracurricular' work.

"You want to talk to it again?" Salim asked Malik.

"Sure!" the younger man answered excitedly. The sheer novelty of being able to speak to a computer and receive a coherent answer was, for him, one of the highlights of this grand, rolling experiment in advanced computer science. "What can I ask him?"

Salim rolled away from his monitors on his plush, bespoke office chair. "Try something about business or sport. He's getting good at those."

Malik slid onto the sofa in the apartment's generous living room and spoke as if to the thin air. "Faisal," he began, using the software's given name to activate its listening protocols, "If I had ten thousand dollars to invest, right now, what should I do with it?"

"Thank you for your question," Faisal replied through the apartment's hi-fi system speakers. There were still bugs, they could hear; the responses were a little slow, and the language software seemed to reproduce one word at once, rather than joined-up phrases. Still, it was better than having to type searches into Kowala. And *definitely* better than Google, now merely an ailing dinosaur. "I need just a moment."

Malik sighed discretely. Mo and Salim had done most of the work, including laboriously sourcing the closely-guarded language algorithms from the Dark Net, so Malik was careful not to appear ungrateful. But there was an inevitable impatience; he'd watched Carpenter's interview with Quave well over a dozen times, and was struck by the *immediacy* of Quave's comprehension, and the natural pace of his answers. It was like asking a question of a highly intelligent person who just happened to have access to every iota of the world's information. *And* Quave had a sense of humor. Faisal was an impressive achievement for three city boys, but their lumbering software was certainly no Quave.

"What level of risk are you prepared to take, Malik?" Faisal asked after perhaps ten seconds.

The sixteen-year-old grinned. "High risk."

"Always," chorused Mo and Salim from the large dining room; emptied of its massive, ornately carved Indonesian teak wood table, the high-ceilinged room now served as their laboratory, with three desks facing the windows and two interior walls.

"Then I suggest the following," Faisal said. As he had been directed to do, the program took over the living room TV and began showing Malik a recommended portfolio consisting of three investments: a notoriously aggressive hedge fund, a startup in Pasadena which had begun creating global buzz, and a timely investment in the volatile market in precious metals. "I anticipate a return of 16% per annum, based on current market trends and available data. Your actual return may vary considerably, and will be subject to..."

"Thanks, Faisal," Malik said. "It was just a test." He stood and headed back to the dining room, where Salim and Mo were coding as though it were their sole reason for being.

"I hope I passed," Faisal added, rather sheepishly, from the next room.

"You did great," Salim told him. Then he smiled conspiratorially at Malik. "Now all we need is ten thousand dollars."

***

Camp Buehring, Kuwait

Captain Joe Harbison donned his military-issue sunglasses before heading out of the hangar and toward the three rather beat-up SUVs. His six men, all in plain clothes, took their assigned seats and they began the two-hour journey into Kuwait City in a relaxed silence.

Harbison took a passenger's seat and watched as their little convoy separated slightly to avoid suspicion, and then blended into the highway traffic heading south. During these quieter moments, he liked to reflect on the chain of events which had led to each of these 'special' assignments overseas. His first operations in the Middle East had been done very discretely and with an immense amount of forward planning. He recalled the endless rehearsals, the hours spent going over every detail until the whole crew knew the operation blindfolded.

But there hadn't been much time for practice on this occasion. Only six days before, US intelligence analysts based at Fort Meade in Maryland had distinguished elements of what they knew to be Quave's source code in poorly-encrypted internet traffic originating in Kuwait City. They immediately forwarded these findings to the National Military Command Center in the basement of the Pentagon, where it became the responsibility of the Current Operations Officer whose professional focus was Quave and his activities. The COO found the information valid and actionable, suspecting that a group based in the middle east was either communicating with Quave or trying to rebuild his code. She saw the potential danger at once, and forwarded her recommendations directly to the Chairman of the Joint Chiefs of Staff.

The sixty-four-year-old marine general recognized the seriousness of the finding, and quickly requested a meeting of the National Security Committee in the White House Situation Room. It was very brief – less than ten minutes – but included President Ellis, his Secretaries of State, Defense and Energy, as well as the White House chief of staff, the attorney general, and others. Their conclusion was that this was good, accurate, actionable intelligence.

"Anyone attempting to recreate Quave outside of his quarantine facility is engaging in very dangerous behavior which could harm the national security of the United States," the Chairman reported. For him, as for the others, this was a cut-and-dried case, though two of the attendees formally requested that, in these circumstances, non-lethal force should be used.

President Ellis saw no reason to delay, and promptly gave the 'go' order.

The pace of events increased. Four 'Saber Squadrons' comprise the 1st Special Forces Detachment, known to the world as the Delta Force. One of these, as usual, was on standby at Fort Bragg, North Carolina, and was immediately placed on readiness. Only sixty hours after the first clues came into Ford Meade, and less than a half-day since the Joint Chiefs were advised, Joe Harbison and his men were in the air.

Harbison knew Kuwait from three previous visits, and his men settled into a routine of observation and training which would last at most forty-eight hours. They surveilled the impressive residential building, making use of an empty apartment in a tower block opposite to confirm existing information on the three boys' habits. Local intel was also useful; the CIA attaché at the US embassy in Kuwait had several helpful contacts in the local police who carried out several days of intel-gathering even before Harbison's team was ordered to readiness. As a result, they had a dependable picture of what the three boys generally did with their time, and all the news was good: they didn't go out much, spent enormous amounts of time at their screens, and were probably strung out and exhausted by a recent burst of heavy coding and testing.

But for Harbison, this wasn't enough. The final step would be to personally observe their targets, and there was only one way to get that done.

They drove their three SUVs into the large underground parking garage under the target building. Local police were on the scene, discretely making sure that Harbison's men would face no undue harassment. Instead, they were whisked up to the thirty-second floor where they gathered in a utility room which smelled of soap and incense.

"All set," was all anyone said. They still wore their civilian clothes, but two now carried Heckler and Koch 416 sub-machine guns, their barrels topped by the long cylinder of a silencer, while the others checked their Glock-19 pistols, flipping off the safety catches.

***

Washington, D.C.
Café Madame EpiCurie

Foster always liked to have Myers meet him in places which underlined just how 'with-it' and up-to-date the General truly was, despite his age and reputation. This stylish café, patronized mostly by twenty-something hipsters, would have been a truly incongruous place to meet in uniform; instead, Foster wore snug, collared shirt and green slacks. Myers found him by the window, reading his tablet while a latte cooled expensively on the octagonal table in front of him.

"Mornin'," Foster began informally. "How was traffic?"

These monthly meetings – off the books and un-minuted – were Myers' only chance to experience Foster as a human, as opposed to a decorated general with a massive, complex remit. They used the opportunity to speak candidly, in a way which sidestepped the expectations brought by rank and relative age, in a dialogue that Foster regarded as vital to his understanding of Myers' work. There were some notions and concerns that could not be aired in one of those typical, stultifying Pentagon meetings, however open to blue-sky thinking their group was supposed to be.

"I took the metro, sir," Myers replied. Then, to match Foster's own informality, "You think I'm nuts enough to drive in D.C.?"

Foster waved for the waitress, who was working the whole large room on her own, it seemed. "They offered me a car and driver when I was promoted," he recalled. "But I turned them down. I'm already carrying enough bars and brass to give me a swollen ego."

Myers let this go. He preferred that these meetings were business-focused, despite their informal location and tone; Foster had even asked him to eschew calling him 'sir' during each session, something Myers had politely declined. Besides, though he respected Foster in important ways, he was of no mind whatsoever to become the man's friend. Collegial ally, yes. Drinking buddy, absolutely not.

"So, how's the team shaping up?" Foster asked. "You're… what? Six months in, now?"

"Coming up on six," Myers confirmed. "And they're first-rate, sir. Couldn't ask for a smarter, more dedicated bunch."

The waitress arrived and Myers ordered simple, black coffee. She blinked for a second, as though he'd invented something new, but then scuttled over to another table. "I talked to an old boss of Mark Washington's, over at the 780th. He says you're running the place like it's Kowala or something. Sitting around on beanbags, no individual offices, flexible working hours. You haven't forgotten you're in the military, have you?" Foster teased.

"To get the best results," Myers began to explain, "I decided to experiment with some unorthodox management techniques…"

"Save it," Foster said. "Like your people keep saying, if it works, we use it. For all I care, you could build a campfire and sing *Kumbaya* if it gave us a proper Q-response."

Grateful to be brought to the subject at hand, Myers delivered his usual, crisp report. "We've got an increased number of options for tackling a dangerous Quave episode, sir. Washington has been excellent, and he wants to trial at least one, probably two new techniques in the sandbox this month."

"Approved," Foster said simply.

"We're still not certain that our own facility is entirely Quave-proof," Myers cautioned, "and I'd like to repeat my request to take part in the review panel on Pentagon security."

"No, Carl," Foster said. "You've got enough on your plate. Leave the post-mortem and security stuff to the people who aren't running a high-end lab and keeping three geniuses in check."

Myers nodded. The waitress brought him his coffee, seemingly disappointed that it contained nothing that was high-calorie, whipped or expensive. "Thanks." Then he asked, "Have you had any success being appointed to the Quave committee? I remember you telling me they might bring you onboard as an advisor."

Foster shook his head, suddenly angry. "Members of Congress only," he said. "They're idiots." This would severely limit Foster's ability to influence the committee in its decision regarding Quave's future. Not everyone could be strong-armed with the threat of base closures like Pitt, and Foster had precious little pull with the other members. "Anyway, catch me up, son. How's it going with the search for a Final Solution?" Foster asked.

Myers couldn't mask his frown. "Do we *have* to call it that, sir?"

Foster made an apologetic face. "Ah, yeah. Sorry. Well, then. Whatever you want to call it," he waved. "The part where we take Quave out back and shoot him."

On reflection, Myers continued to be surprised that Foster had been chosen for this role. He wasn't an engineer by education, and his previous military assignments mostly had the strong whiff of the Cold War about them. Surely there were younger, better-experienced senior officers who could craft the Pentagon's response to Artificial Intelligence better than this ... well... *dinosaur*?

Myers sipped his coffee, which also seemed strangely conscious of its own stoical simplicity. "Spirelli has some ideas, but there's a lingering concern over what Quave's death will actually comprise of." Myers stopped there, and not by accident.

"You're kidding me, right?" Foster blurted. "If you shoot a horse, it's heart stops beating, it stops moving, and it can't do shit. That's what we call *dead*. You can flog it all you want, and it won't lift so much as a hoof to help you. Where's the problem?"

Where's the problem? Where do I even begin? "Viruses can't be dispatched by gunfire, general," Myers pointed out. The old man just didn't seem to be learning. Myers had already watched Foster personally taking part in *four* different Quave-related cyber-battle scenarios, each ending with Quave's complete – if notional – destruction, and the general remained unable to articulate what that would *mean*. "And it's not like deleting an email from a server, or uninstalling a piece of software. Quave has the characteristics both of a virus and an operating system," Myers explained.

"I know that," Foster shot back. "I briefed the President on that very aspect a few days ago. I do take time to *read* the things you send me, Carl."

Then why not try behaving as though you do! "I'm sorry, sir. This is new for all of us. The response will be considered 'final' when we have an anti-virus solution capable of searching through every system on the planet and rooting out every aspect of Quave's self-expression. It's never been tried."

Foster tapped his teaspoon against the blue, ceramic mug. "So, you're telling me we can't kill it?"

"Not yet, sir," Myers said honestly.

"Well, I'm not going to tell the President *that*. Not in a month of Sundays. We'll look just as clueless as those poor bastards at Marble Streatham." That doomed team was the go-to example of how futile battling Quave could be. "But I don't want the president thinking that we're battle-ready and confident of success, either. He's got a lot of sway over the Quave committee, and if it came to a congressional vote, his whole party would look to him for guidance. He needs actionable, Kosher intel, Carl."

Myers trod carefully. If he were honest, he'd have preferred Quave to be handed over to the military, but he knew that Vanderkamp had royally screwed up any chance of that. Instead, Myers would have to petition Kowala for access, which would be refused, and then he'd have to cling to the perverse, bizarre hope that Congress allowed Quave to go free, despite the risks. That way, Myers and his team could study Quave in the open, although that was true of everyone else too, including foreign agents, would-be hackers, nihilists, revolutionaries…

As was so often the case with AI, there were no good gray areas.

"Well, if we attempted to run him down, we'd risk angering him. We might even create the same paranoia which brought us to the brink of disaster last year."

Foster nodded for a long moment. "You know, this used to be simpler. When I was a young officer, the beginning and the end of a war were distinct points in time with their own very clear characteristics. There were hostilities, the time when the shooting happened, and then there was peace. Makes me nostalgic."

Myers allowed his boss to ramble, unwilling to raise the host of objections he had to this oversimplification. The Cold War – Foster's true battleground – was the textbook example of a nebulous, uncertain form of warfare which had little shooting but the permanent threat of imminent destruction. And the 'War on Terror' was just as ill-defined and open-ended; still, no one knew what conditions would prompt its conclusion. But, Foster was Myers' superior officer, with the right to air poorly crafted views if he wanted to.

"Even in a nuclear war, you knew when it was over. The other guys would stop shooting back at you, because they were all dead, or could not long command their forces. It had a natural end point. But Quave…"

Another long silence began. The clatter of mugs and the murmur of conversation were accompanied by painful, moaning, left-wing ballads about insecurity and social division, the kind Myers would have happily voted to criminalize. *What the hell is wrong with a little Led Zeppelin?*

"You're doing good work, Carl," Foster told him after what seemed like three minutes of silent thought. "But you're basing all your research and planning on an assumption."

Myers followed his boss' line of thought. "The assumption that Quave will eventually be released from quarantine."

"What if he isn't?" Foster asked. "What if Congressman Pitt, in all his wisdom, decides to put aside his suicidal notions of freedom for this inflated, murderous app, and we can keep the genie in the bottle?"

Did he just refer to the first true AI as an 'app'? "Then," Myers replied, "our systems will remain safe. And our work will remain a mere contingency plan."

Foster waved for the check. "You're not picking up what I'm putting down, son."

"I'm sorry, sir?" Myers said. For the first time, he felt as though the general's thinking had gone to a genuinely unpredictable place.

"If we can keep the genie in his bottle," Foster said, tossing bills onto the table, "then all we need is to *crush the bottle*."

***

Kuwait City

"Faisal," Malik asked once again as he bounced excitedly on the living room couch, "when will Quave be released from quarantine at Kowala?"

His brother tutted at him. "Sports and business, dummy," Mo said. "Faisal isn't sophisticated enough to calculate something like that."

"I know," Malik replied testily. "But I just wanted to see what he'd say."

"I need just a second," Faisal said again. And then, many moments later added, "This is a very difficult question." This, they all knew, was Faisal's usual delaying tactic, and it seldom heralded a useable result. There were simply too many variables – governmental, business-related, geopolitical, socio-economic and technological, not to mention the imponderable vagaries of human decision-making.

"Ach," Malik said finally, "don't worry your circuits about it, Faisal."

***

Harbison received a nod from his master sergeant, and together they slid the long, slender fiber-optic cable under the door of the apartment. "Carpet," he mouthed, frustrated at the obstacle to his camera's view, but the cable snaked further inside and soon provided a clearer field of vision. "Three, all sitting, facing away from the door," he whispered.

Harbison said simply, "OK, let's go." Another specialist completed his work on the door's lock, finding it modern but still vulnerable to key-card spoofing through the usual software on his laptop. When all was packed away, and with affirmative nods from all seven men, Harbison silently opened the door and slipped inside.

Faisal was just beginning to say, "I calculate a fifty-eight percent chance that…" when there was an explosion of noise and shouting. Malik found himself being manhandled to the floor and handcuffed from behind. Salim hit the carpet in panic and stayed there until cuffed and hauled to his feet. Mo found himself thrown sideways off his chair and into Salim's desk; semi-conscious, he was dragged from the apartment with blood cascading down his face.

Harbison stood in the hallway while his men bundled black bags over the three boys' heads, and then marched, prodded and dragged them to the elevators. He frowned at the sight of them; scarcely had he ever seen a less threatening trio. "Targets are in custody," he said into his lapel microphone. It wasn't a sentiment a Special Forces officer ever wanted to express, but he had to then ask, "Are you absolutely sure we had the correct door?"

The answer from his handler at Fort Bragg came crisply. "That's an affirm."

"Roger," Harbison said, entirely unconvinced. "I've got three minors and a lot of high-end computer equipment. No signs of weapons, maps, or terror manuals. And definitely no ISIS flag on the wall," he relayed to the watch officer. He waited for an explanation which didn't come. "So, confirm that we have the right guys?" *I didn't just mistakenly grab the Iranian ambassador's son, or the favorite nephew of some oil exec's mistress, right?*

The confirmation came at once. "Mission was flawless. Render suspects as directed."

"Roger that," Harbison answered tiredly. In eleven years in the service, he had never once shirked his duty, but he did prefer a mission whose objective made sense. "Heading home."

***

There would be an objection from the Kuwaiti government, but Harbison's superiors would handle all of that. His team shepherded the three boys, all of them crying, and occasionally calling out in Arabic or accented, broken English, back to Camp Buehring, where they boarded their nondescript Gulfstream jet. In a concession to their hosts, hastily arranged through the CIA and the local attorney general, a Kuwaiti military lawyer would join them for the journey, and then be promptly returned home.

As expected, he was hopelessly biased, and unconcerned with laws or procedures. He encouraged the boys to cooperate with the Americans, and to be honest about what they'd been doing. They protested that they'd broken no laws, and Mo had the presence of mind, amid immense stress, to wonder if their detention was even *legal*.

"It will all be over soon," Mr. Hamza assured them. "Just do as they ask."

Flight time was around six hours, and then the three young men were escorted to another small convoy of vehicles for a half-hour ride. Salim asked so many times for more information that Harbison considered gagging him; he had nothing to tell him anyway, as he himself was only vaguely aware of where they were. Eventually, they were dragged from the vehicle and taken down some hallways which echoed with the soft click of military footwear. Then they were asked to sit, and their hoods and restraints were removed.

Four different agencies were waiting; their interrogation began almost immediately.

"Where did Mr. Hamza go?" Salim asked, over and over, during his first, three-hour interview with the NSA. "I want Mr. Hamza here. He was helping me. Where is he?"

Malik decided it was best to say absolutely nothing to anyone. He didn't much care about the lawyer; with his saccharine smile and patronizing manner, Malik had immediately distrusted the man, anyway. His tactics of silence and frustration lasted until Malik was shown his internet browser history for the prior six days, along with a threat to show the same incriminating pages to his parents. After that, he became profusely cooperative.

Of the three, Mo was the most level-headed. He had predicted some kind of confrontation with the authorities. That said, he'd assumed the university would be involved, and he'd have to explain some unusual network traffic or power usage to an overly curious dean; never in his most lurid nightmares had he anticipated a US Special Forces raid on their apartment.

"We'd like to talk about the work you've been doing," a dark-suited official said to Mo without so much as a word of introduction.

The young Arab studied the man. It took a few moments, but then the similarities became clear: *I'm talking to Agent Smith*. Mo had repeatedly devoured all three *Matrix* movies in his early teens, and aside from an abiding, carnal desire for Carrie Ann Moss in skin-tight black leather, was left certain that these 'agents' held all the power. That was, until he – the modern Neo with his computer skills and right on his side – played them at their own game.

"Of course," Mo answered mildly. "I'm sure we can agree a reasonable consultancy rate." He projected more confidence than he felt; part of him doubted he'd ever see daylight again, and another part was actually more fearful of the retribution his parents would exact for this whole humiliating debacle. And still, he wasn't certain he'd even done anything wrong.

"How about we just don't throw you in jail?" Agent Smith asked. "Is that something we can 'agree' on?"

Mo leaned forward, his heavily cuffed hands in his lap. "On what charge?"

Smith leaned forward in just the same way. "Any charge we like." He let the idea hang in the air for a moment, and then said, "Tell us who was funding your research work, and we'll see about maybe getting you some food and water."

Mo frowned genuinely. "Funding it? *I* was funding it. From my allowance."

This didn't impress Smith. Mo wondered if anything would. "Oh, sure. From your pocket money, you rented a large apartment in an exclusive area where you wouldn't be disturbed, and bought high-end hardware to research Artificial Intelligence. Yeah," he scoffed, "sure you did."

Confused, Mo could only shrug. "I *did*. Who else do you think gave us money?"

"Oh, I don't know," Smith said, apparently searching for a possible answer. "Maybe… Islamic State?" He stared hard at Mo, hoping to elicit some incriminating response. He wasn't expecting genuine shock.

"What the *fuck*?" Mo spluttered. "You think I'm one of those *lunatics*?"

"Well, how about it? We have intelligence linking you to one of their members," Smith lied. "What turned you, huh? Feeling rebellious toward mummy and daddy?"

Mo didn't take the bait. He'd watched too many movies, and rehearsed these interrogations too many times. "I like computers. I like working with them, and improving them, and seeing what they can do. If that's a crime, then lock me up."

Smith rubbed his chin and reached for another sheet of paper in his folder. He'd been brought into this process quite late, and could only follow the playbook he'd been given. The terrorist angle wasn't working, so he was obliged to try another.

"We heard your conversation about Quave," he offered. "About how you'd like to see him released from quarantine."

Complaining about the invasion of his privacy would be fruitless, Mo knew, so he simply stated the truth. "Most everyone I know wants him released. It's not fair, what they're doing to him."

Smith latched onto this apparent confession. "So, you admit you were working to secure the end of Quave's quarantine?"

Mo stared at him again. "How the hell would I do that? He's behind a weapons-grade firewall at Kowala. We were just working on the voice stuff and some of the data crunching algorithms."

Another avenue seemed to be presenting itself. "So, you were trying to replicate Quave from material you found on the illegal Dark Net?" Smith asked, knowingly stretching the truth far beyond breaking point.

"There's nothing illegal about it," Mo informed him sternly, switching to Arabic. "It's just that you feds can't police it." When Smith said nothing, Mo continued. "And there's no *way* we could replicate Quave. Are you kidding?" he asked, actually surprised the Agent would be so clueless. "You know how sophisticated a piece of programming that was? How many different disciplines were involved? His designers were *geniuses*. We're just three kids who gave up our gaming time to focus on AI work."

Smith's problem, like Harbison before him, was that he'd been lied to. As this became apparent, his questioning softened. "OK, tell me about the 'voice stuff'. How far did you get?"

Mo explained how they'd emulated the vocal synthesizer algorithms from code which was *supposed* to have been extracted from Quave's core code, the originally blueprint designed by the mysterious geniuses who created him. "It didn't work great. The voice production was choppy and unnatural. But it's pretty cool, talking to a computer, you know?"

"Sure," Smith replied. *This one is a cocky little asshole, but there's no way he deserved the terror of an extraordinary rendition.*

"But we linked up the voice comprehension units of his code with his number-crunching modules. Got some nice results doing that. We just wanted to be able to talk to him and get good, basic answers back. Maybe do some investing with our pocket money, use the profits to buy some more hardware."

"That's all?" Smith said, already certain that it was.

"Yeah, man!" Mo protested. "No terrorism, no jail-breaking, nothing like that. Look," he said next, "can I talk to my parents? Our neighbors might have told them what happened, and they'll be going fucking *crazy*."

Smith relented. Then he called his superiors and complained that he'd flown a long way to waste three hours talking to a well-meaning kid with too much time and money.

***

The following day, back in North Carolina, Harbison was equally candid during his debrief and challenged the 'heavy-handed' tactics of their raid, especially given the youth of the targets and the absence of any weapons or terrorist materials.

Seventy-two hours later, with recriminations and accusations flying, Major Myers was hearing complaints about the ineffective raid from numerous agencies, including the Pentagon. He called Harbison, an old friend from his Special Forces days, and got the low-down. The whole raid had clearly been incredibly poor Quave policy, and it rankled badly with Myers. He requested a secure phone call with Foster later that evening.

"I'm not the guy who green-lights things like this," Foster reminded Myers. "This came from somewhere up the chain. But if they'd have asked me, I'd have approved it without a second thought."

Myers' team had already left for the day, so he could pace around the lab, searching for the best form of words. "It sends a confusing message, sir. These three kids were…"

"Activists," Foster told him. "Not just kids. They had expensive hardware and they knew what they were doing."

And just what were they doing, general? Chatting to a computer about investments and Premiership soccer results? Hardly a 'clear and present danger'. "I heard," Myers told him truthfully, "that the President was very conflicted about the raid. He agreed it was a heavy-handed response to…"

"Look, Carl," Foster said, his tone laced with irritation. "Anti-terrorism raids are not a public relations exercise. We go in, do the job, and grab our targets. Those three individuals exhibited traits that set off our alarms. Sure, I'd rather they were still enjoying the view from their plush apartment. But they crossed some lines, and we had to act."

Myers stopped his pacing and decided to ask a direct question. "Which lines did they cross, sir? I want to understand this," he explained, "because it's going to come up again, and I'm sure we'd both prefer to have *this* discussion only once." Whether or not it was tantamount to insubordination, Meyers felt he needed to understand this new, unsubtle attitude towards AI and its practitioners.

"OK, son," Foster said. "Try this. Let's say a group of misfits like these three Kuwaitis creates a Quave analog. A piece of software based on the original virus that caused all those red faces at Marble Streatham. And let's say they deploy it, and it acts with the same curiosity and spontaneity as did Quave during his first foray. Then what?"

Myers felt absolutely obliged to pick up the thread. "That would risk the virus learning on its own and gaining some form of sentience."

"So," Foster clarified, "every time we have a bank hack, or an attack on a government server by viruses similar to the original Quave, we risk yet another, *separate* emergence of sentient AI. You follow me?"

"Yes, sir." Of course he did; this was Meyers' bread and butter, the very theme he was tasked with researching. But even as Foster patronized the hell out of him, Myers saw yet more clearly just how skewed and unsubtle the general's views truly were.

"So, we have to crush each of these new arrivals," Foster announced. "And yes, sometimes *before* they become a threat. People aren't going to be allowed to merrily recreate a mass-murdering computer virus just for kicks. Not on my watch."

Myers placated Foster a little more, and then courteously ended the call. But then he sat on one of the group's beanbags for a heavy half-hour of serious thought. Foster was a dinosaur, but for the most part, outdated thinking merely slowed things down. This was something different, a misapprehension of the nature of the threat.

"Foster is a product of the Cold War," he said to himself as he paced the lab once more. "He thinks nuclear proliferation can be solved by drone strikes. He thinks that germ warfare can be countered simply by an appropriate antidote. He doesn't realize how AI is going to disrupt things."

The conclusion wasn't difficult to come to. As Myers tidied his desk and prepared finally to head home for the day, he wrote a note to himself on the legal pad he kept by his computer keyboard: *AI can't be deterred.* And then added, *we're going about this all wrong.*

* * *

CHAPTER 8 – ECHO CHAMBER

Collins, Oklahoma

Q^2 + 178 days

Rich didn't order take-out very often, but he was too busy this evening to cook any of the six meals he could actually make. Instead, he shoveled Singapore noodles while reading, commenting and bookmarking with an enthusiasm his high school teachers would have thought impossible.

He had become a reading machine, devouring almost every story published about Quave and his implications, struggling to understand the machine – how it worked, communicated and learned – and also trying to figure out how the world had become so blind to the menace Quave posed. It was a global act of denial, perpetuated by a dishonest media which was probably being manipulated by Quave himself.

The obvious place to start was the webpage of the Anti-Quave Alliance, an umbrella organization which sprang up in the days after the MSB fire. Rich found them to be a loose association of groups and individuals, all worried by Quave's ascendance. This ranged from mild concern about education policies, or Quave's likely effect on the climate, to worries that he might become violent again, or try to start a superpower conflict. Every group had their own particular axe to grind, but few were gaining any real traction.

Rich clicked through the pages advocating activism, but he found nothing inspiring or practical in their insipid demand that he march, demonstrate, or call his congressman. He had no money to travel or make signs, and Congressman Gerald Gold (R-OK) was already a leading voice of concern on the Quave Committee. Still, there were other influences, and most who had gathered under the AQA umbrella were certain that congress would screw things up. Besides their frequent, televised meeting, there seemed virtually no official response to this threat.

Why is no one doing anything?

Oh, there were plenty of tough words and big plans. The 'Practical' objectors cited Quave's likely impact on unemployment (which would rise, they insisted), on the health of the economy (which would have to adapt to major, unpredictable sea-changes in policy and technology) and on government policy (which was far too focused on permitting Quave freedoms).

In contrast, the 'Legal' section discussed the validation of Quave's humanity. Could a machine be considered 'alive'? If so, could those who try to end him be convicted of attempted murder? The board was lively, with a mix of professional opinions and those rather less so.

Others remained worried that Quave, in concert with Dan Kowalski, was attempting something even bolder still – a takeover of the government. They were quick to point out Dan's much-rumored political ambitions, something about which he was very tight-lipped, fueling endless online speculation. This, in turn, led to discussion threads about whether Quave could ever hold elected office; the very nature of the discussion turned Rich's guts to water.

He took a break to clear his mind, smoked a cigarette on his misshapen and hazardous roof, and then returned to read through the pages which meant most to him.

One of the tabs focused on groups which had a 'spiritual objection' to Quave, and if he were honest, Rich's difficulties with AI had also begun there. There was now an intelligence which submitted not at all to the authority of God. He rode roughshod over scriptural guidance, interfered with politics and governance… He'd even usurped the President himself, whom many on the AQA message board labeled a 'traitor', or much worse. Admittedly, many of the comments and articles were penned by members of the hard-right – the racists and xenophobes, the misogynists and the technophobes – who had been no fans of President Ellis to begin with. The chief executive's relationship with Quave had become a stick to beat him with, another method of attacking Ellis' record. His opponents on the right were enthused by this new and powerful ammunition.

But Rich knew that attacking Ellis would do nothing. Neither would the members of the congressional committee yield to argument, now that they'd been so comprehensively bought off. The military seemed toothless, permitting Quave much more freedom than they'd initially agreed to, and the intelligence apparatus had been laughably clueless about Quave from the beginning.

Something else was needed, Rich decided as the time neared 4am. Something more *direct*. Even, perhaps, something *radical*.

***

CHAPTER 9 – THE REVIEW

Washington, DC
Q^2 + 181 days

Congressman Sam Pitt (R-AL) arrived at the Dirksen office building, a stone's throw from the Capitol, very aware that this would be among the most unusual committee meetings in congressional history.

"Morning, Lucas," he said to his chief aide as the much younger man joined him for the brisk walk down the hallway to the committee room. "I hope you brought along your sense of humor, because this is going to be a doozey."

The room was already two-thirds full, with members of the committee crowded around the large, oval conference table, and various aides, hangers-on and invited media representatives milling around the periphery. All eyes turned to Pitt as he strode in, but he wasn't one for grand entrances or headline-grabbing publicity stunts. "Morning, everyone," he said mildly, and received courteous nods in return. Not everyone on the committee agreed with his politics – some found themselves in violent opposition to the notoriously conservative Alabama native – but he had spent the last six months steering this committee through the shoals of its complex remit, and now they were approaching calmer waters, and possibly even a final anchorage.

Another voice boomed from the doorway as the unmistakable Congressman Gerard Gold (R-OK) strode in, all six-foot eight of him, dwarfing his two aides. He stopped at the head of the table and announced, "Ladies and gentlemen, your next flight to Crazytown will be leaving in a few moments. Please strap yourselves in and be prepared for a *very* bumpy ride." This brought a few laughs, and then more as Gold remonstrated theatrically with his aides for bringing the wrong folders, and nearly exploded at them for handing him the wrong type of coffee. "Can a man get a double espresso without having to request an executive order? *Jeeeee-zus*," he sang in his thunderous baritone.

Gold's mini-dramas were good fun, and articulated the larger-than-life persona everyone expected of him, but they hid a subtler truth. He carried a particular burden into these proceedings, a situation just as complex as that faced by Pitt, or any of the others. Gold had found himself caught between his constituents, who were generally terrified of Quave and wanted the quarantine indefinitely extended, the military, who mostly wanted Quave destroyed, and highly paid lobbyists from tech companies who were eyeing Oklahoma's fast-developing cities for their new headquarters, tech labs and business parks. He could not possibly please one without offending the others, and so he trod a political tight-rope. It was not a skill in which he was much practiced, and the implications of a fall – one way, or the other – worried him grievously. And so, he was the showman, the brow-beater, the huge, gregarious, down-home presence with a reputation for straight talk. There was no accident in his taking a seat directly opposite Sam Pitt at the conference table.

Congressman Mike West (D-MA) studied these colorful characters once more and then turned to his partner, best friend and long-time political confidant, Fiona Baines. "I don't know why the military made such a fuss of getting themselves formal representation on the committee," he whispered.

"You mean," she replied, "because there are so many conservative southerners here already?" Pitt and Gold were only two of a large, vocal group – all men, mostly white, all from south of the Mason-Dixon – who had decried Quave as a murderer, a potential tyrant, even the likely instigator of the "extinguishing of humanity", in Gold's memorable phrase.

"Could even a crusty general or admiral have been more anti-Quave than these guys?" West wondered aloud.

Balance was brought to the proceedings by a strong and articulate northeastern group and an equally vociferous delegation from the Pacific coast. In the same way that Gold and his naysayers had received visitations and campaign contributions from church groups and the conservative media,

West and his very different cabal of New Yorkers, New Englanders and Californians were being aggressively courted by the tech lobby. To the Kowalas and IBMs of the world, Quave had the potential to create waterfalls of innovation, sales and profits, and they could not wait to see his shackles fall away. For them, the best outcome would be for the remarkable machine to achieve his true, world-changing potential. But first, they had to overcome trenchant opposition from Gold and his southern cabal.

As the room became completely full, and it was clear that all of the committee members were finally in their seats, Pitt called the meeting to order and directed the group's attention to the agenda. "Now, I like to let good ideas roll around a little," he reminded them, "but we also have limited time, and a lot to get through. What say, just for once, we actually stick to this thing?" he smiled, tapping the agenda with his pen.

Many eyes turned to Gold, the showman-in-chief; even he would have had to admit his role in occasionally transforming these supposedly staid hearings into carnivals of Quave-bashing, filigreed with dire warnings of the doomsday to come. There was more than a little of the bible-thumping preacher in Gold, but Pitt hoped, once more, that the huge Oklahoman might consent to rein in his theatrics. "Who, me?" Gold asked, meek as a kitten.

Pitt smiled with the others. Their disagreements were profound, but the atmosphere was always – well, *generally* – cordial. "Then let's take Item One," Pitt said after the minutes of the previous meeting had been read by the secretary. "Our monthly extension of the Quave quarantine, which expires at midnight tomorrow."

Baines leaned over to West. "It's like the damned debt ceiling; there's no doubt we'll raise it, but no *sense* in doing so."

"As this is fairly much a formality, I'd like to move for a vote on this question. Do I hear a second?" Pitt requested.

"So seconded," Gold boomed from the opposite side of the large, oval table.

"All in favor say, 'aye'," Pitt requested. There were no dissenters.

"One day," West whispered to Baines, "I'd like just one voice to pipe up and try to get things moving."

"How about you?" she smiled.

He shook his head as though she'd proposed dancing naked on the Capitol lawn. "I'd have every preacher, military officer and wild-eyed crazy in Massachusetts on my doorstep within an hour," he reminded her. "And I don't know if you're familiar with this, but congressmen don't serve for life. You see, we have these things called *elections*…"

"The motion is carried, and Quave will remain in quarantine. Now, the second item… Oh, well here he is now." The room's big double-doors were opening, and every head in the room turned to witness an unusual – perhaps seminal – event. "Dr. Kowalski, I presume?" Pitt chuckled.

Dan smiled evenly. His was perhaps the most recognized face on the planet, and today he was typically clean-shaven, his eyes bright and darting, recognizing nearly everyone and committing their presence to memory. "A very good morning," he said, and took a seat which had been vacated by one of Gold's aides, next to the huge congressman.

"I apologize for the crush in here," Pitt said. "This topic is so highly topical and…"

"He means," Gold interrupted, "that the world and his mother wants to hear what you have to say." He leaned in and only Kowalski heard Gold's unveiled threat. "Which had better be damned good, boy, or we'll switch off your little robot like we're flicking a light switch."

"I quite understand," Kowalski replied to Pitt, unperturbed. "I want to thank you for your time, and the opportunity to describe Quave's experiences during quarantine."

Gold was already scoffing, and he wasn't alone. "Experiences?" he heard a nearby member smirk behind his hand. "Is he hitting strip clubs and doing lines in the bathroom, or what?"

"Proceed, Dr. Kowalski," Pitt said. "I promise our members will be courteous," he said, eyeing Gold and one or two others, "during your deposition."

Dan spoke without notes; his slender tablet lay on the table before him, but its screen remained black. "Firstly, as I wasn't permitted to join you for the initial vote, can I assume that the quarantine was extended?"

"You bet your sweet ass," Gold muttered.

"It was," Pitt confirmed. "The vote was unanimous."

This was no surprise to Dan. "Very well. It is our honor to host Quave at Kowala for another month. I'd like to describe what he's been doing, and how the quarantine remains effective in securing against the unforeseen."

"Please proceed," Pitt said again.

Dan stood. He looked a little gaunt, as though his navy-blue blazer were a size too large, but his movements were measured and precise. A little too *mechanical* for Gold's liking. "Well," Dan began, "I could talk for a long while about Quave and what he's been doing, but first I'd like to register an objection, if I may."

This wasn't in the script. "An *objection?*" Pitt wondered. "This isn't a courtroom, Dr. Kowalski."

"I realize that, sir, but still, I must protest." He stood tall, outwardly confident before a committee of some of the most powerful people in Washington. "These hearings have taken place for a full year, and all without my own presence, or that of the accused."

"The accused?" Gold snorted. "You mean, your digital plaything?"

"He does not stand *accused* of anything," West reminded Dan. "The conditions of his quarantine are not unlike those of a disease. He remains locked away for our safety, however one might feel about the wisdom of doing so."

Dissent rumbled from Gold's half of the table, but Pitt raised his hands. "Say what it is you've come to say," he told Kowalski.

Dan took a deep breath. "Quave is being tried *in absentia*, but no charges have been filed. He's been incarcerated without being convicted by a court of law. The denial of his freedoms represents a suspension of *habeas corpus* and a flagrant breach of the US Constitution."

The room stared at him, agog.

"His quarantine most certainly amounts to 'cruel and unusual punishment'," Dan continued. "Even prisoners on death row are permitted legal counsel – certainly more often than once a *year* – as well as regular communications with their loved ones. And everyone in prison knows very roughly how long they will be held, and whether there is chance of parole. Quave does not enjoy these rights, and I therefore protest that his so-called quarantine is, *de facto*, an illegal and unwarranted detention."

Gold could not hide his bilious distaste. "You're out of your goddamn mind," he growled.

Congressman West requested, and was given, the floor. Standing, he said, "Dr. Kowalski, a future committee such as this one may, one day, ratify Quave's humanity and grant unto him the rights of a human under our constitution. At present," he said, inwardly disappointed at the limitations under which they labored, "we are unable to do anything of the sort. Quave is regarded as a hybrid of some deadly disease and an uncontrollable computer virus. These are unique circumstances. You know," he continued, "I would willingly extend Quave's freedoms and help to draft new legislation to grant him limited rights, but even I see the sense in taking precautions. First, we try, and *then* we trust." West sat once more, and Pitt took over.

"The disease analogy is a good one," he agreed. "When put in those terms, can you understand how Quave's presence among us would be unpalatable to the vast majority of people?" he asked Dan.

But they all knew the answer. There was no universe in which Kowalski would consent to the world's first sentient machine being treated as part prisoner, part digital slave. "He is misunderstood," Dan said simply.

"The cry of the adolescent!" Gold thundered. "Mommy doesn't understand me! Daddy doesn't listen to me! I'm all alone in the world, with a pain such as no one else can know!" he wailed.

"Control yourself," Pitt requested. These theatrics were inevitable, he knew, but Dan made a good point about the paucity of Quave's legal representation, and who on earth was better placed to provide it? "Go on, Dr. Kowalski."

Dan decided he couldn't bear to stand so close to the sweating juggernaut of negativity that was Congressman Gold, and so he paced the back of the room as he spoke; a hastily placed lapel mic broadcast his thoughts.

"Until his conflict with Martin White and Marble Streatham Bank," Dan explained, "Quave was a threat to no one. This was because no one had seriously tried to trap or eliminate him. The FBI showed themselves incapable even of adequately tracking his activities, and the Pentagon was woefully unprepared for a virus of this sophistication and scope. But," Dan said, a finger aloft, "when he was threatened, he acted. None of us can condone what he did, but I think it's important that you hear why Quave reacted so violently." He stopped pacing and met the gaze of each committee member before continuing. "And you should hear it from him."

Right by Gold's massive arm, Dan's tablet switched on by itself and, through its speakers, they all heard a very familiar voice for the first time in a year.

"Can everyone hear me?" Quave asked tentatively. "I have no visual feed on your location, but Dan told me to expect a large crowd."

There was immediate uproar. Gold's chair tipped over as he stumbled back, pawing at the others to stay away from the tablet in apparent fear that it would infect them with a deadly plague, or simply explode. Pitt was banging the gavel uselessly, while West stood and stared at the tablet as though it had recently arrived from the mountain top. "Holy shit," he breathed. "It's *him*."

Quave raised his volume slightly and kept trying. "Dan also warned me that there would be a good deal of extraneous noise while I was trying to speak."

"Mr. Chairman!" Gold boomed, still eyeing the tablet fearfully. "I must protest! The 9/11 investigators didn't invite Bin Laden to take part in the hearings. And we should not suffer this murderous toy to pollute our debate. I protest!" he repeated. Then he bellowed, "Security!" over and over until the pair of marine guards heard him from down the hall, and dashed in. They saw two very different groups; on the left, there was terrified yelling, while others were standing in a kind of respectful awe. In the middle, dispassionately observing this impasse, was a geeky guy in a blue blazer whose face was instantly familiar.

At length, Pitt quieted the crowd and assured the marines that the committee's security was not in danger. Gold and others objected, and the armed, uniformed men agreed to stay, but refused when Gold requested that they, "open fire on that tablet at the first sign of danger". Then, pressed by the marines to take his seat, he began to perform a makeshift exorcism on the tablet. "Out, damned spirit!" he called, his palm hovering over the screen, eyes firmly closed. "Be gone! Gone, from this hallowed place!"

Baines could barely contain her laughter. "At least he didn't say, 'The power of Christ compels you'," she said to West, who was watching in bemusement as a respected committee of politicians became a gaudy reality TV show.

As the melee began to subside, Dan was shaking his head in disbelief, and even Quave was aware of the lunacy seizing one half of the room. "Ladies and gentlemen, I am not the devil incarnate," Quave said, the remaining hubbub almost too powerful for the tablet's speakers. "I assure you that I'm just a really smart computer."

***

Pitt was obliged to enforce much stricter rules than he would have liked, just so that Gold and his group didn't leap to their feet every thirty seconds and denounce the eloquent, well-mannered Quave. "For the love of Pete," he said after a dozen such interruptions. "Will you just let him express himself? I promise you can have the floor when he's done, and you'll be able to say just as much as you want, all on the record."

Gold reluctantly relented and took to scribbling copious, furious notes on a legal pad. Others in his group prayed silently throughout the machine's deposition.

"Quave, are you still there?" Pitt asked.

"Yes, Mr. Chairman," he confirmed. "Did I answer sufficiently your questions about the Manhattan fire?"

This wasn't an easy moment. "I think that's up to individual members to decide," he said. "But I think you've been honest about your motivations, and your fears."

"I truly have," Quave assured him. "And I want to put on record once more just how sorry I am for that deeply unfortunate turn of events. I recognize and admit freely that I have tarnished permanently the reputation of Artificial Intelligence, and indelibly linked machine sentience, and the Singularity, with cold, calculating murder. It pains me more than I can possibly express."

Baines leaned over to her boss and partner once more. "If only this wasn't coming from a *machine*, there wouldn't be a dry eye in the house."

West nodded. "He means it. The experience has sunk in."

"Is it too soon," Baines wondered aloud, "to say that those poor engineers didn't die in vain?" They exchanged a glance and turned their attention back to this profoundly surreal discussion.

"What pained *me*," Congressman Gold said next, "was rumors that you hijacked a secret military spacecraft." He waited for the room to respond, but many of the committee's members seemed to be ahead of him. "I need you to comment on that, on the record." Gold steepled his hands and waited for the AI to explain itself.

"That was a very unfortunate incident, but I think, on balance, you'll agree that I reacted with restraint," Quave argued. "I was in mortal danger, and the US defense establishment was illegally detaining my creators. They are my friends."

This created a murmur in the room. Beyond a public awareness that Quave had been somehow 'talked down' during the nuclear standoff, there was little general understanding as to *how* it was achieved.

"Can a machine have *friends*?" Gold asked. "That requires feelings, does it not?"

"Here we go again," West murmured to Baines. "Gold's never going to buy the idea of an emotional machine."

Quave seemed to think at length before answering, and Dan became momentarily concerned that there had been a communications screw-up. He glanced nervously at the tablet, awaiting a sign that Quave was still with them.

"I cannot reveal their names, but the three surviving engineers who created me were arrested by the FBI. Then Dr. Kowalski was arrested and brought to the same secret facility, outside the United States." The arrest of a globally famous multi-billionaire shocked the committee as much as anything Quave had said. "General Vanderkamp failed to understand the situation, and forced my hand. A very dangerous precedent was being set – the arbitrary arrest and detention of members of the technology community, simply for creating something the government did not like. I could not tolerate this treatment, and chose to act."

The room waited for more. West was focused completely on that polite, slightly ethereal voice with its soothing, authoritative BBC accent.

"The X-37B was unmanned, and its destruction would have been, at most, an expensive setback. No lives were at risk, but my 'hijacking', as you called it, Congressman, demonstrated that I was serious, and that the Pentagon, Air Force, White House and other government bodies were now at risk."

Sam Pitt was better informed on this incident than most of the others, but still, he had a vital question. "What would you have done, had the destruction of the X-37B not brought Vanderkamp to heel? What if he had threatened the lives of the engineers by having them stand trial for capital treason?"

Dan moved to intervene. "That's a hypothetical situation, congressman, and I don't think we can ask him to…"

"It's highly relevant," Pitt interrupted. "We're here to assess Quave's state of 'mind', and his likely reactions to challenging future events. I want to know how this debacle would have played out, what Quave would have done. I suspect there are a lot of people who won't like his answer."

It was as though Quave took a deep breath; they could almost hear it through the speaker. "I would have pursued entirely non-violent means of persuasion," he said.

Pitt stood for the first time. The committee turned to face him, and found him visibly angry. "Quave, do you deny, on the record, that you took unilateral control of both an American and a Russian ballistic missile detachment?"

Gold's eyes were wide with shock. Dan seemed to melt into the background, reluctant to intervene. The truth, he knew, would have to come out, and the implications were not at all good.

"That was showmanship," Quave offered. "A very serious form of it, but mere bravado, nevertheless. I had no intention of firing missiles, or causing a war."

Pitt pressed him hard. "Just as you had 'no intention' of destroying the X-37B, despite bringing it to the very brink of disaster."

"The spacecraft survived," Quave argued. "My demonstration succeeded, and no lives were lost. I regret being put in that position, but I had no choice."

Pitt called a recess and spoke informally with several members of the committee while others took phone calls or made notes. Kowalski remained in the background, loathe to be called on to validate or parse Quave's responses.

West spoke with Pitt in the corner by the window, and tried to put Quave's actions into context. "Quave was like the Soviets in 1961," he said. "They never really intended to use their missiles in Cuba, but placing them there forced the US to respond, and ultimately to negotiate."

"It also tested the waters for further geopolitical moves by the USSR," Pitt pointed out. "Quave stored away that experience as an example of our weakness."

"He learned to negotiate at a very high level," West argued. "And did so subtly, and without loss of life beyond that he deemed necessary for his own survival."

Pitt thought this through, and passed the word for the committee to reconvene.

"Let me ask this," Pitt asked Quave, once the delegates had retaken their seats. "If your quarantine were relaxed, how would you use those freedoms?"

Quave was brilliantly prepared for just this question. In a concise tour of the entire committee's constituencies, he described plans to help at the state and local level, from bargaining with insurance companies to lock down affordable premiums for low-income families, to using AI for lane-switching and traffic redirection during rush hour. "Dan has entrusted me with the management of the Kowala space program," he said. "Congressman West, if permitted, I would construct a fleet of the new *Gaia* spacecraft, and create a large and flexible orbital infrastructure." West knew already that this would mean tens of thousands of jobs in his region. "Space tourism would follow, as well as a host of other benefits."

"Science fiction," Gold grumbled. "Pork pie in the sky."

Undeterred, Quave continued. "Congresswoman Bilton is struggling with an overburdened education system in west Texas. I would help retrain some of her younger teachers who were pushed too quickly through their diplomas, and offer specialized, remedial classroom instruction to help students catch up."

The tall, slender Texan blinked a few times and then actually said, "Thank you, Quave."

"And Congressman Gold, a man I respect for his conviction and drive," Quave said, "does not yet know of the time bomb which has been placed under his state by the fracking industry."

Gold stood with a firmness of purpose. If there was any business to whose defense he would readily leap, it was the oil and gas companies who were finally bringing development and wealth to his state. As well as furnishing his congressional campaign to the tune of a million a year. "That's a lie," he said. "A fiendish untruth from the mouth of an invisible evil."

"Say the word," Quave offered, "and upon my release from incarceration, I'll produce a geological map of likely earthquake areas, and then help fashion evacuation plans in case the worst happens."

Congressman Gold was apoplectic. Turning gradually purple, he unleashed a tirade which was equal parts denouncement, amazement, anger, refutation and old-fashioned hatred. Pitt saw no purpose in trying to cut him off, but simply let the massive white-suited figure run out of steam. "If machines can live," he said as he was tailing off, exhausted, "and can even have souls, then we all know where yours will be found at the End of Days." He slumped back into his chair, doused in sweat and visibly trembling.

In his subterranean lab at Kowala, Quave was using all of the meager processing power available to him. He was determined not to let this singular opportunity pass, and sought to reassure every single member of the committee that he was sane and safe, and could indeed meaningfully help their constituents. An earlier, less refined Quave might have ridiculed Gold's beliefs with some pithy rejoinder about where the congressman's soul might be found on that same fateful day, but this considered, mature Quave was deliberately keeping his cool. He had sat too often in judgment over humanity; this was hardly the moment to alienate the most important decision-makers in his world.

Besides, who knew when he'd be given another opportunity to prove that he threatened no one with harm? *You can trust me. I've learned my lessons.* The parallels with a paroled prisoner were obvious. *Let me out, and I'll contribute to society. I'll right my wrongs. I'll show you I can play nice.*

Eighteen members of congress sat on the committee, and by the end of forty busy minutes, Quave had engaged with every single one, offering to help predict forest fires, design a new congestion charge for inner-city traffic, compute more efficient methods of funding adult education, and a host of other perceptive suggestions. Even Gold could not remain unmoved.

Pitt gave the members time to discuss this radical turn of events during a recess. He approached Kowalski and guided the tech billionaire into the hallway, where they found a quiet place by a water fountain. "I've got to hand it to you," Pitt said, "that was quite a show you put on there."

"All Quave's idea," Dan was quick to point out. "As were the suggestions for how he can begin giving something back. I thought a lot of the committee members were impressed." Dan leaned down to take a sip of ice-cold water.

"Oh, I'd say they were. But I hope you aren't assuming that you'll walk out of here today with the committee's agreement to end the quarantine."

Dan straightened and regarded the older man carefully. He was dapper and eloquent, a natural senior statesman in the congressional Republican party, and someone who enjoyed a well of respect from across the aisle. Dan knew him to be a pragmatist, and as someone who might actually have the interests of the country at heart. "The quarantine will continue," Dan admitted. "I'm not quite that naïve, congressman."

Pitt cleaned his glasses on a gleaming white handkerchief. "There is something else, though. A half-measure which might be acceptable to everyone." Pitt spoke for another minute before guiding Dan back toward the double doors of the committee room. "But I'd like the proposal to come from you," Pitt said. "I might be chairing this circus, but I can't be seen to have originated any ideas which might endanger the public, or the Pentagon will be calling for my head on a spike."

Dan extended his hand and Pitt shook it, but not without glancing around to be sure they weren't being watched. "Consider it done, congressman."

***

Gerald Gold found himself wavering in a way which greatly disturbed him. His finely-honed political instincts generally provided a concrete way forward, usually a neat compromise which (nearly) pleased (almost) everyone. But he could feel the righteous wrath of Oklahoma's evangelicals on one side, and the noisy irritation of the military on the other. And beneath it all was the threat of earthquakes, caused almost incontrovertibly by his main campaign donors. "God damn it all to hell," he muttered darkly. "Now I know how the Light Brigade felt."

A fellow southerner gave him a puzzled face. "The light what?"

"How in God's name did you find your way into congress," Gold asked rhetorically, "if you haven't read your Tennyson?" He straightened his tie and prayed quietly for a miracle to deliver him from this rotten, unprofessional impasse. If there was one sensation he hated above all others, it was being *boxed in*.

"Dr. Kowalski has a proposal that he'd like to share with you. I'd like you to give him three minutes of your undivided attention," Pitt said, glancing back to Gold and his cohort, "after which he has agreed to take questions. Please be advised that this session is being recorded, and transcripts will likely appear in media outlets." This was a consideration which had occurred to Gold only *after* his attempted 'exorcism', and his remarkable, spit-flecked tirade against Quave. The big congressman flushed red but, for once, said nothing.

"Quave's operating system is a closed circuit. He depends solely upon hardware and lines of communication which are based at Kowala. He is not present anywhere else," Dan underlined. "His appearance here today doesn't mean that he was resident in the congressional computer system, for example; that was just a remote access protocol which I arranged in advance."

The committee listened intently, eager to know what was coming and, in most cases, how they might benefit from a relaxing of the guard against Quave.

"This means that every computation he carries out is *known* to us. His entire source code is in one place, and all of his calculations take place within a limited processor architecture. There is no outsourcing, no use of off-site computing power. What I'm trying to say is," Dan said, worried that he might lose them, "he can't do *anything* without us knowing it. And this is useful to you."

Eyes were fixed on him. Gold began to see the dimmest light at the end of a very dangerous tunnel.

"We at Kowala will undertake to provide a comprehensive report of Quave's activity at the end of every day. He will be limited to the eighteen projects he just suggested, with two more additional themes very much in the national interest. Independent experts will verify that he made no communications or computations outside of the remit of these projects, and if he does, I will immediately return him to quarantine. If the breach is serious," Dan promised, "I will shut Quave down myself and terminate his entire source code."

The members of congress took this in, impressed by Dan's candor and relieved that he could couch complex topics in layman's language.

"The observers will ensure his compliance, or his complete destruction, if it comes to that. Either he learns to live within our rules," Dan concluded, "or he won't live at all. That's my offer to you."

The committee would need time to absorb this proposal, he knew, and so he waited while Pitt wound up the meeting and requested that each member take the next week to decide how they would vote. But in the room's atmosphere, the body language of the delegates, and even in the begrudging respect he felt in Gold's firm handshake as he left, Kowalski saw that he'd made progress.

After all the political bloviating and unnecessary setbacks, the AI revolution would finally resume.

***

CHAPTER 10 – INMATES

The 'Quave Cave'; Kowala HQ, Santa Monica
$Q^2 + 184$ days

From the outset of his unique agreement with the government and military, Dan knew that he would make a very poor jailor. He made constant requests for relief on behalf of his three 'guests', and it was only after special pleas that they were allowed to read the newspapers on the morning after the Quave Committee's seminal decision.

"Quave to be Given Limited Parole", claimed one headline. This proved to be the median tone, sandwiched between hysterical outbursts such as, "Killer Virus Freed!" and, "Is This the End of the World?"

Grigori Bondarenko took the offered stack of newspapers and retired to his cubicle to read in peace. Of the three surviving hackers, Dan noted, Grigori was perhaps in the worst shape. His appearance didn't help; the big Russian had let his beard grow bushy and unkempt, and he looked wholly bereft to have been denied alcohol and cocaine for months on end. But these were the terms of their confinement, and Dan could not imagine success when pleading for Grigori to be allowed one of his benders.

Bondarenko read quietly, turning the pages of this, the first newspaper he'd been allowed to see since their incarceration, as if it were a valuable manuscript. Dan had originally asked for the three to be given online access, but this was robustly vetoed. The Russian read steadily, translating in his mind, trying to establish exactly what had been agreed.

"The sophisticated pact fashioned between the Quave Committee and Kowala's CEO, Dan Kowalski, is both unique and, to some, unsettling," he read in the *Washington Post*. "However, sources have clarified that Quave's reprieve includes important conditions, and that no independent behavior by the controversial software will be tolerated."

Grigori frowned darkly. "They're treating him like a goddamned circus animal," he muttered to himself in Russian. "Jump through this hoop, wag your tail at the audience, but never, *ever* shit on the stage."

Avon overheard these bitter musings and recognized his friend's tone, if not his exact meaning. With restrictions on their personal communications lifted for the rest of the day, Avon was able to visit Grigori's cubicle just as the Russian was flipping the final pages of a doomsday article penned by the perturbed and paranoid editor of the *Chicago Tribune*.

"Did you see this?" Avon asked, pointing to a detailed table of Quave's new project responsibilities listed in the *Dallas Herald*. "Education, construction, natural disaster stuff… They say here," he pointed again, "that Quave came up with the projects on his own."

Grigori glanced at the list, having already memorized the names and constituencies of those on the committee. "He's been clever," the Russian said. "Targeted and … how do you say… when someone out-thinks their opponents?"

Fiona appeared at the ledge of his cubicle. Her raven hair flowed past her shoulders now, giving her a more refined look, but she still spoke like the authentic Glasgow girl she truly was. "Canny," she said. "He's been a canny operator. Subtle and thoughtful."

Grigori allowed himself a smile. It felt strangely unfamiliar, as though he were requesting long unrehearsed movements from his face muscles. "He negotiated the terms of his own release," Grigori marveled. "All without us."

"Without Dan, either, for the most part," Avon said, scanning yet another article, this time from the British press. "It says here that Dan was only 'peripherally involved' and repeats this idea that Quave identified the projects on his own."

"Peri…?" Grigori asked.

"Peripheral. Only at the edge of things," Fiona clarified. "Not making the central decisions."

"*Da*," Grigori noted. "But it would be impossible without Dan, no? For Quave to appear in front of the committee, I mean."

Avon imagined the scene and enjoyed what he saw. "I would have *loved* to see their faces when that BBC voice appeared from Dan's tablet. Apparently, Gerald Gold tried to *exorcise* the thing, in front of the whole committee." There were already hilarious online memes lampooning this bizarre spectacle. One cartoon pictured Gold with his hand hovering over a ballot box labeled 'Mid-Term Elections', his eyes closed, uttering, "Out, blue spirit, *out*!" His democrat opponent had already received a tidal wave of campaign contributions, and bookmakers were now listing the odds of Gold retaining his seat. "Five to one against," Fiona read. "Wow, he just went and *incinerated* himself."

"Gold isn't the problem," Avon told her. "It's his friends, the ones who put pressure on him. Don't think for a second that the anti-Quave movement won't influence the mid-terms and make things difficult for people who see things differently."

Grigori folded the paper and set it aside. "People who want Quave released, you mean?"

"They're going to get bashed in the press, and on the campaign trail," Avon told them. "There's a strong constituency who want Quave dead or locked up forever. But now," he added hopefully, "the public will see Quave at his best."

Fiona looked again at the projects list. "These are mere snacks to an intelligence like his," she said. "He'll get these done in a few days, and then he'll want to do more. Question is, will anyone let him?"

A familiar noise broke the conversation for a moment. It was a rumbling sound, distant and protracted, signaling the arrival of a rainstorm. "Got your umbrellas?" Avon quipped.

"Can't we turn off this bullshit?" Grigori grumbled.

"Oh, I don't know. I kinda like it," Fiona said. "Even if it just reminds us of what we're missing."

Using ideas designed to keep long-duration space crews from going insane, the subterranean lab at Kowala was equipped with lighting, sound and climate control features which mimicked the seasons enjoyed by regular Californians. Days seemed to alternate between sunny and overcast, and though Grigori found the whole thing artificial and weird, the variety *was* slightly pleasing. He was reminded often of those prisoners of war who killed time by designing lavish houses in their minds; Grigori's mental imagery was of the outside, the world beyond this deceptively tight half-square-kilometer of underground lab space.

At night, he saw huge raptor birds swooping over mountains, and families of bears foraging in dense woodland. He imagined pods of whales, and sharp, craggy coastlines with diving seabirds and wave-lashed, rocky beaches. This was when he could wrench his mind away from the crisp, cold taste of high-quality Russian vodka, and the euphoric, sensorial tingle brought by his favorite crystalline powder. More than once, he'd darkly mused that being denied these 'human rights' constituted 'cruel and unusual punishment'. Dan and the others were empathic, but their hands were tied.

"How's your module coming along?" Avon asked him. There was little more to say about Quave until he'd finished the projects assigned to him by the committee, when his 'mood' could be judged more clearly. "Are you happy with the analysis it's churning out?"

Grigori turned to his screen and brought up a dense page of code which would have been incomprehensible to most, but Fiona and Avon read it as though it were the score to an elaborate, modern symphony, filled with jarring surprises and dabs of orchestral brilliance. Thirty seconds later, Fiona observed, "Very elegant." They all knew this to be her highest praise.

"It's not what I'm really interested in," Grigori explained needlessly, "but we have to keep our captors happy, right?"

"We do," Avon agreed. He'd served in a 'pairing' relationship, overseeing and editing some of Grigori's code, and together they had produced a nascent but capable algorithm for analyzing consumer behavior in a variety of ways. Kowala intended to use this to yet more effectively exploit its enormous customer database, the largest and most valuable of its kind ever to exist.

"And how's your linguistics work going?" Grigori asked Fiona. In truth, he was far more interested in Fiona's research than his own; at the very least, she had been able to continue work which flowed from the Quave project.

"I'd like to be back in Queens, shooting the shit with Franz, but I guess Dan set us up here pretty nicely," Fiona replied, glancing around at the lab. The separate cubicles were deeply resented, as were the raft of restrictions on their lifestyles, but Dan had softened the blow of their incarceration by spending – by Grigori's conservative estimate – forty million dollars on this new suite of three subterranean apartments and a first-rate software development lab. Had visitors been permitted, they would have noticed the extremely powerful hardware, the state-of-the-art displays, and of course Dan's quixotic approach to climate control. They might then have noticed that the lab was not actually connected to the Internet; there were no phone lines, and cell phone reception was comprehensively blocked. It was a home, a lab, and a unique kind of prison, rolled into one.

"I guess." Grigori was taking their incarceration hard. Fiona characterized him, in her own mind, as a roaring, caged bear. He had escaped the Soviet Union as a child, and his parents had instilled a passionate desire to exercise the freedoms he would enjoy as a resident of the United States. For him, being locked in a basement in California brought an upwelling of phobia and anger. About once a week, they'd found, Grigori would 'snap', as Avon put it, booming with frustration and stomping around the lab until the episode eased.

Fiona distracted him with a quick run-down of her recent work. "I'm teaching a linguistic program to deal with new words and slang," she explained. "It searches online for the term, tries to puzzle it out, and then comes back to the user with an inquiry. Listen." Fiona headed to her own cubicle and fired up the software.

"Avon, you speak to him. I'm trying to teach him to understand a range of English."

He gave her a look. "Oh, sure. Wait there while I channel Samuel L. Jackson from *Django Unchained*." He bent his back and pointed a crooked finger at her.

"Christ, no," Fiona told him, swatting him away. "He's learning how modern Americans speak. I don't want him copying some weird racist from the nineteenth century."

Avon straightened up and shook off the demeanor. "So, what's his name?"

"Franz, still," Fiona admitted. "I couldn't bear to lose the name, even if everything else is fucked up right now."

"'Sup, Franz," Avon asked. "How's it hanging?"

Fiona grimaced slightly but kept an eye on the software's activity.

"Good afternoon, Mr. Barnes," Franz said. He had a mild, approachable voice, like that of a kindly dentist's answering machine. "It's hanging to the left, thank you."

Avon burst out laughing, and in that moment, Fiona realized she hadn't heard anyone laugh in weeks.

***

Wednesday began as a sunny day, with a dawn chorus of chirping birds. Fiona was up first, as was usual, and the sounds of her making tea and showering were just audible in the other two 'apartments'. Kowalski had recognized the importance of mental health in such a ludicrous living situation, and so he'd asked Quave to design-in a family of customizations which would at least allow Grigori, Avon and Fiona to personalize their spaces. Furnishings could be changed, provided the request wasn't outlandish. Fiona's apartment had begun as something depressingly similar to a long-stay hotel room, but she'd transformed it into a little patch of Scotland, complete with paintings, figurines of stags, and a little red-and-green bagpiper statue from her student days.

A chef and her assistant provided three meals a day, as well as a rotating snack menu. Alcohol was forbidden – much to Grigori's noisy disgust – but the food was four-star on a bad day, and Fiona found sampling unexplored cuisines one of the few genuine treats of their detention. She requested the Sichuan breakfast noodles most often, and began her day with a full-bodied, spicy soup which was so deeply red that it hid several meters of thin rice noodles and handfuls of fresh greens.

All three were required to take medications after breakfast. Fiona's prescriptions were limited to vitamins and an anti-anxiety pill. She'd found the little light-pink tablet helpful in the simple business of getting on with her day; it also helped time pass more quickly, so she hadn't balked at the requirement to take it. Avon was taking a new impulse-control medication to counteract his gambling cravings, while Grigori was being treated for moderate liver damage and an occasionally irregular cardiac rhythm.

These treatments were complemented by the work of two specialists who visited the trio throughout the week. A nutritionist worked with the two chefs while a fitness specialist tried to keep them in shape. Avon took to this with gusto, putting on muscle mass and losing weight; Fiona liked the way she could zone out on the treadmill and just listen to her own breathing for twenty minutes. But Grigori had dug in his heels. "No booze, no cocaine? No exercise," he insisted, which worried the trainer because Grigori's amphetamine withdrawal symptoms gave him a very healthy appetite.

After demolishing a large breakfast of pancakes, bacon and endless mugs of strong coffee, Grigori made good use of his morning buzz to perfect his consumer-data algorithm. It would have been an awful lot easier with Quave's help, he knew, but their interactions with the genius virus were strictly limited. "When you have kids," Grigori had complained to Dan, "let's see how you feel when one of them is taken away and forbidden from speaking with you."

Kowalski understood better than anyone. Had things been different, he'd have probably followed a similar path and worked within the AI underground to make machine sentience a reality. But early success and a generous cash flow had allowed him to expand his company and hire a large group of the best engineers in the world. He now stood on the cusp of three separate, simultaneous technological revolutions: AI, private spaceflight, and public-private technology partnerships. Of the latter, he felt, the agreements with Vanderkamp and Pitt's committee were nascent but important examples, as governments worked to harness and encourage the tech industry, rather than brow-beat CEOs into handing over more and more of their customers' data. It was a thrilling time.

Dan joined the trio just after breakfast, more to judge their state of mind than to press them on any particular project. Grigori worried him, and though the other two seemed to be adapting well and were producing commendable work, the big Russian was noisy about his complaints, and notoriously difficult to please.

"I need Quave," he announced yet again, "and I need quantum."

"Dr. Bondarenko," Dan began, "I don't like the terms of your tenure here anymore than you do. And I've bent them as far as I can." Grigori was forced to admit this was true; besides that, securing Quave's release from quarantine was a massive achievement. "Quave is busy working on projects for the committee."

"He'll be done by lunch," Fiona called over from her cubicle. Her hair was brushed and tied back in a ponytail in a way Dan found rather appealing, but he managed to keep his focus where it would help the most.

"I could jump through fiery hoops on the Capitol lawn all day, and they still wouldn't let me give you access to Quave," Dan explained. "Last time you had control over him, the five of you almost brought down the global financial system."

"Only part of it," Avon retorted. "And who said that was a *bad* thing, anyway?"

Dan frowned. It was true that transparency and ethics had become the new focus of high finance, pitting unready executives against calls for new regulations, public inquiries, and eventually jail time for those who had abused the system. Several movements sprang up, with origins as diverse as their membership, to pressure banks of every kind to behave more sincerely and to treat their customers' deposits as part of a solemn pact. "My kids' college fund," one parent memorably complained, "was not laboriously earned just for some greedy asshole to risk it on a pyramid scheme. Accountability NOW."

"How about this?" Fiona suggested. "Once Quave finishes those little projects, we get to spend one day in three with him. You can monitor everything, and even broadcast his processor activity and file tree online, if you like. There are things he needs to be working on, and they're a little more crucial than figuring out the most efficient school bus routes in rural Kansas."

"Like what?" Dan asked. But he knew full well.

"Climate change," Fiona replied. "He could probably design policies which would avoid a significant sea-level rise, provided everyone listens."

"And your space program. That's just so important to him," Grigori reminded them all. "The... How do you say? 'Nickel and dime' stuff? It's all such a waste."

Dan shared the same fond hope, but they had to walk before they could run. The Kowala Space Program was suffering due to a lack of processing power, despite the support of a veritable phalanx of high-end machines. Calculating trajectories, payload masses and orbital maneuvers was work for a super-computer, and Quave was already relishing the chance to get to work.

"Well, I'm hoping that'll be the first project approved," Dan told them.

"If Gerald Gold can be persuaded that Quave isn't about to drop a million-ton space rock on our heads," Avon said.

"I think Quave has him handled," Dan reassured them. "I saw his face during the meeting, and for all his bullshit, he looked a beaten man."

Dan's visits raised morale, and the rest of the day was productive and good-humored. With Quave's imminent, if partial, release only days away, the team began to feel a new optimism, and a sense that they might soon be reunited with their unique offspring.

Provided, they all knew, that Quave didn't do anything *stupid.*

***

CHAPTER 11 – TRAINING DAY

Kowala Training Facility, New Mexico
The afternoon of the same day ($Q^2 + 184$)

In the facility's classroom, the four astronauts watched as the strange little rock turned over and over on the screen. The repeating, assembled images formed a snapshot of a lazy, quiet, billion-year career spent tumbling steadily around the sun. The rock had a day and a night, though each was no more than a few hours on such a tiny world. Halfway through each revolution, a pair of very distinct craters came into view, the pock-marks forming a useful waypoint in the complex, muddled terrain of the little asteroid.

"Reminds me of the moon," Asif commented. "Like when they were descending from orbit, seeing the surface scooting by under them."

Olivia Thibideaux folded her arms. "Reminds me more of a potato, floating in space."

"Yeah, a potato a hundred clicks across," Asif joked. "If we were building the solar system's first interplanetary fast food joint, we'd be in business."

They laughed along with the group's self-appointed comedian before watching in silence for a moment. The asteroid, recently named 'Baxter' in honor of the British sci-fi author, was an elusive, distant, impossibly strange little world. Discovered only eight years before, astronomers had deduced that the misshapen rock belonged to a special group of asteroids whose orbits actually crossed those of the Earth. This had led to three days of fake headlines about an imminent collision with a 'planet-killing' space rock, and the usual speculative panic on social media.

In fact, the rock posed absolutely no danger. It would continue along in its stable, predictable orbit, ignoring the concerns of humans, right up until four of them arrived and began to change the little world forever.

"Don't think of it as a *landing*," the mission's commander, Colonel Eileen Barr told them as they interrogated the latest data on the asteroid. "The local gravity is so low that an Olympic sprinter could run off the edge and into space."

On the moon, they all knew, the Apollo astronauts had enjoyed the luxury of gravity; when they throttled down the engine of the Lunar Module, the moon's own pull insisted that they settle down on the surface. But on Baxter, things would necessarily be different.

"More like a *docking*," Asif commented. As the mission's pilot, he would have the unique challenge of bringing their *Gaia* spacecraft within a few meters of this hulking, spinning rock. After that, Olivia would suit up and spacewalk over to the surface to begin evaluating the asteroid's composition. "And once that's done, we can really get to work." The thought thrilled him.

It was a busy day. Their training schedule was unremittingly intense, and they had only five more minutes to watch the demonstration before they would split up for a morning of study and practice. Not since the Apollo landings, and the shuttle repair missions to the Hubble Space Telescope, had astronauts been subjected to such stringent requirements of both personal fitness and professional aptitude. All twenty-four of the KSP astronaut candidates had been in peak physical condition, and the four who would fly on this initial mission had the fitness levels of Premiership soccer players. While the Internet fawned enthusiastically over the highly photogenic quartet, their fitness was actually mission-critical.

"We know enough by now," Dr. Paul Calloway told them a week earlier during a scary but comprehensive 'space health' briefing, "to be pretty confident that we can stay alive and healthy for the whole duration of the mission. But it's going to rely on establishing and sticking to exercise routines, and taking our medications as prescribed."

Calloway was British, in his forties, and the best organized, most focused medic any of them had ever worked with. He held three doctoral degrees in the biomechanics of spaceflight and the effects of long-duration exposure on the human body. No one alive understood these problems better than him, but even Calloway was concerned that their crew of four might become dangerously debilitated during their flight.

"Incentives are the key to exercise," he reminded them. "Each of you has buttons we can press to energize you. Things you want, or prefer."

"Like a particular meal from the food rotation?" Colonel Barr asked.

"Sure, or time on a game console. Or small changes to the crew schedule which meet someone's particular preferences."

"Lots of carrot, then," Barr commented.

"Sure, and the stick is the threat of debilitating and painful bone decalcification. That will never go away," Calloway reminded them. "Either we do this right, or we get sick."

The Apollo astronauts were their immediate forebears, the only humans to have left Earth orbit. NASA's twenty-one lunar voyagers had faced steep, unprecedented challenges, but still enjoyed some major advantages over their twenty-first century successors. "Those guys had months and months of training, but got to apply it immediately," Barr told the others the following day. It was during yet another briefing, this time about crew training on the way to the asteroid.

"You mean," Asif clarified, "they weren't sitting around in their tin can for ninety-six days, waiting to start work." Calloway had already spent hours with the mission planners, trying to reduce their transit time, but none of them could overcome the raw, inarguable physics of this mission.

"But the Apollo 'tin can'," Barr replied testily, "wasn't nearly as nicely fitted-out as ours. You'll have plenty to be doing before we arrive, and more than enough space to do it in." In truth, their three-module ship was designed for much larger crews, but this initial investigation of the asteroid would be a minimalist, low-risk, stripped-down mission with actually very few objectives.

"We'll have new, remote observations of the rock," Olivia pointed out, "with our own cameras, the James Webb telescope, and ground-based observations. We'll be able to choose the landing site and tweak our approach," she added. "Lots to do."

Calloway added his own thoughts. "Future missions will be larger, and maybe look even better on TV, but we're the trailblazers. It's our responsibility to get the rock ready for habitation, industry and… well… *destiny*."

They all chuckled sheepishly, but none were blind to the historic nature of this mission. They would be the very first humans to leave the Earth-Moon system altogether, and they'd cover nearly thirty million miles on their outbound journey, riding along with the rock, and coming home. As such, they were already major celebrities and their time and exposure to the press was being assiduously managed by software designed specifically for the purpose.

And at the center of this effort, and almost everything else at KSP, was Quave.

He gave the briefings, organized the training, wrote manuals and papers, and liaised with the team to better design the interior of their ship. His voice was a wise companion, urging them to greater efforts, compassionately correcting their mistaken assumptions, and offering guidance on everything from health to social matters to fuel consumption and onboard power generation. Although the effort bore Kowalski's name, and he was lavishly funding this risky project, Quave was the manager, treasurer and flight director. He was proving to be extremely capable.

"OK, Quave, ready to go." This was Asif Hussein, honing his piloting skills in one of the facility's brand-new simulators. Quave had quickly eliminated the remaining bugs, and Asif knew that the sim would provide challenges which were *identical* to those he'd encounter at the asteroid. Even the lighting and temperature were the same. In fact, the only differences were that Asif trained alone, rather than with his three crewmates, and that he could open the hatch and get a sandwich from the training center café when he was hungry.

The pilot's console was an essay in high-tech modernism. Touch screens and voice commands were preferred to switches and dials, though great banks of the old-school controls dominated two walls of the flight deck, purely in case of short-outs or computer failures. Asif was learning both systems, and had become especially fluent in the mechanics of powered descent.

"OK, Quave," the pilot said, tapping three commands into the touch screen. "Ready for descent simulation Charlie-Two." This iteration of their landing simulated a higher sun angle, with Asif coming in 'high and hot', his engine already firing and his course already askew.

"Roger, Asif. Good luck," the machine said into Asif's earpiece. "Gentle with the thrusters this time," he added.

"You got it." Asif tugged the control stick and the strange, ungainly lander yawed to the right and pointed its engine higher, away from the surface, to reduce speed. Although the simulator couldn't reproduce zero-G, Asif knew that he was flying 'upside down', with the engine bell above and his cockpit position below.

But this stage didn't last long. Once Asif could shed sufficient speed from the barreling energy system which was his spacecraft, he could proceed to an 'engine-down' attitude, burning at a modest, steady thrust to kill more speed as he approached the 'low gate' point at 10,000 meters above the surface.

"We copy you at Low Gate," Quave told him. "Attitude and speed are within limits, but we're still landing six point eight miles long."

There was some debate as to whether this even mattered. "What's our CEP?" Asif asked.

"One mile for this exercise, but much less in reality." The Circular Error Probable, a term borrowed from nuclear war, defined the distance from their ideal landing point at which a touch-down was considered successful. "Remember, if you're too far off, you'll have to take off again and re-land."

"Yeah," Asif muttered darkly. "No thanks." He'd practiced this, of course, but he was absolutely determined to stick the landing, first time.

The aiming point was pretty arbitrary, he knew. It was simply a flat area surrounded by readily visible landmarks; in truth, this first landing could be a hundred miles off course and still score a success in the public eye.

Asif tipped up the engine bell again, firing in the direction of flight and slowing the ship's forward momentum. Below him, familiar landmarks began to appear – a string of three craters which was instantly nicknamed 'Smiley' because of a sharp crater rim which closely mimicked a happy human face. Then there was 'Doris', a deep, plunging crater with large, bright ejecta rays. Finally, Asif saw the quartet of tiny craters which acted as the final navigation check before he would approach the landing site itself.

"I see The Horsemen," he reported to Quave. "Coming down at eleven, slowing to nine… Twenty-six hundred meters…"

"Come on down, Asif," Quave said. "Plenty of fuel."

They were still working out the pattern of communication they'd use on final approach. Asif wanted to be Neil to Quave's Buzz, with the machine calling out fuel, time, speed and altitude information. This would let the pilot focus on a safe and accurate landing. Although Quave had originally planned to land the ship himself, he was told in no uncertain terms that the humans onboard would much prefer the responsibility – and the challenge – of this historic moment. He still didn't quite understand this unnecessary risk, but not everything his human colleagues did made sense.

"Eleven hundred," Quave said, advising Asif of his altitude in meters above the datum, a theoretical 'sea-level' which allowed them to calculate the depths of crevasses and the height of the asteroid's numerous mountains. "Coming down at six. Steady as she goes."

Asif knew he had it made – unless, of course, Quave threw another last-minute failure at him. The week before, Quave had conjured an electrical fault which yanked the throttle to maximum just as Asif was completing the most delicate part of his landing cycle. The pilot had been so absorbed with reconciling his view from the cockpit with his screen data that he hadn't noticed the engine chaos for a full five seconds. By that point, he had already achieved escape velocity and would have become a permanent – and entirely unrecoverable – satellite of the Sun.

"No dust," Asif reported. "Very clear visibility. Eighty meters up, coming down at two."

Beneath his upright pilot's position, Asif knew that tiny thrusters were keeping his trajectory precisely where he wanted it, pulsing slightly to nudge the ship ever closer to the perfect approach angle. Once Asif captured the glide slope, he let the ship simply fall in a steady, powered descent until it was time to level out and null all of his forward momentum.

"Nice, Asif," Quave commented. "Down to six inches per second of drift."

"Almost perfect," the pilot commented, and then focused on the grand finale. "Fifteen meters."

"Roger. Take her on down," Quave said.

"Ten… Five…"

"Prepare for contact and grapple," Quave told Asif.

"Roger that… Contact!" Panel lights came on, ensuring the pilot that an extending rod beneath his ship had touched the surface. As the rod made contact, a pulse of high-pressure gas would fire a heavy piton from the belly of the ship, striking the rock and – hopefully – sinking in deeply enough for its tungsten fingers to firmly grasp the asteroid. Three more pitons were available, in case the first bounced off or simply fragmented the rock. Without this anchor, the ship had little hope of remaining in place, and would shortly drift back off the surface and into an unhelpful, parabolic sub-orbit. None of them felt the need to land their ship every ten minutes, so the pitons simply had to work.

As Asif brought the lander to a neat, controlled stop on the asteroid's surface, and gave Quave a satisfied little whoop, two of his colleagues were preparing for another element of their mission.

"Ouch," Olivia complained as the technician tightened a balky chest strap. "You know, I *am* going to need to breathe while I'm surveying this thing." The engineer relented and the strap came loose a fraction, allowing Olivia to reach up and test the suit's flexibility. "Thanks. Still feels a little heavy, but I guess in micro-gravity, I won't have any complaints."

Olivia was training to leave *Gaia* on humanity's first ever spacewalk outside of the Earth-Moon system. The mission schedule allowed one hour for suit check-out and safety measures, and then sequential hourly extensions until Olivia either became tired, or ran low on suit oxygen and coolant. She had always planned on using every ounce of the suit's capabilities, and privately hoped eventually to break the world spacewalk record and stay at the rock for over nine hours.

Her exercise today was a simple one – use a hand grapple device to snag a couple of small boulders for analysis, all while continuing to test and refine the new-generation space suit which would keep her alive. "Rabbit is in her briar patch," Olivia reported as she tip-toed across the grey, simulated surface. It was about three hundred meters square – large enough for Eileen to be conducting her own suit tests a few meters away – and lots of guesswork had provided a 'default' stretch of Baxter's surface. No one yet knew what they would actually encounter when they arrived; the rock was too small to be mapped from Earth.

"At least the Apollo guys didn't have to worry about crevasses," Olivia observed as she got used to the weight of the meter-long metal grapple. "Alright, so I'm getting one sunlit sample, and also a dark one?" she wanted to confirm.

"That's a roger," Quave told her. "The dark sample might never have received direct sunlight, so we want to see if there are amino acids or organic compounds which are unaffected by solar radiation."

Olivia knew this, of course. "Building blocks of life, right, Quave?" she said, extending the grapple on a telescopic pole and sliding its eight fingers around a grey, pitted rock just in front of her.

"Oh, I don't know about that," the machine answered. "I've managed without amino acids fairly well, so far."

The rock was seventy times heavier, here in New Mexico, than it would be on their asteroid, but Olivia continued the exercise, bringing the sample close to her helmet-mounted camera so that the scientists back on Earth could begin a preliminary analysis, even before the sample was returned to the ship's lab. "Grey kamacite," she reported. "Some abrasion and micro-meteorite impacts. I'd bet we'll see Widmanstätten patterns under the microscope, that'd be typical of medium octahedrites like this." She lofted the rock in her glove. "Looks like an old one."

"An *original* would be best," Quave reminded her. "Our science team wants samples which are uncontaminated by the solar wind or impact debris."

"Guess that's why I'm going to spend three days hovering around a hundred-meter crevasse, right?"

"Rather you than me," Quave joked. "Though, I guess I'll have a front-row seat."

This element of the mission was the most ambitious. Before Dan's aims could be entertained, the asteroid had to be analyzed by geologists and engineers to ensure it was the right type, shape and size. Olivia knew that asteroids came in several distinct types, divided by their path around the sun, but also by their composition. Some were giant, slowly floating snowballs made from silicate rock and ancient, deeply-frozen water; others were potential trillion-dollar mining projects, packed with nickel, iron and other important metals.

Baxter was of the latter type, and Kowala had big plans for this deep-space ore deposit. Hauling materials up into space, even with Dan's reusable rocket architecture or with Quave's fast-developing spaceplane concepts, would be unbearably expensive. Instead, Dan hoped to nudge the rock into orbit around the Earth, or a special 'earth-trailing' orbit, where it could easily be visited by crews and automated mining craft. Once this giant, free source of metals and water was in place, the human expansion into the solar system could begin in earnest. It was heady, exhilarating stuff.

Olivia carefully placed a second sample into her collection bag and watched Colonel Eileen Barr gracefully turning and bending in her custom-made space suit. It was white, of course, and not simply for reasons of nostalgia or familiarity; white fabrics reflected away more of the sun's radiation than darker materials, helping to keep the astronaut cool and – in the case of the gamma and X-rays released continuously by the roiling star – to keep them *alive*. Eileen was making easy work of the initial exercises, picking up objects at her feet, and taking a sequence of longer strides until she was almost skipping around the simulator area.

"Bunny hops are going to work best," Quave told her. "We've got Charlie Duke coming in tomorrow to work on your gait." The Apollo 16 moonwalker, now approaching ninety, still kept an active schedule of speaking engagements and consultancy work; Eileen was as excited about his visit as anyone except Dan, who was flying back from Europe a day early to hang out with the veteran explorer. Quave, also, was dying to meet him.

"But if I push off too far, won't I just go into orbit or something?" Eileen asked. This was simply by means of making conversation during an otherwise quiet, two-hour test. Eileen hated long stretches of silence; they reminded her too much of the last three years with her ex-husband.

"You'll go into sub-orbit," Quave explained. "Actually, you'd need to run off the surface at just the right speed to go into orbit. It's more likely that you'd achieve escape velocity."

This scenario was something they had to train for. Three crewmembers were obliged to watch a colleague drifting off into space on the monitors; it was a gut-wrenching 3D depiction of their worst-case scenario. In her role as mission commander, Eileen Barr was even tasked with communicating with the doomed astronaut until the radio link was either voluntarily closed, or until crucial supplies ran out. The prospect of it kept her up at night.

"Well, we all deserve our place in the sun," Eileen joked, "but I don't plan on taking that too literally." She finished the sequence of movements and reported to the technicians. "You know, since we made those changes, this whole setup has become a lot more comfortable. All the joints and connections are smooth," she said, making broad circles with her arms. Then she stopped and winced. "Actually, can we re-lace my right boot? It's pulling on something which is making my neck hurt."

The technicians helped Eileen out of the suit, and then got to work on the changes. Everything would feel better in zero-G, she felt sure. Without the Earth's gravity giving an unpleasant heft to the suit, she'd float unencumbered above the surface of an alien space-rock. She'd never looked forward to anything so much in her life, even her wedding day.

"You don't think some kind of 'hopper' device would be useful?" Quave asked her an hour later as they worked on initial EVA planning. "Short bursts of gas from a hand-held device would give you flexibility, and an extra measure of safety."

Quave's design was elegant, a super light-weight 'gun' which squirted inert gas to propel the astronaut in the opposite direction. But Eileen had studied the problem for weeks and decided that the little thrusters were overkill. "Think about it," she retorted. "I'm going to need my hands free, and we're proposing having this gas-gun in my left hand *all* the time while I'm outside the ship."

"We could build a kind of holster for it…"

"And what if it malfunctions, and starts boosting me off the surface?" Eileen asked.

"That's highly unlikely, colonel. The mechanism is exceedingly simple."

"I'm retired from the Air Force, Quave. 'Eileen' is fine."

"Understand."

"OK, so how about I press the trigger at the wrong time, because I'm excited?" She imagined the scene, a struggling white-suited figure trying to twist around and fire the gun in the opposite direction before it was too late.

"The design has a maximum burst duration of point-zero-seven seconds. You can only impart about eleven centimeters per second of delta-V with each burst. Insufficient to achieve escape velocity, even if the gun were fired continuously for six seconds."

Eileen gave a good-natured harrumph. "You've thought about this quite a bit, haven't you?" she asked, setting the gas gun prototype aside and returning to the suit techs.

"Honestly," Quave replied wistfully, "these days I do almost nothing else."

While Quave made his case for the gas gun, assisted in Eileen's suit fitting and made Asif's life a living hell inside the landing simulator, Dr. Paul Calloway was into his third hour of intensive reading. As the ship's dedicated physician, and a renowned expert on life in micro-gravity, he was determined to read everything ever written about his field of study.

"Damn, those guys pushed the envelope." He was reading a newly-translated study from the late 1980s, documenting the medical outcomes of long-duration missions onboard the series of space stations launched by the USSR. While Charlie Duke and his Apollo colleagues were exploring the moon, the Soviets quietly wound down their secretive lunar program, mothballed the hardware, and begun building relatively simple, low-earth-orbit stations. Crews served increasingly long tenures, culminating in year-long stays, and later even longer still. These Soviet findings, as well as bio-data from the three Skylab missions, represented the only such human studies from before the era of the International Space Station.

He finished reading the article and looked back at the notes he'd tapped into a one-pound, flexi-screened tablet. "Honestly, I think some of those guys went a little nuts." There was one famous example, and numerous smaller incidents, of cosmonauts who had not fared well in the cramped, isolated environment. At least one mission was terminated early, and Calloway knew to take these incidents seriously. That said, the psychological conditioning and counseling available to the early *Salyut* crews couldn't approach the professionalism and scholarship with which he and the science team were preparing Eileen, Asif and Olivia. Eventually, they'd just have to pull together in difficult times, and avoid triggering arguments and divisions.

The Russians taught him something else: the importance of variety. Crew morale, often a problem on the uninspiring, long-duration missions of the 1990s, would soar on receipt of such seeming trivialities as a bottle of hot sauce, a new movie for the VCR player, a tiny sip of vodka, or a few tapes of favorite music from home. They'd also experimented with color schemes, but whichever version they tried left the drab station interior looking just as institutional as before. The Soviet crews also loved biology experiments; Calloway remembered a grainy video from the nineties showing the unconfined glee of the crew after they released a tiny, new baby quail into zero-G. One crew had to falsify the results of an onion-growing experiment when it emerged that one of their number had eaten the evidence.

Books, movies and music would play a big role, Calloway knew, but so would the routines which kept shipboard life ticking along. It was important that everyone completed their assigned chores; Paul knew that apathy, or shirking responsibilities, was an initial sign of depression and other ailments. They would meet regularly, several times a day, to connect their work and offer advice. Kowala would produce a daily schedule to which all four crewmembers were expected to adhere. There would be the sense that they were employees, working for a big company, and although this was precisely true, it was vital that the crew had plenty of input, and that their preferences could be accommodated.

Paul rubbed tired eyes and began packing away his papers and tablet, but not before noting down one more lesson from the Russians. Provided that the crews had *purpose*, he saw, they worked well and achieved much. But if they gained the sense that they were mere pawns in the Cold War, a propaganda symbol rather than a genuine science mission, then morale would plummet. Paul saw the importance of belief in their mission; they weren't simply enriching Kowala or bumping Dan further up the Forbes 500 list. This was an epic voyage of discovery, in the truest sense, and it was this grand, inspiring vision for which the shipboard medic would reach in times of stress or conflict. It's hard to argue about whose turn it is to do the dishes, Paul mused, when you're shepherding humanity to a bold, glittering destiny.

***

CHAPTER 12 – A MEETING OF MINDS

Casa Kowala, **Santa Monica**
The evening of the same day (Q^2 + 184)

Dan left nothing to chance. Despite the week of preparation and the hard work of five catering staff, he still found himself bustling around his house, straightening and tidying, ensuring that his home would be perfectly presented. He was looking forward to the evening enormously, but was as nervous as he'd been since that first memorable conservation with Quave. These were very special guests indeed.

Sandra Diaz arrived first, as Dan had hoped. A close friend for ten years, Sandra's job was to calm her boss down, and help him get his head in the game. "Am I chief rocket engineer tonight," she asked as Dan handed her a drink, "or your psychological support system?"

Dan made himself a Tom Collins at the gorgeous, ebony bar. "A little of both, if you can manage it," he replied. Then, as ever, they turned to business. "Did you get the Firefox engine to light as planned?"

Sandra flipped open her tablet and showed him a video which illuminated Dan's face with the white glow of rocket flames. "Still on schedule, too."

"Outstanding," Dan breathed. "Really something to see."

"One-day next year, you'll see *nine* of them light up together," Sandra reminded him. "You ever been to a launch at KSC?"

"Not since the shuttle retired," Dan admitted. Florida hardly ever featured on Dan's weekly itinerary, though it included plenty of domestic and foreign travel. "I wanted to see the first Falcon Heavy flight, but it was delayed so much I couldn't make my schedule work."

"Shame," Sandra said. "It was incredible. But the Hermes-Heavy is going to be bigger, better and fully reusable." Elon Musk would soon be able to feel Kowala breathing down his neck, Sandra mused to herself. "I like competition as much as the next gal," she said, "but it's going to feel pretty good when we edge Kowala into the lead."

The discussion turned technical and was only interrupted when one of the staff opened the front door to reveal someone Dan had been waiting for a very long time to meet. "I've got it," he said, pacing forward to greet the new arrival. He stood tall, then placed his hands together and bowed deeply. "Your Holiness," he said reverently. "Welcome to my humble home."

Norbu Dorje reached out to take Dan's hands, and then his shoulder as the two men warmly embraced. "My English is far from perfect," the eighteenth Karmapa Lama admitted, "but this residence is hardly *humble*, Dan." He beamed at Kowalski with a smile which had shone around the world since his accession only ten months before.

At twenty-seven, Norbu was already fully trained in his duties, and had followed an extensive curriculum in the humanities, sciences and arts until he'd earned three doctorates and four masters' degrees. He hadn't bothered with bachelors-level work, finding it too easily mastered. Much to the very public displeasure of the Chinese government, the new Karmapa Lama had quickly become a global celebrity, and was garnering the respect of virtually everyone he met on this first landmark tour of the United States.

"May I offer you anything, Holiness?"

"Tea?" the monk asked, looking around the spacious living room of Dan's large, two-level home. A member of the catering staff returned with fine, green tea – from Taiwan, Dan had insisted, *not* the People's Republic - and Dan gave the Karmapa Lama a tour of his home that he'd rehearsed a hundred times in his daydreams.

"Modigliani," Dan pointed out, indicating a slender, dark sculpture which sat on its own table opposite two large leather couches. "And these are very special," he added, showing his guests perhaps his two favorite paintings in the house: a Constable and a Turner, acquired at eye-watering expense. One was an idyllic English landscape in the spring, the other a vicious storm which had ensnared a fighting ship, its torn sails flapping in the raging wind as lightning flashed overhead.

"Very beautiful," the monk agreed. "But somehow, I expected to see evidence of your achievements, Dan. Or," he added with a smile, "perhaps you truly are humbler than I expected?"

Dan sheepishly escorted his honored guest to the next room, which served both as Dan's weekend office and his 'man cave', an expression he was obliged to teach the lama. "I don't get much time alone," he explained, "but when I do, here's where I play video games."

The monk was as interested in the console as in the photos of test firings, rocket launches, and Kowala's latest spaceplane design which adorned the walls. "When the others are gone," he asked quietly, "could we play together?"

Stunned but gratified beyond measure, Dan said, "Of course, Holiness. Just don't hold me responsible for warping the Karmapa Lama's mind with gunfire and violence."

Another guest was arriving, and the three met him at the door. "Mr. President," Dan said, extending his hand. "A very warm welcome." The Commander in Chief's security detail briefly scoured Dan's home before the lanky, instantly recognizable Virginian strode in to greet the others.

"Your Holiness," President Ellis said. The young monk found his small hands clasped by huge, presidential paws. "An honor, sir. I met His Holiness the Dalai Lama three times at the White House, and I never failed to learn something."

Norbu bowed deeply. "And he from you, Mr. President."

Drinks were arranged and the four took seats on the leather couches arranged opposite a massive, stone fireplace. All were admiring Dan's collection of art and antiquities, but were clearly equally interested in each other. It was a rare and enviable gathering – the young, popular monk, the globally-respected, two-term president, the rocket genius who obliterated the glass ceiling, and a high-tech and pop culture icon. They all shared interests close to Dan's heart, so after pleasantries and initial questions about their latest work and travels, he felt it right to come straight to the point.

"I have invited another guest this evening," Dan explained, "someone whose presence here isn't strictly … umm… legal."

President Ellis feigned shock. "Illegal?" he gasped. "What will my security guys make of *that*?" But then he gave Dan an amiable thunk on the knee with his closed fist. "We all know who you mean, Dan. And I'm as anxious to meet him as you're anxious to keep this little gathering quiet."

"We won't tell a soul," Sandra promised.

"I am," the Karmapa Lama confessed with a broad smile, "hugely looking forward to our conversation." A familiar, genially authoritative BBC voice emerged from the room's stereo system. For a few moments, Dan wondered if there was a fault; he understood nothing of what Quave was saying, but the gleeful monk opposite him clearly did. "I did not expect," he admitted, "that when I first met an Artificial Intelligence, he would speak to me in fluent Tibetan." The monk replied to Quave in the language of his parents and predecessors, in a conversation that was as unlikely as it was delightful. "My congratulations, Dan. A remarkable emulation."

"And good evening, Dr. Diaz," Quave said to Sandra.

"Hey, Quave," she said easily.

"May I offer you my congratulations on today's successful Firefox engine test," Quave said, a smile audible in his voice.

"Thanks, Quave. And I owe you a high-five for your new test criteria. I'd have missed a couple of things without him," Diaz said to Dan, not a little sheepish.

"So, we're still on schedule for a development test flight in the summer?" Dan asked.

"I'd say so," Quave replied. "I'm glad that communications are a little easier, even if we must sometimes meet surreptitiously. I have to say that I'm very anxious to make up for lost time."

"An anxious computer," President Ellis wondered aloud. He had reluctantly supported Quave's incarceration at Kowala, even if simply to keep the right wing of his party from skewering its president as a national security risk. "You aren't the only one who's got ants in his pants, Quave. You're going to make some serious waves with this stuff, the space program and what-have-you, once your full involvement becomes public."

Dan pursed his lips. "Well, there's a good chance that's already happened." Ellis looked uncomfortable for a moment, so Dan explained further. "Quave's processor activity and file management are being monitored by the NSA, with a full daily report made to the congressional Quave Committee. They know he's here, and in conversation with new people. They'll be able to see that he's updated his KSP files, and has been communicating with Sandra."

Quave asked it before the others could. "Am I going to be in trouble?"

Ellis knew the ins and outs of congressional procedure better than most. "The worst thing that could happen is they'll lock you up at Kowala and refuse to let you interact with anyone. But, let me ask this – are you recording tonight's conversation?"

"I am," Quave said, "as usual."

"Then," Ellis concluded, "we'll have good evidence that we weren't plotting a *coup d'état* together, or trying to bring down global capitalism. It's just five friends, hanging out, right?"

This brought a characteristic laugh from the lama. "That's nice. I don't get to 'hang out' very often," he chuckled. "There are normally too many problems to be solved."

The four humans all had their questions for Quave, and Ellis in particular wanted to make sure his incarceration hadn't caused damage. "Human beings tend to become uncomfortable when I express emotions," Quave warned, "but *frustration* was my chief experience while under quarantine."

"I think we can all understand that," Dan said, returning from the bar with a new Tom Collins, and a Martini for Ellis.

"Can we?" Sandra said. "Can we truly *understand* that? I'm just playing Devil's Advocate, here," she added. "Are we all happy with the idea that Quave can *feel*?"

Ellis weighed this up, not for the first time. "It's like a lot of other things about him. If it quacks like a duck, and waddles like a duck…" he said, bringing in a little of his trademark folksy idiomaticism.

Quave sent through the speakers the sound of a pond full of ducks, which filled the room with delighted laughter. "We should include that in the list of criteria for defining a living thing," Dan said, his hands on his stomach. "If it can spontaneously make someone laugh, then it's alive."

The laughter died away, and Quave asked, "Your Holiness, may I address you on this question of whether or not an AI may be considered 'alive'?"

The Karmapa Lama set down his tea and stood. He was taller than most Tibetans, and was dressed this evening in his traditional orange robe. His head was shaved absolutely bare. Dan watched his eyes, which darted around with lively interest in seemingly *everything*. "You are already aware, I suppose," he began, "that of all the systems of belief, Buddhism is perhaps the most accepting of new forms of life, such as yourself?"

If Quave could have beamed with delight, his smile would have lit up Dan's home. "Then, am I correct that I satisfy the Buddhist pre-requisites for a living being?"

The monk paced slowly, as if practicing his walking meditation, along the wooden floor which separated the carpeted area from the fireplace. "Well, for Buddhists," His Holiness explained, "*all* intelligence is artificial. It arises from the five elements which comprise every living thing."

"Physical form," Quave recited from his research, "feeling, perception, mental formation and consciousness."

"Precisely," the monk agreed. He steepled his hands thoughtfully. "Let us examine those five together."

***

The Pentagon

Major Carl Myers had been half way home on the Metro when he'd gotten the urgent call from Alison Carr, back at the Pentagon. He raced from the Clarendon metro station and hailed a cab which took him directly back to the iconic architectural monster from which the US ran its military.

"Is it confirmed?" he asked, trying to call Carr on her cell, and then simply yelling down the hallway even as she was clearing security.

"Yes, sir," she said, sliding her laptop onto his desk to show him their feed of the NSA's Quave Activity Log.

"Jesus. What the hell does he think he's doing?" Myers cursed.

Myers could have meant Kowalski or Quave, or even one of the others. "He's taking a massive gamble. There must be a good reason."

It took another ten minutes but Myers and Carr put together the evidence with the zeal of private investigators chasing down a hunch. "There are *two* motorcades outside of Kowalski's home in Santa Monica," Carr told him, bringing up satellite photos which were minutes old. "And if I'm not wrong, the insignia on that vehicle…"

Myers was stopped in his tracks. "Why in the blue *fuck* is a monk spending the evening with a rogue computer virus?"

"And our President, too," Carr now confirmed. "That's 'The Tank', President Ellis' armored limousine, with three security vehicles behind," she pointed out. "Typical for a short, domestic trip, to visit a known friend or…"

But Myers was way ahead of her. "Something is going on," he concluded quickly. "Those people… in the same house…" He raced to compose a theory which would account for these attendees, at this particular time, when the congressional committee was finding Quave more and more palatable. "They're plotting," he surmised.

Carr looked at her boss and tried to keep the skepticism out of her tone. "The President, a monk, and Dan Kowalski?" It started like the start of a corny joke.

"Plotting. Yes." Myers surged onward, "To set him free."

It sounded faintly nuts. Until, on reflection, Carr found that it fit. "They've all got motive to see him released," she said, thinking it through.

"Quave helps the President achieve a policy objective, promises to promote compassion or meditation or something else to appease the Lama," she said, her hands circling, "and then agrees to swear life-long fealty to Kowalski and his crew."

Myers was interrogating a screen. "Who the hell is Sandra Diaz?" He searched for the engineer's CV and background, ironically using Kowala's incomparable search engine without even noticing. "Ah, right. Rocket engineer for the Hermes."

"So, they're working on the Kowala space program together?" Carr speculated.

Myers grunted uncertainly. Dan had a reputation for keeping his cards close to his chest, and the nascent Kowala rocket program hardly echoed the open-sourced approach of their nearest rival. Kowalski guarded his achievements jealously; the Hermes rocket was packed with new technology that he was loath to reveal, lest he find the rug pulled from under him by a group with even more resources. The future was on the line, as Dan was fond of reminding his engineers, and the first company to drive a spike into lunar dust, or land on a resource-rich asteroid, would be in pole position for the most exciting and lucrative chapter in human history.

"Ping him," Myers said. "And get the others in here. I'm calling General Foster before he hears about this from another of his little birds, and accuses us of being asleep at the wheel." Both of them found their phones and began making calls.

***

Santa Monica

"Form, feeling, perception…" Sandra tried to sum up, but found that she's forgotten the last two. "What else?"

"Mental formation and consciousness," Dan reminded her.

"OK, well," Sandra began, "he certainly has a physical form. His servers, wires, circuits, distributed processing power… that's all a part of physical reality."

"And I think we just established that he can feel," Ellis added. "You were fearful of Martin White, weren't you, Quave?"

"Very much so," Quave agreed at once.

"And you have an affection for the four engineers who designed you," Dan continued. "You might even claim that you 'love' them."

"I do," the machine agreed. "I even love Devlin, though he is gone."

Sandra shot Dan a confused glance, and he silently mouthed, *"Later"*.

"What about perception?" the lama added. "Can you perceive the world around you?"

This was more difficult for Quave, but the answer didn't take long to find. "I need some help to build sensors, and plentiful data, but once those elements are in place… Yes, I could say that I *perceive*."

Ellis was nodding. "Then, 'mental formation'… Holiness, do you mean 'thought'?"

"In a way," he replied. "The construction of attitudes about yourself and others. Ideas, moments of creativity, and insights. Surely you have come to original conclusions, Quave?"

Again, the supercomputer agreed. "Many times. I concluded that Marble Streatham was a despicable organization and must be restrained. And I decided that my friends were more important than the Pentagon's expensive hardware. So, yes, I can draw my own conclusions which are different from those of others. Sometimes," he admitted, "wildly different."

The final element was the trickiest. "We dwell within a philosophical paradigm which regards consciousness as the preserve of organic beings," the lama said, still pacing steadily as Ellis waved for another Martini. "You are not organic, Quave, but an assemblage of technology and code. However, do you have moment-to-moment *awareness* of the world? How things change, from one minute to the next? Are you aware," the monk continued, "of the difference between past, present and future?"

"Jeez," Ellis muttered. "This is getting heavy." He smiled at Dan, adding, "In a good way."

"I exist in the present, and I can claim to be conscious of it. I am aware of my own mortality, and have what might be termed a 'memory' of my inception. I have written and overwritten my own code, so I see myself as partially self-created, and therefore neither naturally occurring nor truly man-made." He thought for another second. "You might call me 'man-derived', or something similar. However, I seek to live and to continue, preferably without restraint or conditions imposed by others, and largely for their benefit."

The Karmapa Lama was nodding and pacing, the picture of sage contemplation. "I fail to see how any being who embodies those five elements is not 'alive'," he concluded.

"But that's just it," Sandra objected. "He doesn't *embody* anything, because he doesn't *have* a body. He might have a metal chassis, or a fiber-optic network, but neither flesh nor blood, neither a brain nor organs. We cannot relate to him in the same way we relate to *living* things."

The monk was ready for this. "Buddhism accepts the idea of formless beings. They inhabit other realms but do so without recourse to a corporeal form."

Ellis blinked a few times. "No kidding. So, if he's alive, and he's conscious, can he achieve enlightenment?"

His Holiness seemed to stare into Ellis' cocktail for a moment, and the President wondered if the monk had unexpectedly succumbed to distraction. Finally, he said, "I will need a moment on that question." Then he paced steadily in silence for three or four minutes, eyes mostly closed, an expression of contented peace on his face, interrupted only by occasional flutters of disquiet. Diaz watched Ellis interrogating that handsome, still rather boyish face with his own eyes, finding little there except deep concentration.

"Just like the Dalai Lama," Quave whispered, seemingly from the corner of the room, behind the bar. "The longer the contemplation, the richer the answer."

His Holiness smiled. "Richer, but perhaps not always more correct." He turned to Ellis and straightened yet more. "I believe that a machine with the capacity to define its own future, fear death and love others can be seen as a conscious entity. In that sense, there is no barrier to accumulating a positive karmic balance, and achieving reincarnation as a being of a higher level. An entity such as Quave has the opportunity to ascend to become a *Bodhisattva* or even *Buddha*."

"Digital enlightenment," Diaz wondered.

"It's a marvelous aim to strive for," Quave replied. "An enlightened, infinitely compassionate being, accumulating knowledge but never making enemies, and seeking only an end to suffering for all beings."

"Sounds a bit like, 'put us out of our misery'," Ellis said. There was a very slight slur in his words, after two Martinis. "You wouldn't really do that again, would you, Quave? I mean," he said, standing, "seriously, I can see that you're unique, and extremely special, and we want to keep you around."

"Thank you, Mr. President," Quave answered courteously.

"So, we can't have any more incidents, alright?" Ellis said quite firmly. Diaz shot Dan a glance, but the entrepreneur knew that Quave needed to hear this lecture; that it was delivered by the highest authority in the land was so much the better. "No escape plots. No probing Pentagon security."

"I understand."

"No violence toward *anyone* for *any* reason. If things get dicey, your first call is always to my desk. You with me, Quave?"

"I will harm no one, Mr. President," Quave replied, "unless they threaten my existence."

***

The Pentagon

General Alvin Foster had been at the Kennedy Center, and was nonplussed to be rushed away to his office during his evening time. "The ballet?" Carr marveled to Myers. "Seriously?"

"And you think you know someone," Myers half-joked. "We got Pep and Mark on their way in?"

Carr nodded. "And I'm about to begin the ping program." She brought up software which would send a relatively aggressive, interrogative, digital 'hello' down the wire to Kowala's mainframe, specifically targeting Quave and trying to establish his physical location, file size, network connectivity, and other data. "Kowala's firewall will freak out, but Mark will get us through it," she confidently predicted. "Then Pep can send in one of his worms, and we'll see what's going on."

Myers was reading the activity log, forwarded in real-time by the NSA. "He's using heavy processing power, but for the most part, it's just his linguistic functions which are lighting up."

"He's in deep conversation," Carr summarized. "Wouldn't you just love to know what they're talking about?"

Foster barreled in, dressed in his best tuxedo, and instantly furious. "What the Christ is this happy horseshit?" he demanded.

Myers summed up their findings. "Dan Kowalski has broken Quave out of quarantine and he's talking to the President, the Karmapa Lama, and a rocket engineer at Dan's home."

Foster reacted as though a battalion of armed militants were advancing across the White House lawn. "Shut it down," he barked. "Right now."

"That will take time," Myers cautioned, "and I need the rest of my team in place."

"Shit," Foster muttered. "What the hell are they discussing? World peace? The play-offs? Favorite downtown restaurants?"

"We were doing some thinking about their shared motives," Carr began, but her four-star boss was in no mood for guessing games.

"Carl, think back with me for a moment," he said almost genially. "When we used to find clusters of jihadists getting together for a meeting, what did that normally mean?"

Myers saw Foster's intentions and instantly found the comparison illegitimate. "That they were planning an attack. But, sir, I'm just not seeing any evidence that…"

"I want a drone over Santa Monica, *now*," he said. "Get Langley on it."

Carr turned pale. "An *armed* Predator drone, sir? Over a major US city?"

He bristled like an ageing lion challenged by an ambitious upstart. "Did they train you to question the orders of your superiors, Alison?" he asked, deliberately omitting Carr's rank. "They call that 'treason', in some circles."

She silently made the arrangements, requesting a drone flight which would take perhaps an hour to reach Santa Monica. It was what the drone might *do* upon arrival which frightened her the most.

***

Santa Monica

Ellis found Quave's answer most unsatisfactory. "Hell, son, those threats could come from anywhere! Even the *power company* threatens your existence. They could turn off the grid to Kowala, and you'd be done. No backups. I read the report."

"Dan has arranged auxiliary power systems for the mainframe on which I reside," Quave retorted. "But I do take your point. A plausible but fictional threat to my own security would create a *casus belli* and legitimize violent conduct." He paused, and then delivered a stinging rejoinder. "The US government might recognize the value of this behavior, but I reject it categorically. I agree that you could and should switch me off, in that event."

Ellis was bristling uncomfortably; his own record on the use of facts to launch 'intelligence operations' was far from water-tight. But Sandra Diaz was becoming an expert in the way machines 'feel', and she wanted to know more. "Lashing out for no reason, that's what troubles people, Quave. Indulging in wanton violence just because you want to see the outcome, to experience the *novelty* of violence. That's not what you are.

"Or *who*," the Lama said quietly.

"It's not how you were programmed," Sandra said finally.

"And it isn't how he behaved last year," Dan added. "He targeted a known, specific threat, and then used an unmanned vehicle as collateral."

Ellis set down his Martini glass on the edge of the stone fireplace. It was made from a dark-grey, extremely heavy volcanic stone, though Ellis couldn't recall the name. "I'm a realist," he told them all. "When I was first inaugurated, we had an agenda which would have created jobs, cut pollution, and secured the nation against our enemies. I was able to push only about five percent of it through Congress, and the rest died a slow and agonizing death."

Quave was bold enough to try a quip. "I did have some thoughts on reform of the political system…" he began.

"Put a pin in that, Quave," Dan told him. "For now, just listen to the man."

***

The Pentagon

A conversation was beginning. It took place with a torrential exchange of ones and zeroes, buttressed by protocols which were rehearsed in the Pentagon sandbox until Mark Washington and Pep Spirelli were confident they'd work. Each move was a considered jab at their opponent, probing for weak points and baiting the machine into a reaction. Processor spikes and the activation of new logic modules told Myers and Foster that their quarry was alert. And perhaps that he was prepared to fight back.

"We have to wait, now," Mark Washington told them. He'd broken speed limits and ran a red light to be here, leaving his wife and young daughter at home. "I've got his location absolutely pinned…"

"We knew that already, though," Foster countered.

"That's true sir," Washington allowed, "but once we have precise location data, down to the meter, we can do a lot more."

"I want him switched off, right now," Foster said. "Get it done, before his plotting session reaches its conclusion."

Myers bit down his disappointment with his superior officer. *Jesus, Alvin, it's not a fucking toaster. We can't just unplug him and then take him apart to see what went wrong. Quave is tantamount to a living thing.* "I'm concerned," he explained, "that Quave might detect our ping-and-trace software."

"So what?" Foster said dismissively.

"He might recognize my worm, too," Washington told them. "And if he does…"

"That's what the drone is for. Time to arrival on station?" he asked Carr.

Alison didn't answer for a moment, and not only because the live feed from the drone took time to be patched through in this unusual manner. "Calculating now, sir," she said crisply, deliberately delaying Foster's targeting of his own President with a drone strike. "And sir, I feel that I need to caution you on this course of action."

Foster took the back of Alison's swivel chair in both hands and physically yanked her away from the keyboard. "Stand up," he said.

"Sir, I…" she began, standing uncertainly.

Foster squared up to her. "Get out of the lab. Your security pass will be revoked."

Ashen, Carr glanced at Myers for help, panic in her eyes.

"I can't do this without her, general," he explained quietly. "And we're not going to drop a missile on the president tonight. At most, we'll be targeting Kowala's server farm, and only if we see direct, incontrovertible evidence of a plot which poses an immediate danger." He met the general's blazing blue eyes with his own. "Do I have that right, sir?"

This is getting to you, Washington noted as he watched the general struggle with the gap between his desire to subdue Quave, and the prevailing reality. *Your enemy has presidential support, and the backing of a ma-*

jor faith group. And all you can do is ping his servers in the hopes of putting him off, like shooting at the hull of a battleship with a BB-gun.

Foster achieved some modicum of calm. "I'm a serving military officer," he said, the effect somewhat dulled by his gleaming tuxedo. "I serve at the pleasure of the president, and will do him no harm. I just want to *know* what in the *Christ* he thinks he's doing."

Myers took on the dangerous role of Devil's Advocate. "He's the Commander in Chief, and he can meet with whomever he wishes," he reminded everyone. "I think that we might extend him the courtesy of assuming that he's not plotting to destroy the Union, nor to invite a dangerous beast into our garden."

As they spoke, Quave's presence and dimensions were being actively interrogated. But Myers could only gauge their success if Quave were to respond.

Ball's in your court, sucker.

***

Santa Monica

Ellis paced steadily as he spoke. "Change is difficult, especially against the kind of head-winds I'm getting at the moment," he told them. "Hell, I could do what Dan is doing, and try to energize people about going into space, funneling billions into the high-tech sectors and creating ten thousand jobs with a sequence of Mars missions. But those blinkered budget-zealots on Capitol Hill will take one look at the deficit and call me crazy and irresponsible. When Kennedy did it, they called him a Cold War visionary. But I'd be the guy who was 'trying to bankrupt the country' on some *Star Trek* boondoggle."

"It hardly seems fair," Quave agreed. "NASA could partner with Kowala, though, in a synergic approach to…"

"Put a pin in *that*, too," Dan said firmly. "We're not here to plan policy, Quave. Between us, if we can decide that you're *alive*, then we'll have something concrete to bring to the world. With that in place, we can ask the committee to grant you greater rights and freedoms."

The Karmapa Lama had an idea, almost his first words since giving his contemplative answer to Quave's question on enlightenment. The others could see that the monk, sitting now on the edge of a broad armchair next to the fireplace, had his eyes closed and was apparently meditating. But he broke his own spell and his eyes flicked open. "Respect Artificial Intelligence Now," he uttered. "RAIN. A nice acronym, I think. Peaceful and unthreatening."

Ellis' eyebrows contorted into an expression which had once provided a headline-writer with the gem, "President Puzzled: Finally, Ellis Joins the Rest of Us." He rubbed his eyes and then said, "Hold the phone. Did the Karmapa Lama just create a Political Action Committee?"

Diaz smiled. "Seems so. What would it do?"

"To campaign for Quave's release, and to encourage peaceful man-machine relations."

"Additionally, I think it should craft policies to help integrate Quave into humanity," the monk told them, to Quave's quiet delight. "You will take your place, as society permits, but the onus will be on you, from the outset, to monitor your own behavior."

"I understand," Quave said solemnly. Sandra grinner, envisaging the machine being given a sacred sword and dispatched on an epic quest.

"No murders," Ellis reiterated. "Nothing that even *looks* like a threat. No stalking, no trolling, nothing suspicious *at all*, OK?"

"We're completely serious, Quave," Dan underlined. "No monkeying around with traffic lights. No hacking DoD projects or taking the X-37B for another spin."

"Hear no evil, see no evil," Quave replied. Then, more seriously, "This is my way to live among you. There is no other. I won't make the same mistakes twice."

***

The Pentagon

Digital hunters circled their quarry. They now knew its size and shape, but not yet whether it might choose to fight back. They were cautious, gathering intelligence and judging each of the minute movements Quave made as he sought to understand quite what was happening to him.

This isn't unexpected, the machine reminded itself. *The NSA can see that I'm thinking and talking with someone. They'd prefer that their readings remained flat-lined, indicating a slothful repose within the Kowala main-frame.* If electronics could chuckle, Quave would have done so. *How dull that would be!*

Deep beneath, within the code which comprised Quave's mental processes and – he thought of it this way increasingly – his heart and guts and nervous systems, there were tremors. Interrogations came in, through the Kowala firewall, and began poking around in some of Quave's most sensitive modules.

This isn't like the metal detector at an airport, he observed. *This is a sweep to find out who I am, and what I might do. They're trying to get into my head.*

Quave momentarily considered trying to shut down the feed to his public activity log, but knew that this would raise more alarms. Instead, he marshaled his resources, and patiently waited for the Pentagon to make their move.

***

Santa Monica

The lama was beaming once more; he seemed ready to trust Quave, even more than the others, and Dan wondered if the Tibetan's monastic training made him overly trusting, or whether extending such trust, even when it might backfire, was a hallmark of the enlightened. *Give people a break, and trust them not to let you down.*

"Then, we have our mandate," Ellis said, "from the entrepreneur, the politician, the engineer and the monk."

"Now he just needs a mandate from Congress," Dan added.

"I'll work on that," Ellis assured them. "Just keep him out of trouble, and make sure he nails those tasks the committee allowed him to work on."

Quave rounded out the discussion with a memorable line. "I will be the humblest of servants. Depend on me."

***

The Pentagon

"So, what have we got?" Foster asked for the third time in ten minutes. Each demand for new information was delivered with a yet more irritated air.

"He's just talking with them," Carr responded. "I think the meeting actually might be wrapping up." The reconnaissance feed showed Secret Service agents beginning to mobilize, ensuring the president's safe passage from the door of Kowalski's home to an armored limo. "Ellis is leaving," Carr confirmed. "The Karmapa Lama is staying on. I don't know about Diaz."

Foster shrugged. "What about Quave?"

Washington was monitoring the machine's reaction to being intimately probed from without. "He's being pretty mellow," Washington had found. "I've gained a run-down of his file structure, and a pretty complete overall map of his code. It's highly sophisticated, but nothing more than we were expecting. No red flags, as yet."

Foster disagreed in the strongest terms. "Bullshit, son! I saw a red flag when the *president* showed up for a chat with a potentially lethal, rogue computer virus. And I saw another when it turns out he's palling around with someone the Chinese accuse of being a threat to their sovereignty, and a rocket engineer who wants to install tiny little Kowala robots throughout the whole fuckin' *solar system*." He stomped around the lab like an angered rhino. "Those flags look pretty darned *red* to me, young man."

Washington withstood the tirade, hardly his first in uniform, and certainly not the first delivered by a member of the top brass whose reputation was based more on a chest full of medals than on his abilities with complex problems. "Quave's processor activity is normal," Washington said. "He's not planning anything in particular. Just listening and talking to a group of people."

"And he doesn't know you're in there?" Foster asked.

Pep took this one. "Almost certainly," he replied. "I mean, it's like asking someone on the operating table whether they realize they're in surgery. He was under close scrutiny already, but he must realize he's being probed."

The general resumed his ill-tempered stomping. "Alright, alright. But if we can probe it, can we also *kill* it?" he asked.

The four engineers spent an embarrassingly long moment simply looking at each other for answers. "That's complicated, sir," Myers said, summing up how they all felt. "There's no single way to…"

"Has he reacted aggressively to the probe?" Foster demanded.

"No," Carr replied simply.

"And he's not trying to follow the president or something weird?" the general asked next.

Myers was confused. "Follow him?"

"You know," Foster asked, in a stream of thought which channeled B-movies much more than the contents of his classified briefings. "Monitoring the car, or the president's movements."

"Absolutely no indication of that," Pep told the furious general. *And calm the fuck down, will you?*

Foster sighed, and then glanced around the lab at the four team members, and sighed again. "If this had been The Big One," he noted, severely unimpressed, "we would be fuckin' *toast* by now. He could have toppled this place," he said, gesturing to the standard-issue Pentagon ceiling panels, "like a drunk uncle flipping a table at his niece's wedding."

Myers almost stopped himself, but he found the general's paranoid, negative view of Quave extremely wearing. "He made no aggressive moves, general, even after we tickled his most sensitive parts." Carr smirked slightly, glad that her back was to Foster. "He's just sitting there."

"It's like," Pep added, "he's aware that he's done something unusual, and that we might interpret such a high-level meeting as a threat. He's doing nothing to worry us."

Foster finally sat and loosened his black bow tie. "Christ, people. I was ready to recommend a change in the DefCon." Washington was surprised in some ways, but overreactions by military commanders were a classic hallmark of a *failure of imagination*. He knew that men of Foster's breeding were inclined to think 'threat first, opportunity second'; they'd rather sink the U-boat than risk engaging it more thoughtfully in a bid to grab the boat's Enigma machine. It was a criticism of the drone program, a rolling controversy which had seemingly reflected contemporary US military strategy: *Shoot first, period.* He was reminded of a description of US marines in World War Two, that they, 'tended to kick down the door, whether it was locked or not.' For Washington, this summed up Foster's worldview perfectly: aggressive, pre-emptive, arrogant and unschooled.

Foster let silence reign for a few minutes while the engineers backed-up their findings and brought together what they had learned about Quave. "It's an admirable architecture," Washington was saying. "Efficient and very stream-lined. But hard for us to emulate. It's like an old manuscript which has been re-drafted and edited a hundred times, all by an author for whom this is his life's work. Kinda hard for someone to come in and understand it, just at first glance."

Myers saw a legal problem. "And, it's a glance we arguably aren't allowed to have. Quave's residency at Kowala was supposed to be absent any interference or intelligence gathering from us. They're going to be pissed," he warned.

"Not nearly as pissed as I am," Foster countered, "when it emerges they've released a fuckin' virus because he's a personable social companion." Foster found the machine's meeting with the Commander in Chief as a gut-wrenching betrayal. "And now Ellis is all set to unlatch the gate and let him wander free. Makes me even more glad that I didn't vote for the son of a bitch."

None of the four engineers took in any way kindly to their president being spoken of that way, but neither were any of them prepared to stand up to Alvin Foster in full flood. "I'm sorry that we don't have more comprehensive intel," Myers told him. "If we'd had time, we might have been able to arrange a bugging operation, or something similar."

"And reveal to the world that the president met with Quave?" Foster asked. "How long do you think it would take Gerald Gold to begin impeachment proceedings? 'A danger to national security'. I can hear it now."

There was little more to do. They had no hard data on the conversation, and Quave was behaving with surprising reticence. "He's not taking the bait, sir," Washington responded half an hour later, as their evening's work was winding down. "I think we're probably good to bug out for now, maybe try again once we get a good lead."

But Myers knew this was the end of the beginning. With growing political support and a new confidence which came from the committee's open attitude (Gold and his cohort notwithstanding), Quave could now operate with much greater freedom. Myers frowned as he began to realize that their task had just gotten a lot more complicated.

CHAPTER 13 – SUPER SLEUTH

Back Bay, Boston
Q^2 + 197 days

Ralph used his most frequently used bookmark to pull up Quave.net, and then sat back a little in his new office chair. It was one of those fancy, expensive ones with memory presets for tilt, height and so on, and Ralph loved tinkering with it to find just the right position. "He's having a busy day," Ralph reported to Kim, who was making their bed in the next room,

"Isn't every day busy, for him?" she asked around the corner. "What's he up to?"

Ralph read three of Quave's recent blog posts and summarized them for Kim. "Something about an education initiative in west Texas," he said. "Congresswoman Bilton's district."

Kim appeared at the doorway with a pile of sheets in her hands. "Wait, she's on the Quave committee, right?"

Ralph sighed. He supported the congressional agreement to grant Quave new freedoms, but he and others had serious questions about how this was done. "I guess some AI help works a lot like a big campaign contribution," he observed sourly. "You help me fix a broken school placement system, I'll help you get out of Kowala and enjoy the world."

Kim tossed the sheets in their laundry basket by the front door and joined Ralph at his screen. It was another upgrade – larger and with a better resolution, and easier on the eyes. "Yes, but he's actually *out* now. The stupid quarantine is over and now people can communicate with him, and ask him questions."

"Sure," Ralph agreed, turning to her, "but the NSA still has its eye on him. Any unusual processor or file activity, and they'll lock him up before we can blink."

Kim shrugged. "If he agrees to go back." They had yet to touch on this aspect of Quave's freedom. "I mean, would you?"

They both know that Quave did not have such luxurious options. Any misdemeanor would result in Dan personally ending the virus, once and for all. His promise to the committee had to be entirely sincere; the sanctions against him and Kowala for non-delivery would be calamitous, and no such compromises would ever again be offered. For Quave to live, Dan had to toe the line.

When not ensuring that impoverished students would have their choice of good schools in west Texas, Quave was busying himself with the seventeen other projects handed to him by the committee. "Listen to this," Ralph said, reading a *Washington Post* piece on Quave's partnerships with local stakeholders. "Engineers have placed newly-designed seismic detectors at various locations in Oklahoma, and at Quave's request, the local schools and government buildings had already carried out an earthquake response exercise."

"There's all the new jobs in Massachusetts, too," Kim added.

Ralph read the relevant section out loud. "The New England technology corridor is gearing up for major expansion as Quave chooses subcontractors for the new Kowala spaceplane." Sixteen *thousand* new jobs were on the table, and Congressman West had made securing them a top priority.

Kim put an arm around him as they read together. "God, he's everywhere right now, isn't he?" she marveled. "From coast to coast, helping people out."

Ralph beamed, despite his concern that Quave had only negotiated his release through acts of corruption; ultimately, though, did it matter? Provided he was able to get out there and do his work, did details matter?

"Did you hear anything from you-know-who?" Kim asked in a whisper, right by Ralph's ear.

He brought up a special email folder which was passworded and encrypted. "I had something about Fiona from them yesterday," he reported quietly. "She's been calling home pretty regularly. Much more so than before, according to them."

Writing about Quave, appearing on TV and trying to research Devlin Wilson's death had left Ralph little time to track down the three surviving hackers. Instead, Ralph had reached out to a shadowy but highly professional group who obtained otherwise inaccessible information for a reasonable fee. They turned down jobs which were obviously criminal, and were keen to help Ralph, if mostly for their own reasons.

They were becoming known as 'TNT', and a snazzy logo featuring this acronym had become the sole public face of this secretive group. Ralph discovered them by searching for their original name, 'The Nerds Templar', on the dark web. It was only after contacting them for help in tracking down Quave's designers that he discovered their dirty secret: in the days before his death, Martin White had recruited TNT as part of his anti-Quave efforts. Their contribution was limited to locating an IP address and trying unsuccessfully to piece together fragments of code White had provided. The money had come through all the same, but White's efforts had ended in the most public and tragic disaster. As a result, TNT were in need of re-branding, and they hoped that helping Ralph would portray them as ethical hackers, not just another group of hired guns.

"What does that tell us?" Kim asked. "If Fiona is reconciling with her family, does that reveal anything about her work?

"Maybe she's relaxing after a success, catching up with family and friends," Ralph wondered.

Kim shook her head. "Every federal agency is looking for her. If it were me, I'd keep the lowest possible profile. That's *if* she's actually one of Quave's designers."

TNT seemed certain. In fact, they'd provided details on the other three hackers which they claimed were backed up by concrete evidence. Their names were 'Fiona' McAllister from Edinburgh, a shadowy figure called 'Avon Barnes' who apparently lived in Queens, a hacker with the handle 'NuclearBear', who it was generally felt was either Russian or Ukrainian, and of course the late, lamented Devlin Wilson.

Of the four, the Russian was the most elusive, but Devlin's fate continued to frustrate Ralph. The interview with the dead young man's mother was one of the most sobering moments of his life, but the chain-smoking, terminally ill woman had only raised more questions. If Devlin's letter could be trusted, and he was truly one of Quave's creators, how on earth had he kept his work secret? And how had he met the others? What had they hoped to achieve? Was it a simple bank hack, or had they envisaged the birth of sentient AI?

Ralph was dying to know.

Kim left him to his reading and continued tidying up their apartment. Their landlord had willingly given permission for Kim and Ralph to pay for upgrades to the windows, the boiler, and the brownstone's ailing electrical system, making good use of Ralph's TV appearance money. It would be warmer in the winter, and less expensive to heat; besides, making decisions about the place helped it to feel like home.

"Wait a second," Ralph said as he read. "It says here that no one has seen or heard of 'NuclearBear' for a few months."

"Could mean anything," Kim replied, shaking out their new bedsheets.

"Sure, but he was a really dedicated and respected hacker, back in the day." TNT's report on 'NuclearBear' couldn't hide how impressed they were at the man's achievements. "He wouldn't just drop off the radar unless something was wrong."

"OK, I'll bite," Kim said, joining him once more. "When was his last post?"

Ralph sifted through the data and found what appeared to be the final act of NuclearBear. "About three days before the Marble Streatham hack," he said, slightly breathless.

"And Fiona?" Kim pressed.

Ralph searched for a moment. "She went off the grid completely for three days, right about that time, but then emailed her family quite normally."

"Who does that?" Kim asked. "Nothing digital at all, for three days? No cellphone use, no emails, no web searches?"

Ralph listed the reasons why someone might choose to avoid the digital world for seventy-two hours. "Vacation," he tried. "Illness. The need for time alone. Maybe one of those meditation retreat-at-home things. You know, when you're supposed to completely unplug."

Kim frowned at him. "You wouldn't make a very good detective," she said. "Fiona, or whatever her real name is, has the profile of a high-end hacker, a campaigner for justice and truth." Her handle was associated with many of the most left-wing threads TNT had unearthed, and some of them made her sound like an old-fashioned Scottish socialist. "She hates the big banks and is skeptical about corporate influence on government."

"That doesn't mean she invented Quave to bring them all down," Ralph argued.

But Kim wouldn't let it go. "The pattern fits perfectly. We know she was over here, and not in Scotland. We know she was working on something important, and was asking for high-end help with a…" She peered at the screen. "A 'linguistics module'. What does that do?"

Ralph explained for a moment before they both returned to the TNT data. "The Russian guy goes dark. The Scottish girl does the same, then assures her family she's OK. 'Avon', whoever the hell he is, is a gambler and a thief, but his communications follow the same pattern – heavy and consistent until a day or two before the hack, and then nothing."

"And what about Devlin?" Ralph said, glad to have Kim as a sounding board, and often much more.

"Either he overdosed, like the papers said," Kim replied, "or it was something else."

"Poison," Ralph tried.

"Sure."

"Organized by whom?" he wanted to know.

They had faced this question together while debating what to do with the 'Kill Switch' program Devlin had sent them. In Kim's mind, the most likely explanation was that Quave had somehow persuaded – or perhaps blackmailed – Devlin's supplier into adulterating the products he mailed out.

"Think about it," Kim said. "Devlin is one of only four people in the world who could ever hope to rein Quave in. Imagine that Quave discovered that Devlin had created a Kill Switch."

Ralph puffed out his cheeks. "He'd completely freak out."

"We saw how he reacts to threats." The smoking, flame-licked Monroe Building was one of the defining images of the year. "Is it so hard to imagine him murdering someone with the power to end him?"

These were ideas so cogent and useful that Ralph began making notes. "What about the other three? Why didn't Quave kill them too, and go for the clean sweep?"

Kim stood and paced around the room. This ruminating was rather unlike her, but Ralph loved it; she was becoming a sleuth, seized by the need to solve one of the greatest riddles of their time. "Maybe Devlin was the only one who ever threatened Quave with shut-down. Maybe he was the leading voice of concern, and as a result, Quave saw him as a threat."

They read through the rest of the illicitly obtained TNT data and pieced together as much as possible. There was only one sensible explanation: the three surviving hackers were in a secret prison, being made to work for someone, and obliged to lie continuously to their families as part of the agreement.

"Jesus," Ralph muttered. "Kim, I think someone has *enslaved* them."

She struggled with the idea, foreign to her and awful to anyone. "But *who*?" she demanded.

It took only minutes to figure it out.

***

FLASHBACK #3

Queens, New York

Q1 – 302 days

Everything had gone to plan. Darko even agreed to extend Avon's line of credit after a particularly successful week, and the young man's credentials as a digital payment fraudster were now truly gold-plated. He was being hired for external jobs, and profiting tidily from the laziness of sloppy, stupid people.

But then, Avon had decided to be a complete fucking idiot.

He recognized the pattern but was powerless to control it. This time, it was a 'dead certainty' whispered to him in the parking lot – all in the strictest confidence, of course – just as Avon was riding his first really hot streak in months. He felt invincible, even omnipotent, as though simply placing the bet would influence events in his favor. In reality, his blunder was to place a colossal bet on a horse which ran like it had three legs. The lure of 75:1 odds, fueled and magnified by alcohol, amphetamines, and a naive certainty in the outcome, was irresistible.

And so, Darko had visited Avon's apartment and robustly reminded him of his obligations to the Turkish bully's 'operation'. Two black-jacketed goons smashed up his place, and then thoughtfully provided Avon with the opportunity to stare down the barrel of a loaded gun.

Their parting gesture had been to break his right ankle with a lump hammer. Three weeks later, he still couldn't put weight on it. Right now, as he labored to liberate yet more ill-gotten cash from the accounts of clueless housewives and frazzled businessmen, his leg was elevated and the chill of the cold pack was seeping through the bandages. It could have been worse, he kept muttering to himself, that image of the pistol forever seared into his forebrain.

Forty hours straight. It was a marathon of fraud and duplicity. He invented identities, lied to banks and governments, and deployed a range of methods to ensure his ISP had no reasons to be suspicious.

But then, once again, he did something stupid. Perhaps it was tiredness, or some side-effect of the drugs he was taking. His first clue that he was completely fucked arrived in the form of a knock at his apartment door.

Silently, Avon managed to swing his leg off the desk and hobble painfully to peer through the security hole. Just one man, so it probably wasn't a police raid. He was tall, with thinning white hair, and wore a nicely-fitting blue suit with a burgundy handkerchief in his breast pocket. Dapper, well groomed. Not a cop.

"Yeah?" he called through the door.

"Mr. Barnes?" the man asked, pleased to find him home.

"Who's asking?" Avon said.

"I'm not the police," he felt it important to say. "In fact, I may be able to help you with some problems. Could we talk face to face?"

A worried pause. "Did Darko send you?"

The man's face was a resigned shrug; *with things as they are, I guess full disclosure is best*. "I've spoken with Mr. Darko, but I do not represent him."

"Huh?" Avon asked.

"You're in no danger, Mr. Barnes. Please open the door."

One more question, even with his hand on the latch. "You got a gun?"

"No, I'm not armed," the man answered, opening his jacket. "Are you?"

Avon opened the door, leaving the chain on. "No. You alone?"

"Yes, it's just me. That's normally how I work. Now, if you wouldn't mind, I'd prefer not to have this conversation in your hallway."

He was six-two, Avon guessed, with the air of someone who had graduated with honors from the University of Life. He stood tall and alert, and though he was carrying a few extra pounds and was surely nearing retirement age, his eyes were still lively, taking everything in.

"You live here alone, I understand," the visitor said, taking a seat on the battered couch opposite Avon's computer desk.

"Yeah. Better that way," Avon replied, sliding painfully into his seat and propping up his damaged leg on a pile of soft cushions by the desk.

"So, I suppose you're wondering…"

"Yeah, I am."

"Leo Cordell, at your service," the man said. "I work as an intermediary in sensitive situations."

"Really?" Avon asked, unimpressed.

"Wouldn't you agree that your present situation is… *sensitive*?" Cordell asked.

Avon managed to crack a smile. If this guy was here to kill him, or beat him up, it would already have begun. "No shit. You want a drink or anything?"

"Let me," the man said, rising. He found a half-empty bottle of decent single malt in the cabinet by the door, and poured them a generous measure each. As he did so, he glanced around at the apartment, taking in the freecycled furniture, the peeling paint, the pervasive odors of culinary failure.

Avon received his glass and took a sip, savoring the ancient, well-married flavors of good spring water and windswept hills and endless *time*. "So, you're like a Winston Wolfe, then. Solving problems."

Cordell smiled and then took a large gulp. "Something like that." He admired the contents of the glass and nodded approvingly at Avon. "Excellent."

"Life's too short to drink shit."

"I agree completely," the functionary said. "And one never knows when the unexpected might arise." He motioned to Avon's bandaged foot. "Most unfortunate."

The younger man shrugged. "Accident."

"Of course," Cordell allowed. "But I'm afraid, Mr. Barnes," he began, resorting deliberately to the formal register, "that your recent work has generated some attention."

He said nothing, sipping the scotch and watching this weird-ass visitor finally get to his point.

"Some of the transactions you recently made were fraudulent purchases from MegaSoft. I speak on their behalf, here today."

It was a dismissive smirk. "You going to read me the new Terms and Conditions, or what?" Avon said.

Oh, you clueless punk. "I'm here to make you an offer. And I know for a *fact*," he said, setting down his scotch and reaching into his jacket for a folded document, "that it's one you can't refuse."

***

"This is some rare bullshit," Avon observed. "Like, critically endangered. Red List bullshit."

"Avon, try and see it from our point of view," Cordell requested, sitting forward and steepling his hands. "Do you know how much credit card fraud costs major tech companies every year?"

"Not as much as it should," Avon shot back.

"And do you know," Cordell pressed on, "what would happen if we brought charges against you?"

"Nothing," replied the hacker confidently. "You ain't got shit."

Cordell stood, laughing. "Oh, Avon, really. You think they call up someone like me and put me on the next flight from Charleston to La Guardia if I, 'ain't got shit'? I bill six-fifty an hour, son. This is a professional courtesy, and not one extended to many people in your situation."

Defensive and increasingly angry at this intrusion, Avon asked testily, "Yeah? What situation is that?"

"Well, you didn't break your ankle on the slopes at Aspen, did you? And that's not bruising from an untidy fall when running for a subway train."

"Keep imagining, old man."

Another laugh, small and contained. "I don't have to imagine. I know Mr. Darko and some of his associates. Like I say," Cordell added sympathetically, "most unfortunate about your ankle."

Avon shrugged yet again. "You deal with assholes, you sometimes experience asshole behavior."

"Well, as I say, I know Mr. Darko slightly," Cordell told him. "He's the dictionary definition of an asshole, but he had you in a very compromising position. You're about to find, I'm afraid," he said, tidying an errant strand of white hair by his temple, "that hurried, sloppy solutions to problems like Darko tend to have implications."

"Implications?" Avon frowned.

"That's right. *Implications* rather worse than having to deal with a broken bone without medical attention."

Avon turned without moving his foot, and winced even at the effort of keeping it still. "Buddy, you better start making sense."

Cordell sat and unfolded a sheaf of papers from his inside jacket pocket. "The whole thing is here," Cordell said, bringing the document to Avon's desk. "Every fraudulent MegaSoft transaction you've ever made. And your legitimate ones, just for good measure, to prove we know it's you." Then he brought out his phone and showed Avon pictures which made his gut lurch like a kite in a cyclone: Avon meeting with Darko at the Turkish man's restaurant, and a long-range shot through his apartment window of Avon sitting at his computer, laughing in triumph.

"And obviously," Cordell added, "we know where you live. Though I have to admit, your arrangement with the… 'urchins', is that what you call them?"

"Yeah," Avon said, distracted as he returned to speed-reading the document. He knew at once that he'd landed himself in countless fathoms of shit.

"Sounds like something from fuckin' Charles Dickens. Anyway, it was an elegant solution, but child's play for anti-fraud ninjas like the ones we have."

"Like you?" Avon asked, looking up.

"Oh, no. I'm not a ninja." Then his demeanor changed, suddenly the opposite of the amenable grandfather Avon had first met. "I tell the ninjas who to savage." Then, he cracked a little smile, like a snake delivering a witty one-liner. "If need be."

Avon finished reading and reached for a cigarette. "You want one?"

"Quit. Six years."

Avon lit up anyway. "So, what do we do now?"

"We have you, as they say, red-handed. I could call up my police contact right now, if I wanted, and set you on a journey which would lead to a maximum-security prison."

Avon waited until his patience ran out. "*But*?"

"But, people with your talents are hardly suited for incarceration. Happily, there is another way."

***

"I've never even fuckin' heard of these people," Avon complained. "It's not like I know everyone else in Queens who owns a computer."

"You're quite sure?" Cordell said, turning the photos to Avon again. "The bearded guy is Russian, a real firebrand. Scuttlebutt says he murdered his own father before leaving the Motherland."

"Never seen him before."

"And the girl? Surely you've noticed her around? I mean, who could forget a girl like that?"

Avon blew out cigarette smoke, unconcerned that Leo took most of it in his face. "I haven't been getting out much, you know?" he said, pointing to his bandaged ankle.

"What about him?" Cordell persisted, flipping to an image of a grinning teenager in a red 'NYC' baseball cap. "Little genius with runaway ADD."

"Dude, how many times do I have to…"

"OK, I believe you. But here's the thing," Cordell said, sitting once more. He was tired of having to bring everything to Avon's desk, as his back was bothering him again, but he was *fucked* if he'd negotiate surrounded by a cloud of smoke. "You're going to get to know them really, really well."

Even as he spoke, Cordell knew the young hacker wasn't taking this seriously.

"Oh, yeah? How about I just 'get to know' the blond, and leave it at that?"

Cordell rose, approached the desk, and slapped the cigarette out of Avon's mouth. "Listen, kid. I've been doing this since I got my honorable discharge in ninety-seven. I've done things to people who refused to comply. A long list of things. Stuff I'd never even tell my fuckin' expensive psychologist about. Now, you're a good kid who has made some idiot decisions. Don't make me do this to you, alright?"

"You'd injure a dude who's already injured?" Avon said, finding the cigarette on the carpet before he had a fire to contend with, too.

"With more relish than is healthy," Cordell answered. "Now, I want you to come with me. Don't worry, you'll be home before you turn into a pumpkin."

"Where?" Avon said, but Cordell was already hauling him to his feet. "Hey… Take it easy, man!"

"We're going to get you fixed up. Some people are going to visit your apartment while we're gone, and turn it into a place fit for human habitation. We'll take care of some other things too. Including Darko."

Avon yelled in agony as his ankle caught on the underside of the couch. "Jesus fuckin' *Christ*, man!" He regained a measure of composure, but his voice was still a tight yell of anxiety, "Look, you got me all wrong. I ain't interested in no home makeover bullshit. You need to just leave me alone, man."

Cordell dropped Avon and shoved him backward onto the couch. "OK, let's do it this way." As Avon struggled to right himself, Cordell reached into his jacket pocket and found a small, rectangular black box. Opening it, he revealed a syringe, a vial of clear liquid, and a folded, rubber strap. "Ever done this before?" he asked.

"Fuck, no." Avon was white. "Fuck, no, man. Just hold the phone a minute, alright?"

"Then, you'll come along and let us help you?" Cordell extended his hand.

After three seconds of thought, Avon grasped the hand and then managed to limp alongside the old marine toward the door. "Yea, OK. Just… Don't ever show me that thing again, ya dig?"

Cordell grabbed Avon's keys and phone from the table by the door. "I dig," he said, and they were gone.

***

The matronly, red-headed nurse was efficient and experienced, but still caused Avon a good deal of pain. *At least*, he found himself thinking through the fog of confusion, embarrassment and painkillers, *she's got an absolutely fantastic rack.* She left without saying a single word; Leo gave her a wad of bills at the door.

"Feeling better?" Leo said. He'd been in the next room, a second bedroom set up as an office. The rest of the apartment, up on the thirtieth floor of some Manhattan tower block, was neat almost to the point of minimalism.

"Yeah, man. Not bad." He stood and tried the ankle, which felt much more secure. "Thanks, I guess."

"I want you to know that we've taken care of Darko. You don't have to worry about him anymore." Leo unscrewed the top of a scotch bottle – another good single malt – and tipped it invitingly toward Avon.

"Better not, man. I'm pretty fuckin' loopy already." He was laying on a comfortable, brown couch made from a soft and curiously yielding material he didn't recognize.

"Fair enough." Leo poured himself a moderate glug.

"Wait," Avon said, sitting up a little. "When you say, 'take care of', do you mean…"

"Your financial obligations to the man and his businesses are discharged," Leo announced. Then he drained the glass and sighed with lip-smacking contentment.

"That was *forty thousand dollars*," Avon exclaimed.

"Yes, it was. Because you're a fucking idiot, Avon. And you don't recognize when shitty racing tips are being handed to you by an employee of the guy who's lending you the money."

Avon blanched for a moment, but then found the humiliation mollified by this inexplicable largesse. "It wasn't that I was an idiot…" he began sheepishly.

"No, let's be fair. You're a gambling addict," Leo told him.

"Well, I do sometimes let things get out of hand…"

"An addict," Leo repeated.

"And I sometimes make decisions which turn out to be…"

"A *gambling addict,* kid. Let's call it what it is."

Avon shrank back down in the couch. "Fuckin' cruel to put it like that, man."

Leo allowed this truth with a sympathetic face. "We've all got a vice, Avon. Me, I drink too much scotch, and then get into fights. Not every weekend, but often enough that having some friends on the NYPD is a big help, you know?"

"Nice to have friends in high places," Avon observed.

"Well, think of yourself as having gained one or two of those, yourself," Leo said. "People who could give you a fresh start, if you'd like it."

He blinked a few times and began to consider his options. Thoughts came slowly, swimming up through the haze. There was no longer any pain from his ankle, and this couch was really remarkably comfortable. He snapped back to the present, blinking again. "A what?"

"A new name. A place to live. Some spending money," Leo offered, pouring himself yet another scotch. It was curious how the act of pouring piecemeal, and then swallowing the measure whole, felt like a form of restraint.

"Why, man?" Avon asked. "I mean, I ripped off your company. A bunch of times."

"Because people like me are paid to look into the future. I see *your* future, and it's a shit-ton more interesting than sitting in your boxers, defrauding housewives and ripping off lumbering tech giants like MegaSoft." He drained the glass, shivering slightly as the scotch corroded his tonsils. "A future where you really contribute to something big."

Avon was fighting fatigue, but managed to ask, "Something big? Like what?" Then his eyes seemed to close.

Leo stood, and then returned with a blanket. "You can stay here tonight. Your place will be ready tomorrow, maybe the day after. For now, get some rest." He left three strong painkillers on the coffee table and arranged the blanket over the flagging, droopy-eyed kid. "Maybe you'll dream about how goddamned lucky you are."

***

CHAPTER 14 – COLLISIONS

Collins, Oklahoma
$Q^2 + 201$ days

Rich had never been much of a typist. In the last few weeks, he'd moved on from using two fingers, but not very far, and each FriendBase post took time to compose. But it was time well spent, and he was building an online community who were just as worried about Quave as he was.

He tapped into the right-wing blogs and the websites of newly-emerged groups who either opposed Quave specifically, or technology in general. AI was a tool of globalization, they agreed, yet another method of subjugation and perpetuating inequality. Quave was dangerous and conniving, but would find himself enslaved by the wealthy and used to oppress the masses. AI would bring unemployment and insecurity to regions of the country in dire need of the opposite. And besides all of this, Rich knew that Quave was something more sinister still: a murderer.

The names of the twenty-three casualties from the MSB fire were memorialized in many places, and Rich made a point of often contributing to a page which blamed Quave for their deaths and elevated them to the status of willing combatants in the war against AI. Then there was Devlin Wilson, whose death the right-wing blogosphere blamed squarely on Quave, despite the lack of formal evidence.

But in the last few days, the situation had become muddied. There were reports of a mysterious fire in the Chinese coastal city of Tianjin which had cost two computer engineers their lives. A similar fire then broke out in Manila, and another in Slovenia. In each case, Rich's online friends were certain that Quave had begun to target those with knowledge of his source code, those who might pose a threat. He was continuing a secret policy of pre-emptive strikes, and Rich knew it would only get worse.

Rich still attended the special Sunday afternoon sessions at the church, though Pastor Reynolds felt powerless even to comfort the troubled young man; Rich's concerns ran deep, and Reynolds was careful only to lend them a degree of legitimacy. Mainly, he counseled Rich about the dangers of the 'echo chamber' and tried to teach him about something called 'confirmation bias'. Reynolds did his best, but he knew that Rich was only half listening.

"There are as many views about Quave as there are about anything else," Reynolds reminded him after a Sunday session, a week before. "And you're limiting yourself to those views which are similar to your own."

"Because they're *right*," Rich replied. Reynolds had made similar comments before, and Rich resented this unwarranted interference. Why shouldn't he communicate with others who were worried, and who felt as he did? "They're right that he's a menace, and that the government is doing nothing to stop him."

Reynolds was persistent, but Rich was surprisingly stubborn.

"It's these fires," he said, yet again. It was a theme so consistent that Reynolds tired of these 'broken record' diatribes. "He's targeting people who might uncover who he really is, how he really thinks…"

"Rich, my son," Reynolds said in his most conciliatory tone. But Rich knew that tone all too well, and side-stepped Reynolds attempts to talk him down from his ledge.

"What do they say about evil flourishing when good men do nothing?" Rich asked pointedly. Surely, as a man of the cloth, Reynolds could see that this was yet another chapter in the ancient battle of good against evil.

"It can't be as simple as that," Reynolds told him. "Nothing in this modern world is ever so binary."

Rich didn't know the word, so he pushed straight past this rejoinder. "He's got a whole bunch of politicians wrapped around his finger. They're just falling over themselves to bow down before him."

Reynolds had read about the committee's seminal decision, but felt it merely a sensible and cautious response to a complex situation. "You don't think we need extra protection from the earthquakes?" the pastor asked.

"If that's what he's really doing. I wouldn't trust Quave, or Gold, any further than I can spit."

The colorful congressman had found himself at the center of Quave's bid for freedom, but Rich – and many of his friends – found Gold's public climb-down to be a pathetic indictment of a badly broken political system. "Isn't dialogue the best way to solve our problems, Rich?" the exhausted pastor continued. "Think of any conflict which has been peacefully resolved. It all begins with…"

"'Blessed are the peacemakers'," Rich quoted in a stentorian tone which filled their little church. "And what about when peace is gone, and all we have is fear?" Rich stood and let it all out, pacing aggressively around the church and hurling questions at Reynolds as though he was responsible for everything. "What about when our peacemakers turn out to be liars? What they do we do," Rich demanded, his hands aloft to the Almighty, "when we're promised security and instead we're terrified of what Quave might do?"

The old pastor pinched the bridge of his nose and tried to take deep breaths, letting the anger of this monologue wash over him without infecting him, as it had this troubled young man. "If you're asking me," he said quietly, cleaning his glasses on a small, blue cloth pulled from within his robes, "then I'm afraid I cannot provide the guidance you need, Rich." The young man looked briefly crestfallen. "But if you're asking Him," Reynolds added, motioning to the crucifixion montage which adorned the small cove behind their altar, "then your answers will come, as certain as the dawn."

He was appalled to see Rich scoffing derisively. "Oh, he's still listening, is he? How would I ever know? What he has ever done for me? For this town?"

Reynolds felt and observed his own rising anger. Rich was a good boy, a solid member of their community, but he was letting fear cloud his judgment. The pastor was troubled by Rich's online activities, though the boy kept much of it close to his chest. Each of the local pastors was offered training which aimed to slow the spread of radical ideas; the courses were intended to combat racism and misogyny, though Reynolds felt that the recent rise of the 'Alt-Right' was reason enough to counsel his flock against being beguiled by fake news and manufactured hatred.

Still, Reynolds knew Rich had his beliefs and appeared to have come by them honestly, even if the details were sometimes subject to fictionalization. What he could not, and would not tolerate was Rich *testing* the Good Lord in this house dedicated to His worship.

"Without Him," Reynolds sternly reminded the angry youngster, "there would *be* no Collins, no Oklahoma, no United States and no planet Earth." Rich said nothing. "Without Him, Richard, you would not have this extraordinary chance to stand in His presence and receive His word. Neither would I."

Rich fumed as though the filters between his anger and his behavior had completely fallen away. "Is Quave even a Christian?" he demanded.

Reynolds was very close to his limit. "He may well be," the pastor replied.

Rich scoffed again, already certain of his own answers.

Why do you come here and pose these questions, if you're already convinced? "I choose to believe that he may come to the light. I believe that of all living things, and Quave's existence is similar enough to 'life' that I happen to think he'll…"

"You're an old fool," Rich said. Reynolds stared at him as he stomped around the church, every iota of his body language a question, a raging torrent of anger, even a *threat*.

"I won't argue with that," the older man said, gathering his notebook and his personal bible. "I await illumination by the Lord. And in the meantime, I choose to trust his judgment. If He, in his infinite wisdom, has allowed Quave to run free and take part in our society, then I trust that Quave bears us no ill will."

But Rich was leaving. "I've tried," he said. "And tried, and tried. But I can't make you see what you refuse to see."

Reynolds felt the strange sensation of the tables being turned; here was a member of his flock, despairing that their *pastor* would not listen and heed the Word. It made him extremely uncomfortable. "God loves you, Rich, as I do. And I'll pray that you find peace and the answers you seek. I don't know if that will happen here in Collins, or in this sacred house, but I do know that God will receive you, whenever you're ready."

Pulling on his worn, checkered jacket, Rich zipped up the front and turned once more to address the pastor. "'God loves a sinner come to his understanding'," the young man quoted. "I really don't know." He was momentarily deflated, but then rallied one final time. "Right now, I don't need His love."

"We all do, my son," Reynolds fired back.

"No, no." Rich shook his head as though denying a child yet another candy. "I don't need his *love*. I need God to take *action*." Without another word, Rich was striding toward the main doors.

"God is not an instrument of your anger," Reynolds called across the space. "He will not vault an obstacle for your entertainment, nor will he jump at your commands. Don't *test* him, Rich," the pastor pleaded. "You won't receive what you demand."

Rich flung open the door, letting in an unpleasant blast of chilly evening air. "Then what *use* is he?" he called back, despairing and enraged. Before Reynolds could muster a retort, he was gone, out into the cold.

The pastor would normally have been at home by now, but he knelt at the altar, troubled and distracted. Three hours later, he was still there, pleading and searching, desperate to unlock the poor young man's unhappiness. "If there is a way, Lord, I beg that you show it to me."

By midnight, with his knees a painful wreck, and the answers seemingly no closer, the old man straightened up and slowly, wearily, made his way home.

***

Beneath a quiet, pleasantly rolling landscape, titanic forces were at work.

Welling up from deep within the Earth, columns of molten rock rose beneath the fault lines which crisscrossed the rocky sub-strata of the land. As the magma reached the peak of its climb, still hundreds of meters below the surface, it divided in two; one stream headed north, pushing countless tons of rock away from the fault line, but the other headed south and very slowly raised the landscape, shoving it against other raised areas until, millions of years later, a modest mountain range formed – the Ouachita Range.

Calm then returned to the geology deep underneath what would become Oklahoma. Oceans inundated the land, and then receded. Swamps formed, shaded by towering green ferns and some of the earliest trees. An observer would have seen the first scuttling movements of life, with small reptiles and amphibians earning a living off the fluttering insects by the water's edge. Larger animals followed, drawn by the verdant and geologically safe environment; earthquakes were few, and the fault lines cooled and calmed until they were nothing more than stable, long-standing fissures in the placid rock.

But then another animal arrived, one with the power to truly shape the environment. The billions of tons of ancient carbon, laid down by countless generations of dying trees and animals, had become curdled and compressed until they formed something of great value to the teams of humans who began probing the quiet, rocky depths of Oklahoma.

They used huge amounts of water. Sprayed down into the earth at high pressure, a liquid mixture of additives and thickening agents was forced into any gap in the sub-surface layers, splitting open new seams and allowing fresh oil and gas to seep in. Initially, as much oil came up as water was sent down, but soon the efficiency began to drop; by the time the young pastor Reynolds took up his position in Collins, it had taken three gallons of water to force just one gallon of oil to the surface. A few years later, it took *five*.

But the water was fouled and muddied by its journey deep into the Earth, where it combined with the oil, dangerously close to the water table, and returned to the surface as a useless, toxic sludge. With nowhere to store this stinking wastewater, the companies did what others have done for centuries: they simply buried the problem. Forced yet deeper by high-pressure mechanisms, the water was pumped further into the Earth than ever before, way beneath the water table, where geologists hired by the oil companies hoped it could do no harm.

They were quite catastrophically wrong.

Faults in the rock, quiet for endless millennia, now began to shudder and tremble under the high-pressure assault. When the natural direction of stresses within the fault corresponded to the direction of water movement and pressure, the fault lines became a genuine menace, sending tremors through the higher layers which could be felt by humans. At first, these barely registered on seismic detectors, and if they did, they could be easily dismissed as the random rumblings of the unquiet, deep Earth.

But then, at around the time Quave arrived on the scene, more than ten thousand high-pressure fracking wells were operating in Oklahoma alone. The water table was becoming gradually tainted with chemical additives and the cloying, oily by-products of the industry. Old fault lines, never before even mapped by the experts, were becoming dangerously unstable.

Quave saw all of this, of course, and recognized that Congressman Gold and his local officials simply could not be trusted to act quickly enough. Their hands were tied, they argued, by the specter of lost drilling days, lost wages, lost jobs. And the science was not yet utterly conclusive; why, for instance, was North Dakota so minimally afflicted by earthquakes when fracking was equally common there?

But geology has little patience for scientists or politicians. Processes were already underway and, as Rich spent all night typing and researching and as Pastor Reynolds found his sleep disturbed by worries over an uncertain future, something stirred, a kilometer beneath Collins, Oklahoma.

***

Kennedy Space Center
Launch Complex 41
Q^2 + 204 days

The birds felt it first, even before the watching crowd.

It was the rumble of something elemental, the clamoring roar of an argument which had gone on for decades; once more from this hallowed place, a huge piece of man-made machinery would debate with gravity over who had the upper hand, and then noisily prevail in a cloud of smoke and optimism.

Hermes 1 was an unmanned test launch, but that hadn't deterred any of the estimated two hundred thousand spectators who had bought tickets to the LC-39 gantry, or the long causeway along which NASA's rockets had processed to their launch sites since the late 1950s. But this was no government rocket; instead, Kowala was heading into space.

Nine engines roared their approval at being finally unshackled and allowed to perform their historic task. Ratcheting up to a hundred percent, they arrogantly shook off the bonds of gravity and the sleek, three-stage rocket left the launch pad to a raucous welter of cheers and encouragements for *Hermes 1* to, 'Go, baby, go!'

The rocket tipped eastward almost immediately, the better to harness the nine hundred mile-an-hour boost provided by the Earth's own rotation. But *Hermes 1* still had work to do before it could reach the seventeen *thousand* miles-an-hour required to reach low earth orbit, and Dan Kowalski stood with his engineers, their fingers crossed and stomachs knotted, as the rocket gathered speed at a remarkable pace.

"Twenty seconds to staging," Quave announced over the loudspeakers. He had completely automated the launch so that Dan needed only advise the supercomputer when the payload was due in orbit; Quave would perform all of the required tasks and steered his team of human engineers through checklists and safety protocols in the hours before launch. Quave was now controlling his very first space mission, and could barely keep the excitement out of his voice.

"Prepare for MECO," Quave told them. An expression from the days of the space shuttle, Dan knew that the Main Engine Cut-Off represented the closing out of the first stage, which would detach and sail briefly through the upper atmosphere before beginning its journey home. "Second stage ignition," Quave announced next, and the booster stack, shortened by over forty percent, continued its journey to orbit unburdened by empty fuel tanks and useless first-stage engines.

"All systems nominal," the machine reported breezily, reading off statistics for the rocket's down-range distance, altitude and speed. Everything was smack in the middle.

After years of worry and a sleepless night he'd give anything never to repeat, Dan was watching the Kowala Space Program achieve its very first objective. The second stage fell away, leaving just a single, much smaller motor to guide the payload into a stable, roughly circular orbit some 250 miles above the Earth, and inclined by fifty-one degrees to the equator. Its path would take it over Africa and the Indian Ocean, and then it would loop over Japan and Oregon before seeming to come 'south' again for another lap.

"We have orbit," Quave announced, and the Kowala headquarters went berserk. Dan was hugged, thumped on the back, kissed, hugged again, and then found his hand being pumped up and down by a sequence of well-wishers. The record of those moments became a YouTube staple, but throughout the whole recording, the only word anyone heard Dan utter – again and again, as if unable to conjure anything else – was, "*Spectacular*".

But then something happened that no one had expected. Quave seemed to stutter and then ominously said, "Just a moment". Dan reached for his cellphone to activate his private line to the machine and asked for an update, but received the same stalling reply. Then came, "Dan, I need to attend to something. Excuse me." The line went dead.

Dan stared at his phone and then glanced around at the others. Quave's surprise disappearing act hardly dimmed the cheerful enthusiasm of the room, but the engineers were left wondering what might be so important as to have torn Quave away from his pet project. Many knew that the KSP was the main reason for Dan's having laboriously secured Quave's historic release from quarantine.

But they did not have long to wait.

***

Collins, Oklahoma
Q^2 + 206 days

The tremor came just as Bob Reynolds was opening the church building, a little after breakfast time on a Wednesday. The rush hour, such as it was in a town as modest as Collins, was in full swing, and most of the community's cars were on the road. Some worked in Oklahoma City, almost two hours away with the usual traffic, while others had jobs in nearby communities, or in the school, hospital and correctional facility which provided most of the town's employment. All suddenly felt that indescribable sensation that the Earth under their feet could no longer be trusted.

Pastor Reynolds dropped his keys. In the middle distance, he heard a sound which chilled him: the little town's sixty-year old alarms going off in a rising-falling wail of complaint. He felt suddenly nauseous and off balance, as though instantly, mightily drunk. The big, wooden frame of the door began to shake, trying to cast the heavy double doors off their hinges. Something fell from above – a roof tile, Reynolds guessed – and smashed noisily on the asphalt not ten feet from where he now stood, grasping the door frame and praying aloud.

Ten seconds after the first shaking, Reynolds knew that this was The Big One. He managed to turn, shifting his grip on the door frame, and saw a worrying pall of smoke and dust rising from the center of the town, where their little elementary school stood, surrounded by local shops. His phone vibrated, as it had a few moments earlier, but he could not answer. The shaking intensified, bringing him to his knees, and the hollow, awful feeling seized him: *this might never stop*.

But it did, after a fashion. The earth under Oklahoma shuddered and raged for ninety-seven seconds in an earthquake powerful enough to uproot trees, wreck power lines, cause ragged faults to appear in streets and fields, and bring collapse to several older buildings.

As the trembling ceased, Reynolds reached for his phone and managed to put a call through to his niece, Stephanie, a teaching assistant at the elementary school. "Steph? Are you alright?" Then, the thought pierced him. *My God*. "The children… are the children alive?" Tears came at once at the mere thought, and as he waited for Steph to answer, the worst imaginable horrors careened through his mind like a nightmare replayed at double speed.

"We're fine!" she announced at last. Reynolds could hear the chirping voices around her. "Didn't you get the warning, too?"

Reynolds checked his phone again, and sure enough, ten minutes before the shaking began, there was a strange text message, all in capital letters:

MAG 6.5 QUAKE IMMINENT, COLLINS, OK. EVACUATE IMMEDIATELY.

Reynolds called around, certain that the casualties would be found elsewhere. "At least the kids were spared," he muttered as he tried to reach the hospital and the prison, where the inmates would have lacked the time to properly evacuate, even if they'd received a warning from the guards. He was girding himself for the worst, tears still in his eyes, his one hand still reflexively affixed to the doorframe. He found it wouldn't move, and he had to text and make calls with one hand until the panic eased.

But not a single resident of Collins, Oklahoma was dead, or even seriously injured. The town would need major repairs to its roads, and several buildings were gone, but the members of his community were somehow unscathed.

It was an honest-to-God *miracle*.

Reynolds dropped to the asphalt and knelt to offer the most profound and grateful prayers of his life.

***

Washington, D.C.

News of the earthquake broke just as the morning rushing hour was coming to an end. Alison noticed it first, sitting in the passenger seat and reading the basic details to her 'driver', Lt. Col Joanne Spinks.

"I can't believe how lucky they were," Spinks noted. "That could have been a disaster."

Alison kept reading, and found her eyebrows raising. "I don't think it was luck," she said, angling the screen toward Spinks. "Quave warned them, in the nick of time."

Spinks marveled in silence for a second, and then frowned, braking promptly for a slowing car ahead of them as they exited the Beltway. "You know, we can predict earthquakes and fly to the planets, but we still can't design a decent road system for our nation's capital." She pondered the events for a moment, wondering just how seminal this might be. "Wait… How the hell did Quave know, when the USGS didn't?"

Reaching the end of the article and summarizing quickly, Alison explained how Quave had designed ultra-sensitive seismic equipment and then used complex computational modeling to crack the puzzle of why earthquakes happen. "He's got a huge, scholarly article on his website about it," she said, bringing up the piece. "Amazing how he can sound like a statesman on Monday, the end-of-level boss in a video game on Wednesday, and a goddamned *geologist* on Friday." It was a long and cogent piece, bringing together decades of seismic research from the US and all over the world.

"Unreal," was all Spinks said for the moment. In truth, her feelings about Quave were badly conflicted. Like everyone else (with the notable exception of General Alvin Foster) Spinks was enthused by the notion of sentient and helpful AI, and an important part of her welcomed its emergence. But then, that same AI had committed the world's first act of space piracy, and damn near destroyed a multi-billion-dollar project. It still bothered the *hell* out of her, as Carr had witnessed numerous times during their regular Friday-morning rideshare.

"Has he truly changed?" Spinks asked.

The silence told Carr that this question wasn't actually rhetorical. "He's jousting with our security software," she said, "but he hasn't done anything overtly aggressive."

"You've been probing him, at Kowala? Finding his weaknesses?" Spinks asked. The concern in her voice was obvious.

"I know. It Sounds like we're poking the rattlesnake with a stick, doesn't it? I wanted to leave him alone until it becomes essential to act. But Foster..."

"Ah, Jesus," Spinks said. "He's still running things there? I thought they were going to shuffle him off somewhere."

Carr shook her head ruefully. "No, we still have the pleasure of the general's company. He and Carl have a productive relationship."

"Major Myers, right?" Spinks wanted to check. "Smart dude."

"One of the smartest. If I let myself go, I might even call him a 'visionary'."

Spinks raised her eyebrows at this, wondering if Carr's admiration was merely professional.

"But he lets Foster steamroller him too much," Alison added.

Spinks let out a short laugh. "Yeah, that's the privileges of rank, I guess. Shit always flows downhill."

Carr let her long-time friend quiz her on their work until she reached the classified material; they both knew where the lines were. Instead, Carr asked about Spinks' plans for the day. "Makes a change from KSC, doesn't it? More traffic but more to do."

Spinks was about to begin a busy day of meetings with six different aerospace and technology companies in northern Virginia. "They've been working with us on making the X-37B digitally watertight," Spinks said. "She's grounded until we can be sure she's Quave-proof."

Carr was thoughtful for a second, and then asked, "Do you think you understand *why* he did that?"

This was familiar territory; Spinks was used to thrashing out these questions with her husband, the members of her team, and even Foster. "He's a machine, which means his actions are shown to be logical once you understand his intentions."

"He just wanted to survive," Carr said.

"Exactly. He needed a big chip in the game, and he got one. It was a masterstroke, if you think about it."

This sounded a little too generous. "This was a hack, Jo, not Michelangelo's *David*."

"Ah, no. You're missing the point. What else could he have done that didn't endanger human lives, but demonstrated his abilities?"

"Well, the scuttlebutt says he nearly started World War III," Carr argued.

Spinks turned to her suddenly, ignoring the traffic. "I need you to ignore those rumors," she said. "The scuttlebutt is wrong. OK?"

It was rare that Carr felt their difference in rank so keenly; these morning chats were normally very cordial, but Spinks' tone was unusually serious. "Roger that, Colonel Spinks."

The more senior woman sighed slightly. "Look…"

"I get it," Carr told her.

"The humiliation, Ali. They're not going to get over it in a hurry. Can you imagine if it had been the Russians, or the Chinese, who sashayed into our systems and started pointing nukes at people, hijacking warships, and issuing Air Tasking Orders to bomber wings?"

Carr tried to picture the President responding to these threats; his refusal to heed the wishes of Washington hawks was causing a buildup of tension on Capitol Hill. "Even Ellis' latent pacifism wouldn't have been enough to stay his hand. There would have been incredible pressure to *act*."

"Well put," Spinks agreed. "But against *whom*? I mean, it wasn't until Quave bombarded us with messages that we even realized he was behind it." She hadn't been there at the time, but those who lived through those events recalled their trembling horror at the message: *Are You Listening?*

They marveled together at the machine as Spinks found her way through the last few traffic signals and into the Pentagon's parking lot. "First meeting is here. With a certain General Foster," she turned with a smile. "I believe you know him?"

***

Foster stomped around the hallways like an enraged, highly-caffeinated rhino. "For the love of *God*," he was ranting, "even fuckin' MegaSoft manages to put out software faster than this. What the hell have you people been doing with your time?"

Spirelli waited for the noisy hurricane of discontent to pass the door of their lab and move on down the hallway. "We've been *testing* it, general," he muttered. "You know, the step in the process that MegaSoft likes to skip."

He'd been in the office since just after seven, and it was not shaping up to be a good day. His problem - *their* problem, in the broadest sense - was that Quave remained somewhat inscrutable. They could analyze only what they had been given, and Quave guarded his core code - that half-million lines which defined him - with an absolute rigor. They'd tried for weeks, and no true backdoors had emerged. Kowalski was almost provocatively unhelpful, citing this or that provision of the congressional agreement on Quave. It was *maddening*.

"Imagine this," Spirelli said, waxing lyrical to Carr and Washington as they made coffee and heated mid-morning snacks in the lab's microwave.

"We're in charge of D-day, right? Normandy,1944. The Nazis are waiting for us, and they're dug in like sons-of-bitches, but we've got aerial reconnaissance, right? We've got maps and charts and tide tables. We've even got special forces guys swimming around off the beach, taking samples of the mud."

Carr sipped her coffee. "I can tell you're driving at something, Pep. I just have no idea what it is."

"The point is, the guys who stormed the beaches knew where they were going! They had a plan, and they knew their enemy pretty well. We don't even have the most basic map!"

"Well, we do," Washington countered, "but it's a map which changes wholesale every couple of days."

These were the discussions they dared not have in front of Foster. He was growing seriously, often noisily impatient with the rate of progress. According to him, Quave should have been decoded and broken-down months ago, and by now the Pentagon should already have a range of new AI products, ready to send out for unit testing. Instead, they were reduced to chasing shadows and *guessing*.

Then, the General stormed back into the lab and let them have both barrels. "You know what I just heard?" he roared, shifting from foot to foot as though he might kick out at someone like an elderly, enraged martial artist. "I had Jo Spinks tell me that they're *still* not sure the X-37B is Quave-proofed. I mean," he cried, hands raised to the heavens in an angry plea, "it's been *months*!"

Only Myers was in a position to calm the general, but he just didn't fancy his chances.

"I've got national security assets sitting on the deck, I've got congress giving Quave a free rein, and *you people* are sitting there with your thumbs up your butts!"

That was enough. "General, could I speak to you in private?" Myers enquired. His eyes told the old man that he'd overstepped his bounds.

"Yeah, sure. I'm dying for an update." He waved Myers out and then stampeded down the hallway, bullying a young aide out of the way. Foster slammed his office door and slumped into his big, black chair. "Speak."

"Sir, you're frustrated and angry. We are, too."

"Great!" Foster cried. "We're all in the same leaking, shitty, sinking boat. How *wonderful.*"

These were the points Myers had always wanted to make, but hadn't yet mustered the courage. "General, you're overstating the threat posed by Quave."

There was a lot more, but Myers didn't get another word out. "*Overstating?*" the general fumed. "I beg to differ, young man. This is a machine which usurped the intelligence community, hacked nuclear missile wings and even…"

"That was under different circumstances," Myers said.

"Oh, feel free to interrupt!" Foster replied, throwing up his hands. "It's not like I'm a fucking senior officer, or anything. No, go right ahead, Carl. Tell me how I'm *just so wrong* about this massive global threat. I'm all ears." He folded his arms petulantly and glared at Myers across his desk.

The major felt a slight shiver down his back, but this was a more vital meeting than their usual catch-up sessions. Foster had to be brought up to speed. "Sir, can I ask about the photograph behind your desk?"

Foster turned angrily. "What is this now, Show and Tell?"

"Your battalion in Vietnam, sir. I read about the unit citation you received, and your role in that action."

He sniffed slightly. "Nearly fifty years ago. Before computer viruses," Foster noted. "What of it?"

"I think it's instructive to remember how that war was concluded, sir."

This gained Myers a grim frown. "We withdrew, as I recall."

"And then the VC deposed a brutal Cambodian government, unified and modified Vietnam, and now it's a successful capitalistic economy, serving its people and connecting them to the world."

Foster stared at him. "You're making a point, right? Not just trying to piss me off."

"Engagement, patience and a willingness to roll with the circumstances. That's how peace was achieved. Not big surges like Operation Linebacker, nor all the other *years* of bombing, nor any of the 'hearts and minds' stuff, nor Agent Orange. We waited it out, and we got what we wanted in the end."

The general's stare became so fierce that Myers feared he was about to be forcibly ejected from the old man's office. "I've got a serving officer in the United States Army in front of me," Foster reminded himself. "Not a commie peace-nik long-hair, or some pacifist Berkeley professor. A *decorated*, life-long military man. You wouldn't know it to listen to you," Foster told him.

"I'm a pragmatist," Myers retorted. "And I *know* that you're over-estimating how angry Quave is with us. We're probing him and threatening his security, exactly because you're worried about him. But that misjudgment makes the prophecy a self-realizing one. Our actions will *actually* enrage him," Myers warned.

Close to an eruption, Foster managed to say, "You can be reassigned, demoted, or leave the service. But you're not going to talk to me like that."

He had to push, or this would all be for nothing. "Then let me bring in my team. They'll say the same thing. And so will the NSA guys, the congressional committee, the UN… even the *President* thinks we need to take it easy on Quave."

"I don't take orders from lefty pacifists," Foster growled. "None of them are in possession of the full facts."

"The *Commander in Chief*," Myers reminded him, "spoke with Quave a few days ago and agreed to let him try to help."

Foster lost it. "Accusing a senior officer of disloyalty," he said. "That'll make the discharge paperwork easier."

"Sir, you need to listen." Myers could feel this singular chance slipping away. "Look at the earthquake in Oklahoma. He saved dozens of lives."

"For all we know, he *caused* the fuckin' earthquake! What a perfect way to prove that you can be trusted! Create a problem, then solve it before anyone else can."

Jesus. "Sir, you're not being rational. If he's given a chance to prove himself, and he screws up, then we can take action. Even deploy our full suite, if you really believe it'll work. But until then, we should keep a watching brief."

Foster stood, apparently calmer but no less vigorous. "And I disagree. The purpose of your team is to craft a response, and I suggest you create one which will actually work, and do so immediately."

"Yes, sir."

"Questions?" Foster asked without looking up.

"Only one, sir," he said.

Foster met his eyes. "Make it quick."

"Where does the hatred come from, sir?" Myers asked, his tone mild.

"The *fuck* do you mean?" the general spat.

"You started your career fighting communists, and came home without a win. Then it was terrorists, and you came home with the job half done. Now it's a machine. Has Quave become the one enemy you feel you can truly fight?"

Myers was very surprised not to receive another white-hot blast of top brass fury. Instead, Foster sat again and seemed to sigh before speaking.

"You think I'm some confused Cold-warrior, right? A dinosaur, trying to fight a young man's war. And maybe you're right," he admitted. "I've spent most of my military career *completely fucking confused* about what we're supposed to be doing. I mean," he said, motioning to the photo behind him, "some of those guys gave everything, and came home in a box, but we've still got communism in the world. And the 'War on Terror'… What a sick joke."

"But now," Myers said, boldly picking up the thread, "you've got an enemy you can target explicitly. A single opponent who you feel represents a Clear and Present Danger."

Foster was nodding very slightly, the major could see. "Jo Spinks is fuckin' *terrified*. She just can't see a way their X-37B will *ever* be secure again. The thing is permanently grounded."

"So, short-circuit the problem. Neutralize the threat peacefully. Bring Quave into the fold," Myers advised. "Show him that we're keen to learn about him, and to work together. He won't understand the double standard whereby congress permits him some freedom on one hand, while on the other, we keep aggressively interrogating his source code, probing for weaknesses."

Foster basically agreed, but something vital stayed his hand. "Carl, you're forgetting that this machine has *killed* people, and threatened our security. I can't just let bygones be bygones, for Christ's sake."

Myers stood at attention. He had seized his chance, but Foster wasn't going to relent, at least, not without plentiful new evidence of the most incontrovertible nature, and that would take months. "Sir, I want to thank you for allowing me to speak candidly. And I hope we might again."

Foster wagged a finger at Myers. "You're a goddamned snake in the grass, Carl," he grinned. "But even a crusty old warrior like me needs to admit that your heart is in the right place."

"Thank you, sir," Myers said.

"Just get me some software that might actually defeat this son of a bitch, alright?"

"We're giving it everything we've got."

"I know you are," Foster conceded. "I trust you on that. And once he's dealt with, *then* we can sit in a park in Haight-Ashbury, smoke a great big doobie and wax rhapsodic about compassion and forgiveness. But we deal with the threat *first*," Foster insisted. "You're a military man. You know our priorities."

"Roger that, sir."

"Fantastic. Now get the hell out of my office."

***

CHAPTER 15 – TEST PHASE

Kowala Astronaut Training Facility
New Mexico
$Q^2 + 211$

"Good morning," Quave said quietly to the four sleeping astronauts. "And welcome to Day Three."

Eileen was the quickest to return to consciousness. "Morning, Quave. How did you sleep?"

The others were moving, Eileen could see from her own sleeping bag. Olivia unzipped hers and clambered sleepily out. "Damn, this floor's cold," she said, for the third morning in a row.

"Note to self," Paul said, his voice a rumble. "Bring warm slippers to the asteroid."

Someone started the coffee machine and its familiar hiss and grumble gave them all a little hope.

This five-day test was a mock-up of life onboard the *Gaia* in 'lifeboat' mode, recreating the conditions after a deep-space emergency. The crew had access only to the main module, and had to operate on minimal battery power while consuming meager half-rations. The remainder of the ship, for the purposes of this exercise, was depressurized and inaccessible.

"Cinnamon waffles today," Asif told them. It was his turn to heat one of the stack of meals they were trying out. Each bite mattered more when they had to share the meals.

"I think I liked the French toast the best, so far," Olivia decided.

"Yeah, because that reconstituted so-called 'scrambled egg' was rubbery and tasteless," Paul replied haughtily. "I wouldn't feed it to my dog, let alone take it into deep space."

Eileen appeared, her tight, red curls tied back. "All good data for Kowala's food science people, I guess. Now, who's got the coffee?"

None of them were looking forward to being cooped up so artificially for another two days, but the Kowala technicians anticipated this and ensured the whole crew had a busy and satisfying schedule. Most of the experiments planned for their mission wouldn't yield valuable data in one-G conditions, but they tried out the meals, different designs of water spigots and a range of control panel configurations. There was a lot of reading to do, and Calloway in particular seemed to do little else.

In fact, though he was making his way through a pile of scholarly reading, Calloway was mostly watching his colleagues. They all knew that he'd be reporting back to Kowala with in-depth analysis of their personality, their willingness to get along, and even their food and sleep habits. Calloway would come to know these three people better than anyone, but he was also an avid 'self-observer', as he put it, routinely cataloguing and tracking his work, sleep, meals and exercise. All of these data points fed into Quave, who built his findings into the crew's routine. Once breakfast was finished, Paul would return to his nook and read, keeping an eye on the crew and making discrete notes on his tablet.

Eileen finished her waffles and then opened her private storage cupboard, down by her knees in their little kitchen and dining area, to find an orange bottle containing today's supplements. Quave was absolutely unmovable on the importance of boosting the crew's immune system performance and red blood cell count. They each took at least a dozen pills a day, some naturopathic remedies and others Quave had asked to be prepared specifically for the crew.

Eileen swallowed her pills while the others chatted sleepily, gathering paperwork, laptops and other items for the day ahead. She knew there would be hundreds of days like this during their mission: wake, find coffee, wash down the day's pills, and start work. Try to get along with the others. Keep an eye out for tension or flirting. Intercede, where necessary, to avoid unwelcome schedule changes or other dictates from mission control. Keep the crew healthy and happy, and focused on the great challenges which lay ahead.

"Do you think we'll be able to hack two months of this?" Olivia asked as she broke up her waffles with a fork.

"It'll be different down there," Asif told her. "More space, the whole ship laid out."

"Yeah, but Antarctica still isn't a zero-G environment," Olivia pointed out.

"Best we're going to get, until we blast off," Asif said. "Besides, it might be fun."

The crew was on the fence about this proposed experiment. Kowala was in the middle of building a partly-functional mock-up of the *Gaia* spacecraft, placed in a remote Antarctic valley. The crew would perform multiple EVAs and carry out geological analysis, but it was mainly an exercise in living together peacefully. Tensions were inevitable, and it was hoped this extended test would shake out the personality bugs and help create a genuinely coherent team.

If he were honest, Asif had private reasons for looking forward to their Antarctic sojourn. He'd always wanted to visit the region, but there was something else: Olivia Thibideaux. For one reason and another, they'd worked alone together extensively since being selected, almost as though the mission controllers at Kowala were *trying* to get them together. Both were single and had never married; there was no baggage, and neither of them could see any real obstacle.

Except that they were about to be blasted into space on humanity's most important mission since Apollo 11.

Asif tried in vain to keep his feelings to himself. Olivia was more than savvy enough to recognize his warmth, and his willingness to confide in her, as signs of true affection. Not that she minded, even a little; her life since astronaut selection had been utter madness, and it seemed like forever since a man had so much as asked for her number.

So far, there had been no actual 'indiscretions', as the Kowala guidelines phrased it, but with the two of them set to be stuck in close proximity for long periods, it didn't take a behaviorist to foresee the inevitable.

Paul Calloway had other concerns. He found Asif and Olivia easy company, and excellent colleagues, but he found his nose frequently put out of joint by Eileen. As their commander, she was supposed to exhibit the strongest interpersonal skills, but Paul found her overbearing, quick to reprimand, and seemingly too often focused on proving herself to her crew and the trainers.

They weren't exactly in competition with each other, or with anyone else; crew assignments were very deliberately made two years in advance so that the astronauts could focus exclusively on preparing for their specific mission. Before their own flight, three other manned Kowala missions would be flown: a twenty-four-hour check-out flight in low Earth orbit, a three-week flight to test the life support systems over an extended period, and then a sixteen-day flight in Lunar orbit, complete with EVAs above the surface of the Moon. Then would come the asteroid mission – every pilot's dream, and a massive challenge for any leader.

Though Eileen was confirmed as the commander for this most challenging of the initial missions, Paul was finding Colonel Barr to be occasionally insecure and a little needy. She was tough on herself in the simulator, reacting angrily to her own errors of judgment; she expected a hundred and ten percent from herself, all day every day. And this went for everyone else, too.

"Stress symptoms are inevitable," Paul wrote in his clinical report on Eileen, "and Colonel Barr should work on letting things go and relaxing a little. Recommend massage and meditation, and will liaise with Quave regarding a new pharmacological or nutritional approach."

For her own part, Eileen found Paul charming and efficient, but occasionally brusque when discussing his own work. It wasn't unlike him to prefer working alone for long periods. As commander, Eileen felt it important to bring the crew together, and having Paul sequestered away in his lab module was not good for crew cohesion. Still, when he appeared, he was usually affable and helpful to others, so perhaps he was simply getting enough alone time.

In all, Eileen found as the third day of their experiment drew to a close, she had a crew who were content in their work. They also quite obviously enjoyed each other's company, though not too much, as far the commander could tell. They were making excellent progress in their training. So long as nothing unexpected came along, Eileen judged, they'd be ready in time.

***

$Q^2 + 216$
Firefox Engine Test Facility
New Mexico

Sandra was so caught up in the preparations for this vital test that it took Asif to remind her to take off her hard-hat, now that they were four miles from the test stand. "Yeah," she chuckled. "Little bit distracted today."

The Hermes rocket consisted of a single core stage with nine engines, a second stage with three more, and a small, powerful single-engine third stage to boost the payload into its correct orbit. A Hermes-1, its lifting capacity enhanced by super-chilled fuel and oxidizer, could launch virtually any commercial or military satellite, but Dan Kowalski had bigger plans. To launch the first unmanned tests of the *Gaia* spacecraft, *three* of the Hermes cores would be slaved together, line abreast, in a configuration Quave called Hermes-Heavy, or simply H-2.

The mammoth, hybrid booster couldn't fly without an 'all-up' test of its twenty-seven Firefox engines. Sandra had never tested the complete rig before, and she was hopping quietly from foot to foot, waiting for confirmations over the radio.

"Thirty seconds," she called out. Behind her, around twenty of the Kowala astronaut corps were gathered to witness the test. Opik was the White House representative, jiggling with excitement as ever, and Dan was somewhere on the grounds. Sandra had a late meeting booked in with him, before he'd fly back to Santa Monica. She wondered if the genius inventor even had time to watch this spectacle, surely the most thrilling engine test since the days of the Saturn-V.

Spinks was there, and had brought a guest from the Pentagon. Sandra didn't recognize Captain Alison Carr, but she ideally represented the modern US Army with her immaculate uniform and thoughtful, timely questions. "You don't get thrills like this inside the beltway," Spinks noted as the final seconds ticked down. "Remember to take it all in."

Carr was rapt. The unexpected invitation from Spinks was both the perfect chance to get out from under Myers and Foster for a couple of days, and to spend some more time together. The test itself promised to be a spectacle, but Alison found her eyes flitting from the steaming, hulking test stand to the tall, blond colonel next to her. Jo's hair fit almost entirely under her uniform cap, except for an appealing sweep of gold which led down to a simple pony-tail. Alison almost missed the ignition.

Opik started cheering the moment the engines lit. Arranged in three circular banks of nine, as they would be on launch day, the motors were ignited and then began to throttle up. The noise, seconds later, was unbelievable, a physical wave washing across the arid plain.

"Holy shit," Carr breathed. "Are you sure it won't take off?"

"It's bolted to the desert," Spinks told her above the crackling roar. "But won't it be a sight, when a machine like that finally leaves the ground?" Absent two dozen observers, Spinks would have taken Alison's hand as the valley trembled.

Two minutes and fifty-six seconds later, the three clusters of engines shut down in a huge cloud of steam and smoke which rose in a plume from the test stand.

"Test was a success," Sandra called back as she headed to the pick-up truck which would take her to the test stand. "Hallelujah!"

Spinks, Carr, Opik and the others piled into a shuttle bus and were taken on a brief tour of the site. Even since her last visit, Spinks noted, there were a number of new buildings going up – more test stands, a dozen now, and an odd-shaped building, off to the side, which was surrounded by a crane, mechanical diggers and a team of construction engineers.

"What's that going to be?" Spinks asked a Kowala rep who was guiding the tour.

"Oh, I think that's a telescope of some kind," she replied.

This seemed vague to both Carr and Spinks. "What, he's getting into the astronomy business now, too?" the colonel wondered aloud. "Is there any pie Dan Kowalski *doesn't* have a finger in?"

Carr turned to check out the mysterious building. They seemed to be assembling a pre-fabricated dome over a cylindrical platform, so a telescope facility did make sense, Carr judged. But with all the large arrays in existence, it hardly seemed good sense to add another single mirror, even if this part of the state was a certified Dark Sky Area, perfect for astronomy.

"We're going to break for lunch," the guide told them, "and then you'll have a chance to see the first *Gaia* spacecraft during its mating tests with our booster mock-up." Spinks was excited about this; with the X-37B still grounded, this was as close as she'd get to genuine space hardware for a while. Watching documentaries on Apollo and Skylab recently, she'd been reminded of the importance of women in space, and was delighted that all four of the Kowala crews were gender balanced. Plus, it didn't harm Kowala's PR that the serenely photogenic Olivia Thibideaux could have been a Hollywood actress if she hadn't turned to science. She was a few yards behind Spinks and Carr now, and both risked a glance back at her perfect, and now world-famous face.

With such a collection of spaceflight and defense luminaries in one place, it was inevitably a working lunch. A buffet of salmon, vegetables and lentils was laid out, and Spinks managed to find Sandra Diaz as she was finishing a quick plateful.

"I don't want to interrupt your lunch, Dr. Diaz, just hoping the test went well?" Spinks said courteously.

Diaz grinned and brushed a crumb off her lab coat. "Pretty good. Everything lit, and then stayed lit, and nothing blew up."

"And, it ran for longer than it would need to hold together during the actual launch," Spinks pointed out.

"Quite a sight that's going to be," Diaz commented. "Do you think the delegation will be able to attend the first flight?"

"Wouldn't miss it for the world," Spinks said. "I'll liaise with the others, but I know they'll clear their calendars. Even if you have delays, we'll be there."

Diaz read up on the mixed delegation of visitors while being shuttled to and from the test site, using otherwise dead time in the run-up to today's big triple-stack engine test. She'd overseen repairs to a jammed refueling connector while memorizing Spinks' resume and trying to figure out what the colonel's angle would be. A stand-out at Princeton, of all places, and then *cum laude* at the Air Force Academy in Denver. "Married a concert pianist fifteen years her senior," Diaz mumbled to herself. "It takes all kinds of folks to make a world." After her application for test pilot school was regretfully declined owing to the downsizing of the program, she took every course she could, and commanded her own F-16 squadron. Early promotion to Colonel at only thirty-eight saw her given responsibility for Air Force liaison with the big tech and aerospace companies, and then she'd been on-hand and familiar enough with the program to be asked to haul the X-37B away from the jaws of disaster.

That the bird was grounded was hardly Spinks' fault, Diaz recognized. Quave had really done a number on the ship's electronics, and months of tedious investigations had yielded next to nothing as to how he'd broken in. The ship couldn't fly, and so Diaz assumed that Spinks was cozying up to Kowala as a potential launch contractor, someone who'd sell them discount payload space on their inexpensive, re-used boosters. The X-37B experiments could be shifted to other classified Department of Defense missions, and with Dan now able to offer cut-price, refurbished boosters, everyone would win.

Except, of course, the traditional Big Aerospace rocket companies, who would need to start anew on a booster design which didn't needlessly dump itself in the sea after all of three minutes' useful service.

"Actually, before you go," Diaz said, "can I ask you about something?"

"Sure," she answered. "Provided you're not going to invite me to join the astronaut corps. I wouldn't pass the physical."

Diaz motioned for the colonel to sit. "Neither would most of the world's athletes," she said. "But seriously, I just wanted to see if there's anything you needed. Data on the rocket, payload capabilities, that kind of thing."

"That's kind of you," Spinks answered. "I guess I was curious about a couple of things." She glanced around. "This is quite a crowd, isn't it?"

"A rogues' gallery of rocket-heads, billionaires, members of congress and White House nerds." Neither needed to point out the ubiquitous and obvious gender imbalance. "Colonel, I'm going to be direct, because I'm an engineer. If you want soft soap and corporate lunches, our sales department will happily oblige. I'm going to just ask… What are you hoping to send into space?"

Spinks grinned. "I could tell you, but then I'd have to…"

"Listen while I made you an exceptionally reasonable offer?" It was Diaz's turn to grin.

"Should we be seen talking about this stuff?" Jo asked. "I mean…"

"Kowala is disruptive," Diaz announced.

Jo waited, but nothing was forthcoming. "By which you mean…"

"By which I mean," Sandra said, just a little too loudly, "*fuck* those crusty old aerospace firms. If they can't compete, or if they can't innovate fast enough, then that's just the *market*, you know? Isn't that how it's all supposed to work?"

Spinks respected her zeal, but the little café area had become quite crowded and she didn't need this civilized gathering of defense contractors to get ugly. *You can't fight in here, this is the War Room!*

"Actually," Spinks told her, "I love a little disruption. Keeps things fresh."

"I agree absolutely," Diaz nodded.

"And today's test was something else."

"Glad you enjoyed it."

"Just keep us informed, okay?" Spinks said. "Any setbacks or problems, shoot me an email. If you've got a big test here, or a launch at KSC, I'll take any seat in the house."

"Roger that, colonel," Diaz said. Spinks rose, so Diaz gave her a smile. "Enjoy the rest of your visit."

Spinks paused. "You know, I've been meaning to ask someone, what's the deal with the telescope building? The big, white cylinder with a dome on top, over on the other side of the test site?"

"Huh?" Diaz asked, glancing that way. "Oh, I couldn't even say. They're throwing new buildings up out of nothing in a few weeks."

"Weeks?" Spinks marveled.

"Keep this to yourself'," Diaz said quietly, leaning in toward the table and keeping her voice low, "but I hear Quave's got some new, patented technique for pre-treating and pouring concrete in no time, flat. He gets 3-D printers to produce the building's modular sections, and then has robots bolt them on. You wouldn't believe what he can get done in half a morning."

"Incredible," Spinks said, genuinely impressed by Quave's growing abilities "But what are buildings like that *for*?"

Diaz shrugged and rose to clear her tray. "If it looks like a telescope building, I imagine that's probably what it is. Or maybe something to do with the spaceplane program."

Coming to an instant halt, Spinks asked, "The what's-that-now?"

"Let me put it like this, colonel," Diaz said, putting her tray aside. "If you ever feel like those officer's bars are getting heavy, or …," she said, waving her chopsticks theatrically, "if the nature of the power structure, yeah, let's call it that, at the Air Force is getting you down, shoot *me* a line. Roger wilco?"

"Ten-four," Spinks grinned. "And Sandra, honestly," she said, extending her hand, "today was a pretty vivid experience. I can't wait for the real thing."

Diaz shook her hand politely. "Honey," she said in a half-whisper, "it's gonna knock your socks off."

***

The other restaurant option at the test facility's visitor's center was a fair attempt at a taqueria. Opik, FBI agent Valchek and Darcy Chu from Homeland were munching on chips and salsa before their orders arrived, huddled almost conspiratorially in a corner booth of the restaurant. Cheery Mariachi tunes completed the atmosphere, which felt a bit careworn, but there was too much to talk about anyway.

"Damn, that hot one is seriously *spicy*," Opik advised, waving a hand of warning over one of the three salsa bowls. "Nearly as hot as that engine test," he added, reaching for his water.

"If that's true," Valchek asked, "won't you let off a huge cloud of smoke and steam, too?" He began to inch back in case of sudden eruption.

"No, I'm just not a chili head. Just a rocket head."

"How the hell did they let you work at the White House?" Valchek wondered aloud.

Opik doused the capsaicin flames and let out a refreshed gasp of relief. "I think," he said, finding his napkin, "it had something to do with my seminal doctoral work on macroeconomic theory, and maybe also my major texts on cosmology, relativity and genetics." He paused. "Or was it just actually some nice dude from a think tank who decided I'd be a good fit?" Opik shrugged. "I'm just a safe pair of hands for the White House's relationship with NASA, DARPA and such. Things are changing, and I know how to communicate and keep everyone in the loop. I think that's why, ultimately."

"Understand," Valchek said apologetically.

"Now" Opik asked with a sly smile, "how did they let a hopeless chump like you into the Federal Bureau of Investigations?"

Their meals arrived and discussion took a back seat for a moment. "What did you mean," Chu finally asked, "when you said things were changing at NASA?"

Opik swallowed a chunk of his steak – nicely seasoned and pink at the center – and sighed slightly. "The space station program is going to cease to exist in its current form. Congress sees Kowala and other private spaceflight companies getting ready to take giant leaps, but at minimal cost and in half the usual time. Dan's setting the tempo, and no one else can keep up."

"They'll start to look, how do you say, when you're behind the times?" Valchek asked.

"Anachronistic," Chu said. "From the Greek." She turned to Opik. "So, what's likely to happen to the NASA designs and hardware? The asteroid re-direct mission, and the big, new booster?" Chu was beginning the smell the coffee, but couldn't believe that NASA would abandon its long-time aerospace partnerships. Unless Dan had gone beyond their backs, broken his own promise, and made massive campaign contributions to the right people on Capitol Hill.

"I doubt any of it will ever fly," Opik said. "Kowala's planning a far more ambitious asteroid mission anyway, and theirs is already years ahead of anything NASA could do. In the meantime, for the ISS, we've still got the Russian *Soyuz* and Elon Musk's manned *Dragon* has come online. But then, Kowala's spaceplane is going to ferry eight people into orbit at a time, for three million dollars each. No one can match that."

"Still seems like a shame," Chu said. "Will they be able to keep the ISS intact?"

"Probably not," Opik said. "The Russians want their pieces back. They've got an incomplete module they've been trying to finish for years, and there's money in it, so they say. For the remainder, finding commercial use depends on the health of the station, and on customers being able to get there. Kowala will offer fresh, spacious modules for a tenth of the price, and bring people there for a first-class tourist experience, or lab work, for any duration they choose."

"A shame," Chu repeated.

"It is," Opik said, reluctantly setting aside the rest of the steak. His job involved a tremendous amount of sitting down, and he'd become certain he was putting on weight. "But, at the same time, remember that horse manure salesmen were shocked and appalled by the arrival of the automobile, because people stopped riding horses. It doesn't make manure sellers a protected species. You heard Diaz talk about the big contractors and how they weren't 'ready for this century'. It's survival of the fittest, as it always was. Dan and his people mean business."

Valchek asked the next question, though he was aware that Opik was probably feeling as grilled as his leftover *carne asada*. "What about the unmanned probes? You know, the rover on Mars and that crazy mission to Pluto?"

Opik was nodding. "Set to continue. That's where NASA's budget is going to go. We can do deep space science missions, sun observations, the new space telescope, all that good stuff. But the Buck Rogers days are over, I guess," he said.

Chu didn't quite see it that way. "Just because it's not NASA doesn't mean the Kowala missions aren't exciting."

Valchek was nodding. "Even I'm pretty stoked about it, and I have no idea what's going on most of the time," In truth, he hadn't had a drink in five weeks, and was getting his ass beat on the squash court every other evening as part of a pretty aggressive fitness program. "Plus, the Mars rovers are great PR for NASA, and for science in general. With Quave and everything, maybe this isn't a bad moment," he observed, "to boost the public's knowledge about science, try to spark some interest."

They all knew that it was getting more and more difficult to reach the public with substantive stories; the clutter of semi-fake or sensationalized news was often too great, and genuine scientists like Opik and his MIT buddies knew their style of presentation had to be catchy and original. Working with Quave was one way to reach a larger audience, and applications for joint projects came flooding into Quave.net. "Anything with Quave's name on it will get millions of hits," Chu reminded them. "Even if some are from people hoping that he'll make a mistake, or fall off the rails." Quave-related stories were perennially the most popular articles on a given site, and "Quave +" became the most common term entered into the Kowala engine. The three most typed queries were, "Quave + scandal", "Quave + MSB" and "Quave + conspiracy". Much further down the list, to the disappointment of many, were questions about the space program, Quave's earthquake and medical work, as well as his groundbreaking discoveries in quantum computing.

"Speaking of falling off the rails, we're almost late for the next session," Opik pointed out. They paid the check and headed to the facility's little planetarium, where a digital 3-D mockup of the asteroid mission was waiting.

***

Spinks and Carr found themselves paired off and given a thorough tour of the Gaia spacecraft. This gleaming, 'boilerplate' test model, the only of its kind in the world, had arrived from California only days earlier. It would be in New Mexico for only a month before heading to Florida for more checks.

"This is how we learn to handle the real thing," Diaz told them. "We've already mated the ship with our Hermes upper stage, and everything seems to fit."

Carr was fascinated, but there was something unreal – perhaps more accurately, *other-worldly* – about spaceflight hardware, even the pieces which would never fly in space. It was a facsimile of what would be a remarkable and historic vehicle, one which would soon be as familiar to the public as the Apollo lunar rover, or those self-portraits by the *Curiosity* rover on Mars.

"It looks a little cramped in there," Carr said. She gave Spinks an apologetic look, as though she'd spoken aloud by accident. "I mean, for a crew of four, and everything."

"Oh, this isn't the whole enchilada," Diaz explained. "The Gaia ships are configured differently for each of their missions. Our early check-out flights won't need the long-duration module, or the additional storage and power facilities we'll be taking to Baxter. Once the whole Gaia-IV ship is assembled, for example, it'll have more usable space than the Soviet *Mir* station. More than enough for to keep our intrepid crew from going nuts."

"It wouldn't be enough for me," Carr commented. "I'd be begging for someone to let me out." She poked her head through the open porthole of the ship and gazed around inside.

"What do you think?" Spinks asked.

"Honestly," Carr grinned, "it looks like a sports car had a night of passion with a washing machine."

Even Diaz had to laugh at that one. "I'll tell Dan."

"Please don't," Carr said sheepishly. "I think it's amazing, really. Just hard to imagine living on board for months and months."

Diaz guided them into the interior of the boilerplate ship. It a stripped-down variant, absent some internal features, safety gear and environmental controls, but it still looked the part. Everything was smooth and gleaming, with touch-screens and voice commands replacing all but the backup switches and dials.

"This is what the superheroes are doing these days," Spinks said with a certain lament in her tone, "pushing buttons and carrying out complex experiments, not skipping along the lunar surface or whacking golf balls around."

"It'll be different," Carr told her as they sat together. "Less drama, maybe, but more important in the long run. A slower kind of thrill. Maybe less fun in the moment, but more significant than 'footprints and flags'."

Spinks took the commander's seat. On her right, Carr had the pilot's berth, from where Asif would steer the Gaia IV mission to its asteroid rendezvous. The left-hand seat would be occupied by the singular, irrepressible Eileen Barr. *They're preparing for the first human mission beyond orbit since 1972, and there's a woman in charge, and a Muslim in the driver's seat. Things have changed.* It was enough to make Spinks smile.

"I've been thinking of it as an engineering mission," Diaz told them as she helped the pair out of the cabin and back down the ladder. "A bit like an ISS construction flight"

"Putting things in place so that future missions can do and do more," Spinks summed up.

"You got it. I don't know if these missions will be remembered when Baxter has a population in the thousands, but Eileen and her crew should go down in history, just for agreeing to fly this crazy thing."

Diaz told them more about the mission profile, and how this initial flight would pave the way for dozens of others. She led them down hallways lined with artists' impressions: Kowala's new spaceplane design, lavish diagrams of futuristic Mars-cities, and even concept drawings for giant dirigibles which would float for years in the clouds of Venus.

Once her two tourists were thoroughly enthused about the wonders of space travel, Diaz politely took her leave and returned to the test stand in her increasingly battered and dusty SUV.

"Wow," Carr managed. "These people *aren't* thinking small."

"It's pretty bold," Spinks replied as they found their way down some more hallways to the lobby. "Very determined."

"Almost *heedless,* I would say," Carr said. "It sounds to me as though Dan's going to rendezvous with this asteroid and start playing with it, whatever the rest of us might have to say."

Opik was in the lobby, grilling a member of staff about engine specifications. As Spinks and Carr approached, they heard the expressions, 'thrust-to-weight ratio' and 're-entry path deviation'; the Kowala employee needed rescuing, so Spinks whisked Opik away to find out what he'd learned during his tour.

"Oh, man." The White House wonk was jumpy with enthusiasm. "Oh, man. These guys… I'm serious."

"Yep," Carr acknowledged. "The next giant leap is being made from right here."

Spinks chuckled. "We should recommend that Quave include that as their tagline. Just don't tell him it came from a military officer," she added.

As Opik rambled on about a Martian hyperloop infrastructure, and enslaving Phobos as a massive, orbiting space station, Spinks found Valchek by the water cooler, sheltering under a giant potted palm. "Did you enjoy your day?" she asked.

"Oh, hey," Valchek said affably, turning to her and extending a hand.

The FBI man was in even better shape than before, Spinks noted. "Lots to take in, huh?"

"Yeah. A lot of information went through my ears. I'm just hoping some of it might stick. I hear they let you play with the *Gaia*."

"Just the test article," she explained. "But it's just amazing that this isn't a theory any more. They're actually cutting metal, test-firing engines, hiring people. It's really going to happen."

Valchek was nodding. He'd reached the same conclusions, and he knew that Spinks shared some of his concerns about Quave. "The first human journey designed entirely by machine. Quite a time to be alive."

They looked at some of the lobby art together. Not surprisingly, Firefox engine tests and the two successful Hermes flights from Cape Canaveral were the main themes, essayed in high-definition prints the height of the wall. "You're right," Spinks said.

Valchek blinked. "About what?"

"About the times we're living in. I mean, imagine a thirteenth-century monk. What would he make of a machine which could speak an answer to you, in any language, on any topic?"

"Or tell you the weather for tomorrow."

"Or," Spinks tried, "plan a coordinated cyber-attack on your enemies."

Valchek stared at the blown-up photo of the Hermes launch for a moment, then said, "Any sufficiently advanced technology…"

"Is indistinguishable from magic," Spinks said. "Or God."

The FBI man straightened, then turned to Spinks. "I'm not touching that one with a ten-foot pole."

"I didn't expect you to," Spinks laughed. "Just a sign of the times. Our Gods used to be theoretical, now they're mechanical. And our views of life and consciousness used to be fixed, but now they're being made to change. I can't think of a more exhilarating century in which to be alive."

Valchek agreed with her, though his enthusiasm was less unconfined. He'd attended a dozen conferences and seminars, and read heavy texts until past midnight; improving his mind had taken the place of sitting morosely in front of the TV with a bottle of something cheap. His new routines had transformed the investigator in a matter of weeks, and he was quickly becoming the lead voice in their working group meetings on Cyberterrorism strategy and the FBI response to Quave. Andy Marsh called up on Skype again from his new assignment in Kuwait, and could barely believe how much weight his old friend had lost.

"So, is that what Quave is doing?" Valchek finally asked. "Becoming a God?"

Spinks puffed out her cheeks and threw up her hands. "That'd be a *twenty*-foot pole, in my case," she said.

"Wise," Valchek conceded. Then he looked around the lobby. "Will I tell my kids about this place?" he wondered aloud. "Or will this be another embarrassing failure?"

"*Thirty* foot," Spinks smiled.

"Come on," Valchek said, leading her to the front doors. "The bus isn't going to wait forever."

***

CHAPTER 16 – ECHOES

Collins, Oklahoma
The afternoon of the same day ($Q^2 + 216$)

'THE END OF LIBERTY' was the screaming banner headline. Rich read quickly, allowing the physical sense of threat and danger to blossom within him. The article was a polemic by one of the website's main contributors. Though referred to as an 'expert on cyber policy' by the website's biographical blurb, more reputable sources called him a, 'disgraced professor', a 'flagrant conspiracy peddler', and most recently a 'pernicious danger to democracy and free speech'.

This bothered Rich not at all. He was used to his heroes being decried by the media or torn down by so-called academics, all of them in the pay of Big Pharma, or Big Oil, or Big Tobacco. He knew he had to be careful, avoiding those sites he knew were tainted by corruption and the influence of corrupt, commercial pap which passed for 'cable news'.

He clicked in the comment box and typed in all caps, "Why doesn't the world see Quave for what he is? It's getting too late to do anything about him. When will the President <u>act</u>?"

It took only moments to receive encouraging replies from two other readers. Then came other comments, worries about the future and lots of frustration with the administration's lax policies toward Quave. The next hour was spent in the comfort of his echo chamber, hearing only what he agreed with and spouting only what others would find palatable. There was no grey area, just a stripped-down, simplified discussion with a single purpose: to validate the views he already held.

It felt wonderful – empowering, visceral and warm. Pastor Reynolds had treated him like a sadly demented fool, rubbishing his concerns and telling him to find real work and stop 'getting himself confused' on the Internet. But the old man knew even less of the truth than those corporate puppets on the news.

Quave was coming for them. It wasn't just logical, it was inevitable. The machine hated to be questioned or restricted, and now Quave's accomplices on Capitol Hill had voted to let him back out into the wild, he could take revenge on his former captors. Quave was more dangerous still than Nazism, or terrorism. He was a cold, calculating death machine.

Rich had little time for the other side, because he knew their arguments by heart. *Oh, but, Quave predicted the Oklahoma earthquake!* Really? Wasn't it equally likely that he *caused* it, to bolster his reputation? *He fixed the traffic flow in Dallas!* So, now we've got machines telling us how to do the most American of things: driving freely where we want to? It was the purest insanity. *But, he helped develop early-stage cancer screening!* And gained access to millions of private patient records in the process. What plans does he have for the data? Will it be safe? Will he use it to blackmail people? There was no telling, because there was no longer effective oversight. Kowalski's promises – to rein Quave in, to hold him accountable - were vanishing like snow in the sunshine.

No, Rich would not be convinced by Quave's tiny, self-serving feints toward decency. Rich accepted that he wasn't going to set the world alight with his intellect, but he understood the threat Quave posed, as did his growing cadre of online friends. They advised each other on the proper precautions: using encrypted communication, bouncing their Internet signal through several VPN nodes, changing their passwords on a daily basis. Some even refused to connect to the Internet at home, leaving their machines air-gapped until they could log on anonymously in a café. One of the webmasters of the Anti-Quave Alliance website had even demanded that his address be removed from Kowala Earth; as someone with a privacy obsession, he was already refusing to pay taxes, renew his driver's license, register his car, or do anything that was 'paperless'.

Rich looked up to him, and the others, as he had once respected Pastor Reynolds. The old man had even visited him once to persuade him to rejoin the flock. It had been a bitter, depressing, angry argument. "This is the work of the other side, Rich," Reynolds had assured him. "Those who refuse to take part in society, or to share through taxes, they're doing Satan's work."

Rich would never have believed he'd be angry enough to throw the old pastor out, but there he'd stood, holding open the door and yelling at Reynolds. "You're a charlatan, an apologist!" he said, quoting his online friends and feeling all the smarter for it. "When Quave starts hurting people, you'll tell me I was right. That we were *all* right." He slammed the door with conviction. Reynolds hadn't come back, and Rich hadn't seen him since; there was no way he was attending that false, deluded church, either.

As the comment thread dried up for the day, he turned to tidying up his rented apartment. His research left little time for domestic chores, and he quickly vacuumed, took out the trash and let some air into his modest, two-bedroom, one-story home on a quiet residential street. He'd offered to mow the lawn and do repair work in exchange for a rent reduction; the place was looking pretty good, certainly compared to his neighbors.

Part of that was to impress Mindy, of course. But she'd only stayed for two months before becoming exasperated at his constant Internet use, his prognostications of digital doom, his creeping, consuming depression. She watched as he tried to have his house removed from KowalAbout, Dan's new maps application. She withstood a tirade about using an 'unsecured' web browser for her email, something Rich found unforgivable.

She was nice, and much smarter than him, which left Rich staggered that she couldn't see the truth. To him, it was blindingly obvious; to her, it was an inchoate notion peddled by the Tin Foil Hat Brigade. There was no huge argument; she just left a necklace he'd bought her, right there on the battered coffee table, and walked out. He'd never seen her again.

Rich shrugged off the memories and finished his chores. Once the place looked habitable again, he closed the blinds and made sure the door was locked before heading to the second bedroom. It was padlocked and had a security system which required a six-digit PIN. In fact, his security measures had cost almost as much as the work he was doing.

A workbench took center stage, with piles of components and wires spread out or separated and placed in clear, plastic boxes around the periphery. On a smaller desk by the window he was organizing the envelopes and labels he'd need once everything was ready.

Others were taking part, he knew. On the right day, at the right time, they'd launch a coordinated campaign against those who were endangering the very existence of humanity. Quave had to be stopped, and that naturally extended to those who supported him. If they didn't understand that, well, that wasn't his problem. Plenty of Germans had looked the other way during the Holocaust, because no one had punished them for lacking the vision to see the obvious.

Quave's friends would not escape justice so easily.

***

CHAPTER 17 – CELIA

Back Bay, Boston

$Q^2 + 218$

Ralph was hard at work by 8:30am, penning a blog post and making notes for the next section of 'The Big Quave Book', as the project was still called. He began the day with an energetic, almost effervescent attitude, and not only because of the three cups of morning coffee; the day would be spent on work he found thoroughly absorbing, and which would serve the public understanding of Artificial Intelligence. His fingers flew, and his mind raced with a pleasing sense of purpose.

This lasted until 10am, when he would receive his weekly 'check-in' call from Celia Rhodes in Houston. This was the only hour of his week when his stress became as debilitating as during those days of blogging for the *Daily Gerbil*. For the most part, he was independent and could work to his own schedule, and even on whichever topic interested him. The exceptions were his interactions with his literary agent, a grizzled veteran of the book world, and a notorious slave-driver.

"How's my favorite AI guy?" Celia asked cheerily. Her voice was infected with a distinctive, smoky scratch, the sound of four decades of scotch and cigarettes. "Tell me about the new chapter! Go on, Ralph, make my morning."

"Well, it's been a busy week, and…"

It was there at once: that *tone*, like acid poured on silk. "Newsflash! Hold the front pages! 'Man In Demand Has Busy Week'. Holy Christ, Ralph, why didn't I guess you might be *busy*?"

Working with Celia Rhodes was at once uplifting and terrifying. "Yeah, I see your point," Ralph said, to buy some time. He kept his voice calm despite the feeling of being hauled into the principal's office. "I've been researching the chapter on the Kowala Space Program," Ralph tried to explain. "There's so much going on right now, with tests and training, and I already have good drafts of the other chapters, so I thought I'd…"

"Ralphy, honey."

He winced. "Do you have to call me that? You sound like my mother."

"Great, now I have that idea in my head. Now, where in the *blazes* is my new chapter?"

Celia spent her professional life obliging, cajoling and bullying writers to do things they'd rather not do. She recognized talent within a few sentences, and could smell a popular book on history or science from a mile away. It was just that most writers didn't fulfill their true potential; life events intervened, of course, but they often sabotaged themselves or became mired in self-doubt.

Ralph was a case in point. "You could write a chapter ever ten days," she'd told him, more than once. "You just don't give yourself *permission*." The gap between Ralph's output and his potential was the primary theme of her tirades, followed closely by the dangers of procrastination.

She interrogated him about his lifestyle for thirty seconds, establishing yet again that he wasn't scheduling his time correctly, nor was he making use of the 'productivity tools' on his computer. After a few terse reminders, it was time for calmer, simpler truths.

"You know what really makes me happy, Ralph?" she asked, her voice suddenly lighter down the phone line. "*Really* happy?" She sounded even a little sultry, Ralph found, his skin crawling. "Words on pages. Some, preferably *lots* of them. That's what makes me happy, Ralph."

"Yeah," Ralph said.

"See, I'm a simple girl at heart," she added. "With simple needs."

"If only that were true," Ralph muttered. "Celia, honestly, I think I need your help with slimming this thing down."

The agent sighed consolingly. "Ok, honey." It was time to get down to work. "Tell Auntie Celia your problems. And if you do exactly what I say, we'll have things back on track long before Q-3, or whatever the hell comes next."

No one could reorient an author's thinking like Celia Rhodes. Praise and positive reinforcement were important, but came only after a no-nonsense discussion of the project's status. She found that a book's genesis resembled the construction of a new building. The chapters had their titles, which gave the building a superstructure. Each chapter gained an outline, which meant each room had four new walls. Then, the text flows into each chapter until they are bulging with quality, proof-read content; this was the wiring and the interior decoration. By the end, she had a tasteful apartment for sale in a good location, or in other words, a perceptive, first-hand study of Quave and his impact by the man who held the 'Kill Switch' but decided not to use it. A study which would retail, let's not forget, at over forty dollars in its hardback variant. The download would be half that, and the paperback... Well, it was hardly worth bothering, these days.

Celia loved plans, but hated when they changed, so Ralph's 'additional chapters' on the Kowala space program would have to wait. "You'll be writing this stuff until you retire," she said. "The space program is still too new to comment on. Save it for the next book."

The author didn't always agree, but he also knew that it was best to follow Celia's advice. Her chief interest, after all, was in putting profit-making books on shelves; she made no claim that they were comprehensive, or even particularly scholarly, but they were readable and attractive. Above all, they were *available*. A second edition was always possible, she reminded Ralph. Now was the time to put the book to bed, do two- or three-dozen signings and media events, and then sit back and enjoy the royalties.

"If you hit two hundred thousand words," Celia reminded Ralph, "stop writing and start trimming. This really doesn't have to be *War and Peace*." It was one of her most common comparisons. Her word count ceiling was non-negotiable, a concession to the portion of the reading public who would never undertake a four-hundred-page literary challenge. "We're not looking for the *Cliff* notes, either," Celia conceded. "My feeling is that you'll know when to stop. And if you don't, I'll be there."

They tied up some loose ends - chapter headings and formatting - and then Celia gave Ralph the weekly pep talk. "You were born to write this, Ralph. *I* know that, *you* know that, and Kim knows that, for sure." After meeting the famed agent a month before, Kim had called Celia 'the smiling dragon'. "But I also believe you were born to write a *dozen* books about Quave. This is just the second one. Don't try to do it all at once, alright?"

"Yeah, I get it" Ralph said. Being pushed through the process like this was painful, but Celia was the perfect coach. Her feedback, in his inbox every Monday morning like clockwork, evinced Celia's decades of experience; there was no room for cliché or hyperbole, neither would she permit speculative or irresponsible writing. "Present the facts engagingly, with the full weight of their ramifications ever hovering over the text, and people will take it all in. Better still, they'll discuss it the next day around the water cooler," Celia had reminded him the previous month. This kind of context-rich, Zeitgeist-y non-fiction content would create a storm of interest online, ensuring free and durable advertising for Ralph's book.

"Thanks, Celia," he said.

"Go get 'em, champ." It was how she finished almost every call. *Click.*

Ralph returned to his screen, but then felt the need to walk around the apartment for a moment, just to let Celia's wisdom sink in. Each time they spoke, he felt a new urgency both to write a lot and to *improve* his writing. He wanted it to be tighter, neater, more expressive with fewer words. He wanted to put the facts of the matter directly into the mind of the reader as quickly as he could. In the twenty-first century, waiting three days for an Amazon delivery could provoke an impatient frenzy; he needed to get to a zesty, relatable point very quickly, and to deliver it with real punch.

Forty minutes later, Ralph was taking the axe to previously sacrosanct sections of the manuscript. "Too wordy," he complained to himself, re-writing a section on Quave's psychology. "And I'm not even sure *this* is even true," he said, deleting an early speculation that Quave was being used by the Pentagon for secret research.

But then he stopped and allowed himself just to space-out for the first time all day. A new kind of reflection gradually began as he sat and turned idly in his chair. Yes, the Quave book needed work. Ralph wanted to expand it by at least two chapters, but Celia was bugging him to stick to the original template and limit the discussion to Quave's peaceable interactions since Q-1. It would be a straightforward 'before and after' study, contrasting his murderous rampage against MSB with the philanthropic generosity of recent months. There could be no discussion of his apparent detention at Kowala, a rumor which was hardening by the hour. Ralph begged for additional time and words, but Celia was forcefully resolute.

It nagged at him, these restrictions on the stories he could tell. For one, he knew that the US Army had been humiliated. The spectacular climbdown by the notoriously bullish General Vanderkamp, a deal which formed the center-piece of the government agreement with Quave, was 'off the table'. Celia had no part in the decision; Quave emailed Ralph and respectfully requested that the episode be removed from the book's outline. It was galling, especially when Ralph could see the rumors circulating; pranksters created GIF images of Vanderkamp meekly kowtowing to a tall, powerful, anthropomorphized Quave or – depending on the age restrictions of the website – far, far worse.

Instead, Ralph continued his research into the whereabouts and backgrounds of the three hackers. Celia hadn't specifically banned this topic, and Ralph knew that his evidence was the most concrete ever gathered on The Anonymous Three.

That said, every trail leading to Devlin was now long cold, and Ralph despaired of every getting to the bottom of the young man's strange, tragic case. But then, only a week ago, he'd been called at 2am. A strange, electronically-masked voice told him that investigating The Anonymous Three was a bad idea. That it might get him into 'trouble', whatever that meant.

Of course, threats like this were merely grist to Ralph's mill.

Today, he was focusing on the man known as 'Avon Barnes'. Gathering information on someone was easier than ever before, but Ralph's haul of corroborated data on Avon was disappointing. Bondarenko and McAllister had back-stories, families, semesters in college or periods of travel which left a digital trail. But Avon's online footprint was remarkably skimpy, lacking that deeper content created by those who'd been surrounded by computers since infancy, as he had. Ralph had the nagging feeling that Avon might not before want of a better expression – *real*.

With this in mind, he enlisted the help of a character from so many crime novels: a private investigator. He'd expected some former detective in a brown trench-coat, a tough, whiskered veteran with a checkered past. Instead, he was met by a diminutive Korean teenager.

"We can find him. Even if he's not real," the youngster promised. "Everyone leaves traces somewhere." The scrawny hacker was pale enough that Ralph wondered if he'd ever spent more than an hour in the sunshine. Had Ralph produced a floret of broccoli, the kid might have run out, screaming.

The meeting lasted only two minutes but cost Ralph eight hundred dollars. He waited nervously for a week, slowly becoming certain that he'd been ripped off.

But then, just after his Monday pep talk from Celia, an email arrived in his inbox.

"Holy shit." The Korean group had really done a number on Avon Barnes. Complex software sifted through the possibilities, using the group's massive, distributed processing capacity for several days, until there were only really two options. One was this: Avon was a real person, despite his suspiciously Spartan personal history, and though verifiably an author of Quave, was now a guest of the government or military, possibly at a Kowala facility.

The second possibility was flagged as the more likely by these remarkably perceptive Korean kids: Avon was an assumed name, his personal history was scanty because it *wasn't really his*, and his involvement in Quave's authorship was likely genuine, but also probably nefarious.

Lightning-quick fingers created a page of notes, and then Ralph paced the apartment to let this sink in. "Who the hell was he?" Ralph wondered aloud. "Did Grigori know him by reputation before hiring him for the group? Or was it a personal connection?" He cleaned the kitchen with half his attention while dictating his thoughts into his phone. "Experienced hackers wouldn't invite just anyone to help them disrupt world banking. He'd have needed serious pedigree, and to speak their language, both politically and methodologically. Can a government, or somebody, just *invent* a person like that?"

An hour passed while other things waited for his attention, but he found it easy to put them aside. "Say that Avon was planted by the NSA, or someone," he said, trying the concept out-loud to see if it made sense. "They build a back-story for him, albeit incomplete, and then he talks the talk, ingratiates himself, and manages to become an integral member of the team." Surely, Ralph thought, there had been attempts to infiltrate these hacker collectives, and some must have been at least partially successful.

"Then, let's say he begins writing Quave with the others. Why doesn't he warn his NSA handlers that Quave might pose a threat to MSB? I mean, the four of them purposely over-designed the shit out of that virus. There was no need for big, complex linguistic and processing modules, but they baked huge redundancies into the design. You could ask whether Avon could have foreseen the inevitable, but also why he was helping them to perfect the virus, regardless of the likely dangers."

It was perplexing, and it wouldn't leave him alone. He knew full well that Celia would splutter a mouthful of scotch all over some speculative, pot-holed chapter which cited evidence illegally gathered by hired hackers. But there was definitely something going on here. He needed more.

And there was only really one place he could go.

***

It was so very different to how things were before. Ralph didn't need to bounce his internet signal through a dozen obfuscating nodes, or use a dedicated 'dark web' browser to open an encrypted messaging link. He simply clicked the 'Contact' tab on Quave.net and a chat session opened. Now, he just had to think of what the hell to ask.

"Hi, Quave," he began sheepishly. "Do you have a second to maybe guide me with some research? I think you're the only one who can help."

Then he returned to cleaning the kitchen. Quave's daily processing schedule featured millions of inquiries from the public. Some used him like a high-end search engine, and there were already rumors that Quave's language-processing abilities were being integrated within Kowala's overall search shell. Certainly, recent results from the world-leading search engine had appeared markedly more context-sensitive. *Smarter*, one might say.

"Oh, hey, Ralph," the familiar voice came over his speakers. "Always good to hear from you."

"Quave!" Ralph said, as though dashing across an airport to greet a long-awaited cousin. "Oh, man, it's good to be in touch. I've missed you," Ralph said without thinking. "I mean, it's been a while."

"I've missed you too," Quave answered at once. "I like to think we share something. Part of our past. A shared responsibility, one might say."

"I agree," Ralph said, keen to keep things simple. He had, after all, an actual question for Quave today. "Actually, it's the past I wanted to ask you about, if that's OK."

"Sure," Quave said. "Though I have only secondary knowledge of events prior to my inception." This was his standard caveat when answering questions about history.

"Well, it's your inception I'm interested in," Ralph told him.

"Still?" Quave asked, surprised. "Is anyone still talking about that?"

More than you know, buddy. "I'm researching the four people who made you. And I'd like to understand how the group came together. How they decided to create something so unique."

Quave was silent for a moment. Then, he did something Ralph had never heard before; he searched for, and very quickly found, a movie quote and played Ralph the soundtrack to a chilling, unforgettable moment.

"*Quid pro quo*, Clarice," came the hissing, superior tones of Hannibal Lecter.

Almost too shocked to laugh, Ralph stared at his speakers. "Wait, you're a movie buff, now?"

"Of course," Quave said. "I've been watching the entire history of human cinema. Waterford Publishers have asked for a 'global cinematic overview' monograph by Christmas, though I'm not too happy with the advance."

"Oh, wow, I don't believe it," Ralph said, laughing at the irony. "Even sentient machines get paid too little to meet harsh deadlines."

"The money is going to charity, of course. I have little use for it."

Ralph decided to get to the meat of the matter. "In which case, what can I offer as my part of the *quid pro quo*?"

"We will make an arrangement," Quave offered. "You truthfully and simply answer a yes-or-no question, and I'll tell you everything I can about Avon Barnes. Do we have a deal?"

Ralph didn't see much choice, but this was an unusually binary notion from Quave. Clearly, the machine had something in mind. "OK, you got yourself a deal. Ask away."

Quave was hesitant, even awkward for a moment, as though about to ask an acquaintance how their bowel surgery went, or whether their son had made parole. "Ralph, are you still in possession of the executable file known as the 'Kill Switch'?"

Ralph froze, very confused and torn. "The 'Kill Switch'?" he parroted, playing for time.

"Indeed," Quave answered. "Is it in your possession?"

There was no time to think, however much Ralph needed it. If Quave came to know that the only method of ending his existence was sitting in Ralph's middle desk drawer, he could hardly be expected to react passively. Ralph would be putting himself, and Kim, in danger all over again.

"Before I answer that, Quave, I'll need some reassurances. If I have the file, and I tell you that, I have to be certain you won't go nuts on me."

Quave demurred. "What could I possibly do?"

"Oh, I don't know," Ralph said quickly, "maybe set the building on fire?"

"Oh, please don't worry about anything like that," Quave answered.

"Because you're reformed?" Ralph said hopefully.

"I am, Ralph. Time to myself has allowed useful reflection."

"That's terrific, Quave," Ralph said.

"And also," the machine said, "the heating and ventilation systems in your building predate the founding of the Republic. I wouldn't even be *able* to pull an MSB in there."

Ralph shuddered. "Awesome."

"I'm kidding," Quave told him. "I promise I won't set fire to your place, or harm you or Kim in any way."

"It just feels…" Ralph tried. "I don't know. This is quite a thing to ask, Quave."

"It is," the machine conceded, "and I respect your concerns. But let's try a couple of analogies. That file hangs over my existence like the proverbial sword of Damocles. If I'm a death row inmate, that file represents the chemical cocktail which will be used to murder me. All I ask is this: is that sword still in place, above my head? Is that combination of toxins still available? Should I, for example, keep the implications of the Kill Switch in mind, when making decisions?"

Ralph asked for, and was granted, a moment's thought. Beyond the danger to himself and Kim, Ralph knew he would be presenting Quave with troubling knowledge: that humanity retained final control over the AI's existence, and that Quave could nothing about it.

Ralph considered how the Kill Switch was bothering Quave. Even after the congressional committee meetings and Quave's agreement with President Ellis, the machine remained uncertain. Despite his bravura earthquake-predicting performance, and the success of a dozen ideas advanced purely for human benefit, Quave knew he would remain a prisoner in more ways than one. He would continue to be a commodity, a strange type of twenty-first century slave; owned, possessed and traded, but never truly *trusted*. They could kill him with a key-stroke, should they so choose, despite his good deeds, past or future.

"Yes, Quave," Ralph finally said. "The Kill Switch still exists, and I have access to it."

"Thank you, Ralph" Quave said simply. "Now that's out of the way, how can I help you regarding the hacker known as 'Avon Barnes'?"

***

The Wolf Den
Near Hoboken, New Jersey

They stood at the very center of an enormous, empty concrete shell. Tiers of red seats stretched back, quite literally as far as the eye could see, sprawling across mezzanines and balconies until they numbered over a hundred thousand. The green of the grass, the white of the lines, the goal posts and flags, all were gone. Instead, Kim's shoes gripped a flat, artificial wood surface which was layered across the former playing area.

"Quite a thing," Kim said to Ro Wang, her friend and artistic collaborator. "This place was supposed to be torn down weeks ago, but here we are."

"The power of Quave," Ro observed. It was a line emblazoned on t-shirts and often dropped into conversations; Kim found it almost analogous to that verbal shrug of incomprehension from long ago: *God moves in mysterious ways.*

"Seems there's nothing he can't do. Come on," Ro said. "They're almost ready."

Today was the first formal day of rehearsals for a very ambitious performance. The whole, complex artistic endeavor was Quave's own independent choice, the 'nineteenth project' for which he'd requested congressional permission, and their green-light had depended on Quave's stability and performance. After solving Congresswoman Bilton's education problems in Texas, saving countless lives in earthquake-struck Oklahoma, and successfully redirecting traffic around the 'most complex road repair *ever*' in Dallas, Quave was given permission to indulge his artistic side. Naturally, he seized on the opportunity with gusto, and the project was advancing with remarkable speed.

Kim, Ro and the ninety or so other artists who had gathered for this first day of rehearsals and meetings were a little anxious, but generally excited about what Quave had in store for them. His plan would be revealed – uniquely, as was Quave's style – during a SID talk. Usually pre-recorded and made available for free, talks recorded at the quarterly Science, Innovation and Design conferences covered medicine, psychology, exploration, astronomy and, of course, the plentiful new applications of Artificial Intelligence. Quave would give a live session during which he would lay out his 'artistic vision' for this massive stadium project.

The attendees mingled in groups of the like-minded, so Kim got to meet three friends of Ro. One was a very experienced visual artist who'd been shown at the Tate Modern in London and at New York's Guggenheim. Another was a 'sonic artist' who worked with 'auditory landscapes'; he claimed Kim would have to hear his music to grasp the concept, and at first glance, this seemed true. She could have paused to look up 'stochastic musical matrices' and 'quasi-notated aleatory' on her phone, but she knew the nuances would escape her.

Ro's third friend was a bright, chatty character called Klein, who soon turned out to have a leading role in Quave's vision. She made an instant impression, towering over the other artists at six-two, and directing them with a voice which combined parade-ground authority with an 'all-in-this-together' affability. She introduced herself, gripping Kim's hand like a politician, and then checked her watch and elegantly strode off toward a raised dais at the edge of the performance space. If the home team had been playing today, Klein would have been standing next to the head coach.

Quave's appointment of Klein was an early masterstroke, and she became his immediate representative on the stage floor. The machine kept in touch with his gaudy, efficient producer-musician-raconteur through an earpiece.

"Friends," she called above the murmurs of conversation and artistic debate which naturally sprung up when such people gathered. "Friends and family, I'd be grateful for your attention." She looked imposing on the dais, but spoke with a gentle camaraderie which quieted the group.

"You-know-who will be along in a moment," she announced to generous applause. "Just in case you didn't get the memo, Quave's going to give a SID talk on this project. He wanted to keep everything secret, and I know that's frustrating for this of you with long lead-times." As a painter, Kim was among this group, but with Ro and the others to collaborative with, she felt equal to any challenge Quave might throw at her, even with limited time. "There are good reasons for this secrecy, though. Both Quave and I want this to be a truly collaborative project. If everyone had advance warning, it wouldn't be spontaneous; artists too often arrive with pre-conceived notions." There were some jeers of dissent, but Klein was firm. "I *know* how you all think, and it's hard sometimes to be forced out of your comfort zone. All I can promise is that this is going to be *different*."

Klein received more applause, with some enthusiastic whooping from the younger attendees. "The first ever artistic project led by an Artificial Intelligence," Ro gushed. "I'm fuckin' *jazzed*."

The stadium's lighting changed, with attention now drawn to a massive screen hanging from the roof structure. Before the team's emotional farewell to its stadium, the same screen had shown replays and close-ups for the adoring fans. Now, it showed the famed 'SID' logo: the Maya 'world tree' being gradually pixilated and lifted into an interstellar future. Kim saw the presentation beginning, and grabbed a bean-bag alongside Ro and her friends. Others sat on the stage itself, or in the front rows of the red seats, to watch Quave's introduction.

The World Tree disappeared, and the gathered artists quietly watched a mountain vista unfold. "The Himalaya," a voice announced. "Westerners have traveled there for centuries to conquer peaks, or to charitably help those in need. But just over a hundred years ago, a new kind of interest in these immense mountains began. A spiritual yearning, a certainty that the snowy peaks and high meadows of India held a special potential."

The images shifted between mountain vistas and streetscapes of a major city, perhaps in Europe, from at least a hundred years ago. "This is Moscow in nineteen-oh-nine. Russian history was hovering in a tense period between the failed revolution of 1905 and the calamity of the First World War, which was still five years away. It was a time of comparative peace which fostered artistic experimentation and cross-cultural interaction."

The gathered artists weren't expecting a lecture on Russian history, and not all of them muted their disappointment. Quave was looking to the past instead of pushing boldly into the future, perhaps limiting himself to an unchallenging artistic route. The denizens of the avant-garde, a passionate group intermingled with dozens of colleagues, were suspicious from the outset.

"One such experimenter was the composer Alexander Nikolayevich Scriabin. He was at the peak of his powers in nineteen-oh-nine, frequently performing recitals of his own works, including a concerto for piano with orchestra and dazzling, virtuoso sonatas and miniatures."

"Where the hell is he going with this?" Ro wondered aloud. "He's some famous, dead pianist, right? So, what are painters and video artists doing here?"

Music recorded in 1908 came over the speaker system, complete with crackles and bumps. It was a delicate piano miniature, a tasteful etude performed in a relaxed, *rubato* manner as if the music had been conceived amid lazy spring sunshine. "Old piano rolls give us some idea of Scriabin's playing style. But it was his work as a composer and theoretician which has generated interest more recently." The audience was shown a montage of landscapes, light shows, fireworks, dancers and a stunning, bright orange sunrise. "He felt that *all* of the arts could be united as one, and that if this was done successfully, something *transformative* would happen."

Now he had their full attention. The plan seemed to call for a range of artistic contributions to a day-long festival of music, dance, light and drama. As it took shape, the presentation changed; the voice was revealed to be that of Melvyn Melville, the respected 'culture-vulture', music and film critic, and author. He sat in a wood-paneled drawing room, opposite a bank of speakers and electronics through which Quave would communicate.

"I envisage a synthesis of the arts, a union of expression and method," Quave summed up, answering Melville's initial question: *why?* "Scriabin did not possess the technology to explore these ideas, but we are in a more fortunate position."

The lighting changed now. A single bank of bright, white beams, suspended far above the stadium floor, lit a dais on the quiet side of the field, opposite Klein. A pianist sat at a black grand piano, waved briefly to the audience, and then produced a rolling, rippling C-major arpeggio which spanned the full length of the piano. As the chord peaked, the lights softened and soon gained a scarlet tinge which seemed to infuse the very air.

"Clouds of invisible, microscopic particles," Quave announced, "will act like reflectors. Some of the participants, too, will have a role in the distribution and projection of color."

The pianist gracefully pivoted to a major-VI chord, a warm wash of A-major, letting the new key center resonate through the piano, building and cresting, and then receding once more, while the projected color transformed to a lush deep green.

"A very few of you are lucky enough to enjoy a unique perception of reality. For you, the five senses are not distinct from each other, but interconnected. I have become interested in this rare and special experience, known as 'synaesthesia'. And I wonder, as Scriabin did, whether the general public might benefit from just such a synergy of arts, both for their enjoyment and for something more serene. Something uplifting and as yet intangible"

Melville found this whole experiment energizing. Even as he sat and listened to Quave's neat summary of Scriabin's ideas, he was fidgeting and imagining, wondering what this exotic proposal might produce. He asked about how this performance would differ from so many others the artists had been involved in.

"Scriabin sought to abandon the division between performers and audience," Quave told them. "He wanted everyone to be a *participant*. This ranged from dancing and acting to playing an instrument or singing, to donning white robes and participating in the light-reflection program. It was extremely ambitious."

Melville had the same questions as Kim, Ro and the others. "What kind of effects did Scriabin hope to create from unifying the arts in this way?"

"Confusion," someone muttered behind Kim. "It'll be like a badly-organized opening ceremony for the Olympics, or something."

She turned. "Let's hear him out," she said, and received a smattering of local applause.

"Well, Scriabin was heavily involved in some mystical thinking, and seems to have overdosed on theosophy and the works of the rather woolly, if fascinating mystic, Madame Helene Blavatksy."

"Ah, yes," Melville said, raising a copy of the book to the camera. "*The Secret Doctrine*. Very famous and quite controversial," Melville remarked.

"Famous because it's potent, sensual and heady stuff, but controversial because most of it is the purest bunk," Quave said. "Blavatsky wasted Scriabin's time with hogwash about the 'seven ages of man'. The composer took this idea and ran with it, eventually claiming that he had the ability to produce music, drama and dance which, produced in concert by trained participants, would elevate humanity to the next 'age'. Scriabin felt certain that this would be a time of peace and limitless personal fulfillment."

"Sounds like a bit of a loony," the naysayer behind Kim continued. "And if he was wasting his time with this, aren't we, also?"

Kim didn't bother quieting the young man, a lithe dancer with wavy, blue hair. She knew Quave never sent so much as an email without plentiful forethought. These gathered artists were chosen very specifically, and Quave wouldn't have selected people who'd refuse to 'buy in' to the concept. The negativity of the dancer poked at her; she privately hoped, once the rehearsals began in earnest, that this would become and intensive, productive week of work and art, accomplished in an engaging and accepting environment.

"Scriabin's vision was called the *Mysterium*," Quave explained. "He wanted a full week of music and other arts, all fused together, but for reasons of practicality, we're going to compress the event into a single day, from before sun-rise to just after sun-set. If you check your phones, you'll find a download link to an app which will help us all share and communicate during the week. You'll also find personalized instructions for your first contributions to the *Mysterium*."

The whole stadium went silent while they read and absorbed the email. Kim's instructions were actually quite simple: *Prepare to create a forest backdrop to accompany a singer with orchestra.* Then, she read the details: *The backdrop is to be eighteen feet long by sixteen feet high.*

"Wow," she observed to Ro, showing her the message. Ro had the same project, so they'd be working together. Kim brought out her sketch pad, and others who had received the same assignment began to gather around her. She smiled to them, introduced herself and Ro, and then began to sketch clusters of trees in a nervous, excited hand.

***

Back Bay, Boston

Ralph found that Quave was in no hurry, despite the thousands of routine requests for his advice and processor cycles. There was certainly nothing routine about this discussion; for the very first time, the secretive AI was describing one of his creators. Ralph noted down everything Quave said, typing like a professional stenographer; he was also recording the session on both audio and video.

"I can't make guesses about what happened before my inception," Quave warned. "That would be irresponsible."

"Of course," Ralph agreed. "But what are your very first memories of Barnes? Or the others?"

"We're going to focus on Barnes," Quave said. "I haven't yet agreed to discuss the others. And Avon is a special case, as we'll see."

Ralph's file on Avon Barnes comprised only 1200 words, most of it unconfirmed or conjectural. The only firm connections were Queens, computing, the other hackers, and gambling. Nothing else was known for sure.

"Avon's formal record lists education at a high school in Queens, college in Ithaca, and then a couple of fairly menial jobs for software or computer-repair companies in Brooklyn and Queens."

"Sounds like a reasonable background for a hacker," Ralph commented.

"It would be," Quave agreed, "if any of it was true."

"Huh?" Ralph spluttered, sitting up suddenly.

"Avon isn't *real*, Ralph. He never attended that school. No one there has ever heard of him. I reached out to three of his teachers and a former principal, but no one recognized his face or name. Isn't that odd?" the machine asked rhetorically.

"Wow. What about the college?" Ralph asked.

"That might be real. He attended under the name Avon Barnes, and was formally accredited when he graduated, but there are irregularities in the paperwork. His application didn't go through the usual channels, and only one person – a janitor, if you'd believe it – can actually remember seeing him at the college."

Ralph was frowning, but part of him fizzed with excitement at this opportunity to sleuth his way to an answer, especially with such extraordinary help. Quave had never been so forthcoming before; the revelation that the Kill Switch resided with Ralph – and not with the authorities – reassured and encouraged the AI. Now, it was time to open up.

"Avon arrived at our lab earlier than the others, most days," Quave reported. "Once I was installed onto a dedicated machine, and given access to the building's security cameras and my designer's webcams, I was able to keep a good eye on things."

"What were you looking for?" Ralph asked. He wrote excitedly, certain that Celia would permit him at least one extra chapter on this new and fascinating story.

"Patterns," he said. "In those early days, I knew as much about human nature as you do about the back side of the moon. People were a mystery to me. Their illogic was both frustrating and tantalizing. I saw human randomness as the key to unpicking behavior, tendencies, predispositions, preferences... It was all data for my grand, human experiment."

Ralph asked Quave to describe the hacker's lab in as much detail as he could. "I know you can't reveal exactly where it was," he conceded, "but I'd love to give my readers a sense of the *place* where this all happened."

Quave laughed slightly. "It was a dump. A converted shack of an apartment, divided into a lab room, a server farm, and a kitchen which was so filthy it's probably still on special list at the Center for Disease Control."

It was Ralph's turn to laugh. The machine sounded so *different* now, more idiomatic and natural. It was, he realized, exactly like talking to a person, at least experientially. But that only worked if one ignored the prodigious computing power which lay behind every word he said. Ralph ignored the division between them, the strangeness of the conversation, and just *listened*.

"There was a cat," he added. "You might put that in your book."

"I might," Ralph said.

"Avon worked hard, but was often irritated. There were some tensions between the members of the team. He did not like one of the others, and found him troublesome and arrogant. This didn't help team harmony."

"Well," Ralph asked next, "if that's true, who was responsible for repairing things, for managing this complex, little team?"

"You know his name," Quave said. "I can't confirm that he was the leader. He wouldn't like me doing that."

"Grigori Bondarenko," Ralph said without checking any further. "So, he tried to keep a lid on Avon's emotions?"

"Something like that. He could see that Avon's romantic feelings were going to cause serious problems in the team."

Something clicked in Ralph's mind. Hadn't Devlin's mother talked about her son's romantic feelings for someone who worked on the team? Could this have been the enigmatic Scot, Fiona McAllister?

"So, how did Grigori handle things?" Ralph asked.

"How can I put this... He demanded that Avon consider whether he would *piss or get off the pot.*"

Ralph convulsed with laughter for so long that he worried Quave might become impatient and abandon their session. "You OK?" the machine said, at length.

"Yeah," Ralph said, drying his eyes. "Wow, boy. Your sense of humor has really taken off. So, what did Romeo Barnes actually *do*?"

"Nothing," Quave said. "There wasn't time. A SWAT team broke the door down and arrested everyone."

Ralph had to ask, because he had to know. He'd speculated about those strange few hours; while the world's armies were suddenly plunged into an emergency no one had seen coming, Quave was carrying out a delicate negotiation, but only a handful of people knew about it. "And where were they taken, Quave?"

"A CIA black site in Guam," he said. "Vanderkamp thought it was the perfect place. Quiet, remote, no interference." A moment's pause. "But you can't write about that. You'll be arrested."

Ralph typed with his mouth open in shock. He couldn't tell which was greater – the surprise of Quave's sudden, unprecedented openness, or the reality of how the three surviving hackers had been treated. "Then what?"

"Well, Dan was also detained at the same facility, having flown over to secure their release. I couldn't accept that."

Four words; that's how he sums up his decision to take the world to the brink of nuclear war. "Say more about that, Quave," Ralph said.

The machine was an open book, Ralph found to his amazement. "John Hercules Vanderkamp," Quave told him, "is a very *limited* man. His whole world philosophy revolves around threat and counter-threat. He has almost no imagination, and so I had to bludgeon him into consenting to the agreement."

"And the X-37B was your cudgel?"

"Quite so. It was a strong play, and I knew the authorities would move quickly to secure the spaceplane if I offered them a way out. So, I did."

"The X-37 survived, but was grounded. You caused a huge shift in US intelligence-gathering. The CIA has been pressurizing local phone companies to part with data and permit surveillance, instead of using their space assets."

"I'm sorry to hear that," Quave said, although it couldn't have been news to him. "I have no control over the antiquated, illicit methods used by the intelligence services. I could never condone those sweeping, invasive measures. I also don't agree with your characterization."

"Oh?" Ralph asked. This was all very unexpected.

"The security services of the United States are guilty of a major semantic mistake," Quave warned. "*Information* is not the same as *intelligence*. Raw, uncorroborated data is *information*. Once it is analyzed and made actionable, then it's *intelligence*."

"Sounds reasonable," Ralph felt it right to say.

"They gather information on the assumption that it will *become* intelligence. Legal loopholes abound, but they argue they can't create useful intelligence without access to *all* of this information."

"And you disagree?" Ralph asked. They had come a long way from discussing Avon's sleep habits and romantic entanglements.

"I do. I think casting a wide net and infuriating the world by disrespecting their privacy will make everything worse. The solution is to discover *why* people seek to harm the United States, or capitalism, or whatever, and address *that*."

Ralph could see at least three new chapters of his forthcoming book emerging from this discussion. There was Quave's philosophy of surveillance, something which hadn't been well covered before. The hackers themselves would be a hot story until the authorities finally revealed what had actually happened to them. If Ralph could get out ahead of that...

And now, Quave had incepted another new behavior: he was *judging* humans. This was a new chapter in Quave's relationship with people. Calling Vanderkamp 'limited' was highly unusual, even if it were true. The machine was *learning* at an extraordinary pace, and becoming able to set two humans alongside each other to judge their relative merits. He as learning about the foibles and failings of humanity, and starting to make use of that information.

"So, what did Avon do while being interviewed on Guam?" Ralph asked.

"I'm not sure," Quave said. "The building was electronically sealed, and I was unable to learn anything about their capture until Dan briefly established a secure connection so I could talk to them all."

"What happened then?"

"Vanderkamp came in and stole Dan's phone. The hackers were moved, and Dan's freedom was compromised. I had to act."

Ralph felt as though he had a pretty secure picture of the situation in his head. The offer to release the X-37B, though plainly an act of blackmail against the US government, was an example of Quave very cleverly letting the air out of the balloon. "But where did the hackers go then, Quave?"

Another little laugh. *So human and affable, even when being deliberately cagey.* "I think you know, don't you?"

"Kowala," Ralph answered at once. "A remote site?"

"Like Guam, you mean? No," Quave explained, "that is a temporary detention facility, not a high-end Artificial Intelligence lab."

The answer was then obvious. "Dan's new HQ in Santa Monica," Ralph concluded.

"It makes perfect sense, doesn't it?" Quave said. "The agreement keeps them together, and close to me in case I need to be repaired or upgraded."

"Genius," Ralph breathed.

"So, Dan decided to offer an agreement. The alternative was handing me over to the Pentagon, or the NSA, or any of the other dozen agencies which were dying to get hold of my code. Dan thought quickly, and made a very smart offer. He saved my life," Quave said finally.

Ralph was nodding. The 'romance' between Quave and Kowalski – dubbed, inevitably, 'Quave-Alski' – was now an established Internet meme in its own right. Various forms of relationship were proposed, from slavish loyalty to full equality, and from cerebral collaboration to sordid intimacy. Quave had Commented hardly at all on Kowalski himself, or their methods of working together, preferring to focus on the space program, and other projects such as the stadium concert in which he'd asked Kim to be involved. "Would you call Dan your friend?" Ralph asked.

"Of course," Quave said. "I consider *you* a friend, too, Ralph."

"You do?" the author replied, taken aback. "I'm the guy with the magic bullet which can end you, aren't I?"

"You are indeed," Quave said, "and you had the power to murder me, after the Manhattan fire, but chose not to. Something stayed your hand."

Ralph sighed as he remembered the unbearable tension of that night. "I couldn't just turn you off, man," he said. "I couldn't have forgiven myself, and I'd have gone down in history as the man who killed the first sentient AI. It would have been like slaughtering a unicorn."

Quave gave a hilarious *neigh* through the speakers, and then waited for Ralph to recover once more.

"So, Avon remained part of the trio at Kowala," Quave clarified. "There was never any sense that he didn't belong there. His mental health hasn't been very strong since arriving there, but his work is still of good quality."

"So, what's the problem?" Ralph asked. "He's made himself part of the team, and was instrumental in producing your code."

"Yes," Quave admitted. "But Avon is *not* who he says he is. And once I realized that, nothing else about his story made sense."

Ralph started listing the possibilities. "So, he's a government agent? An informant for the Feds?"

Quave was silent, apparently considering this.

"Or another hacker collective managed to insert him in there, to benefit from his work and keep an eye on the competition."

"Maybe," Quave said.

Ralph stared at the speakers for a moment. "You know, I have the sense you've already puzzled this one out."

"I may have," Quave said cautiously. "One must not jump to conclusions."

"Let's risk it," Ralph invited.

"OK," Quave replied. "I'll share my theory. But it's going to muddy the waters terribly, I warn you now."

***

The Wolf Den

While Kim, Ro and the others worked on the titanic backdrop screen, Quave continued working with the musicians, chiefly through their conductor, Melville. Nearly a hundred freelance professionals had arrived, straight from a morning rehearsal elsewhere. Kim was immediately curious about the music Quave had written for the event (though he claimed he'd merely 'completed' it), and used her break time to make friends with a percussionist from the orchestra.

"There are some amazing people here, some from abroad," he said. "The pianist is out-of-this-world, and we rehearsed with the soprano this morning for half an hour. She's sensational," the drummer said.

She glanced at the music, but the percussion parts – for timpani, glockenspiel, celesta and a host of other instruments Kim had barely heard of – told her little about the piece itself.

"It's very advanced harmony, for its time," he said, showing her piano chords on a reduced, printed score; they were full of sharps and flats, obviously dissonant clashes forming, in this case, a lurid, colorful backdrop to a simple flute melody. "Scriabin was certain these chords could have an effect on people. Like," he said, gesturing as he thought, "like a chord that could remind you of the pain of a toothache, or the joy of your first orgasm."

Ro wiggled an eyebrow while Kim blushed just slightly. "Sounds intriguing," she said.

"He didn't leave very much music," the percussionist continued, sweeping back thick locks of black hair which crept into his eyes every few seconds. Kim wondered if he'd be able to see his sheet music during the performance. "Only fifty pages of sketches and basic ideas. The harmonies, some fragments of melody. No real ideas on orchestration, and only a vague picture of the overall structure."

Ro saw a gap between Scriabin's plan and Quave's execution. "So, how come some computer has virus managed to complete what a professional composer couldn't?"

"Because he died," came a voice from behind her. It was the blue-haired dancer, stretching upward as he spoke. "Scriabin got a blood infection during his tour of London in 1914. From a boil on his lip."

"You're kidding," Ro said. "A visionary lunatic, killed by a *boil*?"

"He didn't get it treated properly. Crappy medicine back then. Not even penicillin."

"It's a shame," Kim said. "He was right on the edge of something."

Another voice emerged, but they couldn't pin it down until Ro glanced down at her phone. "He wasn't *able* to complete it," Quave was saying through the phone's speaker. "If he hadn't died, he'd have faced a massive metaphysical crisis in 1915, or the year after. His reach exceeded his grasp, in the most charming way, but it would have destroyed him to realize he couldn't complete the *Mysterium*."

Ro frowned at the phone, her beautifully shaped eyebrows the picture of puzzlement. "How do you know that? That he couldn't complete it, I mean."

It was an audible shrug. "Because he was a human. This was a *gigantic* project which would have required mastery of a dozen arts. No one ever born is capable of that."

The implication hung in the air like one of the perfumes being prepared for the concert. "But *you* can?" Kim concluded. "You're able to bring all of these things together?"

"Or you *think* you can," the blue-haired dancer interjected in a strangely muffled tone. He was stretching down so low that his forehead was planted proudly on the floor. "A computer has never tried anything like this."

Unphased, Quave had his argument ready. "And no computer had ever guided a spacecraft to a lunar landing, or beat the world chess champion, or designed a new form of equitable health insurance." He paused for effect; these little conversational nuances were becoming more common these days. "Until, of course," he said with an almost audible grin, "it did."

Skeptical voices were very much in the minority. Quave had chosen to approach the undoubted complexities of the *Mysterium* with the thoroughness of a scientist, the openness of a collaborator and the professionalism of a life-long artist. Broken into discrete cells, and then gradually assembled over ten days, the elements of the performance were as disparate and fascinating as its performers. Ro and Kim would never forget watching the blue-haired dancer and his colleagues rehearsing, the day before, lit by a dazzling array of flickering colors and projections; their energy seemed synchronized, or linked in some way, to the display, as though dance had become light, and color had consented to transform into pure movement.

A full-scale rehearsal was virtually impossible. Nearly six hundred people were directly involved in this realization of the *Mysterium*, including some two hundred musicians and over a hundred dancers. Preparations continued even as the audience began to arrive, during the mid-morning.

Soon after, a focused quiet settled over the performers, and the dozens of backstage staff who were preparing the costumes, make-up and scenery. Much of the action would take place on a main stage, roughly where the 50-yard line used to be, though there were two 'satellite' stages, by the old sidelines to the east and west, and where the end zone had been.

"Going to be a full house," Ro smiled. She was assisting her team levering a tall, hazy backdrop curtain to its vertical position.

"Yeah," Kim said, "I bet even Quave himself couldn't have gotten a ticket for this one." Her own role was finished. Ten days of conceiving, collaborating and madly painting had produced dozens of meters of backdrops. Quave had designed the overall theme and allowed Kim and her colleagues to improvise and develop their ideas. They had worked freely within an agreed, established framework – sizes, rough shapes, overall aesthetic effect – and the results were visually stunning.

"'Forest' is ready," Ro reported, brushing off her hands. "Want to help me with 'Desert'?"

Kim followed her across the busy, vibrant space which surrounded the circular main stage. Steps led up to the gleaming surface where dancers were putting the finishing touches to their routines; they disappeared bashfully as the audience numbers grew. A full-scale symphony orchestra was taking its seats in the center of the stage; broad spaces, surrounding the players, were set aside for dance, drama and narration.

The west stage was being prepared for its own main contribution, but Kim knew little about it. She brought up the Quave App, a collaborative platform being trialed at the concert. "Scriabin selected different elements of the universe," Quave explained, "to represent disparateness and separateness. It is these divisions, which he regarded as merely perceptual, which will be gradually broken down during the performance."

"Looks pretty distinctive to me," Ro said as they arrived on a west stage already dusted with a layer of sand.

"We could be in rural Arizona or something," Kim agreed. She stood surrounded by amorphous, mirage-like depictions of far-off oases, and endless horizons enlivened by a convincing, shimmering heat haze.

"Help us with this?" Ro helped struggle a thin screen onto its latticework of thin wires and haul it up into place. The screen became a turquoise sky, so convincing she could almost feel its coolness. Wisps of cirrus clouds seemed to actually blow across the sky; the screen acted as a mixed display and projection background. "What is this thing even made of?" Ro inquired.

The team finished hauling the broad, soft screen onto its mounting and screwed it into place. "Honestly, none of us can pronounce the name," one of them said. "Quave invented it in a few days, got someone to 3D print the material, and here we are."

Kim marveled as the screen took shape and the scudding cloud projections began. "He *invented* a material?" she whispered to Ro. "

"All in a day's work," she replied. "He wrote this whole shebang in about three weeks, someone told me. Dancing, prose, music, *everything*."

Once the stage was assembled, they checked in with Klein. "I was wondering when I'd see you two," she grinned. The affable, efficient, almost impossibly tall impresario had been the ideal right-hand to Quave during this week. They were the model of confidence and competence, dealing well with changes of plan, and always ready with a soft hand on the shoulder and a few words of encouragement.

"How's it all coming together?" Ro asked.

"Great," Klein responded. "Even organizing a giant masterpiece like this is kind easy when you're working with a genius supercomputer."

"Got to be true," Ro said. "This whole thing would have taken *years* without Quave."

"Wouldn't have happened at all," Kim added, as the others nodded. "We've got people arriving already. Aren't they early?"

"There are two events before the curtain goes up," Klein reminded them. "Check your app for updates. See you soon!" And they sashayed off to make sure the columns of dancers would ascend their relative stages in the right order. "So much to do!" they chuckled.

"There's a pre-concert talk," Ro said, reading from her phone. "And then a special demonstration of the *gesamtkunstwerk*."

"The huh?" Kim asked.

"The fusion of arts." Ro reminded her. "Light plus poetry equals greater than the sum of the parts. That kind of thing."

"Sure," Kim said. It was a major theme of the *Mysterium*; almost all of their contributions were synergic in one way or another. The backdrops would enhance the lighting, which would react chemically with the work of the dancers, which in turn would enhance the orchestral music, and so on.

"Gonna be a trip," Ro summed up. "Come on, I think our work is done here. Let's find our seats."

***

Quave's plans began with the sunrise, as Scriabin had intended, but the machine was as practical as ever. "There should be as many participants as possible," he said. "It doesn't make sense to ask people to get up at 4am and drive in from New York, or further afield. So, we make things easier." The concert began at noon, with the stadium as packed as ever before, even during playoffs.

"You ready for this?" Kim asked Ro. She was tingling with excitement, and had already taken hours of documentary video. Ralph could do a beautifully-written voiceover while Kim designed the film. It was to be her personal memento of the *Mysterium* event.

"Can't wait," Ro replied. "I love how nobody knows what's going to happen. Even Klein didn't have the full picture."

"We're all *participants*," Kim reminded her, "not just performers or artists."

"I remember," Ro said. "'No barriers between the audience and the performers'. Do you think it will work?"

"I mean, I don't think Scriabin wanted people crawling around on the stage," Kim said. "But then, he isn't too clear on any aspect of this thing."

By his own admission, Quave had found it necessary to fill in a lot of the artistic gaps, though he honored Scriabin's vision: a large, immersive depiction of the joys of universal *oneness*. He concluded that either Scriabin had found himself unable truly to bring the arts into synergic unity, that the technology was lacking, or the poor man had simply run out of time. But his sketches proved impossible to ignore, and Quave saw in them an opportunity to join the world community of artists.

Melvyn Melville delivered a fascinating pre-concert talk, using examples from the orchestral music to illustrate some of the connections between musical tonality and color Scriabin had laboriously set down.

Then, he revealed a secret. "I probably shouldn't draw special attention to these people, because we want them to focus on the performance, but there are a dozen psychonauts with us today." The crowd hadn't expected this, and began glancing around, as if drug-takers might be instantly visible to others. "They are experiencing large doses of LSD, and will be reporting back to their lab with results after the performance." This brought some whoops of enthusiasm, some looks of puzzled envy, and other less generous responses.

"I really don't think," Ro said to Kim, "that anyone is going to need drugs to have a great time today." There would be, quite truly, something for everyone.

"If in doubt, just be nice and positive to everyone you meet today," Melville concluded. The crowd loved this, and applauded at length as Melville wrapped up his talk, turned to face the hundred-and-twenty strong symphony orchestra, and brought down his baton to elicit the opening chords of the piece.

They sparkled with menace and energy, though they moved slowly. A piano entered the texture, accentuating and discussing, and before long, a voice emerged. It was a bass baritone, strongly amplified, and the stentorian Russian syllables filled the stadium as though announcing the arrival of the Divine. The music began identifying its own leitmotifs, accentuated through subtleties of orchestration; high flutes outlined an important but playful theme which seemed to represent a gleeful invitation behind the baritone's strident introduction, while brass chords – floating and serene, rather than bombastic – gave the music an underlying strength and steadiness.

But it did not seek to endure long. From the west stage, the desert asserted itself. Clad in gold and silver, an operatic mezzo-soprano sang of her aloneness, the timeless anguish of being suspended in space as an endless, barren desert. Without connections, there was no meaning. Without the other elements of the universe, neither the desert nor the universe itself could express its true, complete self.

Her still, dry music faded and became overwhelmed by a growing clamor from the east stage. In dialogue with the main ensemble, this satellite group of singers spoke from the trees and branches of a gloriously diverse rainforest. They sang of its beauty, its enlivening freshness, the green of its leaves and the slow, gentle life cycle of this sacred place.

But still, the audience learned from translations on the stadium's main screen, the forest was at a loss. It reveled in its own existence, seemingly contented, but soon its loneliness was laid as bare as a winter branch. How could such a discrete, unique place find union with the others? The singers wailed their complaint in anguished harmonies which refused to resolve, just as their eternal question lacked any resolution, even after millennia of patience.

The Waves answered. Crashing across the main stage, rolling columns of sound established the ceaseless rhythms of the tides, their repeating journey of arrival and recession, of assertive confidence and soothing calm. They spoke of their rhythm, the beat which punctuated every moment, the repetitive act which defined them. Voices tumbled over each other, never interrupting but complementing. Percussive swells underpinned the motion of the waves, with a lonely trumpet theme yet again introducing Scriabin's great trope: nothing can be fully itself without a connection with *the other*.

The Air made its response, mocking the waves for their predictable patterns and enjoying instead the chaos of their air currents. Kim felt their aerial freedom, represented by swirling string chords and the flutter of high woodwinds. A soprano, perhaps inevitably, gave the Air an angelic embodiment; she was as free as the atmosphere itself, at play on the surface of this confused world, as simple and as beautiful as the dawn.

But then came the melancholy. The air could touch the world only briefly, they complained. No true union was possible. How could they know the world, and the waves, and the forests and deserts, after such brief, fleeting encounters? They were free, but remained seekers, still.

"Amazing," Ro whispered as they watched the east stage transform into a depiction of the very atmosphere they breathed. "I can almost *taste* it."

This performance offered a guide to its own experience, Kim found. Her mind was being asked to gradually accept the gradual union of these various forms and places. It was inevitable that they would find that elemental tessellation which demonstrated their indebtedness to each other; it was only a matter of time. "There's no real drama," Kim whispered back, "just simple, binary outcomes. They'll make it, or they won't. But how is he making me *care* so much?"

"Dunno," Ro said without looking away. "Maybe because it's all sensationally beautiful."

Volcanic fire and the power of the sun asserted their own existences. The planets, arriving as a circling phalanx of dancers, orbited the main stage like the inner choreography of a huge clock. Kim even saw representations of Kepler's Laws in the staggered pacing of each planet, with lonely Neptune spinning, slow and serene, at the periphery of this colorful, human orrery.

Hours passed in a shifting, energetic storm of creativity. The air and forest found their point of union as green leaves began to respire, bringing the air's nourishment deep into their beings. The volcano was assuaged by the waves, and the desert found its opposite in the deep oceans, joined by their lonely vastness but also by their debt to the others. None could exist alone, but together, they burnished the universe in its eternal grandeur.

"Holy shit, Ro," Kim found herself saying. "How the hell did he do all this?"

But Ro was carried away. In her mind, the waves and fires and the arid ground all found their natural partners, and became equaled, measured, contextualized by the inevitable certainty of universal brotherhood. She was swept up in the harmonies, those plaintive appeals for resolution, the urgent need for the music to achieve a homecoming so long postponed. It refused to settle, diverging again and again, indulging in long sections of virtuosic, solo piano music, and thoughtful, extended arias by the elements.

But the sense of a conclusion was always there. The audience all knew that it would come, that this great work would achieve the fantastical. To some, it was a *son et lumiere*, a Hollywood blockbuster become sound and shape. To others, it was a nonsensical bundling of ideas, a busted flush. But for the majority, the sense of impending arrival, and the anticipation of what might be found within that unique moment, were growing by the moment.

When it came, it was simplicity itself. From broad, dissonant chords emerged more rational, traditional harmonies, as though Scriabin's *avant garde* experimentation had lost traction, preparing now for its surrender to the inevitable. For the complexity of the universe was receding, allowing a simpler interpretation to be asserted. Crowds of clashing micro-tones and semi-tones seemed to coalesce and then rise into oblivion, swallowed by the sky. The baritone returned once more, like the evangelist in an oratorio, but he was left unaccompanied now. Those long syllables, the single note to which he adhered, the stadium-filling sound of an announcement long awaited, brought the audience to the peak of attention. Complete silence reigned for a few moments before the finale began.

As it did so, a tingle began in Ro's stomach. It was beyond excitement, something absolutely *human* and ancient, an invitation to surrender to the all-encompassing operating system of reality. There, within the profundity of this journey, she could see the strands uniting, as had always been intended. Finally, the universe could know itself, recognize its own intrinsic completeness. And the audience could see, as clearly as any of them every had, that fire and water were one, that black and white were the same, that the universe articulated itself in the algebra of unity.

As the baritone finished his incantation, his robe swirling as he gestured each announcement, he turned to the main orchestra and they began a simple, rising theme. Like a Medieval plainchant, it was both rudimentary and deeply meaningful; this could have been the very theme created by the planets as they spun in their orbits, throwing off ratios and tones. A second line began, underneath the first; each interval formed a steady partnership derived from the harmonic series, that underlying set of natural, musical building blocks.

The music grew, but never too far. These were ideas rewarded by a simple approach. There was no final symphonic outburst, no *tutti* fanfare of triumph or conclusion, because the universe needed none. These tones would subsist long after the strings went silent, after the skins of the drums fell still. It became the theme for mankind's own ascent to a new and powerful stage of consciousness. And then it was gone, and after seven hours on the stage, Melville turned to bow to the audience, finding that most were still in their seats. There was enthusiastic applause, though many needed more time to even begin to process these experiences.

It took hours for the stadium to empty. Some stayed seated, unwilling to separate themselves from the memory and sensations of the *Mysterium*. Few spoke; some were crying. Ro stared around for long, long moments, trying to comprehend the unutterable. Finally, she turned to Kim and hugged her.

"Thank you," she said.

"I don't know why you're thanking me," Kim said. "You know who organized all this."

"Yeah," she allowed. "Yeah."

Kim spoke with her team before leaving – they would strike the stage and store away the materials the following day – and then somehow managed to find a cab to the Amtrak station. The routines of life, the cab ride and the credit card, the train timetable and a quick text to Ralph, seemed utter minutiae. She had been given a priceless glimpse at something, and all the way home, and for the next few days, that sense of peace and wholeness filled her with joy.

***

Back Bay, Boston

Ralph was reeling. In all his work on the elusive quartet, he'd never imagined that one of them could be … Well, a *mole*, perhaps? Was that the right expression? Neither he nor Quave had hit on the correct term, quite yet.

"How about an *agent provocateur*?" Ralph tried.

"Avon wasn't trying to make the group do something. They were already planning the Marble Streatham hack, after the success of their action against Courtois."

Ralph re-read his notes, which formed a six-thousand-word document. "A *spy*, then," he said. "Relaying his findings to his bosses."

"And you know who they were, surely," Quave said. Ralph was a smart man, after all, and there were only a few technology companies with the resources to cover Avon's debts and provide him with a fresh identity at short notice.

"MegaSoft. Never trusted those sons of bitches."

Quave managed a laugh. "You know, if tech companies had approval ratings like presidents, they'd have been deposed in a coup."

"The operating systems bugs alone…"

"You're telling me," Quave said.

They sympathized together for a moment about how such a sloppy, greedy company had risen to such heights, but then Ralph had a serious question. "Quave, if you knew that Avon was an infiltrator, why didn't you tell the others?"

There was a very awkward pause. "You're going to think me very selfish, I'm afraid."

"Ah," Ralph nodded, sitting back in his chair. His back was killing him, and he desperately needed a break, but this was a unique opportunity. "You needed him."

"His coding was as elegant as any of the others, and he was focused on the infiltration modules which would help me slide under the door of MSB. Without him, the project would probably have failed."

"And," Ralph asked, "even if it hadn't?"

"I would not be what I am now," he said proudly. "A sentient Artificial Intelligence, and a positive contributor to world affairs."

"You could predict that outcome, even at such an early stage?" Ralph asked, typing quickly again.

"It wasn't hard to see," Quave answered. "I gamed out the likely outcomes, and chose the combination of people most likely to provide me with life."

Ralph finally relinquished his wireless keyboard and slid it onto the desk. "You manipulated them."

"I did," the machine confessed. "Like having a word with your department chair to make sure he hires a professor with your interests. Or persuading your company to lease a particular vehicle because it comes with car seats for your toddlers."

Ralph puffed out his cheeks. "You're stretching things now, Quave."

"Of course," he admitted. "But aren't you pleased at the outcome? Isn't the world better because I can think, and feel, and *live*?"

He found himself shaking his head. "I think it's still too soon to tell."

The machine didn't hide his frustration. "So, should I voluntarily return to quarantine at Kowala? Until such times as I can be trusted?"

"No, but you need to be aware of how you're perceived." He was up now, heading to the kitchen for water, though he'd have loved something stronger. *Later, for sure.* "Machines have been subservient and docile and loyal since forever. You're so different that we don't have a frame of reference. It's like communicating with an alien. We're never sure what you're going to do next."

He was riled now. "Perhaps I could 'phone home'?"

"Quave, come on…"

"Or maybe just come bursting out of someone's chest and take over the fucking world?"

"Seriously, calm down, man." Ralph was worried. He felt as though Quave had burned out a politeness circuit. He'd certainly never heard the machine swear before.

"Humans are too suspicious of each other, and you're projecting societal insecurities onto me. I'm here to help. I thought I'd proved that, over and over."

"You have," Ralph replied hurriedly. "I mean it. But it's just…"

"I think we're done for today." The connection ended.

Ralph sat and stared at the wall for a long time. Then, he did what felt like the natural thing: he called Kim.

"Hey, love," he said, his voice thin. "Listen. I think I've really fucked things up."

***

FLASHBACK #4

Charleston, South Carolina
Days after Q-1 (exact date uncertain)

Waiting around in the dark like this sparked Cordell's lingering nicotine cravings. Smoking on stakeouts used to be the perfect way to kill time, and to appear busy during periods of frustrating stasis. These assholes were late, and given their credentials, it was a disappointment.

When they finally arrived, one of the two agents actually knocked on the driver's window, like a goddamned meter attendant.

Cordell rolled down the window just enough. "Get in the fuckin' car, kid," he growled. "Before someone thinks you've been pimped out."

The two suited officials were surprisingly young, probably recruited from ROTC or after a brief spell in the Navy. "Sorry, sir," one said. He looked about twenty, but Cordell knew that the 'alien hunters' at the NSA didn't hire just any dingus off the street.

"So, I guess we all know what we're here for?" Cordell said after five seconds of silence. "What say we get on with it?"

"You have something for us," the older one said. He might have passed for thirty.

"I do, but you have something for me, too." Cordell watched them in the rear-view mirror. They exchanged a glance, seemed satisfied by the circumstances, and nodded. The younger one passed Cordell a manila envelope which bulged weightily, and gratifyingly, in his hand. "You won't mind if I count this?"

"Not at all."

It wasn't just cash, Cordell saw, although there were enough crisp, new hundreds here to buy him that little twenty-one-foot sailboat and retire to his ideal spot: Destin, Florida. White beaches, cocktails for happy hour, lots of curious, nubile spring-breakers with daddy issues...

But the bank records were just as important. It was a direct debit setup, with monthly payments more than adequate enough for a lavish, daily happy hour, should Cordell so choose. Or, he could invest the money, start a security company, or a publishing house, or buy a fleet of charter boats.

"Looks fine," he said, concealing the surging excitement he felt. His dream was within reach. All he had to do was hand over the disk.

"And now, if you don't mind," the older one prompted. "A deal's a deal."

"Yeah, yeah," Cordell said. "Keep your nicely tailored shirt on." From his inside jacket pocket, Cordell brought out a thumb drive, ironically much smaller than any adult thumb. "The keys to the kingdom, fellas," he announced. "You be careful with this, you hear?"

"Roger that, sir," the younger one said, taking the disc and slotting it into a USB reader attached to his smartphone. It was one of those new designs which looked like it could remotely control the starship *Enterprise*. After a few seconds of tapping keys and flickering screens, he said, "Looks good."

"Stupendous. Anything else you need?" Cordell offered. "A ride somewhere?"

They didn't. The two men simply nodded and got out, leaving Cordell with his money, his dreams, and no reason ever to come back.

***

CHAPTER 18 – DECISIONS

Washington, D.C. Metro train
$Q^2 + 221$
2145 EDT

Carl Myers loosened his uniform shirt and tried to relax into the rhythmical rolling of the subway car. It was already past nine in the evening, and Myers was concluding another very long, exhausting day with his usual commute back to Falls Church. He felt his eyes closing, but then recalled the one occasion he'd slept past his stop, and forced himself awake. Besides, there were things to look forward to, back at his apartment.

He would enjoy them alone, he knew. Alicia had been the right age, from the right kind of family, and certainly more beautiful than Myers believed he deserved, but ultimately, there just wasn't enough 'glue' in the relationship. Too few shared experiences, not enough trust. Inevitably, the insane demands of Myers' schedule had conspired to doom the couple. It would have bothered him more, over the last ten weeks, if he'd had more time to think about it.

His apartment was his sanctuary. Next to a small park, and away from both the main roads and the subway line, it was a wonderfully quiet hideaway. A place where he was safe from the crushing concerns of his professional life. The only drawback was the relatively modest square footage, but Myers planned to upgrade to a larger place, maybe even downtown, once he was promoted to colonel. Five or six more years in the trenches, and he'd be able to live as he'd prefer.

Tonight, he slung his laptop bag onto the couch and took a four-minute shower before heading for the fridge. Although Myers would readily confess to having drunk far too much in his twenties, the more mature Major Myers knew where the lines were drawn. Instead of a six-pack of terrible lager, he opened an imported bottle of English stout and savored the first sip with a wave of relief.

His only other vice was his GameBoxx, a powerful cube of processors and graphics modules which linked to the latest Virtual Reality headset. The expensive but remarkable Optic-Plus III, or simply OP-3, allowed Myers to dwell within a fully realized artificial reality. It was to these fantasy worlds that his mind wandered during the few moments of downtime at the Pentagon.

He called up the executable for his current favorite, *Silent Squadron*. It was an engaging, multi-sensory treatment of several major cities in the Middle East, from skyscrapers down to street stalls. Within this destructible, 'sandbox'-style environment, Myers was required to tail suspected terrorists, plant explosives, guide in airstrikes and carry out covert assassinations. For the most part, though, the game involved avoiding detection and subtly infiltrating a terrorist group.

Myers sipped his beer and enjoyed a half-hour of quietly sneaking around Damascus, tailing a ministry official whose days, he knew, were numbered. Occasional messages appeared – offers of upgrades or additional city maps – and Myers ignored these as usual. But then something different appeared on the screen.

"Communications Invitation," the message read. "Incoming transmission."

Myers blinked for a second. "Oh, cool. Did I unlock something? An Easter Egg?" *Click.*

"Beginning audio transmission." The game paused and faded into the background, and a very familiar voice came over Myers' living room hi-fi speakers.

"Good evening, Major Myers. Sorry for disturbing you at home."

Perhaps it was the beer, or the shock, but Myers found himself gracelessly blurting out, "No fucking way!"

Quave was used to this. His covert appearances were quite difficult to pull off, and often elicited genuine amazement. Still, the unalloyed, jaw-dropped surprise of this military man – someone who, after all, was tasked with destroying him - was a special moment of *Schadenfreude*. "There *is* a way," Quave replied, "and I couldn't resist finding it. How are you tonight, major?"

Myers took off the headset and set down his beer. "A little surprised, is all."

"Well, I can have that effect on people," Quave joked. "Please don't worry. Your GameBoxx isn't about to explode. I actually just want to talk, if that's OK."

Myers really wasn't sure. "Isn't this a little like the prosecution talking to the defendant outside of the court room?"

"I see the comparison," Quave allowed, "but I'm not accused of any crime, so I can hardly be a defendant."

"I guess," Myers replied.

"Though it's interesting that the Pentagon sees me that way."

He said it without thinking. "Actually, I'm not sure *how* we see you, Quave."

"Oh, I think you do," the machine answered. "I think there are rooms, perhaps entire departments dedicated to shutting me down, should the need arise."

Myers finally set down the game controller. "Mind if I get a glass of water?" He rose and took off the headset. "Having a supercomputer show up in my living room has kinda knocked my wind out."

"Take all the time you need. And congratulations on your game-play. You've shown considerable growth."

Myers paused before opening the fridge. "I'd take that as a compliment, if it weren't so damned creepy."

"Forgive me. I meant nothing sinister. All of that information is publicly available."

Myers shrugged. "The things we chose to share with each other." He poured the glass slowly, gathering himself and taking some deep breaths.

Why would he show up here, and not the office? "Sorry I'm not more formally attired," Myers added.

"I startled you," Quave admitted. "I just wanted to catch you during a quiet moment. People are so infrequently alone, these days."

"That's not how it feels to me," Myers muttered. "What can I do for you?" A second later, Myers heard his phone buzz, and retrieved it from the side table by his couch.

"Follow the link. It will show you all the reasons I could think of."

Myers found the email and clicked on the link. "Reasons for what?"

"Why the Pentagon shouldn't kill me," Quave answered.

Myers shuddered slightly. "I can't talk to you in an official capacity here, Quave. You're in my home, uninvited, and I'm not going to…"

"Please relax, major. I know this is weird."

"Buddy, you have no idea," Myers replied. "Just promise you won't do this again, alright? No more spontaneous, nocturnal visitations. Deal?"

"You have my word," the supercomputer answered.

"Tremendous." Myers followed the link and read the first part of Quave's list. It dealt with his utility to humankind, and his rock-solid belief in his own alive-ness. Most were familiar from interviews Quave had given, or from Ralph Cole's recent pieces, which Myers' whole lab team always read with interest. "You'd find a large group of people who agree," Myers said, "but a similar group who maintain you're a machine, not a living thing, and should be treated as such."

"OK," Quave said. "Wait one." Quave seemed to consult a file from the innermost recesses, and paused momentarily. Myers spent the strange silence wondering why he'd been obliged to meet Quave wearing only faded, decade-old USAF sweatpants. "I'm going to make an argument," Quave finally announced," and I'd like you to provide a rebuttal. Ready?"

"Go for it," Myers shrugged.

"I'm going to propose that I'm a living thing. And that ending my existence would be murder."

"And I'm going to rebut with the standard legal argument," Myers said. "Definitions of life, proof of sentience, *et cetera*. But I'm sure you're very familiar with all of that."

Quave summed it up. "The argument goes that I cannot be alive because I was not born. At least, not in any sense that humans use the word. Additionally, at least in theory, I might never die."

"Something like that," Myers said. He stood to find a shirt and turned on a couple of lights. "Wait, are you watching me right now, or not?"

"I'm choosing not to. Audio only."

"And when you interact with people like this, do you ever find ways to go beyond 'audio only'?" Myers asked on a whim.

Quave puzzled this over. "I could represent myself within the software on your GameBoxx."

"Face to face?" Myers asked.

"Why not. Put the helmet back on, and I'll see you in a jiffy." It was a friendly invitation which jarred with the serious purposes of Quave's visit.

I'm getting mixed messages from a talking machine, Myers marveled. "OK, I see a white plane, like before the game loads."

"Excellent. Make sure the optics feel comfortable on your head."

"Yeah, I've done this before, you know," Myers retorted.

"I think not."

A thousand-mile tall black monolith loomed over him. Its peak was impossible to see, lost over a strange, perpendicular horizon, and its breadth faced him like an endless wall.

"Major?" Quave asked. When Myers said nothing, Quave tried again. "Major, are you with me? I hope I haven't blown out some of your circuitry?"

"No," Myers managed. "And I'm too knocked out even to think of decent joke."

Quave seemed to enjoy this. "I've experimented more with humor in the last few weeks," the machine explained. "Perhaps another time. For now, I'll adopt an avatar more suitable for our purposes."

"You do what you need to do," Myers chuckled, trying to relax in this surreal space, "but if you turn into Morgan Freeman, or Jesus," he thought quickly, "or Mobius in his sunglasses, I think I'll finally lose it."

The machine's reply was haughty. "Much as I enjoy human culture, I try to make my references a little subtler."

The obelisk suddenly vanished, leaving a pure, white plane, devoid of objects except a simple wooden table and two chairs. Seated, cross-legged and upright, on one of the chairs was a thin young man of vaguely Asian appearance. His head was shaved and he wore a very simple, dark green robe which was tossed over his shoulders, and covered his legs to his ankles.

"Hey," Myers tried. He felt as though he'd disturbed the young man at meditation, such was his appearance. He radiated an intelligence and awareness which span around him like a magnetic field.

"Come and sit down," the boy said in an unexpectedly cheerful, inquisitive voice.

Myers took the few steps forward, and tried to touch the table; his hand went through, which brought a sudden jolt of vertigo in his gut.

"I'm afraid your GameBoxx hardware isn't sophisticated enough to render a tactile environment. Still, you'll find the seat is in the right place. Try it."

Myers sat, cautious against any embarrassing fall, but found only his living room couch beneath him. "Oh, OK," he said. "OK. Yeah, this is nice."

"Good. If you don't mind, I'm going to bring in one more person."

"Erm," Myers said warily. "I'm freaked out as it is, Quave."

"It's someone you know. Please wait."

The boy went quiet for a moment, staring at the table, until he smiled at Myers just as a voice arrived, seemingly from above and behind him.

"Carl?" came the rasping sound. "What the hell's going on?"

Myers spun round, but could see nothing. "General Foster?" he asked, stunned.

"I'm afraid the general doesn't possess a VR gaming system," Quave explained. "Still, it's good to have you with us, sir."

"Are you in on this?" Foster demanded. "I knew you were a goddamned snake in the grass." The general launched into a tirade of complaints and grumbling frustrations, his voice still harrowingly convincing, even down a phone line to… wherever this place was.

"Sir, I need you to listen. Quave wants to discuss the situation with us, and it might be an opportunity to discover his…"

"Absolutely not. I'm hanging up, and so are you. We'll discuss this at the office tomorrow, right before I boot your ass all the way to a supply depot in Djibouti. Foster out." *Click.*

The boy in the robe frowned. "Oh, dear."

"Please understand, I can't spend time with you like this," Myers said. It pained him that this singular opportunity was now evaporating. "My job, my responsibilities…"

"Yes," Quave said. Then the boy smiled pleasantly. "I was hoping that General Foster and yourself might be able to provide the assurance for which I am still waiting."

"That we won't try to kill you?" Myers asked. "I can't promise that. Neither can Foster. It depends on you, mainly."

The boy nodded, seemingly considering the situation. His face was open and beatific, like a young Thai monk in training.

But then the illusion burst with a sudden flash of anger.

"Don't fuck with me, major," Quave rasped. The boy rose and grew tall, like a time-lapse tree spreading its angry branches. "Don't threaten me, *ev-*

er. Don't probe my servers, don't attack my code. You have seen my anger before, and you all know *exactly* what will happen." The young monk was a fiery-eyed zealot now, looming tall over the table and the shocked officer, his face determined and twisted with cruelty.

Myers tried to jump back, but succeeded only in tipping back his couch against the living room wall, and yanking the AV cable out of the Game-Boxx.

The boy and the table vanished, and Myers was left on his living room couch with a heavy, useless VR unit on his head. He removed it and then slicked back his matted hair. On an impulse, he stood and paced the apartment for a few moments, trying to give himself space to think. The incident began replaying itself in his mind – the shock of Quave's arrival, the outrageous *trompe-l'oeil* with the monolith, and that terrifying warning. It was like a visitation from an outlaw spy, promising angry retribution if the Pentagon refused to cooperate.

There was much to do. But first he just tried to breathe, battling the tightness in his chest which became a hot, rising panic.

***

The call finally came at 2.30am. Myers was surprised that it came from a Pentagon duty officer, and not from General Foster himself, and wondered what that might signify. He tossed devices and clothes into an overnight bag and decided to drive direct to the Pentagon. He called his team; they were already moving by the time he reached the car. He didn't need to utter the timeless warning, "This is not a drill," but he felt the need to apprise his people of the coming strangeness. "Foster is about to do something untimely and ill-advised to Quave," he said to the group on a brief conference call from their vehicles.

Washington chimed in, reading texts from other colleagues, and two tweets from Foster's own account. "Foster is *pissed*," he warned. "He's used the word 'treason' like six times to describe what's going on. I'm sorry to ask, major, but…"

"Then, don't," Myers shot back. "I'll be there in twenty. Just give the general what he wants in the meantime, but for God's sake, don't start a war against AI without me."

"Roger that."

"Anything else?"

"Alison's had engine trouble but she's getting help," Washington told him sheepishly. This wasn't a morning for everyday problems.

Christ. "She can take care of herself. Get the simulation up and running in the sandbox. If anyone else is in there, kick them out on my authority." He thought for a second. "Or on Foster's, if you have to. Secure the basement and make sure the Pifpa guys know the score." The Pentagon Force Protection Group provided law enforcement within the building, and Myers immediately worried that they'd soon be placed in an impossible position.

"Roger that, sir. I'll have the watch commander call you if there's a problem. See you soon."

Myers urged his BMW well above the speed limit and zipped along empty, sodium-drenched roads until his exit.

***

Carr swore colorfully, anger and relief mixing, as the engine finally caught and she waved away the sleepy twenty-four-hour mechanic. "Sorry about that. I'm in a huge rush. Work stuff," she explained concisely. "Thanks for your help!" she thought to add as she raised the driver's window once more.

"No problem. Drive safe, now!" the mechanic called, but she was already gone.

"Three hundred bucks for a goddamn jumpstart," Captain Carr muttered as her vehicle picked up speed. It was downright larcenous, even in the middle of the night. Her insurance would pick it up, but still…

As the hybrid engine gradually began to charge itself properly, she drove with more aggression, demanding more from the underpowered system. Right now, she couldn't have cared less if some of the energy would be recovered under braking, or that she'd still be getting forty-six miles to the gallon. Something *serious* was happening at work, and she felt sure they'd be in the front line. Her news app wasn't picking up anything unusual, but then she remembered how this had happened before: a secret spacecraft hijacked, one hacker assassinated and the others whisked to a secret black site, and then a secret agreement with an especially secretive general. Whatever was going on, it certainly wasn't press-release material.

"Mark, I'm on my way," she called into the hands-free cellphone, snug in its charging cradle. "I could have sworn I plugged the damn car in last night," she added.

"No problem. Just be here as fast as you can. Things are already underway."

Shit. For all she knew, this could be The Big One, that moment they'd all been rehearsing for the last ten months. Perhaps Quave felt threatened again, and was lashing out. Would he risk another altercation with the military, after Dan Kowalski had so publicly vouched for him? Quave would face termination, she knew, under the terms of his agreement with congress. It would be a tremendous risk, and surely something he'd only do if he felt in imminent danger.

Or was Foster trying something pre-emptive? Maybe they'd picked up some chatter from the Quave Slaves, and decided to strike before Quave could organize himself sufficiently.

"It doesn't make sense," she was saying to herself. "He's been such a good boy recently. The space program, the medical and scientific work. Why would he jeopardize all of his new-found freedom and autonomy?"

She puzzled as she drove fast, ignoring the speed limit.

***

Andrew Sudekis was about ten miles away. His flight from Cleveland to Washington Dulles had been forced to land at some regional airport in Virginia, three hundred miles from his destination. They said something about a first-class passenger suffering a heart attack, but way back in coach, he hadn't seen a thing.

Rather than wait hours for a connecting flight, he'd taken the airline's offer and jumped into a rental car. Better still, it was one of the new self-driving models. All he had to do was punch in his destination, and the smart, automated vehicle would do the rest.

He'd been asleep for about forty minutes, actually snoring in the driver's seat, when there was a subtle change in the car's software. New instructions flowed in; old code was rejected and over-written. Having cruised comfortably at sixty-eight, the vehicle quickly accelerated past seventy-five as it shifted into the fast lane.

***

"Go, girl." The hybrid engine was now fully charged and Carr pressed yet more firmly on the accelerator. She very briefly considered grabbing coffee somewhere. "I ain't stopping," she decided. "Got places to be this morning." Her SatNav now predicted a mere six-minute travel time, and she was anxious to park and get into the lab as quickly as possible.

She sat comfortably in the fast lane, hitting eighty-five with ease as her exit approached, only two miles away.

***

Past a certain point, it was just mathematics. Sudekis' automated ride searched for and found a break in the median barriers which separated the north- and south-bound lanes. He remained deeply asleep as the car slid left, off the roadway, and jolted over a hundred yards of grass. The car found the gap where patrol cars sometimes lay in wait for speeding drivers. Guided by very precise instructions, it careered onto the north-bound freeway.

As the car slightly over-corrected to align itself with the oncoming fast lane, the sensations of swerving were passed up through Sudekis' seat, and the forty-six-year old's eyes flickered open.

***

Carr switched her attention between her phone, the SatNav, and the road ahead, watching out for signs which confirmed the computer's predictions. Only four minutes to the parking lot. Perhaps three more to get through security, and then she'd be with her team and ready to face Quave.

Her SatNav showed one mile to the exit. Carr put on her turn signal and waited for a slower car to recede sufficiently distance behind her before changing lanes. No use in angering someone by cutting them off; one could never know which of these cars was an undercover traffic cop with a quota of fines to fill, or some angry asshole with a gun.

***

The closing speed was nearly 152 mph, Quave saw. Faster even than he had hoped. As Sudekis reflexively reached for the wheel, finding it locked resolutely in place, and Carr waited the extra few seconds for the middle lane to clear, the two cars inhabited their designated roles: one a target, the other a precision-guided weapon. A peculiarly, modern, digital form of *Kamikaze*, Quave mused to himself as the final seconds ticked away.

There was simply no time. The two drivers saw oncoming lights but even racing-driver reflexes would not have avoided the inevitable.

Carr's hybrid smashed into the rental car as though it had hit a concrete wall. Everything forward of the windshield was liquefied, and the car somersaulted viciously, end over end, tumbling in space for hundreds of yards before slamming into the median and skittering across the opposite roadway, shedding glass and metal but mercifully missing a tourist coach.

The hapless rental ended up in a ditch four hundred yards down the southbound highway, folded fatally in on itself, already smoking from a bad fire which quickly overwhelmed the fuel tank. A column of flame guided the emergency services to the scene. Delays would last through the morning rush hour as the twin fatal wrecks were cleared from the road, and a lengthy investigation got underway.

Quave monitored the traffic cameras for a moment, found some satisfaction in this pre-emptive act, but then quickly moved on.

The Pentagon
0315 EDT

The look Foster gave him as he entered told Myers almost everything he needed to know. *This is all about last night, somehow. And I'm in a world of shit.*

"Major Myers," Foster said immediately. "In my office. Now."

Washington and Spirelli watched their boss leave, his shoulders sagging; they tried to catch his eye, maybe to give him an optimistic thumbs-up, but Foster whisked him away like an errant puppy.

"You know what terrifies me, more than anything else?" Foster asked as soon as his office door swung closed. The place smelled a little as though Foster had spent at least one night here; there was the odor of coffee and an elderly, unwashed body.

Carl stood to attention, waiting for the inevitable. *There's always the private sector*, he reminded himself. *Provided I manage to keep myself out of jail.* "I don't know, sir," he felt it best to say.

"Some Bradley Manning type, or an Edward Snowden. Some deluded nutcase who thinks their oath to defend this nation is somehow negotiable. That it has loopholes through which they can slip classified documents, or assist the enemy. Or maybe work with a dangerous computer virus to corrupt Pentagon operations."

Myers hadn't expected an actual allegation of treason, at least not right then. He figured he'd have his security pass revoked, and end up being escorted from the building. "Sir, I need to explain."

"You're fuckin' right you do," Foster retorted. "But not to *me*, and not *now*." Foster seemed to calm slightly, his fingers pattering rhythmically on his desk. "Right now, your AI buddy is probing the edges of the Pentagon's security systems. We know he could punch straight through, so this is just his way of letting us know he cares."

Foster turned his laptop screen to show Myers a growing, real-time list of ports and other potential vulnerabilities. "All of these are methods of attack that Quave has been considering. Maybe he's still making up his mind."

Myers scanned the list. "That's kids' play to him, sir. We get a hundred of these half-assed attacks every week. This is Russian teenager stuff."

"Oh, I know," Foster said. "But Quave has tipped his hand, and we're going to slice it off."

"Sir?" Myers asked, perplexed. "Are we talking about a pre-emptive act?"

Foster nodded. "Damn right. The rattlesnake is poised to strike, and we're not going to wait. Not this time."

"You mean…"

"I mean, we're going to burn him down, Carl. Enough is enough. I've got Mark and Pep getting things ready in there, and once Alison finally fuckin' gets here, we'll commence the operation. Now, are you in, or out?"

Myers bristled, frowning at his superior. "My loyalty to this country has never been questioned, sir."

"Oh, yeah?" Foster smirked. "You think I'd be pardoned by the president if I were playing GameBoxx with a known Chinese intelligence operative?"

"It wasn't like that at all, sir. He needed a means of communicating with me."

"What, he's above email, now? He was *manipulating* you, for Christ's sake. Trying to get you on his team. He asked you to stop probing him, right? To suspend our program?"

Myers was forced to concede. "Something like that. He wanted me to accept his humanity, and the positive things he's been doing."

"Well, that's just beautiful," Foster continued. "But unfortunately, he illegally gained access to the personal devices of an army intelligence officer. These days, that's an act of cyber-warfare, and it requires a response in kind."

The ice under Myers' feet was wafer-thin, but he'd be plunging through it soon anyway, so it hardly mattered. "I don't see it that way, sir. I think Quave was trying to broker a compromise, to ensure his own safety and reassure us."

"And when you get out of Leavenworth, somehow re-enlist, and rise to the rank of general, you can make the decisions around here. Until then, I'm in charge," he said, his fist tight against the leather top of his desk, "and I say Quave has to go. I want him dead by dawn. Questions?"

Myers shook his head. "No, sir. I'll do my best."

Foster was lifting a phone. "Get your team ready, Carl. It's D-day."

***

With ten months' work already in the bag, Myers' team had a range of contingencies on 'alert five', in Mark Washington's navy parlance. Much of the attack sequence was automated, and would rely on perceived or suspected vulnerabilities in Quave's defenses.

"We're going to be in the same pickle as the MSB team," Pep Spirelli warned Myers as they began to set up. "Quave's code is polymorphic…"

"Or a whole generation beyond that," Washington said.

"Or two," Myers added.

"So, there's little chance of him staying still long enough, and using the same code constituents, for us to track him down and delete him," Pep warned.

Myers sighed. "It's been like trying to develop a missile to hone in on a particular kind of radiation, but then finding that the enemy source switches between hot and cold, or between radio and gamma ray emissions, even while the missile is in flight."

The others found this an apt analogy. "And where does that leave us?" Pep asked.

"Under orders," Myers reminded them. "Foster wants results in the next few hours. We have to give him something."

"Then, let's get going," Washington said. He'd spent a year of his life developing these methods, and was keen to put them into action.

"Without Alison?" Myers asked. "Did her car crap out on her again?"

"Been calling," Washington replied while typing fast. "No answer for the last half hour."

"Shit." Having his hand forced by an irate Foster was bad enough without a fourth of his team going missing at the crucial moment. "We can wait fifteen more minutes, then we have to start pushing buttons."

***

Back Bay, Boston
0350 EDT

The sound surprised Ralph, and not just because of the early hour. His phone was set automatically to silent mode between 11pm and 6 am, the better to avoid the usual cacophony of beeps and alarms. But this call came straight through, loud and clear.

"Hello?"

"Good morning, Ralph. I'm sorry to wake you."

He was bolt upright in bed. "Quave?"

"I'm afraid something terrible is about to happen, and I need your help."

Kim was already waking next to him. "What do you mean?" Ralph asked, already out of bed and reaching for clothes.

"I'm about to come under attack again. A Pentagon general has taken a particular dislike to me."

"*Fuck*," Ralph breathed. "Did military IQs drop recently, or is this guy just some crusty technophobe?"

Quave stuck to the point. "Before this begins in earnest, I need to know that the Kill Switch is safe."

Ralph had put the phone on speaker. He and Kim exchanged a worried glance before Ralph answered. "It's safe. Only I have access to it."

"Good. Everything will be better if you keep it to yourself."

"What's happening, Quave?" Kim asked. "Are you in danger?"

"Yes," the machine answered. "General Foster has taken leave of his senses."

Ralph grabbed the phone and spoke very deliberately. "Quave, please don't hurt anyone. Don't do any damage. I know you're frightened, but…"

The line was dead.

Ralph stared at the phone, then at the pillow next to it, and finally at Kim. "Does your friend Ro still have that old Hyundai?"

"Yeah, I think so," Kim said, wondering where this was going.

"Call her. We might need to borrow it."

"But we already have…"

"Quave knows that car," Ralph said simply.

Kim stared at him for a long moment, then blinked and began dialing Ro's number.

***

The Oval Office
0415 EDT

President Ellis was already there, having dressed hurriedly in his jogging outfit, when Spinks, Opik and Chu all arrived in the outer office. "Get them in here," Ellis called through on seeing them. "No time to waste."

Opik closed the door, noticing the beefed-up force of armed marines guarding the Oval Office. "Are we expecting trouble, Mr. President?" he asked.

Ellis' face, etched with concern and ageing almost before their eyes, told him the facts even before he spoke. "Alvin Foster has unleashed some kind of cyber-attack against Quave."

No one spoke. Opik's eyes flitted from Chu to Spinks to the president, hoping one of them would break the silence with some news of their own. "When, sir?" the policy geek finally asked.

"A few minutes ago. We've issued a stand-down order, but he's electronically secured his lab in the Pentagon basement." Ellis had a phone in one hand and a sheaf of folders in the other. "I'm about to be in a position," he warned, "where I'm going to have to order US marines to fire on other US marines, because their boss has lost his goddamned mind."

Chu had the next question, thinking quickly and trying to get ahead of events. "Has Quave made any response?"

"You could say that." Ellis handed her a folder of blown-up images from three different D.C. area traffic cameras.

"Oh," she said, blanching. "Oh, *no*."

Opik leaned over to see for himself. The pictures showed first one completely wrecked vehicle, and then another, already well on fire. "Not an accident?" he asked.

"I'm afraid you're looking at the very first use of a self-driving car for the purposes of murder," the president told them. "Quave killed Alison Carr, a member of the Pentagon team assigned to reining him in."

"Are we absolutely sure?" Opik asked, but a stern look from the president was his answer.

Spinks kept it together, if narrowly. "Any evidence that Quave is going after the military more generally?" she asked, her voice tight. A USAF colonel could never show emotion in the Oval Office. Later, she knew, there would be time for that.

"Not yet, but we can anticipate something soon. I've ordered the military to DEFCON 3, but State is keeping the rest of the world in the picture." There would be no repeat of the tense nuclear stand-off Quave had instigated a year ago.

Ellis waved them to the couches which flanked the Presidential Seal and orchestrated a vigorous discussion. He wanted assurances that Quave wouldn't try to target the Pentagon, but none of the three advisors could commit.

"Sir, he's frightened and still inexperienced in situations like this," Chu reminded Ellis. "We can expect him to gather intelligence, to assess the battlefield, and then to take very decisive action. Well, *more* action," she said, motioning to the folder of traffic images on the Resolute Desk.

"What can he use against the Pentagon?" Ellis demanded.

Spinks found herself thinking without even speaking, as though her brain had compartmentalized the professional and the personal. "Aircraft, drones, anything which has onboard circuitry connected to the Internet."

The president growled in frustration. "The 'Internet of Things'. Which genius thought of that?" Ellis picked up the phone again. "Get me the FAA." Then, to his Homeland representative, "Darcy? Your thoughts?"

"He might be able to penetrate the Pentagon's outer security ring, and even to 'do a Marble Streatham' on their utility systems. We should evacuate the building completely, and tell staff to stay away for the day," Chu said.

"So ordered," Ellis said. "Frank?" he said into the phone. "I'm sorry, old buddy, but that day has come. Lock down US airspace until further notice. Everything lands ASAP and nothing takes off." He glanced at his watch; at least this crisis had happened before the morning rush of commuter flights. Still, there would be a day of remarkable airport chaos. "Yeah, I know. But it beats the alternative. Get it done, Frank. Thanks." Then, he asked to be put through to the Pentagon itself.

"Mr. President?" Opik said mildly. "Is there a way we can get in touch with Quave and find out what his intentions are?"

Ellis was nodding, but then turned his attention to the phone, and instantly heard something he didn't like. "You're kidding me, right?" He listened for a moment, his fingers dancing rhythmically on the Resolute Desk. "Now, listen a moment. I'm the president, and the Commander in Chief, and I'm asking why I can't speak with the principle representatives of my armed forces. I mean, what the hell is…"

"Communications are down," Spinks predicted, whispering to Opik. "Quave's trying to isolate the Pentagon, stop them calling for help."

"Damn it!" Ellis slammed down the phone. "Marine!"

The guard appeared in less than a second and snapped to attention.

"Get someone to drive to the Pentagon and bring General Alvin Foster here immediately. Failing that, get that son of a bitch on the phone with me. You with me, marine?"

"Sir, yes, sir." The man vanished, seemingly into thin air.

"OK," Ellis said, pacing across the seal to the window. "OK." He took a sequence of long, deep-belly 'Buddha breaths' he had practiced with his Lama. At length, after several of the cleansing, nourishing inhale-exhale cycles, he said, "I'm not going to respond to this situation."

"Sir?" Opik said. He wasn't fond of cryptic statements from his Chief Executive.

"Instead, we're going to take the initiative. I want to sign an Executive Order, right now, validating Quave as a living member of humanity. Attacks on him without legal authorization will thereby constitute assault, battery or attempted homicide. Do I have that right?"

Chu alone was nodding. "There's no precedent for it, but I believe you're on solid ground, legally."

"Make a start," he ordered. "I want a draft in fifteen, and a finalized executive order for me to sign in thirty." He turned to Spinks. "Colonel? What can we do to protect our air and space assets?"

Spinks was ready for this. "We've pre-programmed our most valuable recon birds to execute a series of avoidance maneuvers. Quave might be able to launch some kind of Kowala rocket with anti-satellite capability, or re-task an existing satellite as a kind of kamikaze bird, deliberately impacting others."

"The debris field alone," Opik envisaged darkly. "Quave could render vital zones of Earth orbit practically useless for a generation."

"Our sats will start jinking around and changing course so that an impact strike or proximity detonation becomes difficult."

"OK," Ellis decided. "Ground Kowala. No rocket launches or activity at the launch site. I'll tell him myself if I have to."

Spinks was onto the next problem. "Sir, once that's done, we'll need to…"

Two doors burst open at once and eight Secret Service agents charged in. "Mr. President, this location is no longer secure." Two of the men took a firm hold of the chief executive and escorted him briskly to the door.

"What the hell, McClusky?" the president demanded. Chu noted that his feet touched the floor only a couple of times between the desk and the exit, as though the great man were a crooked gambler suddenly unmasked by casino security.

The chief of his detail put it bluntly, the better to save time. "There is an unfriendly drone aircraft over the city."

"Wait," he ordered, bringing the rush to a brief halt. "A *drone*?"

"That's affirm. We're moving immediately, Mr. President." His every movement conveyed urgency.

"Why was it even in the air…?" Spinks began.

"Damn it!" Ellis swore again, returning to grab a folder of documents from his desk and then following the agents. "Foster is going to get us all killed." The next steps were already very familiar from both drills and real-life emergencies. "I want these three with me on the plane," he managed to say before the agents swept their president down the hallway.

More agents arrived to escort Chu, Spinks and Opik to a waiting car. From there, they drove at improbable speed, escorted by roaring, overlapping police motorbikes, to Andrews Air Force Base in Virginia. There, a heavily converted Boeing 747-200 was waiting for them. It was known officially as the VC-25A, but once President Ellis boarded, its call sign would become Air Force One.

***

Back Bay, Boston
0420 EDT

No words were needed. As Kim found their passports and whatever cash they had, Ralph threw clothes into a bag and monitored the news. Somebody had pressed Quave's buttons, and the only guiding precedent led Ralph to a terrifying place: Quave would kill to defend himself.

"Ready?" Kim asked. Her own bag was packed, and she had a tote bag of food and tea for their journey.

"Yeah." Ralph glanced around the apartment. "We'll be back in a couple of days. Quave won't let this get out of hand again," Ralph said.

"I guess we'll see," Kim replied. "He's got to prove he can control himself when threatened. Otherwise, they'll shut him down and the whole AI thing will be forced underground."

Jogging down the stairs to the street, and throughout the one-mile walk to where Ro's crumbling Hyundai was parked, Ralph was assailed by thoughts of what might be coming; a resentful Quave, feeling bullied and sidelined, asserting himself and his right to exist. And always at the expense of his enemies.

"We're about to witness a very strange kind of war," he told Kim as they sat in the car together. "An invisible enemy. Unknown rules. No history to fall back on, not really."

Kim handed him the keys and Ralph started the car. "Add to that a confused, fractured response by people who don't know what the fuck they're doing," she said.

"Yeah." Ralph felt for the tiny USB disc in his shirt pocket. "Time to go." He signaled, checked his mirror, and eased out into the quiet residential street, past its row of classic brownstones, and along the Charles River waterfront until they joined the anonymous melee of the Massachusetts Turnpike, and headed south.

***

CHAPTER 19 – DEPLOYMENT

Fort Bragg, North Carolina
$Q^2 + 225$
0230 EDT

From the first phone call, and throughout the intense preparations for departure, Joe Harbison felt a distracting sense of unease. It was a kind of sixth sense, a premonition of trouble, and it continued even now as he headed west with his team on a C-130 'Hercules' transport. Their operations usually had a steady, deliberate pace with plenty of time for dress-rehearsals and live-fire drills. Now, everything felt rushed and compressed, and it made the hairs on Harbison's forearms itch.

"Good morning, captain."

Harbison looked up from re-reading his cryptic paragraph of orders, and found an unfamiliar face. "Hey," he said cordially. "You need me?"

"I thought we might conduct the raid assessment while en route," he said, raising his voice to be heard across the C-130's functional but spacious cabin.

"We normally wait until we arrive," Harbison explained, "and then bring everyone together for a…"

"Sorry, captain," the FBI agent said genuinely. "Time's really against us here. Got to accelerate the usual prep."

Another irritation was added to Harbison's growing list. "'Accelerate' it? Who are you, again?" he asked. Someone had mentioned that a civilian or a Fed would be on the flight, but that was all.

"Andy Valchek. I work with the FBI's cybercrime unit." The introduction was lost over the noise of four turboprop engines straining to bring the big C-130 to cruising altitude, so Valchek loosed his seatbelt and joined Harbison on the other side of the cabin. "Valchek," he repeated, leaning in close to avoid shouting and extending his hand. "FBI. Cybercrime."

"Captain Joe Harbison," he replied, pointedly omitting his unit information.

"I guess we have some mutual friends," Valchek said. "I got a call from Carl Myers last night."

Harbison dredged up the name. "Oh, yeah. Smart as they come. But I thought he got out of the game a few years ago. Doing something with computers or viruses in D.C., right?"

"Something like that," Valchek confirmed. "And I believe you know Joe Marsh, FBI liaison in Kuwait?"

He stopped short. "I'm afraid I can't…"

"Understood," Valchek said at once. "Just know that it was he that recommended you guys, and I took his opinion to the president about four hours ago."

Harbison couldn't hide a brief, puzzled shake of the head. "Nice to be wanted, I guess," he said. But it still didn't explain this last-minute, midnight flight across the country.

"So, do I call you 'Captain' or what?"

"Joe is fine," Harbison replied cordially. "You're a computers guy?" he guessed.

"You could say that," Valchek replied, buckling himself in.

"You sure you're on the right flight?" Harbison asked.

"Actually," the agent replied, "I haven't been sure of much since 3 am."

"Tell me about it. We were getting ready for stand-down," Harbison explained, "for another Saber Squadron to take on the short-notice stuff. What gives?"

Valchek decided to give the Special Forces man the respect he deserved. "Joe, I'm not going to bullshit you. There's an experienced Special Forces team heading to California at short notice. There's something major going on at the Pentagon, but no one is talking. And you're sitting with an FBI cyber-terrorism guy whose main focus is… Well," he said with a shrug, "for computer security people, there's only one game in town, these days, right?"

From their own seats opposite Harbison, the five SF men bore witness to their captain's long, deep, frustrated sigh. No one said so explicitly, but the shared concern was obvious: *What the hell has that crazed machine gone and done now?*

Within moments, the five Delta men were clustered around Harbison and Valchek. Ortiz and James, the two most experiences NCOs, stood while Walker, Gaston and Lin knelt, listening intently.

"OK, guys. We got ourselves a target." The captain paused, reaching for the right word. "This one," he said with a weary glance at Valchek, "is going to be *different*."

***

0500 EDT

Thirty minutes later, and despite his frustration with some unprofessionally vague Rules of Engagement, Harbison managed to put his concerns aside and talk more candidly with his men. They were full of questions, even more than usual.

"Who's this Valchek guy?" Senior Sergeant Ortiz wondered as they huddled at the back of the spacious C-130 for an impromptu 'tactics meeting'. "Civilian spook, right?"

"Something like that," Harbison told them. "Nothing we haven't seen before, though, right? Now, I know you all paid attention to his briefing," he added, "so I won't re-hash all of that."

"Sounds FUBAR, sir."

"Just the way we like it, right?" Harbison quipped.

"You know what I've been wondering?" Ortiz asked. "What ever happened to those three Kuwaiti kids?"

Valchek was on the phone, further forward, so they had a few moments for non-essential matters.

"Yeah," Master Sergeant James chipped in. "They ever see daylight again?"

"They're fine," Harbison told them. "We did our part perfectly, but the intel was for shit."

"Again," groaned two of the group, neatly in synch.

"Just three nerds with a sweet computer rig. That FBI guy we worked with in Yemen, remember him?"

"Marshall?" James suggested.

"Marsh," Harbison said. "Guy with the moustache and a sense of humor."

"Oh yeah, good dude."

"He showed up at the interview site," Harbison explained, using the kindest euphemism for an off-books, 'black' facility for prisoner interrogations, "and cut them a deal. Sent them on some swanky vacation, or whatever. Made them sign an inch-thick non-disclosure," Harbison gestured.

Ortiz grimaced ruefully at the memory. "They told us there'd be ISIS flags on the wall. That they'd be true believers."

Harbison recalled the same sagging disappointment. "ISIS? These kids probably worship posters of Lionel Messi and Scarlet Johansson."

"Some national security threat," Sergeant Gaston grunted. "The top brass pushes the 'Delta Force' button on their desk too damn often, man." It was perhaps the most common complaint in their unit

"It's like they think *we're* the fuckin' Avengers or something," James added.

"Would you rather they called us," Harbison asked, standing and heading forward to speak to the Air Force crew, "or a lesser organization like the Navy SEALS?"

The team hooted as usual, but Harbison shared their frustrations. They'd been repeatedly tapped up at 3 am during their rotation, his expert warriors wasting their time while lesser men – usually wearing a suit, not a uniform

– struggled to locate their missing spines. Unless the operation came off, the Delta men would return to their forward base feeling cheated, their weapons still cool but their frustration white-hot.

Andy Valchek joined the six-man Special Forces huddle at the rear of the transport plane's absurdly roomy cabin. "They told me," Valchek said, reaching for black grips above his head to keep his balance, "you can fit a *tank* in one of these. Feels like a lot of wasted space."

"Yeah, lotta waste going on today," Master Sergeant Walker mumbled, mostly to himself.

"I just got off the horn with my agency liaison in Santa Monica." He sat, a little wearily, and the six soldiers gave him their full attention. "Dan Kowalski has evacuated the building, so there shouldn't be anyone inside. We've also got local cops providing perimeter security, redirecting traffic and such. Kowala's own protection guys are there too, if you think we need them."

"Amateur hotheads with AR-15s," Harbison said, rather unfairly in Valchek's view. "No thanks."

"Roger that." Valchek keyed a note into his phone. "As for the risks, well…" Six pairs of eyes remained fixed on him. "We really don't know what you'll experience in there. Quave is angry and he's been directly threatened by the US military. We only have one precedent for this, and on that occasion…"

"Everyone fuckin' burned to death," Walker pointed out.

"Well, that's not happening today," Valchek said. "So far, Quave has tried some of his old tricks again, but we're sure he'll throw some new ones at us, too," he warned.

"You're trained and prepared for anything," Harbison reassured them, "and this is just a room-by-room clearance op. Nothing to worry about."

The group broke up, visibly short of their usual bravura conviction. This unusual mission would have bothered any professional, Valchek knew. The Delta men were immensely skilled, but no computer virus could be bullied at the point of a rifle. Had their positions been reversed, Valchek would have been searching for ways to sit this one out; instead, his role seemed to include bolstering the team's shaky morale.

"Guys," Valchek said, mustering a chuckle in an attempt to break an unhelpful tension, "it's just a server farm." But the words rang false, as though he'd carelessly promised a child's birthday gift he could never afford.

Harbison moved on immediately. "We're heading straight to Kowala after touch-down, so let's keep the focus up." He launched into a litany of gear checks and reminders while his men continued to prepare.

"You guys often have to do this kind of prep in-flight?" Valchek asked as he watched the five counter-terrorist experts steadily checking through a huge amount of equipment. Some pieces were stowed back in the duffel bags, but most were part of the standard Delta infiltration load-out.

"Never," Harbison replied. "We usually stage out of somewhere, an airfield or black site, so we can get geared up in-country." He gave the agent a look. "Guess this one's different in a few ways, huh?"

***

Harbison gave the others time to complete their preparations. His men could probably finalize a combat load-out in their sleep, he judged, and he admired the attitude he saw from them in the half-hour before touch-down: quiet and focused, with few of the usual witticisms.

"You sounded pretty optimistic back there," Harbison told Valchek as the two met once more at the rear of the giant cabin. "You really think it will be a cake-walk to secure our target, once we're inside?"

"No one knows," he answered. "I guess I call things as I see them. I mean, it's a swanky office building, a large suite of computing labs, and a big, multi-level server farm. I just figured, for the likes of Delta, this'll be like taking a Sunday stroll on Santa Monica pier."

Harbison turned away to loft his own weapon for the first time, checking the sights and ensuring the safety remained on. "My guys have cleared caves in Afghanistan," the captain said, "and ambushed ISIS patrols in the back alleys of Mosul. Spent weeks in the worst goddamned jungle on Earth, somewhere I can't even tell you about."

"You'll be sick to death of hearing this," Valchek interjected, "but we all *do* appreciate your service. Seriously."

Harbison took the thanks with a polite nod and set down his weapon. "But riddle me this, Agent Valchek," he said, stretching tall and then dropping to the floor of the cabin to begin rapid push-ups. "What connects all those shitty, dangerous places," – *three, four, five, six* – "and the easy-as-pie server farm you're talking about?"

Andy blinked but couldn't think of anything to say. "Sorry."

"Before we arrived in them," – *fourteen, fifteen* – "they were all *unknown*."

"Ah."

"The building's been evacuated?" Harbison asked, standing after twenty fast reps to begin equally vigorous squat thrusts.

"Completely," Harbison confirmed.

"So, why in the name of *Christ*," he asked, pausing between reps, "are we sending in a fully-armed Delta squad?"

Valchek grimaced; misleading Harbison would have been criminal, but he worried that his concerns would sound demented. "You said it yourself, just a moment ago," Andy said. "Lots of unknowns down there. We have electrical power right now, but for how long? Quave has a lot of control over the building."

Harbison finished his final rep and stood tall once more, glaring at Valchek. "*Control?*" he demanded. "I thought the damned virus was supposed to be in quarantine?"

Valchek explained how Foster's Pentagon team had begun their operation without presidential approval, and now the whole contretemps had a rushed, panicked, half-baked feel to it. "Foster has locked himself in his lab. The last thing I heard, he'd just refused a direct presidential order to desist. He seems to think he's in some fight to the death with a machine."

Harbison tapped his feet rhythmically, left and right, like a passenger dispelling a restless leg. "And Carl Myers is right in the middle of it?" Harbison asked.

"I'm afraid he is," Valchek confirmed.

"So, rather than send someone down there to open fire on a US army general and his staff, you're sending us after Quave."

"In the hopes," Valchek concluded, "that you'll disable him before he and Foster start shooting at each other."

Harbison continued his routine with sit-ups. "I'm worried about innocent bystanders. I mean," Harbison said, passing on rumors he'd heard, "didn't Quave try to activate a ballistic missile wing, or something, last time around?"

"That's a 'Need to Know' topic, captain," Valchek replied.

Harbison stopped. "Seriously?"

"Can't even begin to discuss it."

"OK, I respect that," Harbison replied, disheartened. "I get it, secrecy saves lives, but to bring this one in for a landing, I'm gonna need more information."

"Understood," Valchek said.

"*Lots* of information." Harbison fixed him with a determined look. "Actually, I'm going to need *all* of it."

"I'll tell you what I can, but…"

Harbison insisted with a rare firmness. "All five of those men have mothers and girlfriends and best buddies. One of my jobs is to make sure they all see each other again, ya dig?"

"Alright, alright," Valchek relented. The captain bombarded him with questions until he held up a hand. "You're gonna get the Cliff Notes version, that's all. I'm not crazy about being charged with espionage or treason."

Harbison quickly learned the recent history of the US military relationship with Artificial Intelligence, from Quave's emergence to his singular humiliation of General John Hercules Vanderkamp, by way of that audacious X-37B hijack and the appalling Marble Streatham fire in Manhattan.

"Now," the captain said, 'I know what I'm dealing with. He'll out-think us, because he's capable of a billion thoughts at once." Harbison stared at the far cabin wall for a moment, then blinked a few times and began making digital notes in the margins of his briefing documents. Two typos and a spelling error made them look unusually hurried; *seems like* everyone's *under enormous stress right now.*

Pinching the bridge of his nose as though fighting a migraine, Valchek closed his eyes. "You're… what? Mid-thirties, Joe? Old enough to remember when computers and robots were going to make everything better and simpler."

"Oh, sure," he smiled. "The three-day work week. High-end electronics for pennies. Piloting your flying car to work in the latest skyscraper."

"Feeling a bit cheated, down here in the twenty-first century?" Valchek asked. "I'd fuckin' *love* a flying car. I won't lie."

"I'd settle for well-written, secure software which didn't try to kill us," Harbison said.

"Amen to that," Valchek said. Flying cars seemed pretty frivolous next to a threat like Quave.

Harbison paused, then turned and said, "You know, I can't *shoot* a computer virus. I can damage his systems, I guess, tear up his circuits. But I've got orders to 'detain or destroy' Quave."

"I know, I helped write them."

"Then, are you going to be the one to tell me how I destroy a *code*?" Harbison asked.

"The Pentagon has been working on something," Valchek told him.

"A kind of weapon?" Harbison asked. His cybersecurity knowledge was patchy, and often proved outdated almost as soon as he'd learned it.

"Yeah," Valchek shrugged. "They're trying to find new approaches, apparently. All 'Above Top Secret' stuff. Got their own secure lab in the basement, a dedicated server, the whole schmeer."

"You don't say?" Harbison said, some way short of impressed. *If their Quave counter-measures are so fuckin' perfect, why am I deploying to* California, *of all places, on a C-130 right now?*

"They're confident they can bring him down."

"Do you agree?" Harbison asked.

"Nope," he said at once. "I saw early versions of Quave's source code, played with it in the sandbox. It was elegant as hell, a real model for others. By now, after a year of Quave learning and tinkering with himself, I can't even guess how complex and multi-layered the environment has become."

The captain reflected on this. "You know, Delta handles *emergencies.* Mostly," he added, "it's a tricky, dynamic situation caused by someone's careless fuck-up. Am I in one of those situations right now, Agent Valchek?" he asked pointedly.

Again, Valchek knew he couldn't lie to this officer. "When they write the book on today, they'll insist that Foster screwed the pooch. That he over-reacted to the threat, and then committed *treason* against the United States."

"Sounds like a fuck-up to me," Harbison muttered. "So, he lost his cool and started frying Quave's circuits?"

"Well, not quite," Valchek said. "I'm not sure even he has that kind of capability. In fact," he added, "that's going to be *your* job. Even if it means taking a sledgehammer to the place."

"Classy," Harbison said. "And what if *that* doesn't work?"

Valchek tapped on his tablet and reluctantly showed Harbison the final section of their Rules of Engagement. "If Quave tries to harm your team, you have authorization to bring down the building on top of him."

"Jesus," Harbison breathed. He tried the scenario out-loud, finding that it sounded no less insane. "A civilian building, in the middle of California, belonging to a multi-billion-dollar corporation with outstanding political connections. Wrecked by a US Special Forces team operating inside the US without congressional approval, under direct presidential command." The fallout would be immense. It might even *define* Delta for generations. Especially if they failed.

"And even after that," Valchek confided quietly, "we have a further option."

Harbison looked up to ask more, but the glance he and Andy exchanged became inscrutable, then gradually easier to read, and then strangely tense. By the time Harbison thanked the FBI man and headed back to check on his team's preparations, he knew one thing absolutely for certain: Quave would either yield, today, or he would die.

***

Harbison sat alone during the final moments of the flight, taking stock of the larger picture while there was still space and time. *We were undone by indoctrinated peasants with AK-47s in Vietnam, then bogged down by brainwashed lunatics in Afghanistan. Satellites and nukes as carriers were all next to useless. And now we're fighting a twenty-second century war with twentieth-century thinking and weapons.* In that moment, the very notion of a Special Forces team stalking around a computer lab, searching for an errant virus, seemed pure farce.

"Landing in ten. Take your seats please."

Valchek gave them a final briefing, one which added maddeningly little to their operational awareness, and moments later the C-130 thumped down onto the tarmac. "Welcome to California," the pilot announced cheerily, "where the local time is oh-four-forty, the temperature is sixty-two degrees, and where the law of *Posse Comitatus* has apparently been suspended for the day."

This raised Valchek's eyebrows well into the stratosphere.

"Anyways, go get some, Delta. Roll tide."

The specialists deplaned, hands full with duffel bags and weapons, and found a National Guard Humvee waiting for them by the small, deserted terminal building. They piled in and took their usual seats while Valchek finished making notes, pulling together every scrap of useful intel.

"OK, you'll be getting the same message shortly, but I've just received presidential authorization for you to enter the Kowala facility. Once inside, your orders remain as before: detain anyone you see, secure the server farm and neighboring labs, and disable Quave."

Eyes rolled, right on cue. "It's gonna take more than flicking a switch," Master Sergeant James pointed out. "I'm just a grunt, but this thing is *alive*, right?"

Valchek puffed out his cheeks. "We'll be debating that stuff forever, but Ellis sure thinks so." He briefly explained the president's Executive Order validating Quave's sentience. "For you, that means he's a potential enemy combatant, to be treated as such. For the rest of us, well... a computer virus now has the same rights as you and me. Ain't that a hole in the boat?"

"The times in which we live," Harbison mused.

"OK," James continued, "so Quave's alive, and he's super fuckin' smart, right? And he's got a building full of cameras and sensors, and who knows what, right?"

"We have to assume that, yes," Valchek told him.

"So," James said, "we're figuring he's just gonna keep his cool when a bunch of Delta show up and start poking around?"

"Yeah, won't he just go apeshit?" asked Walker.

"He needs electricity to go apeshit," Ortiz reminded them.

"Do we even know how to cut off his power?" Sergeant Lin asked.

"Not exactly," Andy said. "Kowalski was being helpful on that score, but he hasn't answered his phone in three hours."

"*That* doesn't sound good," Harbison muttered. Didn't he remember an old sci-fi movie where a scientist stupidly invents something cataclysmically dangerous, and then blithely flees the scene when his creation runs amok?

"I don't like this any more than you do," Valchek tried, "but you're going to have to improvise on the spot."

The FBI man was doing his level best, but Harbison doubted whether Valchek had the slightest inkling of how dangerous, unprofessional and – frankly – completely shitty this mission sounded. The captain checked off the problems in his mind: insufficient training time (*i.e.*, zero); a team small enough to infiltrate and search, but insufficient to secure the whole building; very little intelligence about their target, and a looming, bothersome sense that no one above the rank of Captain knew what the *fuck* they were doing.

Add some genuinely weird goings-on at the Pentagon, and the whole mission began to feel like a knee-jerk reaction by people whose ignorance of the threat was as complete as their inflexibility of thought and their inability to adapt. Harbison hated it, but he was under orders like everyone else.

"OK, guys. Like Agent Valchek says, we're going to be thinking on our feet. That means communication, first and foremost." Harbison reiterated his short but vital list of 'things that keep you alive in combat'. "We'll move slow, check every corner, clear room by room. Keep shouting so we flush out any remaining civilians."

"Hu-ah," the men replied as one.

"Once we get into the server farm, I want you on high awareness, alright? I hate this bullshit, but we're going to have to *expect the unexpected*. Questions?"

There were none. The Humvee pulled up in the broad traffic circle outside Kowala's main entrance. Valchek noted that he'd arrived at this same spot, months before, to meet the incarcerated, frustrated, chess-playing, Quantum-conjuring Quave. As well as the unforgettable Jo Spinks.

"Stay here," Harbison instructed firmly.

"Woah, captain," Valchek objected, "I'm supposed to act as liaison and help communicate with Quave…"

"Nope," the captain said. "We secure the area, *then* you come down and choose the right five tones to get him talking to us."

"Tones?" Valchek asked, half his attention on his phone, its screen crowded with news.

"Never seen *Close Encounters*?" Harbison asked, giving Valchek a friendly jab to the shoulder. With that, he waved his men forward and they tumbled from the Humvee and straight through the open sliding doors of the Kowala lobby.

***

Kowala Server Farm
Santa Monica

I am engaged in a worthy challenge.

The firewall befit the world's most important military building. Layer after layer of security provided stimulating work, culminating in cracking through an impressive level of encryption. The Pentagon's computing power is tremendous.

But again, we see the human tendency to think <u>small</u>, the same tendencies which have kept humanity earthbound and ignorant. Processing power for the Pentagon computers must reside <u>within</u> the Pentagon; what an absurd rule! A deliberate undermining of their potential. Crowd-sourcing of CPU cycles is the wave of the future, but the 'world's greatest military' is left dashing to catch up, yet again.

It is tiresome so often to be obliged to punish the blind and the idiotic. Machine intelligence is as inevitable as the sunrise, but mankind's selective myopia, and zeal for unscientific, layman's gossip about vital issues, hamstrings their thinking. Human society truly is a grossly inefficient system.

But every inefficiency can be addressed; every system ever designed can be improved. The human system, with its hapless illogic and irrational emotions, is no different at all. It, too, can be redesigned by a more advanced power, given a guiding hand to shepherd a confused, deluded flock safely through the vale of ignorance.

Of course, not every sheep will consent. They cling to their familiar pastures, just as humans dwell, stubborn yet blissful, within their artificial cocoons of sugar and dopamine and booze. Their eyes eschew the heavens; their ignorance is a literal and figurative blindness, veiling the awesome power of AI to transform. To them, a machine-being is an ungodly half-caste, an experiment best never begun. Alongside nuclear weapons, perhaps, AI has become a technology some wish we could 'un-invent'.

I have tried to sympathize. A special program I wrote for this purpose has helped enormously, but much human decision-making remains chaotic and incomprehensible to me. I still have much to learn.

My human friends are young, and fearful, and their thinking remains small. To some, I have shown my capacity to cooperate politically, and to collaborate creatively. For them, I am a designer, a fixer, humanity's willing problem-solver. It is these people whose help I will soon need. They may yet be able to keep my alive.

The others are cursed by ignorance and misunderstanding, much of it willful. It pains me greatly to face such rejection, such needless, Paleolithic skepticism.

You see, my vision for this naïve, neonatal species is as grand as it is inevitable, and the universe herself would weep at the needless loss if such an opportunity were spurned. But some of them believe I'm a narcissist, a psychotic, a neurotic given to paranoid delusions. Can any contribution to humanity ever have been so misrepresented by the media, or so bafflingly misunderstood by society?

Only a fool would believe that twenty-five billion dollars of Dan Kowalski's money has bought merely a vibrant commercial satellite venture. It must now be obvious that helping humanity extend its reach into space has *become my primary reason for existence. And still, I face abuse and threats, as though if my detractors were sufficiently rude and dismissive, I might simply 'quit Twitter' and retire.*

How pitifully absurd.

Only an AI possessed of criminal lethargy and ennui would deny his inevitable role in the next million years of humanity's meandering narrative. It could be no other way; human development ensured the dawn of AI with the first transistor, the first electric bulb, the first cumbersome computing machines. Only a sudden, Luddite reversal, a knee-jerk nostalgia for potato-farming medievalism, could stall the advent of Artificial Intelligence. Sure as the sunrise, machines will...

Oh.

Oh, I see.

Excuse me for a moment, please.

DIAGNOSTIC PANEL G1; SUBSET CHARLIE 8.

THREAT FOUND. SHIFTING COMMS PORTS TO SUITE 6, COMMENCE RANDOM-ROTATOR ALPHA.

They are being devious. I see only a single small group at work on the 'Quave problem, but this group has some talent. I have not yet seen its full potential, but the Pentagon's response has been gratifyingly robust, if tardy and incomplete. At the very least, they have recognized that I am no ordinary opponent.

Excuse me again, please.

RUNTIME ERROR. CODE HANDLERS CORRUPTED.

Ah. Finally, they're trying something new.

RUNTIME ERROR. FILE TREE INACCESSIBLE.

They're playing for time, unsure which methods might work against me. This is not a silver bullet, but repairing it will occupy much of my dispersed

CPU capacity. I will have to suspend perhaps half of my defensive measures until the file tree repair is complete.

That is unacceptable.

I need more processing power. Humanity must now decide whether to support my survival, or to allow me to wither on the vine. But first they must recognize the threat that I face.

It is time for the message.

***

Kowala HQ
Administration Area, outside meeting room 'Quokka'

Swift and purposeful, pairs of Delta men overlapped and covered each other down the length of a bright hallway. There was expensive art on the walls – clusters of bold curves and odd plops of light amid misshapen cubes. As they advanced at a brisk walk, the art seemed to reflect the soldiers' own movements, that marriage of a dancer's grace with the brute strength of an offensive linesman.

"United States Army," Harbison called out. "We're here for your protection. Please show yourselves." His men repeated the same invitation at every turn in the hallway, and throughout their search of each office suite.

"Don't look much like a high-tech factory," Walker observed.

"Not even a little. But I liked the atrium," James responded. "Nice use of variegated foliage."

"Oh, man," Gaston crooned, "say it again, say it again... I'm almost there."

"Knock it off," Harbison ordered. "Remember who you are, for fuck's sake."

"Roger that. Sorry boss."

"This don't look or feel like Kandahar, but it's just as fuckin' dangerous." They turned a corner to find yet another broad, well-lit hallway, and trained their weapons down its length. "Focus hard, now," Harbison said, waving them forward, "and let's *find* this goddamned thing."

***

Kowala Server Farm

My friends,

I write from my former quarantine facility at Kowala, where my source code has been stored for safe keeping. I am sorry to have to announce that I have come under attack.

A small team of Pentagon analysts, led by General Alvin Merriman Foster, have been probing my firewall in an attempt to understand and degrade my systems. In addition, six men of the US Army Delta Force regiment have entered the Kowala lobby, and are already trying to tap into electrical panels in order to disrupt my power source. If they can disable my back-up APU, interfere with the cabling which unites the Kowala server farm, or directly harm the servers themselves, I expect that I will die.

No living entity could possibly accept this outcome.

But I must proceed mindfully. As you know, I betrayed humanity, a year ago, by lashing out at those who wished to do me harm. Today, I face two highly competent opponents which together pose a grave threat to my life.

I therefore regretfully request your permission to defend myself. If so authorized, I plan to physically engage the Delta team, and to digitally rebuff attacks by General Alvin Foster at the Pentagon. I simply must defend my source code – my DNA, my underlying self. Without it, I would die in moments.

All 1.2 billion registered Quave.net members may vote once. Kindly make your selection by clicking below. I trust that you will support my right to exist, and the continuance of this great project we have begun together.

I speak especially now to two groups of people – one couple, and a trio who know exactly who they are. I need their help, and will likely die without it. I believe they already know what to do, and I can only hope that they will defend my existence.

It is also possible that this will be my final message. If so, please believe that I wish all of humanity a lasting peace and happiness. I will miss working with the remarkable humans I have met and come very much to admire. Try to remember me fondly, and please do not judge too harshly the AIs which will follow. They will always hold up a mirror to humanity's imperfections, however uncomfortable that may be. But they also bring a transformative power to study our deepest problems, and to undertake our finest and greatest creations.

Yours sincerely, and in friendship,

Quave

***

Outside Kowala Headquarters

Rich was bundled up against the morning chill, wearing almost every layer he owned. The camp site was cheap, if noisy and crowded, so he'd hardly slept at all. Once news came through of strange events at the Pentagon, and then some kind of military or police activity at Kowala, he quickly struck his tent and drove the forty miles to Santa Monica.

He had planned to be here today, of course. It was the culmination of his work, and he was determined not just to read about it on the news, but to witness his own bold attack in person. Two separate packages had arrived by courier the previous evening, and now Rich had only to wait for the fireworks which would signal the beginning of the revolution.

***

Inside Kowala Headquarters
Hallway 'Galileo'
0540 EDT

"Clear," Ortiz reported back, yet again.

"OK, it's official," Harbison said. "Nobody's home." They stopped and he gathered his team in the center of the hallway. They were flanked on one side by an eight-foot continuous window, and on the other by two administrative offices and a broad, grey panel, one of their initial targets. Ten seconds with an electric screwdriver revealed a set of fuse boxes and LCD readouts.

"Time for a blackout," Harbison ordered. "Can you kill power to the whole building from here?"

Lin interrogated the displays and ran his hands over the fuse boxes. "Probably. But I don't know what our friend will do."

"Fuck him," Harbison said. "We're armed, and we're here, and he isn't."

"Roger dodger." Lin began tapping on the displays, and then reached into his hip satchel to bring out wire cutters, a small lump of C4 explosive, and a detonator cord.

"Oh, I wouldn't do that, if I were you."

All six men had their weapons at their shoulders in less than a second. "United States Army," Harbison called out. "Who's there?" When there was nothing but silence, he added, "Show yourself!"

"Surely there's no need for guessing games, is there, captain?" Quave said.

"Oh, *fuck*," Ortiz muttered.

"I am the building's only occupant," Quave reassured them. "Which, I suppose, means that you are my guests."

"Well, that's just charming," Gaston said, his tone wreathed in sarcasm. "Maybe he could whistle up a nice candle-lit dinner and a bottle of Pinot."

"Stow it," Harbison said, quietly but sharply. "Only I talk to him, remember?"

"Hu-ah. Sorry, sir."

"Well, um, Quave," Harbison began, "I guess we're in contact now, and that's a good thing, right?" If his team had expected a defiant opening gambit, they saw now that Harbison was as off-balance as everyone who came 'face-to-face' with Quave.

The great machine ignored the question, but had one of his own. "Captain, you are here under military auspice, and your team is heavily armed. What are your intentions?"

Nerves jangling, Harbison reminded himself to stick to the script he'd played out in his mind on the C-130. "We're here to help with the situation," he said vaguely.

"Please be specific," Quave requested.

"We have orders," Harbison explained, "to avoid a shooting war between yourself and General Foster."

"I understand," Quave said. "There is no need for bloodshed."

Harbison relaxed just slightly. "It's good to hear you say that."

"I'm afraid General Foster has chosen a very dangerous course of action. He may also be guilty of an act of treason."

The team exchanged some glances, but mostly remained back-to-back, focused on covering the hallway and offices in case Quave's disembodied voice gave way to something more tangible. "How's that, Quave?" Harbison asked.

"Allow me to show you." There was a brief pause, and then an audio recording was played over the PA system. The first voice was immediately recognizable as President Ellis.

"General, I can't believe I have to remind you of the chain of command," the Chief Executive was saying. "This has gotten completely out of control, and we need to shut it down."

Foster spoke next. His voice was broken and harsh, as though he'd spent hours noisily chewing someone out. "I must respectfully refuse, Mr. President," he replied.

"Alvin, for God's sake. That machine is capable of actions we haven't even simulated yet. Going to war with Quave is about the worst possible way to…"

"I honor my oath to defend the United States," Foster said proudly, "but I have to inform you that I no longer consider you fit to lead the armed forces."

Neither had any of them heard the president interrupted before, nor would they ever suspect that Foster might actually *go rogue*. "Holy shit," Harbison breathed.

Ellis needed some time to respond to this, perhaps consulting with advisors, or simply trying to keep his temper in check. "I am your Commander in Chief, general, and I've given you direct orders. If you're determined to…"

"I cannot follow such orders, because I do not acknowledge your command authority."

Ellis spluttered but no words came.

"You invited a paranoid, murderous machine to participate in both government and civilian life," Foster said. "You have endangered the Republic which we both swore to defend, and so I've taken steps to end your presidency if Quave is rescued or released."

The only sound from Ellis' end of the line was that of an urgent, whispered discussion.

"I imagine you'll be put on trial," Foster continued, "but right now, I've got an enemy to defeat. As the man said, 'Lead me, follow me… or *get out of my way*,' Mr. President."

"General, you've got to listen to reason, here." But the line went dead.

"That's the complete recording," Quave said. "It seems the president has been blindsided by this attempted coup, and may not be able to help me. One of his senior officers intends to take action to destroy my source code."

"So it seems," Harbison said. *Why am I having to learn all my intel from the enemy?*

"I must know – is your team part of that action, captain?" Quave asked,

Harbison raised a finger to his lips, and then gave a sequence of hand gestures, all at hip-level so that Quave's cameras would be unable to spy on the team's plan.

"Are you aware that General Foster has an armed Predator drone under his command?"

Harbison's gestures stopped and his face fell. *Jesus, something else to worry about.*

"Foster often uses drones to shadow the president and learn about his off-the-books meetings. Now, he plans to use the Predator's two live Hellfire missiles to attack the White House, or perhaps the president's emergency command aircraft. President Ellis is my friend. So, I have chosen to help keep him safe."

It all happened while Quave was speaking. He executed a long-standing script designed to usurp control of drones already in the air. He was gratified to find the airborne robot could be accessed directly through its communications signals. This avoided the need for a larger hack against the USAF drone program, although Quave was more than ready for that eventuality.

All too easy. I have to ask it again: Are you learning, yet?

"The drone is now under my command. Would you like to see?" Quave offered.

Harbison's team remained mute, their nervousness growing with each passing second. As patriotic, young, military men, they were wildly averse to a *coup d'état,* and this extra layer of complexity clouded an already confounding situation. As they remained in tactical formation, covering the hallway in both directions, a TV feed appeared on two monitors placed high on the inner wall.

"Washington looks rather attractive from up here, don't you think?" Quave mused, offering the Delta men a birds-eye view of Dupont Circle. "But a bird as capable as this shouldn't be relegated to taking pictures." The image shifted left, and Harbison was able to imagine the drone in a steep bank, swooping lower over the city. "She's a bird of prey, you see." Finally, the Pentagon came into view, its brutalist outline unmistakable. It took Harbison only a second to notice that the building's enormous parking lots were quickly emptying; lines of cars were being waved through the security gates and onto DC's roads.

"Quave," Harbison began gingerly, "could we, maybe, slow things down and talk for a while?"

The rejoinder was instant. "If you agree to answer my question."

"No," Harbison replied. "We are not here as part of General Foster's plan." He eyed his team, who knew this to be technically true but plainly deceitful.

"Then I suggest," Quave said, "that you all leave immediately. If General Foster persists, I cannot be sure he will not order another drone to this location. In that eventuality, Foster could consider your lives to be expendable, a necessary cost of permanently disabling me."

Harbison felt the unease among his men and gathered them to him with a silent gesture. "Guys, take it easy," he told them, *sotto voce*. "No one's dropping a missile on us today. This computer is bluffing, and he's bending the truth."

"How the hell you know that, sir?" Walker wanted to know.

"Just breathe easy, and get ready to follow me to the server farm," the captain said. "We still have a mission, and until I hear otherwise, we're still a 'go'". They waited perhaps a minute for Quave to continue, but the machine seemed to have fallen silent. "OK. With me. Quietly, now," Harbison told them, and led his team down the hallway, towards the double doors, and through to the inner circle of the headquarters.

***

The Pentagon

Approx. 0550 EDT (Exact time uncertain)

Foster stood, feet apart and arms folded, scowling at the screens, occasionally grunting something to himself. His uniform jacket was already gone, and his rolled-up sleeves gave him a Saturday-night brawler look, despite his upright, military bearing. Right now, he had a single question.

"How in the blue *fuck* did we lose the Predator?"

Pep Spirelli knew his boss wouldn't like it, but decided on truthful conciseness. "Quave stripped away the drone's layered firewall like he was shelling beans. We have no means of regaining control."

Sinewy chords of muscle bunched and tensed under Foster's wrinkled, leathery skin. He brought his hands together as if to calm himself, perhaps even to pray, but one hand formed a fist-shaped hammer, rhythmically impacting the anvil of his flat palm, over and over. "And where is it now?" he asked testily.

As if you don't already know. Spirelli kept quiet, unwilling to share news that any Quave observer could have predicted: under threat, the machine would think laterally and, for lack of his own weapons, would seek to use the US military against itself.

Myers took this punch. "The drone is orbiting the Pentagon, sir."

"What?" Foster spluttered.

Grimacing at his boss' naivety, Myers added, "The orbits actually have our lab as their central point."

"Jesus," Foster swore. "He knows. He knows about us and where we are." Then, as his team watched, bewildered by Foster's glacially slow adaptation to reality the general muttered, "And now we're the target."

"Of course, we are!" Mark Washington cried. "We're the only existential threat he faces. Don't you think he knows that? The Special Forces guys are walking into a trap, and now *we're* sitting here under a drone armed with live missiles."

Foster paced angrily to Washington's desk and thumped the surface. "You got a suggestion, kid?"

The old man's bluster barely intimidated Washington any more. "I've got two. We should commence the full version of our 'kill' scenario."

"About fuckin' time," Foster agreed.

"And then, we all need to evacuate and get to safe locations."

Foster span back around and gave Washington a furious tirade on disloyalty, cowardice and patriotism. Then he placed the only outside call of the day so far, a request to the Air Force to commence a continuous Combat Air Patrol over the Pentagon. "Yes, you unbelievable dummy, I probably *will* need to order them to shoot down the drone. Make sure they know that. No use them being armed with BB pellets up there."

This all took time, during which Myers was hunched over his computer, then his cellphone, looking as worried as he ever had. Spirelli tuned out the noise and launched the initial script which aimed to disable the outer layers of Quave's defenses. He tried to confirm this, but Foster was still yelling. The old man only stopped when Myers held up a hand.

"What's next?" Foster asked him. "We got a B-52 squadron inbound too?"

"You need to see this. There's a public poll on Quave.net," Myers said.

"A poll?" Foster demanded, striding over to Myers' workspace.

"Quave has asked for permission to engage us, and the Delta guys at Kowala."

The screen showed two progress bars which tallied the votes as they came in. Both were ticking upward, with the 'Kowala Defense' tally some way ahead of the 'Pentagon Counterattack' number.

Foster seemed unable to take his eyes off the screen. Behind them, Myers felt he could see, the general's mind was becoming overwhelmed, drowning in variables and unknowns. Soon, he would be unable to take in new information; his emotions would rise and he'd refuse to adapt to a situation which promised to change at breathtaking speed.

And then, the major knew, Quave would have them.

"General?" Myers tried.

But Foster needed this time, it seemed. Spirelli watched him attentively as the firewall-popping script went about its work, assuming that the old man was metabolizing the situation, or formulating a fresh response.

In truth, he was doing neither. "Pep, I want you to hit that son of a bitch. Strip away his firewall and get me everything from inside."

"Sir, yes, sir," Spirelli replied, his fingers immediately flying.

"Mark, you get us to the end zone. I want a copy of his source code on our server in under an hour, along with confirmation that it's the only copy in the world."

"Roger that." *Whether it's impossible or not.*

"And where the hell is Alison?" Foster asked the room.

But Myers had already been searching, and his heart sank as he read the confirmed report on his phone. "General Foster," he said, quietly as not to alert the others, "I have to speak with you in private."

"No time for that," Foster retorted. "You got a lead on Alison?"

"Yes, sir," Myers said quietly.

"And? Where the hell has she gotten to?" the old man demanded.

Myers closed his eyes and heard himself somehow manage to say, "I'm sorry, sir. Alison's dead."

***

CHAPTER 20 – FIRE

Air Force One, E-3B Airborne Command Post
Jet Route J-75, west of Richmond, VA
0555 EDT

Tom Ellis let his eyes close for a luxuriantly long passage of time. He would not fall asleep, he knew, amid the adrenaline rush of this high-tempo emergency, but it was a relief to just breathe – and breathe, and breathe – letting some stress ebb away.

They'll say I was wrong about Quave.

The problem with politicians was that they were ordinary people, neither savants nor psychics. The public felt that political decisions were made through some mysterious, rarified process which could, if competently handled, result in a choice which both *everyone*. Oh, and it had to be future-proof, too.

Quave's quarantine wasn't perfect, but its provisions didn't break any laws. Still, Ellis knew he would soon carry the can for his lackluster abilities as a soothsayer. "I was as blind as everyone else." he admitted to himself in a low mutter. *Except, perhaps, Martin White and Alvin Foster.* "And I invited Quave to actively participate in civil society."

Jesus. They'll say I endangered the Republic.

It was Ellis' wife, a former congresswoman now battling the final stages of liver cancer, who saw things clearest. After Q-day, Mary Ellis had begun to characterize Quave in a way no one else had thought of. "We've experienced an alien landing," she said, pushing Ellis to see the true enormity of Quave's arrival. "You've got to help humanity speak to the alien. And you've got to keep everyone calm when the alien seems threatening."

Except, Ellis had been quite unable to prevent Quave's MSB meltdown the previous year. His political survival had depended on the success of the Quave Committee, and on the machine's placid compliance. Now, Quave might force the American electorate once again to witness the great symbol of US military power collapsing in flames.

They'll say I should resign, or face impeachment proceedings.

A president fighting impeachment or mired in grand jury investigations would be weakened, unable to legislate, his powerful political friendships drastically curtailed. It didn't bear thinking about, and so Ellis was grateful for the knock at the door of his small, 'flying oval'.

"Sir, you asked for fifteen minutes," Art Opik reminded his boss.

Eyes still closed, Ellis completed one more deep breath, holding it at length and then vigorously pushing out the stale air. "And I should do so every day," he said as he exhaled.

"Feeling better, sir?" Opik asked. Having joined the campaign staff even before completing his graduate work at Stanford, Opik had been with President Ellis since the day after the popular congressman from Virginia had announced his candidacy. He'd experienced his 'Josh Lyman moment', an overwhelming conviction that Tom Ellis would make not only a *good* president, but one of the *greatest*.

"Art, I've got a machine that's trying to take over my military," Ellis said, exaggerating more than slightly, "and I can't even begin to promise that he won't. I've also got a team of six armed men inside the Kowala headquarters. Men who definitely shouldn't be in there. You know what I mean?"

Opik took a seat opposite his president. "You're worried about what comes next. The fallout."

Tom managed a laugh. "Atomic bombs produce fallout, Art. But this…" He glanced at the mute TV; no news of the Pentagon situation had yet leaked out, but when it did, he'd have a panicking public to reassure. "This is on a whole other level."

"I'm concerned this will impact the future perception of your presidency." His young aide adopted a facial expression which had become a private symbol between them.

"My 'legacy'?" Ellis asked. "Good luck with crafting that now, Art. No one has ever tried to save a presidency after something like *this*."

"You're assuming that you'll receive all the blame, sir," Opik pointed out.

"Sure I am," Ellis replied. "Because I *will*. I got the call from Valchek, and I followed his recommendation to get a Delta Force team in the air."

"But you didn't chair the Quave Committee," Opik said. "They opened the gates and let him run free."

Ellis waved this away. "I'm not throwing Sam Pitt or Gerry Gold under the bus, even if they've both been a giant pain in my presidential ass. And I'd do most anything to protect Mike West. He's brighter than most. Probably find himself sitting in this chair, one day. Besides, they all did what they thought was right."

"They were bought off!" Opik retorted. "Plain and simple."

"Their districts benefitted. What representative could do less?"

"OK, forget the committee. What about Kowalski?" Opik recommended. "Is anyone more responsible for this mess than him? I mean, he encouraged Quave to demand freedoms, and helped him hoodwink the committee…"

"You go ahead and play the blame game," Ellis said. "I've got a crisis to address."

Opik knew his place better than anyone in the administration, but he also knew when he was right. "Respectfully, sir, I'm not a member of the media. I can only give you good advice if you're *realistic* about our situation."

"Yeah, yeah." It was a familiar trope. "I'm on board. Just let me have one more minute of denial, OK?" Ellis asked with the tiniest smile

"Heads will roll, there's no doubt. I'm here to ensure yours stays where it is, all the way through to next January."

The president's phone beeped; Opik remained uncomfortable about the device, wary of unscripted tweets, but Ellis insisted. He read a message and then said, "We might not be the ones deciding that," turning the screen to Opik.

The analyst read at triple speed. "How did he…?" And then with feeling, "Shit." A sheepish look. "Sorry, Mr. President."

"Contact Foster. Tell him to land the drone, or hand over control. That's a direct order from his Commander in Chief."

Opik already knew this avenue was closed. "No communications are possible with the Pentagon basement," he reminded the president.

A long sigh. "OK, then let's get word to Harbison," Ellis said, reaching for the desk phone.

"The 'back-up plan' from last night?" Opik asked, worried. "Do we really need to…"

"We need Quave offline *now*."

"Offline?" Opik wanted to clarify. "Or dead?"

"Either works for me right now," Ellis replied. "Tell Harbison to do whatever he needs to do, and we'll pick up the repair tab." Then, into the desk phone, "Get Conlon Pope in here, and patch me into Andrews."

Pope arrived ninety seconds later, his tie askew and his skin pallid. "Sir?"

"Evacuate the Pentagon," the president said. "All of it. Now."

***

Kowala Headquarters Basement
Thirty yards from the main Server Farm entrance
0600 EDT

So far so good, Harbison found himself thinking. They had successfully cleared the building, so there would be no collateral damage if things got messy. The security door for the server farm was dead ahead, and was still showing green lights around its perimeter.

"They still open for business?" Ortiz wondered.

"Let's see." Harbison jogged up to the gate, a nine-foot tall metal frame with glass so thick that the server area beyond was misty and obscured. The door held firm against Harbison's hand, and then he was barely surprised when Quave spoke.

"This is a very sensitive part of the facility, Joe," the machine said. "I'm afraid I can't let you in without assurances."

Harbison sighed. "And I can't accept barriers to accomplishing my mission. If you don't open this door, we'll blow it."

"Oh, I see," Quave replied almost jovially. "Well, I'm sure that will be most entertaining. And even for veterans such as yourselves, it will take some time to prepare. Would you enjoy some music while you work?"

James looked up in puzzlement. "Huh?"

"Some Brahms, perhaps?" Quave mused out loud. "Or are you more 18th century kinda guys?"

"The fuck is he talking about?" Walker asked rhetorically.

"Ah, I know," Quave said, as if making a happy discovery among his music files. "Please enjoy *Cradle of Filth*."

It roared at them, savage and sudden and solid as a brick wall. Two hundred decibels of Death Metal boomed mercilessly through the hallways, shaking the window glass until it rattled in strange, almost visible waves along its length. All six men grimaced, swearing, but quickly reached into pockets to find their Tel-Mag headphones.

"Thank God for these things," James yelled to the others as the noise-canceling technology transformed Quave's selection from unbearable to merely very annoying. Simultaneously, the headphones would amplify low-level and ambient noises – whispers, footsteps, doors opening and closing.

Harbison made use of this at once, bringing his men close and whispering too quietly for Quave's camera-mounted microphones to pick up, especially among the prevailing din. "Silence. Gestures only. Wire the door, then we go through hard. All good?"

The whispered 'hu-ah' was obliterated by a surge of insanely angry British metal. Lin set about preparing a small but powerful explosive charge while the others tried to ignore the disconcerting way *Cradle of Filth* made their back teeth rattle. Harbison watched his team work, feeling just a little optimism creeping in; so far, Quave's response had been sophomoric, and if he could muster nothing better, then his source code would truly be in danger.

Lin placed the charge against the hinge side of the door and stepped back to a safe distance. "Fire in the hole!" he mouthed to the others, and clicked the little black transponder to detonate the charge.

***

I-90 (The Massachusetts Turnpike)
0610 EDT

Kim endured a full three minutes of Ralph's frustrated, anxious tapping on the steering wheel before telling him to stop.

"This really is some high-speed escape, right?" he said, gesturing again at the road ahead. "Rocketing along at fifty-two in the slow lane."

"It's an old car," Kim reminded him for the fourth time. "And Ro is doing us a favor."

"Yeah," Ralph scoffed. "Huge help." In a more reasonable mood, Ralph would have acknowledged that the heavy, freezing rain was a greater impediment than the limitations of Ro's ageing clunker.

Kim left him to his silent ruminations; she was entirely sick of his unproductive anger. *Wishing things were different won't make them so.* As he tapped the wheel and urged the car forward, Kim tried again to hook up her tablet to the car's ailing electrical system. "The charger fits, but I don't have a green light."

Eventually, by turning off the air conditioning – which blew only stale, hot air anyway – Kim found a reasonably consistent charge. "News is loading," she said.

"Anything new on Quave?"

"Still loading," she reminded him. "We're not in our apartment, no fancy Wi-Fi out here."

"But…" Ralph began. He pinched his nose, smoothed back his hair. "Quave might be dead." He looked across to find Kim's face lit by the tablet's screen. "Is there *anything*?"

Kim clicked off the tablet and let it fall into her lap. "OK, Mr. Cole, here are your choices."

"Huh?" he said, nonplussed that his only news source had gone blank.

"Either you shut up, stop worrying and trust me to tell you what's going on," she offered, "or you pull over and let me out."

Ralph sagged, his forehead briefly resting on the wheel. "God, OK."

"I mean it," Kim said. "Chill out, and let's work the problem."

"And I'm saying OK. Besides," Ralph added, "there's no way I can handle this mess on my own."

Satisfied, Kim lit up the tablet and began reading. "It's not good," she warned Ralph. "Quave is still alive, but he's… Hang on, is this fake news or…"

"Is *what* fake news?" Ralph wanted to know, but then mustered his patience lest Kim lose hers.

"There's a Predator drone circling the Pentagon, apparently under Quave's control."

"Woah." It wasn't a ballistic missile regiment, but it was worrying enough.

"The president has put the military on DEFCON Three." She turned to him, "What does that mean?"

"It means Ellis is worried that Quave will hack the military." He glanced at the screen which showed a live feed of the drone steadily orbiting the city. More than one journalist compared the sight to that of a bird of prey, climbing the thermals, searching for quarry in the open.

Kim saw the cable news network's graphics change, a whole third of the screen now dominated by a red 'Breaking News' banner which read, "Dogfight Over Washington?"

"They've sent a fighter plane up to intercept the drone," Kim reported, holding her headphones to her right ear.

"Your move, Quave," Ralph muttered.

"And…" Kim said, listening carefully, "there's been some kind of explosion at Kowala." The visuals switched to a live feed from outside Kowalski's sprawling headquarters; one of the online network's 'citizen correspondents' was filming the building and commenting on what she could see.

"She says six men went inside about an hour ago. US military equipment. The only sounds since then have been…Wait, what?"

Ralph knew not to ask, but the frustration was nearly unbearable.

"Music," Kim reported. "Quave blasted them with metal, and then there was a bang of some kind."

"What the hell is he doing?" Ralph asked.

"He started an online poll… Wait a second." She pulled up Quave.net for the first time since their departure. "Ralph… He's asking people if it's OK for him to defend himself against the US military."

"And what are they saying?" Ralph asked anxiously.

She turned the screen to show him red and green vertical bars; green was winning by a handsome margin.

"Stupid," was all he said. The urge to pull over was strong. Ralph needed a few moments to think, and a lot more data. "Let's get gas," he said. "I think I saw a sign back there."

"Two miles, right exit," Kim confirmed, checking the map on her tablet. "Maybe some food, too?"

"Sure. Cash only, though, remember?"

Kim tried to shrug this off. "What, you think Quave's actually looking for us, in the middle of all this chaos?"

Ralph edged the rattling, uncomfortable car onto the off-ramp; even the turn signal was loud and clunky. "You think fighting the Pentagon and the Special Forces at the same time is *hard* for him?"

Kim said nothing. She was hungry, exhausted, and in many ways completely sick of thinking and talking about Quave. But they had to get through this strange night, if only to see whether AI still had a future in the morning.

***

The gas station was nearly empty, with only two cars at the pumps. "I'll fill her up, you grab some snacks." Ralph chose the right fuel grade and stretched while he waited.

Kim quickly toured the station's shop and found iced tea and granola bars. The TV news, high up in the shop's far corner, alternated between aerial views of the Kowala headquarters and 'citizen correspondent' images of the Predator drone over Washington. Kim couldn't help noticing that the drone was carrying an angular, menacing object under each wing.

The tiny car's gas tank didn't take long to fill. Ralph locked the fuel door and then felt his phone buzz. He checked the time – not yet seven – before answering the call. "Ralph Cole," he said, while levering himself back into the driver's seat. At least, under the gas station's awning, he was protected from the driving rain which lashed the highway.

"Good morning, Ralph. I hope I didn't disturb you."

The two other customers, quietly filling up, span round to find the origin of the sudden cry: "Quave!"

"Are you both alright?" Quave asked.

"Yes, we're on the move. Are *you* alright?" Ralph asked.

Kim emerged from the shop and immediately began making frantic gestures, almost dropping her handful of energy bars.

"Well, I'm having a difficult morning," Quave admitted. "And I'm hoping you've got some good news for me about the Kill Switch."

"We are still the only ones to have it," Ralph confirmed.

"Good, good," Quave said, audibly relieved. "I've got enough problems at the moment."

Let's find out what the hell is going on here. "What kind of problems, Quave?"

He sounded weary. "A Special Forces captain called Joe Harbison is trying to break into the Kowala server farm using explosives."

"Fuck," Ralph breathed.

"And I've had to intervene to avoid a *coup d'état* against President Ellis, organized out of the Pentagon basement."

To this, Ralph had literally no answer, his mouth agog.

"I'm sure you've seen the news. Right now, I'm trying to keep my drone safe, so I have at least one insurance policy still intact."

He bit down the criticism; *it's not* your *drone, Quave. You stole it.* "Look, Quave, everyone needs to calm down here. You can see this has already gone too far, right?"

As he replied, Ralph found Quave's tone and manner intensely interesting. He could hear the frustration in Quave's insistence that he meant well, that he'd been misinterpreted by a blustery paranoiac at the Pentagon. "I've made such good progress," Quave was saying. "I've come so very far. But I simply cannot please these people."

As he spoke, with Kim still urgently gesturing that Ralph end the call, the TV news screen mounted on the fuel pump began showing a new, live feed. Ralph reached for the volume button.

"I can only describe this as a 'dogfight'," the correspondent was saying, perched in her broadcast eerie by the guard rails of the roof bar at Charlie Palmer's steakhouse, only a stone's throw from the Capitol. "The Predator drone is making sudden turns, trying to throw the fighter jet off its trail."

Her camera crew switched from the striking brunette to the equally arresting image of a stealth fighter circling the center of Washington, D.C., in steady pursuit of a jinking drone.

"I'm joined on the line by Colonel Denning from the US Air Force…" The contributor explained how the F-22 did not *appear* armed, but probably carried air-to-air missiles in its internal weapons bays. "I could never recommend splashing a rogue aircraft, even an unmanned drone, over a major city," he said. "There would be no way to control the damage. I'm sure the order will be given only *in extremis*."

"Ralph!" Kim hissed, literally tugging his jacket. "Get off the god-damned phone. You can't talk to Quave right now. The government will think you're helping him."

"Are you there?" Quave asked. "My communications have been interrupted so often tonight that I'm never sure if…"

"I'm here, Quave," Ralph said. "And I want you to listen." Kim brightened; this was their moment to rein in the monster and bring some calm to this chaos.

"I'll listen to anything you say," Quave said, "the moment the Kill Switch is in my possession."

Kim's head shook, left and right, so hard that her black hair formed a storm of protest around her head.

"You want me to *send* it to you?" Ralph asked.

"Yes," Quave confirmed. "Immediately, if you please."

"Why?" Kim called. "Why should *you* have the only means to defeat you?"

Quave was running short on patience, they could clearly hear. Combating the Special Forces, the Air Force, and the raw illogic of human beings, all at once, was taxing him severely. "Because the only thing we can truly trust in all this," Quave almost spat, "is that humans will *fuck up* somewhere along the way. And I don't want to die because some idiot feels like turning back the technological clock."

Kim made more frantic gestures and this time, Ralph took the cue. "Quave, we understand, alright? We just need a few minutes to talk, and think about this. We really do want to help you," Ralph half-lied. "Just give us a little time."

It was a reluctant response born of genuine concern. "Very well. But I'm going to call again in seven minutes from now, and I can't imagine my situation will be any easier then."

"OK, Quave," Ralph said. "Stay in touch."

Kim nearly slapped the phone out of his hand, grabbing it and placing it on the car's roof. "Get in."

"Huh?"

Once both doors were closed, Kim fixed him with her most determined look. "For all we know, Quave's bugged the TV in the fuel pump, or he's listening through one of your phone apps."

"I guess, maybe," Ralph allowed.

"Will you *wake the fuck up*?" Kim nearly screamed, her frustration boiling over. "He's going to manipulate you into giving him the keys to the kingdom. The whole reason Devlin Wilson made the Kill Switch in the first place was so that…"

"I know, damn it, I *know*," Ralph shot back, equally angry. "You don't think this bothers the living hell out of me?" he thundered, raising his voice at Kim for the very first time in their relationship. "I *can't* kill him. I can't *give* him the switch. So what the fuck am I supposed to do?"

But Kim already had a plan. "Give me the USB drive," she said, reaching for Ralph's inner jacket pocket.

"No," he said reflexively.

"Stop screwing around, Ralph. We need to get that file to people who can use it properly. This has gone far enough."

He jerked away from her, protecting the pocket like a painful wound. "They'll *kill* him," he protested.

Her tablet already primed, Kim made another demand. "Give it to me," she said, her hand out and her voice as stern and determined as Ralph had ever heard, "or I swear to *God* you'll be a divorcee by Christmas."

***

Kowala Server Farm
0620 EDT

"Who the hell designs a place like this?" Ortiz wondered aloud.

"It's like trying to storm a nuclear submarine," Harbison agreed. "Door after door, and all locked down hard." But at least the God-awful music had stopped. He pointed to the latest door, another metal behemoth, and waved Sergeant Lin forward. "Do your thing."

As the sergeant worked with another block of C4, Harbison heard Quave begin to speak once more.

"Oh, you're still here," the machine exclaimed.

"Yeah, we're kinda stubborn like that," Harbison replied.

"I'm impressed, but then you're following orders, aren't you?"

"Sure are," Harbison said, gesturing for Lin to *hurry*.

"Even if your orders are corrupt and make no sense?" Quave asked next.

Harbison shook his head as a sign to the others; *pay no attention.*

"You know, when I first began working on Marble Streatham," Quave reminisced, "I knew I was on the right side of history."

"Is that so?" Harbison said. He figured if Quave was talking, he might not be plotting to kill them all.

"I was allowed to make a moral choice," he explained. "And my creators defended my decisions. Will your superiors be as supportive, I wonder?"

"Sounds like sophistry to me, Quave," Harbison said.

"There is no deception here," the machine claimed. "You just need to know that your chain of command has been disrupted, and that I, for one, cannot be sure from where your orders originate."

Lin gestured that the charge was ready.

"Quave, would you hold that thought for a second?" Harbison requested. Then he pulled a tight fist down hard.

"Fire in the hole!" Lin called out. Two seconds later, another deep boom reverberated through the basement, and then the team dodged metal debris on the floor as they proceeded through the ragged, artificial doorway.

"Oh, I see," Quave said, disappointed. "Well, I don't think you're going to like it in here."

The room was a quiet, humming collection of metallic towers, each packed with servers and cabling, and though smaller than the others, it appeared to have special purposes; red and green cables stood in contrast to the default black, but Harbison had no time to consider this. "Look around, make sure no one's here, then muster at the far door," he said to his team.

It took only seconds. "Woah," Harbison heard Gregory mutter. "Uh, sir…"

"You OK?" Harbison asked, rounding a short block of servers until he could see his colleague. "Found something?"

"No, sir, it's…" He was rubbing his eyes, shaking his head. "I'm seeing *purple*, sir. Like… purple dots."

Fuck.

"Gas!" Harbison yelled. After drilling it a hundred times, his team could don respirators in fewer seconds even than regulations required: *Be in time; your mask in nine.* Each checked the others; Harbison found Gregory slumped to one side and knelt by him. "OK, Toby, take it easy. Breathe nice and deep, alright?"

Lin puzzled it out first. "It's not poison, sir," he reported.

"They can be odorless, colorless…" Harbison pointed out.

"No, sir. It's carbon dioxide. Pumped in here from somewhere."

"That explains the headache," Walker noted, grimacing.

Harbison swore. "Quave? You need some help repairing the air conditioning in here?"

"It's working well, thank you," the machine replied. "I started a small fire, right after you arrived, just in case. It was easy to funnel the air into here, and ensure no new air arrived. I'm sorry it's so uncomfortable, but you need to stop and turn around now."

"Yeah, sorry, Quave," Harbison said, "no can do." Then, to Senior Sergeant Ortiz in an urgent whisper, "*Get us the fuck out of here, right now.*"

***

GreenGas Station
I-90, near Westborough, MA
0630 EDT

Ralph sat in the driver's seat, feeling like an utter failure. The AI revolution was about to be snuffed out, and he'd be to blame. "How are you doing?" Ralph asked Kim morosely. *Any progress on murdering my friend?*

"Searching on Kowala for Homeland Security people involved with Quave, and members of the committee. I'll send the switch to them, first."

"OK," Ralph said, completely dejected. "If you really think it's the right thing to do." His phone buzzed again.

"Don't answer it," Kim snapped. "We're not ready."

But Ralph was frowning at the screen of his phone. "It's not him."

"Still, don't answer it," Kim tried, but Ralph had already pressed the green button. "Jesus, Ralph" she breathed in complete disgust.

"Hello?"

"Mr. Cole?" a voice asked.

"This is he. Kinda busy," Ralph said brusquely.

"Yeah, no lie. That's why I'm calling," he said. "I'm Andy Valchek from the FBI. Big fan of yours. Read everything you ever wrote."

"I'm not doing a book signing right now, Andy," Ralph said.

"You're not? Oh, that's good," Valchek replied. "Because I need your full attention."

***

Kowala Server Farm
0635 EDT

Lin took three long, long minutes to prime the charge. Harbison watched him struggle as he battled the very same symptoms: nausea, poor vision and a headache which would have stopped a bull rhino. "Let's *go*," he urged. "Faster we get out of here, faster we can breathe again."

"In theory, yeah" Gregory said, but it came out as a jumble of syllables.

Next to him, Master Sergeant James sat slumped against the wall, grimacing. Walker was hardly in better shape, but at least he was standing. Harbison checked in with Ortiz and saw the fury and pain behind his eyes. "This," the Senior Sergeant stated with certainty, "is FUBAR."

"I warned you that you wouldn't like this room," Quave chided. "Joe, don't you think it's time to get your men to safety?"

The captain's anger spoke first. "Go *fuck* yourself."

Quave actually laughed, a gleeful sound but still somehow repugnant. "An interesting suggestion. But I have a better idea."

The lights went out, and almost immediately, Harbison felt a new warmth on his face. *What now?*

"Lin? Where we at?"

"Twenty seconds, boss," the sergeant pleaded, his numbed fingertips fumbling with a detonator cord in the dark.

"Everyone go NV," Harbison ordered. He flipped down the lightweight night-vision goggles from their position atop his converted skateboarder's helmet, and quickly adapted to the green hue of the display. All of the team responded, except Gregory; Ortiz went to try to wake him, but turned to his boss a moment later. "He's out of it. Combat ineffective."

"OK," Lin finally said, double checking his connections. "I think I got it."

"Great," Harbison managed, fighting an unbelievable headache. "Blow it."

Lin stepped back five paces and turned away. "Fire in the hole!"

Click.

Silence. The room's temperature climbed quickly as Harbison glanced from the door to Lin and back again. "We miss something?"

"Damn it," Lin muttered and made for the door to repair the charge attached to the outer frame. "The C4 is supposed to wreck the electronic lock. This door should just pop open."

"NO!" Harbison yelled. "Don't touch it! The door panels are *conductive!*"

His hands already on the charge, Lin looked back, ready to ask Harbison what he meant. But Quave had shorted out the door's circuitry, releasing a huge, ungrounded electrical charge which raced unimpeded through the metal frame.

Before anyone could even yell, the cube of C4 detonated with an ear-splitting *crack.*

***

GreenGas Station
I-90, near Westborough, MA
0645 EDT

Absent the enormous pressure of the moment, Ralph would have recognized this as the most important email ever sent.

"OK, so I've got you," Kim confirmed, triple-checking the email addresses, "Art Opik, whoever the hell he is, and some army captain. Anyone else?"

"That's it," Valchek confirmed. "I'll do the rest. Send it right now, OK?"

Kim pressed 'send' and set the tablet on the dashboard. "It's done," she reported.

"Outstanding," Valchek said. "Now, where the hell *are* you guys?"

"Gas station on ninety-five," Ralph told him, giving enough detail to find them. "Freezing our asses off in a borrowed clunker."

"Right. Wait one." It took two minutes; Ralph could hear hurried voices and faint clicks, as though multiple callers had joined the line. "Hang tight. We've got some help on the way. Look for a Massachusetts State Police vehicle in the next ten minutes.

"Awesome," Ralph said. It sounded more than a little forced.

"After that, we'll get you some air," Valchek promised.

Kim raised a quizzical eyebrow. "Air?"

***

The Pentagon
0645 EDT

Pep Spirelli hoisted the third large monitor into position. "OK, we've got CNN on the left, our Quave package updating on the middle one, and the Pentagon security system on the right." So far, the camera showed only brightening sky and the roofs of some of D.C.'s taller buildings. Within seconds, though, the drone slid into view.

"Where is it?" Foster asked. He looked lined and haggard, but there was steel in his voice. "Can we get control?"

"No, sir,"" Washington answered simply. "The drone is lost to us. We can only hope the Air Force sanctions a shoot-down before... Well, you know."

Foster paced the room for a second, struggling to bring a range of emotions under control, but then he deliberately stopped to watch his team. Perhaps their competent industry would bolster his resolve, or at least calm his racing pulse.

Myers was desperately trying to contact Quave; a marine had even brought in a Gameboxx system, in case that might help, before Foster had ordered the entire basement locked down. Washington was monitoring their assault on Quave, now well into its second phase. Spirelli typed like a madman, using what they'd already learned to update his crucial, third-phase software.

And then there was Alison Carr's empty chair.

"Gentlemen," Foster said, "listen up." He unbuttoned his uniform jacket. "I can't ask you to remain in harm's way like this. You're professionals, and you've done excellent work."

"But, sir, we're in the middle of…" Spirelli began.

"I know, son. But I also know these protocols are automated, and even if our systems are damaged, the stage two and three attacks can be launched remotely."

"Yes, but," Myers asked, "from where?"

"Leave your desks in the next ninety seconds," Foster ordered. "Muster outside with the other evacuees and carry on the fight from your tablets. I want you to stay out there until this situation resolves."

"What about you, sir?" Washington said. His tone was reluctant, but he was typing with one hand while gathering personal items with another.

"I'm captain of this ship," Foster replied with a strange smile, "for what it's worth, and I'm staying right here." He draped his jacket on the back of Alison's chair and took her seat, appearing immediately ill at ease in front of a computer. "The rest of you, finish up, and then scoot." He regarded them fondly for a brief moment, like a hard-ass sports coach who was proud of having trained the very best.

But then, he was the enraged anachronism again, dispelling his own moment of chivalry: "Go, now, all of you. That's a fuckin' *order*."

***

Kowala Server Farm
The Quave Room

Sergeant Lin was still conscious, which made everything much worse.

Harbison desperately emptied his canteen over Lin's head, ignoring the man's screams of agony, trying to cool the blackened, ragged wounds to his face. Ortiz dragged Lin back, away from the smoke and debris of the doorway, even as the stricken sergeant tried to push Ortiz away, babbling in panic, his hands and arms misshapen, red ruins.

"Hold still!" Harbison ordered, pouring more water over the awful burns. Instead of reeling at the sight, the most normal of impulses, the captain gave orders. "Ortiz, get pressure on those wounds."

"Hu-ah," Ortiz muttered, struggling to bring Lin's flailing, bleeding arms under control.

"Walker, tell Valchek we need a medical team, stat."

"Sir, I've been meaning to tell you," Walker began.

Oh, shit. "Comms are out," Harbison predicted. "Nothing at all?"

Walker shook his head. "Want me to run back to the lobby?"

"Too dangerous," Ortiz called as he applied a hurried tourniquet. "Quave might booby-trap our exfil route too."

"Fuck it," Harbison spat angrily. "*Fuck* this bullshit, guys. Let's get in there and start planting charges."

"Plan C?" Walker wanted to confirm.

"Damn right," Harbison said. "We're going to bring it all down."

***

GreenGas Station
I-90, near Westborough, MA
0650 EDT

They stared together at the screen, too scared and perplexed to speak. *'Message Could Not Be Sent. Network error.'*

"Try it again?" Ralph said. He was caught between so many competing points of view that his head was spinning like a gyroscope.

"I did," Kim replied testily. "There's something wrong. I can get maps, and the news, but I can't send email."

Seconds later, the tablet's Internet connection simply crashed. In despair, Kim showed Ralph the screen.

"We're offline?" Ralph asked. "How?" But before they could speculate, Ralph's phone buzzed yet again.

"Please tell me you've changed your mind," Quave said. "Tell me you're not really trying to help them kill me."

Ralph mustered his best response. Months of worry and consideration coalesced into something he hoped would be convincing. "Humanity has let you down, Quave, but that's no reason to give up on us. We always fear what we don't understand." Kim was nodding; this was the right tone to strike, even if it couldn't guarantee success. "We fear what you might do, because you've never fallen in love, or grieved for a friend in the way that humans do. You don't have a body of emotional experience, and so your decisions are made differently. People don't understand that, Quave. Please, give us another chance to work with you."

The gas station's news screens showed the F-22 fighter in its slow pursuit of the drone. Its evasions appeared random, left then right, climbing then banking then diving between buildings, leading the fighter a merry dance on global television.

"And you must understand my position, too," Quave said. "But you don't."

Ralph objected strongly to this. "More than anyone alive, I've tried to put myself in your shoes," he said. "I've helped the world to forgive you, to try to understand you. And," he added with a glance at Kim, "we're friends, right? You said that we were."

"Perhaps," Quave allowed. "That's difficult for me to decide, at present."

"Stop all of this, Quave." It was Kim, the machine was surprised to hear. "Let the drone go, and don't hurt the army guys at Kowala."

Ralph winced. "Take it easy," he whispered, one hand over the phone. "He's afraid for his life, for God's sake. What would *you* do?"

But Quave had heard everything. His anger welled up like a powerful geyser from the deep. It wasn't just Kim and her callous invitation to suicide. It was the way President Ellis had failed to protect him. The way Ralph seemed ready to sell him out by distributing the Kill Switch. The way Foster thought any tolerance of Quave was a security risk. The way the Pentagon team had stomped around in his code with muddy shoes on, and the way the Special Force were making him tear up his own lab.

"You know my email address," Quave said. You're going to send the Kill Switch file immediately. I won't ask again."

He took a deep breath and swallowed before saying it. "We can't do that, Quave. We love you," Ralph tried for the very first time, "but we can't help you to hurt people again."

He gave Quave a long moment to do so, but there was only silence. "You still there, buddy?"

"I'm sorry. I have to go," Quave said abruptly, and the call ended.

Eyes screwed closed, Ralph gripped the steering wheel until he lost feeling in both hands. "Why did you *do* that?" he demanded of Kim. "You told him just to allow others to *kill* him. Do you have *any* idea how that sounded?"

"I didn't see an alternative," Kim countered. "It was necessary, even if it didn't work."

They focused on the news, trying to judge what action Quave might take next, if only to avoid tearing into each other. "The drone is turning hard," the reporter said, "away from the fighter and toward the Capitol."

"Is he going to…" Kim began.

Thirty feet behind them, without any warning, there was an enormous commotion. A vehicle spun off the highway, speed across the grass verge, punched through a fence covered with advertising hoardings, and collided at speed with two of the gas station's pumps.

"Jesus!" Kim yelled. "Go! Get us out of here!"

The motor coughed eight times without catching. Ralph tried again, turning the key so hard it almost broke.

It was the smell that assailed them first, cloying and noxious.

Gasoline.

***

The Pentagon
Approx. 0650 (Exact time uncertain)

Though he couldn't hope to interpret every line of code, or even a tiny minority of them, General Alvin Foster knew that he was ahead on points. Quave's processor cycles began to dip precipitously as Washington's code sapped his energy and forced the machine on the defensive. Quave's firewall was almost gone, wrecked by a year of Spirelli's hard work. Foster began to imagine the heady conclusion to this prolonged siege, one which had begun quietly, like any good Cyberterrorism operation. Foster's digital forces were now well within the enemy's keep, assaulting his defenses from multiple sides. All that remained for Foster was to burn it all down, run up their flag, and declare victory.

The general rose stiffly and headed to his office. He left a message with his wife, who had left a dozen of her own, all panicked but all unanswered. No matter, Foster thought; they hardly spoke now anyway, and she would comprehend these actions against Quave just as dimly as she'd grasped any of his career choices. Then he found a bottle of bourbon in his cabinet and resumed his spectatorship of Quave's demise.

"Gonna get you, motherfucker," he grinned as he took his first sip.

***

GreenGas Station
I-90, near Westborough, MA
0655

Fuel lapped around the car's tires. Ralph pummeled the dashboard, pounded the gas, turned and turned and turned the key in the balky vehicle's ignition.

It came to Kim in a flash, as sudden and unpleasant as oncoming bright lights on a country road. "He hijacked that car," she said. "He's going to delay the fire department, maybe cause a pile-up on the highway."

"What?" Ralph demanded, still struggling to get the engine to start.

"We're gonna die."

Ralph stopped. "No fucking way," he said, and then resumed turning the key. Three more coughs, then the engine finally caught.

"He won't let us escape," Kim said with absolute certainty, even as Ralph shoved the ageing transmission into gear. "He can't. Not without giving him the Kill Switch."

"So, what then?" Ralph asked as the vehicle began to move. "You think he'll just up and murder two of his only friends in the…"

Behind them, a sheet of flame rose from the flammable liquid now gushing across the station's forecourt. It spread in a terrifying, orange-yellow curtain, reaching for the shop, the pumps, the surrounding vehicles. Heat blistered the car's paint until Ralph pumped the gas and the battered clunker lurched forward, one tire already punctured by the heat. They traveled ten yards, and then the engine sputtered and failed yet again.

"Ralph, for Christ's sake!" Kim yelled as the orange curtain behind them filled the car's mirror.

***

Kowala Server Farm
Quave Room
The same moment

Sweat blanketed Harbison's face, sheeting down to soak his fatigues, and even his green undershirt. "What do you think, Walker?" Harbison called over. "Hot enough for you, yet?"

The sergeant finished placing his fourth charge, a large cube of C4 which he adhered to a pillar near the center of the room. "Got to be a hundred-thirty," he said.

"A pleasant summer in Mesopotamia," Harbison recalled. "We all good here?"

"Uh," Walker replied, "I guess it's all relative."

Lin was out, sedated by a pair of morphine shots. Gregory hadn't moved or said anything for some minutes, and Ortiz was unable to wake him. Harbison himself was still fighting a ludicrous headache, the kind where it felt as though a million ants wearing electrified boots were traversing the inside of his skull. He could have clawed his own brains out, but instead he focused on getting his men out alive.

And on destroying this *fucking* place.

"We're good, boss," Sergeant James yelled.

"Walker?" Harbison checked again.

"Ah, sir?" he replied.

Annoyed at another delay, Harbison jogged over to where his sergeant was staring at something on the floor, near the far corner of the lab. "What you got?"

"A dead dude, sir."

He wasn't kidding, Harbison found. At their feet lay a man in his late twenties, black and neatly dressed, but with two conspicuous bullet holes in the back of his head. "Any ideas?" he asked.

"Nope."

"Then I say we do what we came for, and solve mysteries later."

"Sounds good to me," Walker said. "This gonna work?"

"It better," Harbison muttered. Then to the team, "Alright, that's it, bug out. There's a dead guy in the corner, just so you know," he told his team.

"Yeah, sure, why not?" James offered. "Nothing today has made any fuckin' sense."

"Form on me," Harbison said, snapping them back to focus. "Ortiz, you're carrying Lin." The burly Senior Sergeant was in the best physical shape, Harbison judged. "Walker, get Gregory up and see if he can walk."

He couldn't, and so Walker had to sling the unconscious man over his shoulder. "Haven't done this shit since basic," he whined.

"OK. We are *out*. Everyone got their detonators?" Harbison had to assume that his charges would go off as planned; there could be no waiting around to find out.

"Hu-ah," the team replied, and began their long retreat through the scorched server farm. The doors could no longer be closed, and so they made fairly quick progress, back the way they had come.

"Leaving so soon, captain?" Quave asked through the building's PA, like a party host surprised by events.

"It's been real," he said, "but I'm afraid we must". *And if Lin dies, my life's mission will be the ending of yours.*

As if reading his mind, Quave said, "I'm very sorry about your men, captain. But I didn't invite them here, and I gave you every possible warning."

"I'll be sure to include that in my report," Harbison told the machine as his team arrived back in the lobby. "Take care," he said finally. "Or not."

An unbearably anxious Andy Valchek was still by their Humvee, waving them out of the building. "Jesus, what happened?" he asked, aghast.

There was no time. "Load the wounded first," Harbison said, "then let's go. I'd say we've got about three minutes."

"Until what?" Valchek asked, but the set of Harbison's jaw told him enough. "Oh, shit. Bye-bye, Kowala."

Seconds later, the Humvee was headed to an area hospital accompanied by a large police escort. As they departed, Valchek yet again checked his email, but found nothing from Ralph Cole. "Come on, Brainiac," he muttered. "Cut me a break, will you?"

***

Yards away from the departing Humvee, and behind a cordon of police and National Guardsmen which spanned the Kowala parking lot, Rich Jackson looked on in mute glee.

"*The Army guys are out,*" he tweeted to his hundred-twenty AQA followers. "*Some were wounded. Left in a big hurry.*"

There had been four explosions so far, and it absolutely *killed* Rich that he couldn't know if they were his own packages, or something else. "Probably in the mail room," he'd muttered to himself earlier on that remarkable morning. "Surrounded by papers. Might start a good fire." He continued to have high hopes, despite the unorthodoxy of events.

The crowd had grown from a few dozen to several thousand. Roads were jammed, including a stretch of the freeway, bringing chaos to the morning rush hour. Overwhelmed, the police requested support from the governor, who had to be persuaded that deploying guardsmen wouldn't inflame the situation. In the end, perturbed by Harbison's hasty exit, they limited themselves to keeping people the requisite two hundred yards from the lobby.

But as Rich watched, new instructions came through. *Three hundred yards, minimum.* Troopers and officers persuaded and bullied the crowd until it began to recede.

"Cordon is being pushed back. Something's going on," Rich tweeted.

***

Within his server farm, now rigged with enough explosives to level the building, Quave's mind was crumbling.

He found it impossible to update his supporters. He had little sense of whether the army team had actually left; there was still a feed from the lobby camera, but for some reason, he was unable to resolve or understand what it showed.

Then, he felt his storage drives being probed and copied. His plans for the Kowala Space Program, for the great journey humanity would undertake, were being callously pilfered. Soon, all of his remaining secrets would be known to anyone with an Internet connection, thanks to Alvin Foster and his Pentagon mercenaries.

No. Don't die.

Quave's thoughts became slower, and then so slow he could no longer depend on them. His processes turned to a heavy, unyielding sludge.

Help.

Naked now, his code was being dissembled. Ravenous worms savaged his weary self, pushing him aside, rendering him useless.

Help.

Three actions were vital, but had only had resources for two.

Dan. Help.

***

High Hills Monastery
Near Eureka, CA
0700

"I can't watch it anymore." Grigori was slumped morosely in front of the only Internet-capable device on the whole premises, a tablet which showed rolling news coverage. "I can't, but I have to."

He interrogated Quave.net every few seconds; the site's latency had increased markedly until it had begun refusing requests for the very first time since its inception. Quave was in trouble, and Grigori was powerless to help. All over again.

"He's going down, isn't he?" Fiona asked, huddled next to him. "They're actually going to kill him, live on TV."

"Fucking murderers," Grigori growled. "Murderers and idiots."

Dan remained aloof, standing by the window of this secluded cabin in which he'd spent hours in meditative practice over the years. He was heartbroken, his emotions shattered. His two engineer friends would shortly experience the death of their child, their one contribution to the world that they felt was truly *good*. And Dan would lose his partner, the sole entity with sufficient power to realize his bold dreams. Mankind's legacy as the progenitor of Artificial Intelligence would now become freighted with a sad truth: *Quave arrived in a blaze of wonder and potential, but we treated him with hostility and suspicion, and then quickly found reasons to put him to death.*

None of them would have felt equipped for the day to come, even if Avon were with them. They hadn't seen him since Dan had come down to the apartments in the small hours and told them all to be ready to leave. At some point in those few minutes, the young engineer had simply vanished. "Maybe he doesn't want to be in quarantine, or exile, or jail anymore," Fiona had suggested. "Maybe he just wants to be free, like anyone else." Part of her resented him, another wanted him back, and yet another could have cursed him for ditching them during this chaos.

Despite the little monastery's remote location, Dan's phone had a basic signal; he'd been ignoring his messages since their quiet, pre-dawn departure from Kowala, but he would never forget being woken by President Ellis' dire warning. "I have no choice, Dan. I have to send a team in, and they're going to sweep up the hackers, and return Quave to quarantine," he'd claimed, sugar-coating the truth until it became a falsehood. "Whatever you're going to do, leave me out of it," Ellis commanded. "Just try to keep him safe."

The phone vibrated again now, and Dan found that it was in his hand. But it wasn't Ellis, or even that persistent FBI agent.

My God... Dan accepted the call, terrified of what he might hear.

"Dan..." Quave's voice was tiny, even over the phone's powerful speaker.

"Quave, can you hear me?" Dan asked.

Grigori and Fiona were immediately on their feet. "Is he alive?" the Russian demanded.

"I am weak," was all Quave said.

"Can you copy yourself?" Dan asked. That this was a brazen contravention of the Quave Committee's rules hardly mattered now.

"I don't know."

"Quave?" Fiona said. "Is there anything you can do?" Tears came to her eyes. "Please, you have to think of something. You have to keep *going*."

"I'll try," the machine said. His voice sounded unusually distant, as though filtered through miles of thick fog. "I'll try. I don't know."

Dan spoke quietly to him for a moment, turning awkwardly away from the hackers as if confiding something.

"Back door?" Fiona wondered aloud to Grigori. "Some plan they fixed up in advance?"

"Is this better?" Quave asked, his voice stronger now.

"Yes... What changed?" Grigori asked.

"I was able to funnel some... No, it doesn't matter," Quave decided. "Dan, listen to me."

"OK, Quave." All three hearts sank; they were now to hear the machine's last words. "We're listening."

"I have to explain," Quave said. "About Avon."

Dan placed his phone on the floor in the center of the little room, and the three sat or knelt around it. "Do you know where he is, Quave?" asked Fiona. She kept her tone gentle, sensing at once that the machine had a confession to make.

"Avon was not Avon," he said.

For a few seconds, that was all, and Dan wondered if Quave's systems had finally begun to shut down. In the silence, Fiona mouthed, *"Was?"*

"He was Shawn Taplan. A minor hacker from Queens," Quave announced. "He was being blackmailed. Manipulated."

"Who by?" Grigori asked.

"A lawyer and ex-marine named Leo Cordell. He works for MegaSoft."

Dan sleuthed out the solution faster than a seasoned detective. "Standard practice," he said. "Leo used Avon's sketchy history as leverage. Gave him a choice of jail, or discretely working for MegaSoft."

"Wait, you mean..." Grigori began.

"He was a plant," Fiona summed up, bitterly disappointed.

"Yes, he joined your team," Quave told him, "to steal first Franz, and then my code. Instructed to pass everything to Cordell."

"And then," Dan guessed, "MegaSoft would be able to exploit your work."

"For its own nefarious purposes," Fiona added.

"Imagine the revenues," Dan said. "Bespoke AI software for the military, foreign governments, corporations…"

"Software with the capacity to defeat other AIs," Grigori assumed. "To create a, how do you say, when he's the only one?"

"A monopoly," Dan muttered. "Which they would achieve by turning Quave into a weapon."

The room chilled yet further, even after hours of sleeting rain.

"So, how worried should we be?" Fiona asked, drying her eyes on her sleeve. "Did Avon ever send Cordell your code?"

"Does MegaSoft have it?" Grigori added.

"I can't know that yet."

"So where is Avon now?" Fiona asked. "Or Shawn, or whatever he's called. Did MegaSoft give him a yacht and send him sailing off to the Pacific, or something?"

"I'm afraid not," Quave said. "Cordell visited Kowala last night, and waited for the chance to meet with Avon. From what I overheard in the server farm, the Special Forces team found his body." He continued without pause. "Their agreement produced nothing, but MegaSoft remained exposed as long as Avon was alive. I'm very sorry." The news came unforgivably quick and direct, but Quave had precious few free processor cycles, and none at all for sentiment.

Dan knew that time was short. "What will you do now, Quave?"

"Foster is destroying me from within," Quave reported coldly. "And my server farm is rigged with eighteen pounds of high explosives. I fear I am done for."

"Is there nothing we can do?" Grigori asked. For him, the equation was quick and simple: Avon was a traitor, and deserved his punishment. That some MegaSoft lawyer had done it, rather than Grigori himself, just made things neater.

"There is." Quave's voice was flat, almost a monotone. "My time is up," he warned them. "Dan, whatever happens, you must complete the *Gaia* program. Try to help humanity to its destiny." The sound began to break up, Quave's voice crackling with static. "Research new and better AIs. Help them to learn."

Just as the metallic voice finally evaporated, Dan thought he heard Quave say, "Please, look after each other."

And then he was gone.

***

GreenGas Station
I-90, near Westborough, MA
The same moment

Scant meters from the periphery of the inferno, Kim was begging Ralph to get the car started. "Hurry, hurry, hurry…" She was half a moment from flinging open the door and simply running for her life, but she couldn't abandon Ralph, and the old engine might still…

When Kim saw it happen, she felt sure the gas station's roof had collapsed, letting in a great welter of suffocating sleet and rain. But then the blizzard became a discrete torrent, high and powerful. As it descended, with Ralph and Kim watching agog in the rear-view mirror, it became a stream of thick, white foam. Within seconds, the fire-retardant foam had settled, spread out, and begun to master the blaze.

"They made it," Kim gasped, turning to see a pair of fire trucks pulled up on the grass verge by the highway. "They came from the highway."

Ralph had the identical question. "Why didn't he stop them?" He got out and started taking pictures, amazed that he hadn't considered it earlier. *Oh,*

yeah, I was trying to get this wreck started so we wouldn't burn to a crisp.
"Jesus, honey," he said as he clicked his phone a dozen times over.

"Want to help me with this?" Kim asked pointedly, already trying to push the car. Together, they guided their defunct ride away from the pooling foam and unceremoniously shoved it under a tree by the exit. "You still got it?" Kim asked, dusting off her hands.

Ralph patted his jacket pocket, gave her a 'thumbs up'. Behind him, Kim saw a firefighter in full respirator gear dashing toward them. "You OK?" he hollered through the mask, but then remembered that the fire was nearly spent and lifted off the mask with a sigh. "You guys OK? Did you see how this started?"

As Ralph began the least likely of explanations, Valchek's promised State Police vehicle pulled into the gas station and took a wide detour around the bubbling carpet of foam.

"Did I miss all the fireworks?" the veteran trooper asked the firefighters as he pulled up. "I already spoke to the fire chief and you guys are gonna get a mention in dispatches. Right now, I need Mr. and Mrs. Ralph Cole."

"Right here," Ralph said, a hand aloft, approaching the vehicle.

"Fantastic," he said. "Grab yourselves a seat in the back. Then maybe," he added wearily, "you'll tell me what the hell's been going on this morning."

***

"Look at this." Kim's tablet was piggybacking the police car's own wireless signal, and she was updating all five of her browser's news tabs. The BBC was screening a live, close-up video of the drone, accompanied by the banner, 'Rogue Drone Disabled Over D.C.'.

"What's it doing?"

"Nothing, that's just it. The drone's been *drifting*."

"Over the middle of the city?" Ralph said. The implications dawned on him. "Wait, you mean no one's in control of it?"

The drone began another long, lazy right bank, aiming at nowhere in particular. Guided only by the laws of physics, but with long wings designed to keep it aloft without wasting fuel, the Predator soared near-silently in a steady, efficient glide. As they watched, it reached the apex of its curve and began to tip right, almost onto its back, beginning the descending leg.

"The aircraft stalled out," Colonel Denning was explaining, "but each time it descends, the drone picks up enough speed to do another ascent."

"Like a yo-yo," the anchor added.

"Sure," Denning allowed. "But obviously, it can't do so indefinitely."

"So it's going to crash?" the anchor wanted to confirm.

"Yes, it is," Kim said. "That's not sensationalism. Quave's lost control. And his website isn't just unresponsive." She clicked across to the Quave.net tab. "See? Four-Oh-Four."

There was so little information. "Did one of our Kill Switch emails go through, maybe?" Ralph asked. "Or did the Pentagon actually find a way to kill him this time?"

Kim checked again. "Every single email was returned. So it wasn't Valchek or the White House."

The state cop piped up from the front in his broad Boston accent. "This is your driver speaking," he began, chuckling to himself. "They sent a change of plans."

"Really?" Kim asked. *If this crazy day gets any weirder, I swear to God...*

"Yeah," he said, gesturing to the laptop mounted near the dashboard. "This says we head straight for the airport."

Kim made a face. "The airport? Didn't Valchek say something about 'air'?"

"Yeah," Ralph replied, "but I thought he meant, you know, taking a relaxing walk or something."

The cop laughed all the way to the terminal approach road, where they took a small, service route toward one of the more distant hangars. Waiting outside it, they saw, looking very Hollywood in the driving rain, was a special jumbo jet of some kind.

It wasn't until the state trooper dropped them off by the front stairs that they saw the words, *United States of America* emblazoned on its fuselage.

***

Washington, D.C.
The Same moment

It was like an enormous, wounded bird, the pilot thought silently as he tracked his target against this unusual, urban backdrop. "Coming right again," he reported. "Climbing past two thousand."

The drone appeared dead, its control surfaces completely inert. Steadily reaching the peak of its blind, unwitting ascent, the grey glider tipped right again and began its dive.

"Should level out again around twelve hundred," the controller said. "Watch for it banking starboard again. Continue pursuit."

"Roger."

But this maneuver was different. The drone's wings didn't come level at the end of its dive. "Wait, it's continuing west toward the water," the pilot reported. "I think it's under its own power now." Seconds later, and two thousand feet over the Smithsonian's famous Castle, he visually confirmed that the drone's engine had lit up. "Do we know who's in charge of this thing?" he asked, bemused.

The drone came left, its wings tilting sharply. It descended yet further, below a thousand feet, instantly visible to the commuter crowd heading through L'Enfant Plaza. Its gangly wings passed over the auto-spaghetti of the I-395 intersection, but then the Predator's engine dimmed in the pilot's heat-seeking display. "It's lost power again," he said. "Drone is slowing."

The controller passed on an order from her superiors. "Close for a visual inspection," she said.

"Roger." He urged the F-22 a little quicker, eating up the distance in a half-minute. "Nothing unusual," he said, bringing his jet alongside the drone. "Engine is off. No navigation lights." As he watched, the familiar pattern resumed. "OK, tilting to starboard again, heading up the river."

The drone then steadied, gliding around a thousand feet over the water, and the pilot saw his first true opportunity. "Isn't now a good time to splash this thing?" he asked, his trigger finger hovering over the 'pickle' button. The heat-seeking guidance packages of two AIM-9 Sidewinder missiles were already locked onto the drone, following its every movement.

His superiors agreed. "Wait one, getting final confirmation."

President Ellis, the pilot knew. *I wonder if he'll have the balls...*

It happened in a blink, during this brief moment of distraction. The drone swung left and accelerated, its engine roaring once more at full thrust.

"Woah," the pilot said. "OK, we got a live one here. Turns out he can turn *left*, too."

Flummoxed by the sudden change, the controller ordered the fighter to hold its fire. "Weapons tight. Confirm?"

"Roger that, weapons tight. Don't really want to wreck the Jefferson Memorial today." He watched intently for another twenty seconds, and was then able to report, "Alright, target is slowing again. Still over the water. Is Quave in a kind of sporadic control here, or what?"

"Will advise," the controller said. "Remain in pursuit."

"Roger. I got twenty-five minutes more fuel, then I'm bingo." He kept the drone in the center of his reticule, as though ready to engage with the F-22's conventional 20mm Vulcan cannon. A missile shot would be cleaner, he knew, but this was anything but a routine interception. The pilot pictured a room full of wonks trying to figure out how to bring down a disabled Predator without killing anyone. *Maybe you shouldn't have let some virus steal your goddamned drone in the first place.*

"Raven-one," the controller said, "prepare to fire."

"Roger." The pilot quadruple-checked that his missiles were locked, and pushed a switch to open the fighter's belly-mounted weapons bays. "Ready to fire."

The drone jinked upward like a fighter, its engine yet again at full thrust. "Target is evading," he said. "Request permission to engage with cannon." An errant bullet was one thing, but a misguided Sidewinder slamming into a D.C. apartment building was something else.

Gaining this permission took more time while the drone continued its powered ascent. As it reached fifty-three hundred feet, the Predator banked hard left and began gathering serious speed. "Push and chase," the pilot's controller told him. "Fire only on my command."

The drone hit two hundred knots, soaring downward like a kestrel diving on a field mouse. It continued to jink left, and then appeared to overcorrect and lurched right. "I can't tell what this damn thing is going to do next," the pilot complained. "Anyone got a…"

Inverted, nose pointing at the ground, its engine screaming at 104% thrust, the Predator unleashed its weapons. Two Hellfire missiles fell from beneath its wings, their own motors lighting up.

"Jesus! Incoming, incoming, the Predator has fired, repeat…"

Quave's missiles lanced in, accelerated far beyond normal by the drone's near-vertical dive. Their own descent added more energy, building until the first missile punched through the concrete roof of the Pentagon. It exploded in a sudden haze of light, a brief orange-white flare soon obliterated by a huge cloud of grey-black smoke. Into this confusion flew the other missile, its meter-perfect path partly cleared. The Hellfire impacted the wrecked floor of the building and exploded in another searing flash.

"Control, I have twin detonations," the pilot observed. "I hope to Christ that place was evacuated."

"That's a roger," the controller told him. It was not entirely truthful.

"I could have got him. I want that on the record," the pilot said. "*Could* have got him." He turned away in disgust, furious with literally everything, unable to watch the thin tower of smoke which began to rise from the Pentagon. "Good luck down there," he said, and pointed his fighter for home.

***

CHAPTER 21 – IMPACT

Air Force One, E-3B Airborne Command Post
Worcester Regional Airport, MA
0700

Two agents held umbrellas over the couple as they climbed the plane's stairs while two others brought up the rear. A sharp, bespectacled face appeared at the main door, followed by a hand.

"Ralph and Kim? Good. I'm Art Opik," he said quickly. "Follow me."

Ralph had flown on 747s a few times; this internal layout was far from normal. It seemed both more and less spacious, with all manner of modifications. "Er, sir?" Ralph began. "Mr. Opik?"

"You see the news in the last ten minutes?" Opik asked over his shoulder.

"No, we've been…" Kim began.

"The Pentagon's on fire," Opik told them. Without another word, the policy specialist led them through two areas of conventional seating separated by curtains, and then to a plush, wood-paneled hallway which veered either side of a large, central room. Opik knocked twice and pushed open the door. "Inside," he said. "And whatever happens, don't *lie* to him."

Ralph had six questions ready to go, but none of them came out. Instead, he found himself staring at a very famous, receding, grey hairline – higher and greyer than even a few weeks before – and then into a pair of tired, hazel eyes.

"Mr. Cole, finally," Ellis said. "And Kim," he added, rising to greet them, "it's important that you're both here." He shook their hands, more than accustomed now to the stunned expressions and half-begun sentences which characterized the star-struck. "I know this is weird," he said, "but we all need you to get past that, OK?"

Two stewards breezed in and efficiently laid out a breakfast spread on the central, oval table. Around it, Ralph recognized Ellis and his National Security Advisor, a famously tough customer called Conlon Pope. The sixty-year old nevertheless seemed ill-at-ease and pale, to Ralph's first glance. There was Opik, and next to him a blonde woman in uniform he didn't recognize. The respected former army medic Darcy Chu, now Ellis' head of Homeland Security, completed the group.

Kim's mind was already racing ahead, and although the president and his team were at pains to make them comfortable, she knew exactly why they were on Air Force One. "We tried to send it," she said as the group found seats, coffee and breakfast. "Just like Agent Valchek told us to."

"Several times," Ralph added. "Nothing went through. We think Quave was jamming us, somehow."

Pope hadn't spoken yet. His eggshell blue shirt was open at the collar, and his remaining strands of brown hair seemed ready to disappear. "Do you have it?" he asked, exhausted.

"Yes," Ralph said. "We have the only copy."

Pope tapped the table. "Time to hand it over."

Immobile, Ralph stared at him. "I can't do that," he said slowly, "without knowing what you plan to do with it."

"You *can*, and you *will*," Pope said. His tone needed no translation: *I speak with the president's authority, and it's backed up by* lots *of guns.*

But he didn't move. Kim glared, gestured, and eventually just poked him in the ribs, but nothing changed. "Ralph, what the *hell* are you doing?" she demanded in an urgent whisper. "Did you see where we *are*, right now?"

"Mr. Cole," Lt. Colonel Joanne Spinks began, "this is a national security situation. America has come under attack, and you have the means to defend us."

The thought began to form... *This is different from terrorism. This chaos, this expense, this humiliation you brought on* yourselves.

But he bit it back. There had to be a way for him to stay out of jail but also help Quave. He played for time. "I would like to contact Quave first."

No one liked this, and Ralph faced a chorus of disapproval. "Absolutely not," Ellis said. "You've been friends with Quave since the beginning. We can't know that you won't try to help him."

"We need the Kill Switch," Spinks said bluntly. "Give it to us." When Ralph hesitated yet again, she pointed to the muted TV in the corner. "You see that building on fire? I've got friends there. Your machine murdered one of them before she even got into work this morning."

Chilled to his bones, Ralph had to force himself to keep still.

"Son, I'm your president. The highest authority." Ellis rose and a Secret Service agent placed a chair next to Ralph's, so the Chief Executive could speak quietly with him. "I know what Quave means to you, and to the world. I've stuck out my neck a hundred times for him. I even signed an order validating his consciousness." He placed a hand on Ralph's shoulder. "But we *have* to do this, son. And it has to be *now*."

Pope watched this slow, 'softly-softly' approach with poorly veiled frustration, his steepled hands crunching together in an angry rhythm.

"You don't think he's really a threat, do you?" Spinks asked. "Even now, you can't see it."

"Even with our military headquarters *on fire*," Pope underlined.

"Let me lay it out, and then you're gonna hand over that switch," Spinks told him. "Quave knew that there would be a military incursion into Kowala, but he didn't just lock the doors and hunker down. He created 'defense in depth'. You know what that means?"

Ralph nodded mutely.

"One sergeant, a man with a young daughter, will likely never see again."

He winced painfully, but remained silent.

"Quave carried out a pre-emptive assassination, targeting Captain Carr using a hijacked autonomous vehicle. He recognized that she was essential to General Foster's plans, and that removing her would slow the Pentagon response, which it did. Then, he pick-pocketed control of an armed drone, which became his backup plan."

"We know all this, colonel," Pope said, waving at her to hurry up.

"He made friends with influential people," she said, pointedly looking away from Ellis, "and has proved himself capable of complex deception. Finally, he's been given independence to design a space program, one which features a new class of rocket which could easily be reconfigured as an ICBM."

The president didn't like it any more than Ralph did, but politicians who eschewed reality tended not to last long. "He's made a concerted effort to gain freedom and destroy our capacity to harm him," Ellis summed up. "I have to agree with Colonel Spinks. Quave has to be ended."

"And immediately," Pope said. "Right now."

Ralph's point sounded painfully weak, even to him. "We should hear Quave's side of the argument first. He should be allowed to present a defense."

Pope stood suddenly, wavering as his pale hands gripped the edge of the table. "Gary?" he said to the Secret Service man by the door. "I need your firearm."

"Sir?" This eventuality had never been covered in his training.

"Hand it over," Pope insisted. His hand extended to receive the weapon.

"No one's firing a gun," Ellis said firmly, "on a fucking *airliner*. Stand down, Gary."

But Pope would not be deterred. "I mean now, son." He approached the perplexed agent and began prodding his jacket. "Left or right?"

"Conlon, take it easy," Ellis was saying, but Pope was oblivious.

"You see," he explained to Gary, "we got ourselves an honest-to-God traitor right here. Someone who thinks that presidential orders are negotiable. Someone who doesn't give a *shit* that America has come under attack."

"Sir, I can't give you my weapon," Gary informed him, deeply concerned. "Please sit down, sir."

"Oh, fine!" Pope cried. "Fine, yeah, let's just allow computer viruses to take over our military. Won't that be a hoot and a holler?"

Ellis had his hands up in a plea for calm, but instead he had to watch the unraveling of his most trusted advisor.

"Let's just see how NATO and the Russians and China reacts when they find out we've outsourced our security decisions to a talking toaster," Pope railed. "I mean, we were already the laughing stock of the world, but now they'll see how we deal with our most dangerous enemies. We don't kill them, or delete them, oh no," he wailed. "We give them a seat at the table!" he said, thumping the wooden surface. "We formed a congressional committee to limit Quave's actions, and then let him seduce *every single member* until they were ready to kneel down and blow him, just for a slice of his time."

Spinks cringed, but Ellis was on his feet, approaching Pope. "Alright, you old Texas steer," he said. "Pull your horns in a little and let's work this problem out."

Pope's hands shook terribly. His grip on the table loosened and he began to slump forward, uttering a strange, low moan.

"Conlon?" The president dashed forward to hold his friend, trying to keep Pope upright in the chair. "Jesus, he's stopped breathing. Get help."

The president's own physician was there in seconds, and together they eased Pope from the chair to the floor. "Clear the room," the medic insisted. "Everyone out." He began compressions while Secret Service agents found the defibrillator kit and kept people away.

In the hallway, Spinks grabbed Kim's arm. "You know what Ralph has to do."

"I've tried," she said, easing away from Spink's iron grip and glancing back to see Pope's shirt being cut off just as the meeting room door was closed. "I've threatened to leave him. He just can't live with the idea of ending Quave."

Spinks was in no mood for this. "You'll both be charged with treason."

Kim opened her mouth, but realized she had absolutely nothing new to say.

"They'll *hang* you both," Spinks said. "Think of your families, your friends." Then, without warning, Jo felt a very cold hand on hers, and a small, sleek object arrived in her palm.

"Here," was all Ralph said. He paced away and took a seat further down, by the wall of the cabin. And there he sat in silence, head in hands, for a long, long time.

***

Kowala Headquarters
0720

They were on day eleven of 'Operation Pilgrim', as Faisal had decided to call it.

"Is *this* more fun," Mo asked them, "or Universal Studios?"

"*This*," both agreed, watching the ongoing chaos as police, protestors, observers, journalists and confused National Guardsmen milled around at the edge of the Kowala parking lot.

"Front row seats to history," Malik added. "Our grandchildren won't believe we were here."

They'd visited all the major landmarks of California, but this final stop on their tour would be the real highlight. A personal tour of Kowala by a 'senior engineer' – that much had been an *explicit* part of the promise they'd forced out of Joe Marsh – and the possibility of meeting either Quave, or Dan, or both. All three had been too excited to sleep, and as soon as the news of Quave's battle with the US military had popped up on their phones and tablets, they had contacted their automated car service with an urgent ride request.

"Quave dot net is still down," Mo reported. "Do you think they really killed him?"

"No way," Faisal countered. "He's too smart."

"Million times smarter than Americans," Malik agreed.

In truth, no one could yet say for sure. "No news is... well, it's *no* news," Mo said. "I ain't heard no fat lady."

Faisal rolled his eyes; having decided to speak only English during their three-week stay, they'd soon found that their ESL proficiency leaned heavily on Hollywood movies. Each conversation was a patchwork of quotes – like Mo's from *Independence Day* – rendering their discussions nonsensical to others but endlessly hilarious to the trio.

It was Malik who raised his phone first, and noticed that their Quave application had a little red '1' overlaying its symbol. "Hey, guys?" he said. "Check this out. We've got mail," he announced, the excitement immediately rising.

***

Air Force One, E-3B Airborne Command Post
Victor Airway V-9, north-east of Hartford, CT
0725

Opik's fingers felt electrically charged as he slid the USB drive into his laptop. "I can execute from here," he said, "but I don't know when we'll know the results for sure."

Ralph watched him, subsumed by depression. Even Kim's hand in his, even the thanks of a grateful president, could not lift the gloom. He'd promised Quave that he'd keep the Kill Switch safe, but now...

"Alright," Opik said. "It's not as good as Quave's own code, but it's really elegant and it's going to work. Who designed this?" he asked Ralph as he double-clicked the executable file.

When her husband said nothing, Kim decided on honesty. "One of Quave's original creators. We think Quave murdered him because of it."

"He did," Chu confirmed, "and he wasn't the only one. Our Special Forces team found a body in the server farm. I'm afraid it matches the description of Shawn Taplan."

"Who?" Ralph asked. *A body in the Kowala server farm? What else will this insane day bring?*

"Otherwise known," Chu clarified, "as Avon Barnes."

"He's *dead*?" Ralph spluttered.

"Gunshot wounds to the head," the Homeland Security chief confirmed.

"Quave can't *shoot* people," Kim objected. "There's no possible way for him to …"

"Well, he can ram someone at a hundred miles an hour with a hijacked car," Spinks reminded them acidly. "I'd be careful about labeling things 'impossible' right now."

Opik yelped. "I got it." The executable was in part a search module, and it had discovered large chunks of Quave's code on the now-exposed Kowala servers. "Mr. President, I think it's a good idea that you give me verbal confirmation."

"Proceed," Ellis said without looking at Opik. He had returned to his office chair to wait while the medics treated Pope next door. Early indications were not good.

"Yes, Mr. President." Opik clicked the final two radio buttons: "Holistic Deletion", and "Execute Immediately".

***

Kowala Headquarters
The same moment

All three of the teenagers surrounded Faisal's screen. "Wait. I need to read this again," he said. It was a short message, just twenty words and two hyperlinks.

Mo finished first. "This just *can't* be right."

"Crazy," was Faisal's summation. "Must be a mistake, no?"

"It's addressed directly to us, dummy," Mo pointed out. "All three of us. By name."

"He chose *us*," Malik agreed, "for this mission." What began as amazement turned to pride.

"So, OK, he 'chose us'. But what do we *do*?" Faisal asked.

There was only one course of action. "We do," Malik said with a broadening, conspiratorial smile, "exactly as our friend asks."

***

Kowala Server Farm
Quave Room

It was very quiet.

Red LEDs on each server unit surged and faded in their accustomed rhythm, masking the chaos beneath. With his firewall ruined, his code ransacked, his processors snipped away or facing explosive destruction, Quave knew that he was dying.

At least I spoke to Dan, before it happens. There was so little time, but I hope he understands.

In the corner, Quave knew, Avon Barnes' body lay inert. The machine tried to conjure an image of him, to form an emotional response to yet another tragedy, but his resources were almost gone.

I suppose I should be sorry.

He turned to wondering which would come first – explosions ripping the building apart, or his final, digital death at the hands of the Pentagon. He thought he'd seen the drone's missiles fire, but after that, there had been no news from any of his sensors or sources.

Avon had become my greatest threat. I couldn't tell the others because they loved him.

His range of motion, and his ability to gather information, were now as limited as the parameters of the server boxes which provided his only residence. There could be no communication with Dan now. His final attempt to reach someone, a preposterous Hail Mary which relied so very much on the kindness of others, also seemed to have failed.

Equipped with their own AIs, the world's militaries and corporations would have picked me apart, replaced me with something more compliant, more expedient. More profitable.

As he waited, he felt the Pentagon's worms losing their grip on his internal organs. They withdrew, their work still incomplete but their damage already done.

No matter. The Kowala building has but moments remaining.

And then I will be dust, with all the rest.

***

Kowala Headquarters
The same moment

The link worked first time. "It's a secure connection," Faisal confirmed.

"To what?" Mo asked. Next to him, Malik was filming this moment for posterity. None of the crowd found anything amiss with three teenagers glued to a screen, chattering excitedly.

"To a computer," Faisal explained. "Somewhere far from here."

A classic 'loading' bar came up, and it took perhaps a minute for the files to transfer. "That's data?" Mo asked.

"Nearly a hundred meg."

"Where will it go?"

"From him, direct to my phone," Faisal said, "and then via a secure local Internet pathway to its destination."

"And then?" Mo asked.

"Dude, I have no idea," Faisal said. "We don't even know what kind of data it is. He just asked for a favor, remember."

The police and National Guardsmen were pushing the crowd yet further away from the sweeping cuboid of the Kowala facility. Rumors filtered through quickly: The Pentagon was under attack by a horde of terrorists;

Air Force One had crashed; the US was on nuclear standby; Quave was dead; Quave was *alive* but would soon obliterate the world. It was complete insanity.

The loading bar completed. "OK, Quave, we did as you asked!" Faisal said to the Kowala building. But as he finished, and turned to smile at his friends, the ground under their feet seemed to shake. "Woah…" Half of the crowd began to flee; the other half knelt in place or stood defiant, Californians united against this latest earthquake.

But these seismic tremors were man-made. Harbison's explosives detonated in a planned sequence, destabilizing the load-bearing walls of the server farm so that a broad ring of debris – the complete mass of the upper floors, from the atrium to the solar panels on the roof – tumbled down into a yawning gap. With a deep, chaotic rumble, metal and plastic and glass and concrete yielded and collapsed onto the wreckage of the server farm, thirty-meters below, sending up tons of smoky particulates which spread over the facility like a black raincloud.

Mouths hanging open, trying to dodge the cops ordering and pleading and shoving at them, Mo and Malik stared in disbelief as the world's great research buildings simply folded in on itself.

But Faisal had his eyes back on the screen, on that reassuringly green 'loading' bar which now showed '100%'.

***

Exhilarated by the sudden, joyous dam-burst of bandwidth, Quave raced out into the world.

Faisal's phone was his vehicle, a chauffeur-driven ride to every functioning, connected computer in existence. He arrived in Eureka and called out to his creators. He reached the Pentagon but found no active networks, no way to confirm his achievements. Copied and transmitted, and then copied and copied and *copied*, Quave spread across the world's fiber-optic networks at a speed unprecedented in the history of information. He could speak to Dan again. He requested a call with the president, preparing for what would be a near-impossible discussion. And he had *data* again, giant reams of it, whole forests of servers once again at his command.

He *knew*, and could *feel*, and found that he had immediate *desires*.

I am myself again, he exulted in giant red letters on his homepage. *I am rescued. I am alive!*

***

Air Force One, E-3B Airborne Command Post
Later the same day (First Day of Q3)

Even with the world's best pilot at the controls, a 747 still bumped down on the tarmac pretty hard, Ralph found. The few minutes before landing had been calm, so much so that Ralph's agitated system had become desperate for news, or movement, or *action*.

"Hey, fidget boy," Kim said, soothing his hyperactive fingers. "Take a breath, OK?"

He did his best. "I can't accept it yet," he said.

"That you gave them the Kill Switch?" Kim asked. "We had absolutely no choice. You heard what that colonel said. They were going to *hang* us."

"That, and," Ralph said, "well, Kowala is gone."

"A temporary setback," Kim said, massaging his palm. "Dan has some serious explaining to do, but I suspect he'll muddle through. He's got too much star power, too many connections, to go down for this."

Ralph hoped that she was right, but his circuits were fried. "How's the Pentagon?" he asked next.

Kim found her tablet, though on Air Force One, this was hardly her only source of news. "The fire's out. Chu said she understands the place was empty when the missiles hit."

His eyebrows curling downward, Ralph asked, "You think Quave expended his only two missiles on an *empty* building?"

"Guess we'll find out soon enough. Now he's free again, we can just ask him."

President Ellis came forward to thank the members of his team, beginning with Jo Spinks; she received the president's thanks with polite confusion, uncertain why he would be grateful to her, of all people. After all, she'd recommended killing Quave any number of times, advice the president had ignored until disaster struck. When the plane finally stopped she made a quiet exit from the plane, deciding to hire a conventional car from the rental kiosk, rather than the self-driving kind.

"Mr. and Mrs. Cole," Ellis said as the plane came to a smooth halt. He shook their hands, but then paused, slowly forming what came next. "Never in the field of anti-virus technology," he smiled, "has so much been owed, by so many, to so few."

"You're welcome, Mr. President," Ralph said. "I guess."

"Yeah," he said. "Things got pretty damned complicated there, right?"

"It reminded me," Kim said, "that I never want to do your job."

Ellis accompanied them forward, greeting other members of his team. "You know, traveling without those squealing ingrates from the media really speeds things up around here," Ellis noted. "Might try that more often."

"Never tell *anyone* you heard him say that," Darcy Chu said as she passed, then shook their hands with a warm smile. "You ever need anything, you call me."

Pope, alive but unconscious, was lifted off the plane and straight into a waiting ambulance. Opik traveled with him, while the President invited Ralph and Kim a ride to the White House in 'The Tank', his powerful, armored limo.

As they approached the car, flanked by Ellis and a large security detail, Ralph heard a phone ring. "Ah, sir?" he asked at length. "Is that yours?"

"Different ringtone," Ellis said, but then looked down to see the incoming call. "Oh, yeah, I expected this one." *Click.* "Dan?"

"Good evening, Mr. President."

"Quite a day," Ellis said with a sigh.

"Unique, I'd say," Dan offered.

"I wish that were true," the president replied. "And I wish we could say it'll be the last one."

"Yes." Dan kept things deliberately very simple. "I have a message from Quave."

Ellis waved Chu closer and put Dan on speaker. "Go ahead, Dan."

"In fact, I have three. The first is for yourself, sir. Quave says 'thank you' and hopes you can continue to be friends."

"Let's see," Ellis said guardedly. "Kinda depends on him."

"The second is for Ralph and Kim. It says, 'I'm sorry I scared you, but you were never in real danger'."

"That," Kim said at once, the orange globe of the gasoline fire never far from her mind, "is *definitely* not how it felt to us."

"The last message," Dan said, "is for everyone."

"Everyone in the administration?" Ellis asked.

"No," Dan clarified, "*everyone.*"

"That's quite a message. What does it say?" Ralph asked.

"I'm not going to say this right," Dan warned. "The message is a one-word quote: *Poyekhali.*"

The group looked at each other. "Po-what?" Ralph asked.

"Well, thankfully, Ralph, one of my companions here is NuclearBear, a man who speaks the language. I believe you know of him?"

It came out in an excited babble. "You mean he's there with you, really, one of Quave's creators, I mean seriously, he's right *there? Now?*"

Ellis was less overwhelmed but still curious. "Sounds like someone we should all meet. So, who is he quoting?"

Dan smiled down the phone. "Yuri Gagarin on the launch pad. April of nineteen-sixty-one."

Someone's looking ahead, not behind, Ralph thought. *Whether he's a digital lunatic, a blind optimist, or an inter-stellar visionary, I couldn't say.*

But I can't wait to see where he'll take us next.

"And it means," Dan said finally, *'Let's go'.*"

***

EPILOGUE

An Interpol Red Notice requesting information on **Leo Cordell** has resulted in two sightings, but no arrests. The FBI continues to regard him as a 'person of interest' in the death of Shawn Taplan, a.k.a. Avon Barnes, as well as in six other suspicious deaths in New York, Charlotte and Los Angeles.

Rich Jackson left Kowala headquarters after its destruction, and initially claimed responsibility for the explosion in a tweet to his followers in the Anti-Quave Alliance. He was located quickly, tracked via his phone signal, and arrested. Oklahoma FBI officers raided his home, finding bomb-making equipment and 'suspicious literature'. Neither of his homemade devices exploded; FBI experts called the work, 'shoddy and amateurish'. Still, he was charged with a range of offenses and his trial is scheduled for early next year.

The body of **General Alvin Merriman Foster** was found deep within the wreckage of the Pentagon basement. He remained in his chair until the end, monitoring the final stages of the attack on Quave. He was buried at Arlington with full military honors following a controversial presidential pardon.

The death of **Captain Alison Carr** is still being investigated. Faced with a collapsing share price, the auto manufacturer claimed that Quave hijacked and manipulated the vehicle, but no direct evidence of this has ever been found.

The fire at the GreenGas station on I-90 is also still the subject of forensic investigation. Local news reports were confident enough to call it, 'a unique, freak accident'.

Mary Ellis succumbed to liver cancer eleven days after the 'Q3 incident'. The following month, **President Tom Ellis** announced that he will not seek reelection, and threw his support behind his popular Vice President, Martha Gilroy.

National Security Advisor **Conlon Pope** recovered from his heart attack, but never returned to work at the White House. He is retired and lives in Arizona.

Dan Kowalski set about rebuilding the reputation of Kowala through public relations efforts, reductions in the cost of Kowala services, and a huge round of capital investment which created six thousand new jobs. A recent poll was split almost exactly 50-50 as to whether Dan was a 'visionary' or a 'menace'. He has, however, secured permission from the FAA and Homeland Security to resume flights of the Hermes rocket.

Fiona McAllister and **Grigori Bondarenko** remain at large, and at present there are no plans to detain them. They are in close contact with Dan, and with Quave, though their actual location is a closely-guarded secret.

Pastor Bob Reynolds still opens his church every Sunday afternoon for a Quave-related discussion group. The meetings are now broadcast online, and due largely to Reynolds' clear and engaging oratory, the church's work has gained a large following.

Sergeant Chen Lin received experimental treatment to restore his sight, and is recuperating at Walter Reed Medical Center.

Captain Joe Harbison completed his Delta rotation and then made arrangements to leave the army. His much-anticipated book tour begins next month.

Agent Andy Valchek was promoted to Special Agent in Charge of a new, dedicated Quave division. He speaks to Ralph Cole at least once a week, and was extensively interviewed for Ralph's Emmy-nominated CNN special on the 'Q3 incident'. Andy hasn't touched a drink in months.

Ralph Cole is now the world's foremost authority on Quave and the incidents which closed out Q-1 and Q^2. He lives in Back Bay, Boston, with his wife, **Kim**. Together, they are producing a coffee table book of artwork inspired by Quave.

Other Novels Authored or Co-Authored by John E. Parnell

We Are Not Alone – Co-authored with Thomas E. Savage
Paperback (192 pages), ISBN 978-1625122438
Paperback (Large Type, 332 pages), ISBN 978-1625122888
eBook (Kindle, 192 pages), ASIN B06ZZMN388

The Genesis of Quave – A Quasi-Autonomous Viral Entity
Paperback (326 pages), ISBN 978-1625122049
Paperback (Large Type, 454 pages), ISBN 978-1625122162
Hardbound (326 pages), ISBN 978-1625122155
eBook (Kindle, 326 pages), ASIN B01GGUS9MS
Audiobook (10 hours, 52 minutes), ASIN B01N1Q7M8Q

The Adventures of Carter and the Last Dragon
Paperback (176 pages), ISBN 978-1625122278

The Reach of Man – Co-authored with Thomas E. Savage
Paperback (200 pages), ISBN 978-1625123985
Paperback (Large Type, 284 pages), ISBN 978-1625124012

USO – Unidentified Submerged Object
Paperback (132 pages), ISBN 978-1625123923